FAST LANE ENTERTAINMENT PRESENTS

MONEY AIN'T EVERYTHING

EYONE WILLIAMS

"THE KING OF STREET FICTION IS BACK" -DC BOOKDIVA

ISBN-13: 978-0-9836279-1-3

Library of Congress Control Number:

First Edition, January, 2013
Printed in the United States

Publisher's Note

Fast Lane Entertainment
#245 4401-A Connecticut Ave.
NW, Washington, DC 20008
Facebook.com: eyone.williams
Twitter: eyonethewriter
Instagram: uptowneyone

DEDICATION

Shout out to my man, Panama
Death before dishonor

ACKNOWLEDGEMENTS

At this point in my career I have paid my dues. I have dropped a number of novels, made bestsellers lists, won awards, hit town after town selling my books, and met the people that support me. I am very grateful for it all and give all praise to Allah, The Most High.

My family, my team, and my supporters mean the world to me. They have all helped me a great deal with this project as well as others. DC Bookdiva, you know what it is. Thank you so much for everything. You have brought so much to the table, helping me start Fast Lane Ent. We did it big with that Secrets Never Die and Lorton Legends joint (wink). Thanks for believing in me. All my peoples from the Lattisaw side and the Williams side, much love—family is everything.

Much love to the book stores that show me love and support my movement: DC Bookdiva, TLJ (Quita, Shawn, Ty), Cartel Café and Books (T. CW, and Lakisha), A New Quality, Sidi, Barnes & Noble, Source of Knowledge, Black and Nobel, Horizon, Official Connections, The Bronx Bookman Chris B, Frugal Books, Akieon, Afrikan World, Brian the bookman, Expressions, New York Star, Rodney at the Shrimp Boat, Curt at In Style, and all the hood spots that carry my books out of love. Thank you. Michelle The Official DC Book Reviewer, Scarlett Brock, Breeze, Flo Schoolfield, Vernita Brown, Allison M. Edwards, my man Martin Gross that held us down on Minnesota Avenue, Darren Rochester, D. Jones, Moe, and the whole TDCB much love, thanks for the support.

Much love to OOSA, Ms. Toni, Crystal Gamble-Nolden and the whole crew. Just Read Book Club, Mary Green, Monica Forbes, Marissa Palmer and all the great people I kick it with. Black Faithful Sister and Brothers Book Club, Sandy Thebookconnoisseur Barrett Sims, Carla Towns, Zaneta Powell, Lee Reagan O'Neal, and Gabrielle Dotson; keep reading the bangers and letting people know what's up. Kisha Green and everybody over at Literary Jewels, you know what it is: Real is Back! ARC Book Club Inc. showed me a lot of love, giving Lorton Legends a chance; thank you SiStar Tea, Locksie Locks and all the great people over there.

It's a pleasure to have met you all. Much love to AAMBC Book Club, thank you for supporting me and honoring me with the award for Male Author of The Year for 2012. Ollie Moss, Micole Walker, Charlene Richardson, Jeanette McMillan-James, Papaya Wagstaff, Ondrea L. Davis, Cali Kim, Karen E. Quinones, Patrice Reesie Avery, Tami Briscoe, Shon Perry, thanks for the support. Shot out to Jeff Gatsby Wilson, good look on The Talk Show and all the good things you have going on.

It's always great to have the respect of your peers. Since I've been out here in the free world and been able to move around I have been able to connect with so many people. Many of them have shown me nothing but love. Salute to my DC Bookdiva team: Nathan Welch, keep your head up; Kwame "Dutch" Teague, never lay down, fight till the end; RJ Champ, grind homie; Darrell DeBrew, you are in a lane of your own and I respect that; Pinky Dior, they ain't ready for you sis; Frazier Boy, welcome home; Mikeo, what they know about 1000 Grams? Much love and respect to Wahida Clark, Uncle Yah Yah, Nuance, Ne Ne Capri, Mike Sanders, Anthony Fields and the whole WCP family. Shot out to T. Styles, C. Washington, Seven, Davida and the whole Cartel family. Salute to Gorilla Convict, Seth, see you out here soon, homie. LCB, CEO Azarel, Miss KP, Kendall Banks, C.J. Hudson, and the whole team, I love the grind and the love you all show me and mine. Ashley & JaQuavis, big up to you two; had a great time with you all in New York for the release of Cartel 4—continued success always. Much love to my man Treasure E. Blue, I'm ready for your next book, we gon' rock down here in DC. Much love to my sister Envy Red, thanks for coming out and supporting me at Barnes & Noble, that was real and it meant a lot to me. J.M. Benjamin, you showed me a good time in Atlantic City homie, see you again soon, much respect. K'wan, Charlotte and Team Animal, look forward to hooking up every time I hit NYC. Big up to my sister Nikki Turner, we had a ball in B-more.

Salute to my man Al-Saadiq Banks, realness ain't in the talk; it's in the walk. My man and homie, Real Live. What's up G Street? Shot out to George, Shawna, Qiona Drummond, Joe Awsum, and your whole team. J.W. Smith, Jimmy Da Saint, Erick S. Gray, Deborah Cardona, June Miller, Rahiem Brooks, Michael McGrew, Ni'cola Mitchell, Tamika Newhouse, James Tanner, Maurice Pittman, Shoney K., Iesha Brown, Michele Fletcher, K.D. Harris, Amen Meadows, Aaron Bebo, Mack Mama, Teresa Seals, Yafeesa Johnson, Cha' Bella Don, Caleb Alexander, Amanda Lee, Blacc Topp, and everybody else that I deal with in the game, much love.

Free my nigga Jason Poole, look out for his next book, Prince of The City, with Wahida Clark Publishing. J-Rock, I got you homie, I'm gon' rep for you!

Much love and respect to my homies doing it big on other levels. Tabi Bonney, you on top of your game. I see big things. Big thank you to you and Zelle for the opportunity to do the film. My nigga Real Live and Gutta Da Goon, salute to Da Mob! What's up Lil Devil, FMF, I see you. Salute to my Hard Workin' niggaz, Roc, Hermo, Krazo, Choc, 40 Boy, KRU and that whole movement; yall real niggaz. That song we did together got the streets talking still. Shot out to Mo-Mo for making it sound the way it needed to. Fat Trel, good look for the love on Minnesota Avenue; you supported Lorton Legends and I respect that. Uno Boss, pleasure to have met you, I respect the way you think. Shot out to Big Wax, "That ain't law ak!" Shot out to my man Tony Lewis Jr., DC or Nothing! Salute to Cornell Jones, you make a nigga feel like a star every time I run into you down the Stadium Club.

Cap City, Mardi, Trick E and the whole movement yall got it going on, salute! Garvey The Chosen 1, your CD was the first CD I bought out of a store in over twenty years; keep doing your thing! Howard Brown and my Dark City team, thanks for allowing me to do my thing in the movie; I'm an actor now. Shit is unreal how things come together. Good look on the video for I Wonder too. Bernard, thanks for letting us do our thing at Twelve, respect that! Kev and Tiff, salute!

For all my men still behind the wall, keep your head. It's death before dishonor for life with me. Moose, you still be supporting me, buying my books from the feds. Much love for that. Black, out there in Atwater, love you my nigga. Corky, keep your head up, you gon' be back out here before you know it. Kobi, salute! Get that book out. Wee-Wee, Tone, Cinquan, Sop Sop, Tony Lewis, Freeway, Marky, Mario, Rome, Lil Lu, Twan, Roy Tatum, Roy Middleton, Trey Manning, Big Greene, Eddie Mathis, Butch Wood, Ned, Creek, Reel, Face, Brion, Monkey D, Fatts from Rittenhouse, Conrad, Debo, Eyez, Brook, Rah Rah, Philly Black, Mike Boone, Bryan Burwell, Miguel, Nappy-Bey, Salah, Mad Dog, Fice, Raff, Sean Branch, Wendell Smith, Nate Bailey, Frank, Rick, Lou, Talib, T.R., Al, Puddgie, Norvell, Donnell, and all the other good men that I have walked the yard with. Big shot out to my men in ADX, Mustafa Zulu, Nkosi Zulu-El, Baby Face, Dom, Dion Green, Fly, AJ, Supreme, and the rest of the men fighting for their lives in the belly of the beast. You are not forgotten.

Panama, this project is done. I put my all into it, now I intend to make this joint a bestseller. Salute!

Real is back!

Fast Lane Ent. over everything!

CHAPTER 1

September 1981
Downtown Panama City, Panama.

Crowds of tourist and local pedestrians filled the streets taking in the great weather and shopping. Traffic was thick up and down the streets. Streets cops were out in full force keeping an eye on everything moving. Street crime was their main focus. Off to the side, two Panamanian teenagers strolled out of the alley and mixed in with the crowd. They stood out like a sore thumb. They were of West Indian decent and had the look of local thugs from the nearby projects. They teenagers were on a mission.

"The police on the other side of the street." Vicioso said in his thick West Indian accent. He made it his business not to make eye contact with the police. He was calm on the outside, but on the inside he could feel the butterflies in his stomach.

"They look like they watchin' us, too." Pete cut his eyes at the police.

Both teenagers kept their cool. Being watched by the police was nothing new to them. Cops were always suspicious of the local youth. "Let's take care of business." Pete said as he and Vicioso made their way through the thick crowd. At 16, they had been living a life of crime for over five years and knew what they were doing.

"Come on, laope." Vicioso was ready to make his move, police or not. He took off first, already having his eye on what he wanted. Pete took off as well, pulling out his knife. Vicioso went after a white, American tourist; in one well timed motion he snatched the man's wallet from his pocket and ripped his camera from his hands. The tourist tried to struggle for his property but Vicioso wasn't having it. He shoved the tourist to the ground and took off running. It all went down in seconds. Unrest and confusion spread throughout the crowd of tourist. The screams of frightened women grabbed the attention of the police who pulled their guns without a second thought. It really took balls and audacity to pull a caper in downtown Panama City. It was a known fact that the police had a green light to shoot to kill. Nevertheless, Vicioso and Pete had to do what they had to do.

The police gave chase, but they didn't have a clear shot at the two teenagers who were bulldozing their way through the crowd trying to make it to the nearest alley so they could make their escape back to the projects of Santa Cruz.

As soon as the teenagers stepped into the middle of the street the police opened fire, in broad daylight. The gunshots seemed to come from all directions. Bullets flew by Vicioso's head and slammed into the brick wall. Never looking back, the teenagers hit the alley and slipped into the building. They made their way through the building and came out the back door at top speed. They'd lost the police just that fast. Minutes later they were back in Santa Cruz where they stopped to catch their breath behind Vicioso's building. People were everywhere in the projects, but no one was paying them any attention.

"I'm 'bout to go in the house for a second. We gotta get the hell out here." Vicioso said, still trying to catch his breath.

"Me too, compa." Pete said, still holding a wallet and a gold watch in his hand.

"Catch you later." Vicioso gave his comrade five.

"See you in the mornin'." Pete said.

As Pete stepped off and ran across the basketball court to his building, Vicioso went inside his building and an upstairs to the third floor. Carefully, he walked down the hallway, watching his back every step of the way. He knocked on a door at the end of the dimly lit hallway. A tall brown-skinned man with a gold tooth opened the door. He looked at Vicioso and shook his head with a smile on his face. "You got balls, Vicioso." Serio said as he let Vicioso into the apartment.

Serio was in his early twenties and had watched Vicioso grow up in Santa Cruz. He had a lot of love for Vicioso and saw a lot of himself in the teenager. It was Serio who gave Vicioso his nickname; he said Vicioso was vicious when it came to robbing tourist downtown. The name Vicioso stuck, and as time went on, Vicioso got more vicious with every caper. Serio had come up the exact same way. He'd made a name for himself by robbing tourist in down town Panama City. Serio was well known throughout the projects and other parts of Panama City, by all means he was considered a legend. Vicioso looked up to Serio like a big brother and had the utmost respect for him.

Serio shut the door behind Vicioso and said, "You getting' real bold movin' in broad daylight like that. I see you been doing' that on the regular now." Serio said with his thick West Indian accent. "You act like the police won't kill your raas." He sat down next to Vicioso on the sofa.

"I got to do what I got to do, mena." Vicioso said with a serious look on his face.

"I heard them shooting' like shit today." Serio said.

"Yeah, they was trying' to take us out today, but we got the hell outta' there in no time." Vicioso smiled, showing his gold tooth.

Serio lit a cigarette. Vicioso asked for one. Serio gave him one and he lit it for him. "What you get today?" Serio asked blowing smoke in the air as he picked up the camera Vicioso had sitting beside him.

Vicioso checked the wallet he'd taken and counted the cash. "Eight-hundred dollars."

"Not bad." Serio said with an approving nod.

Standing 5' 9" at 130 pounds, brown-skinned, with a small afro, Vicioso nodded. It was a nice take. He'd seen worse takes. Like the time he'd been shot by the police on a caper and ended up doing juvenile time at Butri. Poverty was the norm in Panama. There was no such thing as welfare. When the refrigerator was empty there was no stopping the hunger pains. Vicioso's mother worked two jobs to provide for him and his younger brother, Pimpo, but that wasn't enough. Vicioso wanted what he felt the world owed him: a better life. If it took risking his life, robbing tourist, Vicioso was more than willing to roll the dice. He was down for whatever.

"What you want for the camera?" Serio asked.

"For you … give me a hundred dollars, laope."

"Here you go." Serio pulled a bankroll of money out of his pocket, he then went in the other pocket and pulled out some weed and said, "Take this too. A little somethin' extra."

"Thanks." Vicioso said, looking at the clock on the wall. It was 2:34 P.M. "I gotta run. I'll catch you a little later."

"Okay." Serio walked Vicioso to the door with his arm around his shoulder. "Check wit' me later on. I got somethin' in the makin' that you might like. It's a few dollars in it for you to." He smiled.

"Oh yeah, cool, compa."

Vicioso walked into the apartment that he shared with his mother and brother. He found his mother in the kitchen

4

washing dishes; she looked over her shoulder and said, "Where you been all day?"

"Hangin' out a little bit." Vicioso took a seat at the dining room table.

"Please," his mother rolled her eyes. She was far from green. "I know what you been out there doin'. And you got Pimpo runnin' right behind you, followin' in your damn footsteps. Y'all gon' get your raas killed out there in the streets."

Vicioso sighed. "Ma, I ain't got Pimpo followin' me, and I ain't been doin' nothin', why you keep sayin' that? It's like you want me to be doing somethin'."

"Harvey, cut the shit. I wasn't born yesterday. You know damn well that Pimpo looks up to you. Everything you do he does. You need to think about that." Melly said.

Pimpo was two years younger than Vicioso and stayed in a world of trouble. His violent streak was off the meter. He had his own little crew and they were known to terrorize shit on their downtown capers. They had stabbed a number of tourists who had underestimated their seriousness.

"I work too damn hard for you and Pimpo to be runnin' the streets, riskin' your lives, Harvey. You two are worryin' me to death. This shit has to stop somewhere." Melly's West Indian accent got thicker as she fussed and her anger grew.

"Ma, I'm not runnin' the streets no more. I keep telling you that." Vicioso shook his head in frustration. He was tired of hearing the same thing over and over again from his mother. In his mind, he was only doing what he had to do, what any other young man would do that was in his situation.

"Stop talkin' to me like I'm some damn fool, Harvey." she yelled. "I hear all the stories about you and Pimpo every time I leave out the house. It's a shame, it's down right foolishness. You think people don't talk? You think what you are doing is some kind of secret or something? It's not. Keep taking everything for a joke and you gonna' find yourself dead or locked up somewhere. What the hell is wrong wit' your raas?"

Vicioso smiled. He knew his mother was speaking the truth. She always spoke the truth, no matter what anyone thought about it. "Ma, I'll talk to Pimpo and tell him to slow down, okay? That's all I can do. Pimpo is his own man. You know that."

"Yeah, yeah, you keep saying the same thing every time I say something to you. Get your shit together!"

After nightfall, Serio was standing in the back of the projects talking to his man, Polee, about a caper they were working on. The caper was a serious mission that they'd been waiting on for a while. The stakes were high, but the money was going to be good if the job was done right.

"This is goin' to change everything for us." Serio said as he blew cigarette smoke in the air. "I got my end covered. It's all mapped out. As long as things are done right the move is as good as gold."

"You want me to take care of Padro?" Polee asked. He was five years older than Serio, but they were partners in crime equally.

"Nah, let's keep you clean on this one just in case somethin' goes wrong, that way I can be the bad guy in the eyes of the Colombians. You know how they are going to look at shit after everything goes down. Always remember this is a thinking man's game. We plan to be around for a long time to come. No mistakes, no room for error."

"I like that." Polee smiled. He loved the way Serio's mind worked. They made a good team. Polee looked at his watch and said, "I gotta go meet Padro, I'll let you know what the deal is when I get back."

"Cool, make it happen." Serio and Polee gave each other five and went their separate ways.

As Serio bent the corner headed towards the front of the projects he ran into Vicioso. "Vicioso," Serio called out. "Let me talk to you, mena." He pulled Vicioso to the side in the shadows of the projects and said, "Remember what I was tellin' you about earlier?"

"Yeah you said you had somethin' in the makin' and it might be a few dollars in it for me."

"That's right." Serio put his arm around Vicioso's shoulder, like one would do with a little brother.

"Well, what's up, laope? Tell me what the deal is, Serio. I know it's somethin' nice if you got somethin' to do wit' it."

"I got a caper set up at the hotel, but I can't show my face there or the police will be all over me. You know how that goes. Anyway, that's where you come in. The Colombian that Polee deals wit' wants us to do a job for them. It's a diamond dealer comin' to town to meet some Colombian jewelers; he'll be carryin' all the diamonds wit' him." Serio smiled as he laid the plan out. "You up for the job?"

"Hell yeah. No question. As long as you tell me what's what and where everything is, I can pull it off. You know that." Vicioso wasn't afraid to do any job if the price was right. He was down to make a dollar any day of the week. "What's in it for me?"

Serio smiled. "Let's go up to my apartment and talk for a second."

Inside Serio's apartment he explained the whole situation to Vicioso. The diamond dealer was from Belgium and sold stolen diamonds to Polee's Columbian "friend." Serio told Vicioso exactly where the diamond dealer was going to be staying and how he carried the diamonds. All Vicioso had to do was take the goods and get out of the hotel without getting himself killed by the police.

"All you gotta do is dress up like a hotel worker and do the job. Simple as that. It's dangerous, but it can be done, and I know you can do it and get away with it."

"I want Pete to do the job wit' me. I need somebody I trust to watch my back." Vicioso said.

"That's smart." Serio rubbed his chin, thinking about how much he was willing to pay the two teenagers for the job. "How does two thousand a piece sound?"

Vicioso had never had $2,000 at one time before in his life. For $2,000 it was no telling what he would do.

"Say no more, I'm in, mena!"

Serio smiled and gave Vicioso five. "I knew you would like the job, but keep in mind that this is not your everyday downtown robbery. This is big shit. You know they'll kill your raas on the spot if you fuck up."

"I won't fuck up. Like I said, just tell me what to do and I'll get it done, no questions asked." Vicioso was honored that Serio had picked him for the job. There were countless other teenagers in Santa Cruz that would do the job for free just to get down with Serio and Polee. Vicioso could tell that Serio saw a lot of potential in him. That made him eager to pull the job off right.

"Meet me here Friday evening. Six on the dot. Don't be late." Serio said in an authoritive voice.

A short while later, Vicioso was in Pete's bedroom telling him about the job Serio had lined up for them. Pete was ready; there was nothing to talk about. He knew that they were onto something big by fucking with Serio and Polee. If all went well there would be no looking back as far as he was concerned.

8

"This is the kind of caper we need right here." Pete smiled as he sipped his cup of ice water. "How much you say we get a piece?"

"Two-thousand dollars."

"Ofee." Pete smiled and nodded. "I can't wait!"

Friday evening, Vicioso and Pete were sitting in Serio's living room dressed like young hotel workers as they listened to the final instructions about the caper. Serio had a connect inside the hotel that had given him a key to the garage door that the hotel workers used to enter the back of the hotel. Vicioso and Pete would have no problem getting inside the hotel from the back where no one would pay them any attention.

"Y'all ready?" Serio asked the teenagers, smoking a cigarette as he stood in the middle of the living room.

"Yeah." Vicioso nodded. He was focused on the cash pay off at the end.

"Reego will be downstairs waitin' for you." Serio said, giving the teenagers an examining look. He felt confident that they were the right ones for the job.

Vicioso and Pete headed downstairs and jumped into the back of a cab that their older homie Reego was driving. Reego was already down with Polee and Serio; he'd paid his dues within their circle. Reego spoke to the teenagers as they jumped into the cab. On the way to the hotel he coached them through the game plan again, just to keep them on point. "Make sure y'all take the back stairwell goin' in and comin' out. Don't even make eye contact with nobody." Reego said.

"Got it." Vicioso said, looking out the window into the night.

"Where the cops be at?" Pete said.

"It's only two, and they be in the lobby." Reego said.

"We can deal wit' that. That ain't nothin'." Pete said.

Once they arrived at the hotel Reego drove down two levels into the parking garage and parked in the rear corner. Vicioso and Pete both felt butterflies in their stomachs, but they were still ready to take care of business. "Here you go; make sure you keep your eyes open. I'll be right here waitin' for y'all when you finish takin' care of business." Reego said.

Vicioso and Pete made their way to the door. The garage was almost empty, there were two white women walking to their car. The white women paid no attention to the teenagers; they were no more than "help" in their eyes. Vicioso and Pete slipped inside the hotel through the workers entrance and headed for the back stairwell smoothly. They made it to the eighth floor and headed down the hallway carefully. A few tourists passed them along the way but paid them no attention as they made their way down the hallway.

"Young man," an old black woman with a French accent called Vicioso. Acting the part, Vicioso stopped and looked back. "Yes, you." The woman pointed at him. "I'm about to get some rest, can you please return my food cart to the kitchen."

"No problem, ma'am." Vicioso played the role to perfection. He grabbed the food cart and continued down the hall with Pete as the woman went back inside her room. Once her door was shut, Vicioso pushed the cart to the side and bent the corner.

Vicioso and Pete were right on time. The diamond dealer was just leaving his room, heading for the lobby to meet the Colombians. The two teenagers followed the diamond dealer to the elevator. They kept an eye on the metal suitcase he was carrying. "We gettin' on the elevator wit' him." Vicioso whispered to Pete.

"Let's do it." Pete kept his game face on.
"Cool."

10

As soon as the elevator doors opened the diamond dealer stepped inside. Swiftly, Vicioso and Pete slid inside right behind him. They were the only ones on the elevator. Sweet! The doors shut and the elevator began descend. Quickly, Vicioso hit the emergency stop button right between floors.

"What the hell?!" the diamond dealer looked scared and confused all at the same time. Vicioso and Pete then whipped out their knives with the quickness. Vicioso snatched the metal suitcase. "What the hell is going on?!" the diamond dealer put his hands in the air.

"Just keep your cool and you won't get hurt." Vicioso said with one hand around the diamond dealer's neck. Pressing the button for the bottom floor, Vicioso shoved the man against the wall. The diamond dealer began to look more angered than afraid.

"Do you little thugs think you are going to get away with this? Do you know who I am?"

"Don't really care." Vicioso said with a serious glare. "I'm callin' the fuckin' shots. Listen to me carefully, when this fuckin' door opens you stay right. If you so much as make a fuckin' sound I'ma slit your throat right here." The look in Vicioso's eyes made it clear that he was not playing.

The elevator doors opened and Vicioso and Pete jogged to the back stairwell. They hit the door and ran down the steps to the garage. Dashing across the parking lot they saw Reego already coming their way in the cab. Jumping inside the cab they off into the night.

Back at Serio's, Vicioso and Pete were paid $2,000 a piece for their work. It was a big take for the youngsters. Serio gave them five and said, "Good job. I knew I could count on you two. Shit will only get better from here. Trust me."

"Thanks for givin' us the job. That says a lot." Vicioso said.

EYONE WILLIAMS

"No problem. I'll catch you two later. I have a few things to take care of." Serio said as he let the teenagers out of the apartment.

Serio shut the door and went to sit at the dining room table with Polee. The metal suitcase sat on the table. Lighting a cigarette, he opened the suitcase. "Well, the plan is comin' together." he said. Inside the suitcase there were four black velvet pouches. Serio opened one and dumped the contents into his palm. Huge, heavy diamonds sparkled in the light like small cubes of ice. "I'll take care of Padro. Tell him that you sent me to drop the diamonds off."

"I'll give him a call as soon as I get in the house." Polee said. He then looked at his watch and said, "Everything should fall right in place now. In a minute we'll be in New York and all this shit will be behind us, Serio. We won't have to ever look back."

"That's the idea. Never look back." Walking over to Polee and putting a brotherly arm around his should, Serio continued, "We come from nothin', nothin' at all. We will one day be at the top of the food chain where we belong. Men like us are destined to be at the top. We refuse to be less than leaders. Never forget that."

Polee shook his head in agreement. "So true, brother."

Serio gave Polee five. Their plans were in the final stages.

The next afternoon, Vicioso walked into his apartment with his arms full of grocery bags. He had steaks, chicken and ground beef. It felt good to put food on the table. It was what he was supposed to do, he believed. Providing for the family was the most important thing in his mind. He took pride in it.

After putting the food up, Vicioso went into Pimpo's bedroom to check on his little brother. He found Pimpo lying on the bed watching TV. His eyes were bloodshot red. The bedroom smelled like strong weed. The 14-year-old looked

12

just like Vicioso, only a little smaller. Vicioso and Pimpo were as close as brothers could be. They'd always been that way.

"Damn, you high already. You ain't even brushed your teeth yet." Vicioso joked as he picked up Pimpo's pack of cigarettes and took one out. "Give me a light."

Pimpo gave Vicioso a light and said, "You act like you don't smoke when you first wake up. Don't come in here on that bullshit."

Vicioso laughed. "Don't let Ma hear you talk like that. She already blames me for all the shit your rass be in."

Pimpo smiled. "Yeah, you a bad influence. I learned everything I know from you." Pimpo joked as he lit a cigarette and changed the subject. "I heard about the hotel job last night. I know that was you. I seen you talkin' to Serio. Why you ain't take me wit' you? You be holdin' back. I'm your brother. You need to start cuttin' me in."

"It was too dangerous. I couldn't risk somethin' happenin' to you. You know Ma would kill me. When the time is right I will cut you in. I promise."

"So it's okay for you to do the job, but it's too dangerous for me? What kind of sense does that make, Vicioso? I'm not a little kid. I can hold my own wit' the best of them. You know that."

"Come on, Pimpo, you know how it goes when you are the youngest. I know you can hold your own. That's not the question. It's Ma. You know that. Ma gon' always worry about you more than me. I can't not think about her."

"Cut the shit, you know I can handle myself in the streets, I'm gon' be okay, Vicioso. You need to start cuttin' me in on some of the capers you got your eyes on. We brothers. Ma don't have to know everything. She can't control everything I do in life. I'm gon' do what I want to do. I'm my own man. You already know that."

Vicioso smiled and let out a frustrated sigh. "You right. Everything you sayin' makes sense. Let me think about it. I'll get back wit' you as soon as somethin' right comes my way."

There was a knock at the front door. "I'll get it." Vicioso said as he left the room. When he opened the door he saw Niecy standing in the hallway with her hands on her hips. She was wearing a pair of tight white shorts and a white T-shirt. Her sexy brown legs were glowing and the curves of her sexy body made Vicioso forget about the conversation he was just having with Pimpo.

"Damn, you look good, mami." Vicioso said with a smile. "Come in."

Niecy smiled and gave Vicioso a hug and a kiss as she walked in.

"I was just about to come upstairs." Vicioso said as he led his girl to his bedroom.

"I saw you comin' back from the store so I thought I'd drop by and check on you, make sure you stayin' out of trouble. You know how you are, you get in all kinds of trouble if I don't stay on top of you." Niecy sat back on the bed.

Vicioso sat beside Niecy and put his arm around her. "You don't have to worry about me. I got everything under control. Trust me, mami."

"Please." She playfully rolled her eyes. "I trust you."

"On another note, I got somethin' for you." Vicioso pulled $1,000 out of his pocket and handed it to Niecy. "I want you to put that wit' that other money. I want us to go ahead and get our own apartment. We gotta save our money if we want to have anything in this world. We need to start thinkin' for tomorrow. Put a few dollars to the side for a rainy day."

14

MONEY AIN'T EVERYTHING

As Niecy took the cash in her hand her eyes lit up with excitement and surprise. "Papi, where did you get all this money?"

"Shhh …" he put a finger over her lip and gave her a soft kiss. "Don't worry about that. Just get on top of gettin' the apartment. I got big plans for us."

"Okay, Harvey. I'll take care of it."

Niecy was two years older than Vicioso. They'd been together for a little over two years. She knew what kind of young dude he was, everybody in Santa Cruz knew what kind of young dude he was, but Niecy loved him all the same. She trusted him and knew that he'd always had her best interest at heart. Coming from the same back grounds they had a lot in common and mostly wanted the same things out of life: something better.

"Let's go out and get somethin' to eat downtown. I want to spend some time with you." Vicioso said.

"Okay." Niecy flashed a bright smile. "Sounds good to me."

Serio sat on the sofa in his living room, smoking a cigarette as he watched TV. He was thinking about the money Polee got for the diamonds: $300,000. $150,000 of that belonged to Serio. Padro must have thought they were fools. He had offered them $25,000 for the diamonds; they said fuck him and put another plan in motion. A plan that could mean death for both Serio and Polee, however, in life, as far as they were concerned, they had to take risks to get where they wanted to be. Now Serio had to tie up the loose ends with Padro who was expecting him to deliver the diamonds shortly. Like a skilled chess player, Serio was many steps ahead in the game. He had his shit mapped out like an army general.

The TV special that Serio was watching came back from commercial. It was about the Panama Canal and how it played

15

such a huge part in Panamanian life. Most of the stuff they were talking about Serio already knew. The host was talking about how most of the black Panamanians came from the West Indies seeking employment in connection with the construction of the canal. He also spoke about how Panama was once a province of Colombia and that in 1903 Colombia refused to allow the U.S. to build the Panama Canal after the French had failed. A chain of events went into effect and the U.S. encouraged Panama to revolt against Colombia. When the smoke cleared, Panama became an independent nation on November 3, 1903, sitting between Costa Rica and Colombia.

A knock at Serio's door grabbed his attention. Slowly he went to take a look through the peephole. He opened the door and saw Padro standing in the hallway with a smile on his face. In Spanish, Serio told Padro to come in. They both headed for the dining room table where a metal suitcase was. Serio walked close behind Padro and offered him a cigarette. Wanting to get down to business, Padro declined the cigarette and reached for the suitcase. In a flash, Serio grabbed Padro by the collar and put him in a deadly headlock. Surprised, Padro struggled to get out of the headlock as he began to gag. Serio was cold, calm and collective. His blood pressure didn't even raise a notch as he choked Padro out with ease. As Padro began to fade to black, Serio pulled a shiny blade and slit Padro's throat in one quick motion.

Holding Padro in the chokehold until he breathed his last breath, Serio squeezed the life out of the Colombian with no remorse. When Serio was sure that Padro was dead he let the lifeless body fall to the floor. I was over in no time. Walking over to the phone, Serio picked it up and called Polee.

"Yeah." Polee said.

"Come over. I need some help cleanin' up. Everything is done." Serio said.

CHAPTER 2

Living from caper to caper was all Vicioso and Pete knew; it was their way of life. After their hotel job they ran through their money in no time and were back at it again, robbing tourist. As nightfall covered the city, Vicioso and Pete were running for their lives and ducking bullets at the same time. The cops were on their back and shooting to kill. Vicioso and Pete had just robbed a group of American tourist. As they cut down a dark alley a bullet flew by Vicioso's head, he never looked back. Santa Cruz was only a few minutes away, but they had to get there and at the moment the police seemed to be everywhere. It was an all out chase.

"Come on!" Pete said as he cut into the back of a dark building. "Let's hide inside here. See if we can duck 'em."

"Hell no, we gotta keep movin', if they catch us down here they gon' kill us." Vicioso said.

"Freeze!" a cop yelled as he bent the corner. Vicioso and Pete dashed inside the building and down some dirty steps into what looked like a store basement. Gunshots rang out behind them. Pete yelled out in pain as he tumbled to the ground holding his leg. Blood was gushing. He'd taken a bullet. Vicioso pulled his comrade into the darkness behind some old dusty boxes where they tried to remain as silent as possible. They could hear the cop coming down the steps; they knew that death was near.

"Come out and I won't kill you bastards." The cop hissed as he made it to the bottom of the steps, waving his revolver in the dark.

"Shh," Vicioso whispered to Pete. His heart was beating so loud he could hear it over the cop's voice. Pulling out his knife, Vicioso said, "I'm goin' to get us outta here alive, mena. Don't worry about it." Peeping around the boxes Vicioso saw that the cop had his back turned. In a flash, Vicioso sprung out of the darkness and stabbed the cop in the back with three quick swings. The cop yelled out in pain. Vicioso got more aggressive, taking swings at the cops neck.

"Aaaahh! You bastard!" the cop yelled as he dropped his gun and watched it slide across the floor. Growing weak, the cop fell to his knees. Vicioso saw a lead pipe in the corner and grabbed it. He then began to bash the cop in the head with the pipe until he was no longer moving.

Dropping the pipe, Vicioso walked over and helped Pete t his feet. Pete's whole left leg was covered with blood. The pain he felt in his leg was extreme. He didn't think he was going to be able to walk.

Wiping sweat from his forehead, Pete said, "I can't feel my leg. I can't make it home. You need to get out of here, Vicioso. You can still get away."

"Fuck all that. I'm gon' make sure we both get out of here. Trust me." Vicioso said as he helped Pete up the steps. When they got back to the door they had entered they looked out into the dark alley. They could still hear the police in the area but they didn't see any. "Come on, we almost home." Vicioso helped Pete down the alley as fast as they could move. Pete's wound left a trail of blood every step of the way.

The next morning, Vicioso was laying in the bed sleep. It had been a long night, but he and Pete had made it back to Santa Cruz safely. After they had made it back to the projects

18

they went to Serio's apartment so they could get Pete's leg fixed up. Serio called a woman over that worked at the hospital and she took care of the gunshot wound in no time.

"Vicioso! Wake up!" Pimpo came into his room with urgency and began to shake him.

"What the fuck is up?" Vicioso was dead tired.

"They got the bulletin on TV!" Pimpo was loud and excited. "A cop got killed last night, beat wit' a pipe and stabbed to death. The police say the killers are from Santa Cruz. It's a manhunt in progress. Police are going door to door. They even have the army with them. Shit is crazy."

"Fuck!" Vicioso jumped up and grabbed his clothes. "You sure they said the cop got killed?"

"Hell yeah, they showed pictures of the body bag."

Vicioso knew the police would be out for blood. The walls began to close in on him and felt like there was no turning back. He didn't know what to do next, but he was sure they he couldn't allow the cops to get their hands on him. "I gotta get the fuck outta here. Did they say any names?"

"Nah." Pimpo said. By the way Vicioso was acting Pimpo knew his brother had something to do with the murder of the police officer. "Where you goin'?"

"I don't know yet, but I gotta get the fuck outta here." Vicioso tied his shoes. "Look, Pimpo, I'm goin' over Reego's. Don't let nobody know where I'm goin', not even Ma. You got that?"

"Yeah." Pimpo said. "Are you okay? You gon' be alright?"

"Yeah, just do what I said. I gotta get a move on." Vicioso left the apartment and crept to Reego's spot. He had to figure out what to do next.

The heat turned up fast! The policed began kicking in doors left and right, turning Santa Cruz upside down. They hit

Vicioso and Pete's apartment but the teenagers were nowhere to be found; they were both hiding out in the shacks behind Santa Cruz. The shacks were called "Hollywood" because countless notorious criminals came out of the shacks and they were known like movie stars.

Pimpo met Vicioso late at night in the shadows of Hollywood to bring him news of the raids. "Ma is worried about you, laope." Pimpo said. "She said the police are goin' to kill your raas if they catch you. Shit don't look good."

"Did you tell her where I am?" Vicioso asked, looking over his shoulder. He was on edge like a man with nowhere to run.

"Nah, but she knows that I know where you are. She wants you to turn yourself in. She said that since you are still a juvenile that you and Pete will only go back to Butri. I think you should listen to her, Vicioso. The police are goin' to kill you if they catch you out here in the streets. I don't want it to turn out like that. You how this shit goes."

Vicioso sighed. " Let me think about this shit. I got a lot on my mind. Don't worry about me. I'm gon' talk to Serio and find a way to take care of this shit."

"Niecy keep askin' me where you are. She knows I'm lyin' when I say I don't know. She's worried about you, too. The police raided her mother's apartment."

Vicioso sighed with frustration. "Look, tell Ma and Niecy that you talked to me and that I'm okay. Tell them I love them and that I need time to think this shit out. Okay?"

"Okay."

Vicioso gave his brother a hug and disappeared into the shadows of Hollywood. He needed time to think and get his thoughts together. Whatever was to happen next would be a matter of life and death.

MONEY AIN'T EVERYTHING

While the cops were hot on the trail of Vicioso and Pete, Serio was sitting on the sofa in his living room waiting for Polee to come over so they could take care of business. A knock at the door grabbed his attention. He grabbed the .38 he had beside him and put it behind his back as he checked to see who was at the door. It was Melly, Vicioso's mother. She was like a mother to Serio as well; she'd help raise him in the projects. Serio open the door and let her in.

"How are you, Melly?" Serio asked as he shut the door.

"I need to speak to you, Julio." Melly got straight to the point. There was a stern look on her face and Serio knew exactly what was on her mind.

"How can I help you?" Serio asked as he eased the gun into the small of his back without her noticing.

"Don't play dumb wit' me, Julio." Melly folded her arms. "You know why the raas I'm here. The police are all over the place, lookin' for Harvey and Pete, kickin' in doors and shit. I need you to help me find Harvey and talk some sense into him. You know he looks up to you. You need to help me save his life before the damn police kill him."

"I respect you too much to play dumb wit' you, Melly. I swear I haven't seen Harvey or Pete since the night before the police bulletin. I will try to find them for you. Give me a little time and I will work it out. I promise."

"Do that for me. I've already called the news people and asked them to be present if I can get Harvey and Pete to turn themselves in. Otherwise, the police are goin' to kill them in the streets, you know that. They are still juveniles so it's not much that can be done to them if they turn themselves in. I need you to talk some sense into them; make them understand the situation. Can I trust you to do that?"

"I can do that. Sure." Serio nodded. "No problem. I'll find them for you tonight. Okay?"

"Thank you, Julio." Melly gave Serio a hug and left, trusting that he would be a man of his word.

Later on, Serio went to holla at a few people to see if he could locate Vicioso and Pete, although he had a feeling they were hiding out in Hollywood. Walking through the projects in the dark he noticed that there weren't a lot of people hanging out. The manhunt for Vicioso and Pete had turned Santa Cruz into ghost town. A creepy feeling began to spread through his stomach. All of a sudden he became more alert than normal, Heading toward Hollywood through the dark cut behind the projects Serio didn't feel right.

Out of the shadows came a voice: "Don't move or you're a dead man." Serio turned around and saw two police officers coming his way with their guns pointed at him. "We only want to talk, Serio." the tall one said. Serio didn't try to run; he knew they had the jump on him. He took his chances. If the police wanted to kill him they would have done it without talking.

"What the mada raas y'all want to talk to me about?" Serio asked, not making any sudden moves and paying close attention to the cops.

"Someone important wants to talk to you." The officer said as he searched Serio and removed the .38 he was carrying. "I'll keep this for you." The officer tucked Serio's .38 between his waistband.

"Who is this person and why do they want to talk t me?" Serio kept a close eye on the cops. A police car pulled up and stopped in front of them. Nervousness over came Serio but he played it cool.

"Let's take a ride. You get up front." The tall officer said, directing Serio into the car with a pistol. Serio went with the flow. Once inside the car, the tall officer said, "Serio, you're no longer a regular thief from the gutter anymore. You're

22

moving up in the world and people in high places are starting to take notice. I must commend you for that."

"What's that supposed to mean?" Serio asked, feeling uncomfortable with the whole situation.

"Your name is comin' up a lot in big circles; it's come to the attention of some important people. You're no fool. You know what that means. I don't have to spell it all out for you. If you were slow there would be no way for you to get away with the type of shit you get away with. Nevertheless, you are starting to think big and that's what separates petty crooks from big time shot callers."

"Is that right?" Serio said as he looked out of the window. "Well, for what it's worth, I'd like to know who really cares about how much of a shot caller I am."

"You are smart, you will see a lot in the opportunity that is about to come your way." The officer laughed. "If you don't see a lot in it then you are not as smart as I think you are."

Serio laughed and said nothing else for the rest of the ride.

A short while later, the police car pulled up behind an old warehouse in a very remote part of town and parked in the shadows. Serio was marched inside and told to sit at an old wooden table with a bright light hanging above it. A decorated police officer sat across from Serio with a smug look on his face as he puffed on a cigar. A suitcase sat on the table between them. The whole scene was like something out of a movie. Serio paid close attention to everything. One of the officers that had rode in the car with him was now standing behind him holding a pistol.

The decorated officer sitting across from Serio was the chief of police. He took another puff of his cigar and said, "Let me get straight to the point. I want to be very clear with you about a few things." He threw his cigar to the floor and grounded it out with his foot. "Your Colombian friend, Padro, that disappeared the other day after the little diamond deal at the hotel was doing business with me. Me and a few other very important people. People that don't play about their money. I know you and Polee had a hand in his disappearance." The chief leaned forward with his elbows on the table. "I really don't give a fuck about his disappearance, but what I do give a fuck about is my money and he was making me a lot of money. In more ways than one. So to make things very clear to you, understand this: You will fill his shoes or me and you will have a serious problem. Understand?"

"Fill his shoes how?" Serio asked.

"I offer you a business deal, the same deal I had with Padro."

"Why me? You care nothing about me. I'm sure there are a number of other people that can do your dirty work for you."

"Serio, I've taken notice of your rise from a little project vagrant, stealing small stuff to get by, but now you are thinking much bigger. I like that kind of thinking. The world is a big place with a big playing field and a man has to be willing to play the game at all costs. Money makes the world go round. You understand this. From the slums to the top government offices, it's all the same. It's about money. Why do you think America controls the Canal Zone? You think they care about our country? No! They care about money and its big money in the drug trade. If Colombia would have let them build the Canal we would still be a shit hole in Colombia. When you make money you are important, you make a difference. Otherwise you're just another bum, good for nothing." The chief stood up and opened the suitcase. He spent it around and pulled out a tightly wrapped block of white powder in a plastic bag and placed it on the table in front of Serio. "Do you know what this is, Serio?"

"Cocaine."

"Do you know how much cocaine this is?"

"No. How bout you tell me."

"It's a kilogram. It's the drug of the future. It's dirt-cheap here, but it's worth thousands of dollars in the U.S. and other places. I have access to so much of this shit that I don't know what to do with it. Padro was getting rid of tons of this shit for me like it was nothing, but you put an end to that. So, as far as I see things, you owe me. I offer you the same deal that I had with him. You can get rich. Very, very rich, beyond your wildest dreams. Trust me. I'm offering you a piece of the pie, Serio. A piece you had better take if you know what's good for you."

Serio couldn't believe his ears. It was too good to be true. "What if I say no?" Serio rubbed his chin, testing the water.

The chief shrugged and said, "You accept the deal or you disappear, just like Padro."

Serio weighed his options. He knew what he was dealing with. He could either make the best of it or he could disappear. He knew that if he played his cards right that he could always make the best of the situation. It was a no brainer.

"Fair enough, let's do business." Serio nodded.

It was a deal and a new business relationship was born.

Surrounded by news crews and family members in the heart of downtown, Vicioso and Pete turned themselves in. Serio had talked them into doing so in an effort to make sure the police didn't kill them. The same police chief that now supplied Serio with kilos of cocaine was on the scene to oversee the whole thing. He assured Serio that the teenagers would be safe and he kept his word.

"They're goin' to be okay." Serio said to Melly. "They'll be home in two or three years. Don't worry yourself, okay."

Melly gave Serio a hug and said, "Thank you Serio, I was so worried that they were going to kill them. At least I know they are safe now."

CHAPTER 3

Vicioso and Pete did two years in a juvenile facility called Chapalla. They did their time as thorough young dudes that took no shit; they made names for themselves by doing so. In countless encounters the two street thugs from Santa Cruz didn't think twice about stabbing anything that got in their way. Most of their beefs were with dudes from Colon, another part of Panama. Word about how Vicioso and Pete were carrying things on the inside made it all the way back to their projects and by the time they hit the streets again at 18 they were well respected men. They had a lot of pull in Santa Cruz by this time. Everyone knew they had paid their dues. By this time, Serio and Polee had made their way to Brooklyn, New York and were setting things up in a way to bring others from their projects over. Getting to the U.S. and having a chance at a better life was every young kids dream in the projects of Panama. Vicioso had plans of taking the trip to the U.S. himself after hearing stories about how Polee and Serio were getting rich there, but he needed Serio to find a way to get him there. Vicioso's top goal was to make it to the U.S.

Walking through the projects on his way to Niecy's apartment, Vicioso saw Pimpo and a few of his comrades. At 16, Pimpo was all about his business and was known as a no nonsense young nigga. Pimpo and his crew were pulling off the biggest downtown robberies in the city, wreaking havoc on the tourist and anybody else that had what they wanted. The police couldn't stop them, although they had made it clear that they were going to kill them the first time they got the chance to. Pimpo had already been shot in the back by the police but that didn't slow him down one bit, he was on a mission to get money by all means.

"Pimpo!" Vicioso called out as he walked up on his brother and his crew.

"Que sopa?" Pimpo said as he walked over with his gold tooth gleaming in the bright sun.

Vicioso gave his brother five and said, "What y'all up to for the day?"

"We trying to get rid of these gold chains we got last night. Why, what's up, mena?"

"I got a job you might like?" Vicioso lit his cigarette.

"Tell me about it, laope."

"I know where a safe at, but I need some help gettin' to it."

"When you wanna pull it off?" Pimpo got right to the point. He wasn't into a lot of talking. Money came before everything.

"Later on tonight. Where you gon' be at?"

"Over Me-Me's." Pimpo said.

"I'll call over there when I'm ready. You gon' like this move here."

"Cool." Pimpo gave Vicioso five and stepped off with his crew.

Minutes later, Vicioso was letting himself into Niecy's apartment.

"Que sopa, mami?" Vicioso said when he saw her sitting on the sofa in a long white T-shirt that was somewhat see-through. Her black bra and panties were outlined underneath. She smiled when she saw him and got up to give him a hug and a kiss, pressing her sexy body against his. Rubbing her back, Vicioso said, "Damn, you smell good."

"I just got out the shower, papi." Niecy laughed.

Niecy and Vicioso were closer than ever now. While he was locked up she did everything in her power to make his time go as smooth as possible. Her letters and pictures gave him something to look forward to from day to day. It made their love for one another grow stronger than ever. Although Niecy didn't have much money to send since she was taking care of herself, she still made sure she sent him a few dollars here and there for him to buy the things he needed. That meant the world to Vicioso and he swore that he would always be loyal to her for that. He told himself that one day he would be on top of the world and that he would make sure she wanted for nothing. Vicioso swore that no matter what he did when he got out of Chapalla that he was going to show Niecy that he loved her with all of his heart. She was the one for him and he knew this out of the gate

"Pete just called here lookin' for you." Niecy said. "He said he'll be ready later on."

"Okay." Vicioso said as he and Niecy took a seat on the sofa. He put an arm around her and gave her a kiss on the cheek. They talked and touched and hugged and kissed like young lovers, enjoying the time they spent together. Just as things were about to get real heated the phone rang.

"Damn." Niecy said. "I wonder who the hell that is." She got up and answered the phone. After exchanging a few words with the caller she cut her eyes back at Vicioso and said, "It's for you."

"Who is it?" Vicioso wasn't in the mood for talking, he wanted some alone time with his woman.

"Serio." Niecy said, handing him the phone.

After making a small fortune by dealing with the police chief back home, Serio fled the country and went to New York where Polee was already waiting for him. Things worked out exactly as planned. In the process, Serio beat the police chief for close to twenty-five kilos and sent the cocaine to New York through Polee's connect. Polee and Serio along with Reego were taking full advantage of the booming drug trade in the U.S. Things were in full swing.

"Serio!" Vicioso said. "What's up, compa? I got the pictures you sent. Man, y'all niggaz look like movie stars up there. Y'all got on all that gold and diamonds, sittin' on BMW's and shit. America must really be the land of milk and honey. I can't wait for my turn to shine."

Serio laughed. "Yeah it's beautiful up here. Your turn is coming real soon. Believe that. Ain't no snatching no wallets up here though. This is the real deal. Niggaz can get rich up here, I swear to God, Vicioso. You'd love it up here. Shit moves a hundred times faster, money is everywhere. It's like the shit grows on trees. I ain't never seen nothin' like this shit. Everything you ever heard about shit up here is true. Even the police act different, they can't shoot you like they do down there. They gotta' have a reason to shoot. Can you believe it?" Serio laughed, he'd only been in New York for about a year and a half, but he'd caught on to the American way of life overnight.

Thoughts of New York flooded Vicioso's mind as Serio glorified the infinite opportunities of the drug trade. "I'm tryin' to get a taste of that." Vicioso said. "You know I can carry my own weight. Y'all gotta have a spot me for me up there. What's up, let me know somethin', mena."

"We runnin' a tight ship right now, we done ran into a few problems. Some light shit, but we still need to make sure everything is what it's supposed to be. But give me some time and you got my word that I'll get you up here. By all means, I need you. Just be easy for a second." Serio said.

"Cool, 'cause I need a change. I'm right back doin' the same shit I was doin' before I got locked up. This shit gettin' old, real old real fast. I need some new avenues."

"Vicioso, I got you. That's my word." Serio said. "Let me run it by Polee."

When Vicioso got off the phone with Serio he looked at Niecy and said, "Can we finish what we were doin'?"

Niecy smiled, pushed Vicioso down on the sofa and got on top of him. "I'm waitin' for you."

Brooklyn, New York.

Serio pulled up in a black Nissan 280 ZX and parked in front of a tall apartment building in Crown Heights. Polee controlled a lucrative coke spot inside the building that was making close to $10,000 a day, easy. It was Serio's job to make sure the spot ran smoothly and he took pride in his job. Having no problem with playing his position, Serio was the number two man in the drug operation, mostly because Polee was in New York first. However, Polee and Serio had a deal that would give Serio his own drug operation in due time. For the first few months in New York, Serio did all the security work in connection with the drug operation. Serio understood that murder had to be part of the game if he and Polee were going to survive in the U.S. as Panamanians. They made it their business to play no games. On more than one occasion, Serio put his Uzi to work in defense of Polee's coke spot. After the first murder the stage was set and the law was laid down firmly.

Sliding his .45 in his waistband as he grabbed the shopping bag between his legs, Serio looked around and got out the car. There was a lot of traffic moving up and down the busy streets. He made his way into the building and up to the coke spot on the fourth floor. Along the way he passed dealers and addicts that lined the hallway. At ten in the morning the traffic was moving like it was ten at night. Cocaine seemed to move around the clock. Polee wanted to make sure that his spots never ran out of work.

Serio knocked on the door and Reego let him in.

"What's up, Serio?" Reego shut the door behind them. The small apartment that Reego was working out of had nothing more in it than a sofa, a TV, a table where the drugs sat, and an M-16 leaning against the wall.

"How shit goin'?" Serio sat the shopping bag on the table. It contained $5,000 worth of coke.

"Shit movin' fast. The police shut down the American spot on the second floor. Business done picked up like shit in the last hour. Money comin' in faster than I can count it."

"Oh yeah, picked up like what?"

"I done made over a thousand dollars in the last forty minutes or so." Reego said. A knock at the door grabbed his attention. It was a sell. Two more followed back to back. Reego served the free-base through the hole in the door where the peephole used to be. "We gone sell out before four o' clock. I'm tellin' you some good shit."

"I'ma drop some more coke off after I take care of a few things. You gon' be okay. Trust me. I see what's goin' on." Serio said, looking at his brand new gold Rolex. "I'll be back in about an hour or so."

"Cool." Reego gave Serio five.

Serio left the Crown Heights coke spot and went to pick up some money from two other spots. It was a real job. He then headed to one of the apartments that Polee had set up as a stash house. Inside the stash house Serio put up the money he'd collected which was close to $50,000 and it wasn't even

noon yet. He then ordered some take out food and waited for Polee.

Polee showed up a short while later carrying a mid-size gym bag. He was returning from a meeting with his Colombian connect in Queens. In a red short set and a gold Cuban link chain with a diamond Jesus piece, Polee looked like a million bucks. He sat the gym bag on the dining room table and said, "Everything cool at Reego's spot? I heard the police ran up in the building."

"Yeah, everything cool. The police raided the Americans' spot on the second floor." Serio said, smoking a cigarette. He told Polee how fast the coke was moving while he was in the spot with Reego. "I'ma have to take some more work over there when I leave here. It's movin' that fast."

"Sounds good to me." Polee smiled.

"I put all the money from the spots in the safe."

"Good." Polee said. "Take a look inside the gym bag. Get one of them new guns. It's some serious shit in there."

Serio looked inside the gym bag and pulled out a small Uzi.

"I got them from our Colombian friends. They said we can get them for dirt-cheap. I want us to give all our workers one of them. Having one of them with you is like having a small army by your side." Polee went in the refrigerator and grabbed a Pepsi. "Did you take your cut of the money yet?"

"Nah, I'll do it when we collect all the money tonight. The shit ain't goin' nowhere."

"Cool. We got a shipment comin' in tonight. I need you to ride wit' me to get it. You know how shit is up here. I always need my right hand man with me to make sure shit is straight."

"Say no more, it's done."

Polee had sweet connect that was giving him kilos for $10,000 apiece as long as he bought fifty or more at a time.

"Let's get this money. We are doing good right now, but it's so much more out there for us. When it's all said and done we will be richer than we ever dreamed." Serio said.

Time began to fly for Polee and Serio. They were getting paid by all means and setting the pace for other Panamanians in Crown Heights. In a way, Polee was seen as the man, he called the shots and had the connects. However, Serio was very much a part of the team's success and had no problem playing the background, it was part of the plan. The plan was to get rich, not famous. Together, Polee and Serio had established a cocaine distribution network throughout Crown Heights that was far greater than they had ever wished for. They had coke spots that were pulling in more than twenty thousand dollars a day. Nevertheless, it was time for the next phase of the New York plan, as far as Serio was concerned.

Inside Polee's Crown Heights apartment, he and Serio sat back smoking weed and watching a little TV. The conversation was nice and smooth, they were talking about how good business was going and how they were going to bring up some more of their homies from Santa Cruz to make their numbers stronger.

Blowing weed smoke in the air, Serio looked at Polee and said, "I think it's time for me to open my own spot, Polee." Serio had been mapping out his next move for some time.

Polee twisted up his face and gave Serio a funny look. The look rubbed Serio the wrong way. "I thought we talked about that already, Serio. I thought we was building somethin' big together. Team work is what makes us strong."

With a slight frown on his face, Serio said, "We did talk about it, but I don't think you understood where I was comin' from, Polee. It's time for me to do my own thing. We put everything together the way we said we would now it's time for me to branch out. I'm a team player, you know that, but

34

what we got goin' on right now is all yours. All you want to do is focus on Brooklyn, I want to take this thing on the road and open up spots in other places, maybe even other cities. We got people that we know gettin' rich all the way down in Miami and shit. I want a piece of that action."

"You want more money, Serio? Is that it?"

"Nah," Serio shook his head. "I just told you what I want. I want my own thing."

"It's not the time yet, Serio."

"Polee, I don't think you understand, I'm not askin' you. I'm tellin' you that I'm about to do my own thing." Serio looked him in the eyes. "We will always be brothers, but I'm looking forward to making some other moves."

"Who the raas you think you talkin' to, Serio?" Polee yelled.

Serio smiled and shook his head. "Choocha, Polee, you're lettin' all this money go to your head. Let's not forget that we put this shit together as equals. Remember?"

"I'm the boss!" Polee shouted. "I call the shots! You don't tell me that you're about to do your own thing! Don't forget who runs the show!"

"You don't call the shots for me!" Serio shouted as they both stood up, standing face to face. Tension was thick. He didn't think Polee would try to pull rank on him. Serio was offended that Polee was talking to him like he was just a "worker" or something.

"It's the money ain't it?! You want it all to yourself! Don't you?!" Polee shouted.

"This don't have shit to do wit' money, Polee! We do things two different ways! You know that. If you think it's anything different than you're wrong."

Polee sighed and shook his head as he walked away. He was heated. "Okay, you wanna do your own thing. Cool!

You do that, Serio. Just remember that you are turnin' your back on the family. I got the manpower up here. I got the connects and the respect---"

"Fuck that shit you talkin', like I need you. I helped you put this shit together! You ain't put this shit together by yourself. I'm the one that killed Padro. You forgot that?!" Serio was heated now. "I'm the one that got the diamond job done right to set all this shit up! I played my part; don't forget that! Don't you ever forget that!"

Reego was in the other room sleep when the heated argument woke him up. He walked into the living room to see what was going on. "What the fuck is goin' on?!" Reego shouted, trying to get Serio and Polee's attention. "What y'all yellin' and shit for."

"Fuck this shit!" Serio walked out the front door.

Polee yelled after him, "You on your own, Serio! You makin' a big mistake! You ain't shit without me!"

"What the raas is goin' on?" Reego asked Polee. "We family we ain't supposed to be fightin' each other. We got too many other motherfuckers against us up here."

"Serio wanna be the boss; he think he know best. Fuck him!" Polee shut the front door.

"But we all fam---"

Polee cut Reego off. "Serio ain't family no more, he picked his side. He ain't wit' us no more, he on his own. You got his spot now. Can you handle it?"

"Y'all just had a little argument, Polee. It ain't the end of the world. Y'all brothers, y'all gon' get past this shit. We all brothers." Reego didn't want to see Serio and Polee fall out; they were both family to him. He felt caught in the middle being as though he was loyal to them both. However Polee was the boss.

36

"Listen to me, Reego." Polee sighed out of frustration. "This New York shit ain't about doin' your own thing. It's about teamwork. Whoever got the strongest team wins every time. We are all outsiders up here. If we want to do our own thing then we can't say that we are family because family sticks together, no matter what. Serio has always wanted the whole world for himself. That's the way he wants it so fine. Like I said, you have his spot. Understand?"

Reego just shook his head and sighed.

"I understand. Say no more."

Serio was living with a badass broad by the name of Yasmin. He met her shortly after he hit New York and they began to grow on each other. Months later they moved in together. Yasmin was a Panamanian that had grown up in New York so she understood the way things worked in Brooklyn. She was the first person to show Serio around when he didn't know how to make it to the corner store and back without getting lost in the busy New York streets.

Lying in the bed with Yasmin after a strong session of love making, Serio gazed at the TV with a blank look on his face. Yasmin looked into his eyes and knew something was wrong.

"What's wrong wit' you, Serio? The pum-pum wasn't good or somethin'?" Yasmin joked.

Serio smiled and rubbed her silky hair. "You know the sex was good, baby girl. It's always good."

"Well what's wrong, I can tell that something's on your mind."

"Me and Polee fell out today." Serio said as he lit a cigarette.

"Fell out like what? An argument or somethin'?"

"A little bit more than that. It got bad. We said shit to each other that we may not be able to ever take back." Serio explained the situation to Yasmin. "I'ma go ahead and start my own spot. That was the game plan from the start. I ain't never been good at being number two anyway. Either I'm equal or I'm gone. For a man like it'll never work any other way." Yasmin was rubbing Serio's thigh as he explained the situation to her. "It's time for a change. A lot of time change is better. You know?"

"I understand. Do what's best for you, popi."

Over the next few days, Serio set out to put his plan into effect. He and Polee didn't even try to clear up their differences. The tension between them was a big topic amongst Panamanians in Crown Heights. Serio found out that Polee had him black balled. None of the Panamanians he knew from home would do business with him for fear of getting on Polee's shit list; they all had bullshit reasons why they couldn't sell him any coke. Frustrated, Serio had to try the Colombians that he knew in Queens. It was his best shot.

Sitting in the back offices of a corner store in Queens, Serio discussed business with a Colombian man by the name of Vick. Vick was in his early thirties with light skin and dark, curly hair. His potbelly made him look a few years older. He and Serio knew each other from Panama. Although Vick was Colombian he'd grown up in Panama and then moved to New York in his late twenties to take advantage of the booming drug trade.

"Serio," Vick said. "May I ask what happened between you and Polee that has you here talkin' business with me? Not to get in your business, but something doesn't sit well with me about this whole thing."

"Word travels fast I see." Serio smiled. "Nevertheless, me and Polee are family, but right now we are doing our own thing. That's it, that's all."

"I understand." Vick smiled. "So, how much business are you tryin' to do? Let's talk numbers."

38

"Depends on how much you gon' charge me for a key." Serio said.

Vick raised his eyebrow and said, "For you... we go way back, so let's say ten-thousand a kilo. You were kind to me back home; I want to repay your friendship."

"Sounds good to me." Serio smiled. "I see that you honor friendship. That's says a lot about you."

"Helps you live long in this business."

"Makes sense."

"Here's the deal, Serio. Money makes the world go round. Long as we can make money together we have a partnership."

Serio shook Vick's hand. "Deal."

Serio spent the rest of the week plotting his next move. Now that he had a connect he had to open a spot. He knew he was in for a struggle, but there was no turning back. He was only going to return back to Panama one of the two ways: Rich or in a box.

Riding down Franklin Avenue in his black Corvette, Serio saw Reego coming out of a Panamanian store. Reego waved Serio down. Pulling over, Serio watched Reego walk over to the car. There was no love lost between them. Serio was sure of it.

Reego jumped in the passenger seat and said, "What's up, Serio?"

Serio sighed and said, "Just tryin' to put a few things together out here. You know how it goes."

"Cut the shit, Serio. You and Polee need to stop actin' like y'all ain't family. We came up here as family, ain't nothin' supposed to come between us." Reego was hurt about the whole situation. "If we can't stick together up here what's it all worth; we supposed to have each other backs up here. Why don't y'all cut that shit out, man."

"You're right, Reego, but it ain't me. Polee thinks he's the Godfather or some shit. It's his way or no way at all. I ain't kissin' nobody's ass. If it was my mother I would still feel the same way."

"I understand that, but y'all still need to work this shit out, Serio. You know better. We family, I can't say that enough."

"I'm sure we will work it out sooner or later, but right now it's best that we do our own thing and go out own ways." Serio lit a cigarette. "Polee done let his head get big. He done lost sight of the game plan. We all supposed to be getting rich, not just him. That's not how this shit works."

Reego sighed. "I know, but it gotta be another way to make this shit work for us to all get along."

Serio put his hand on Reego's shoulder and said, "Me and you gon' always be family, we brothers. That ain't gon' ever change. Me and Polee always gon' be family, me and him just ain't gon' be doin' business together. This shit will blow over. Until then we gon' just let it play itself out."

Serio pulled up and parked his car in the Red Hook Projects. He had met a girl who lived in the projects by the name of Lisa. She was sexy, down-to-earth, street-smart, New York girl that he'd met in a club in Flatbush a while back. They hooked up from time to time. As Serio made his way to Lisa's building he noticed people everywhere and they all seemed to be watching him. He was an outsider. Serio didn't let the mean glares bother him. He was on a mission. Making his way through Lisa's building with his hand inside his coat pocket on his .45, Serio headed up to the third floor and knocked on Lisa's door.

"What's up, Serio?" Lisa opened the door with a smile. She gave him a hug and let him in. She was a light-skinned girl with long black hair that was peppered with streaks of blond. She stood 5' 4" carrying 130-plus-pounds in all the

40

right places with a body that made Serio look her up and down twice. "I thought you were comin' over last night."

"I got caught up." Serio walked over to her sofa and took a seat, taking his coat off. "How you doin'?"

"I'm okay." Lisa said in her sexy New York accent. Her jeans were so tight that Serio could see her panty line. "I just finished doin' my hair." She sat beside Serio. "Bam should be here in a minute."

Bam was a young dude in his early twenties that Serio met through Lisa. Bam and Lisa's younger cousin used to mess with each other in high school. From time to time, Serio would give Bam a few $500-packs of coke to sell. Serio told Bam that he planned to open his own coke spot and offered Bam a job. Bam was all for it, so Red Hook would be the base of operation for the coke spot.

"You hungry?" Lisa asked, walking toward the kitchen.

"Nah I ate breakfast before I came over. Thanks though." Serio got up and turned the TV on. Minutes later there was a knock on the door. Serio answered and let Bam in.

Giving Serio five, Bam said, "What's up, Serio?"

"You ready to put this thing in motion?" Serio asked.

"Hell yeah!" Bam said as he and Serio sat down on the sofa together.

"I'm cookin' some eggs and bacon. You want some, Bam?" Lisa asked from the kitchen.

"Yeah, I could use something to eat. Thanks Lisa." Bam said.

"Bam," Serio said, "I'ma be straight up wit' you. I'ma fuck wit' you, but I don't want no shit out of you about my money. I don't know no other way to say that. We see eye-to-eye on that?"

"Serio, you don't gotta worry about that wit' me. I just wanna make some paper. That's all." Bam said.

"Cool, we gon' open up shop tomorrow."

"Where at?"

"Lisa said we can use this spot until I can get another apartment in the building. You know me, I don't give a fuck as long as it ain't no bullshit. Just look out for me here and there."

Serio said, "No problem. That's how we'll do it then."

Bam rubbed his hands together with excitement. "I'm ready. Let's put it in motion."

The next morning, Bam and Serio got down to business pumping coke out of Lisa's apartment. Bam gave away a few free hits to get the word out and then the sells began to come slowly but surely. Within a few hours, business began to pick up faster than expected. Word got out that the new spot on the third floor had high quality coke. Bam was serving coke through the hole in the door left and right. Serio sat on the sofa smoking weed and watching TV with an Uzi beside him; he wanted to make sure things ran smooth. There was no time for games. The plan was coming together well. From 8:00 A.M. to 4:00 P.M. the operation ran strong and smooth. At the end of the day the count was $7,500. Not bad at all.

As Serio and Bam finished counting the money, Lisa walked into the living room and said, "Serio, you gon' look out for me today or at the end f the week?" She understood how things went. Her uncle used to use her apartment the same way before he went to prison.

"Here you go." Serio gave her $1,000 and said, "This should hold you for a minute, but I'ma still look out for you at the end of the week. This is just for starters."

Lisa gave Serio a kiss on the cheek and said, "Thanks. I'll see you when I get back. I gotta run to the store."

"I gotta make a run, I'll see you later on tonight." Serio said. His mind was really on all the money he could make if the spot could continue to run smoothly.

"Okay." Lisa smiled and left.

"I told you the spot was a sure thing." Bam said, playing with Serio's Uzi.

"You was right." Serio handed Bam $1,000. "That's for your pocket. From here on out I'ma pay you at the end of the week. You cool wit' that?"

"Sounds like a plan, son." Bam said.

"We gon' open up shop first thing in the mornin', eight on the nose. Make sure you ready." Serio put his money in his coat pocket and grabbed his Uzi and placed it in a shopping bag. "I'll see you tomorrow." Serio gave Bam five and they left together.

CHAPTER 4

The next three weeks moved smoothly and business picked up fast at Serio's Red Hook spot. Bam was a breadwinner, pulling in close to $10,000 a day for Serio. The first hadn't even rolled around yet. Bam had recruited two Red Hook teenagers to function as lookouts; their names were Gee and Miles. Serio didn't have to sit in the spot all day long after the first week, he would drop the coke off in the morning and come back to collect the money around four in the evening. However, he was very hands-on with the spot so he made it his business to hang out at Lisa's most of the time just for the hell of it.

Serio walked into Lisa's apartment just before 8:00 A.M. carrying a shopping bag with a $10,000 pack in it. He also had breakfast for Lisa; he always brought her breakfast when he dropped the coke off. Sitting the shopping bag down on the coffee table he took the McDonald's food to Lisa's bedroom.

"What's up, mami?" Serio said as he walked in. She was laying in the bed still sleep.

Rolling over, she smiled when she saw Serio. "It's time for you to find another spot to work out of." She joked. "I'm gettin' tired of getting' up all early in the mornin'. This is really not for me."

"Don't worry your pretty self." Serio sat on the bed beside her and rubbed his hand through her silky hair. "I'm workin' on that." He kissed her forehead. "You need to get up and get dressed if you still want me to drive us to Atlantic City."

"Let me take a shower." Lisa got up and headed to the bathroom in her bra and panties.

Serio let Bam in a few minutes later. "Everything you need is in the shopping bag. I'ma take Lisa shoppin', I'll be back before four."

"Cool." Bam hung his coat up. "I got this here. Don't worry about shit, son."

A short while later, Serio and Lisa were gone and Bam was on the grind. Hours seemed to fly and the sells never stopped coming. By 12:30 P.M. Bam had made $4,500; he was taking no shorts. A knock on the door grabbed his attention. Bam walked over and looked through the hole in the door and saw Miles. He opened the door and was taken by surprise. "What the fuck?!" He shouted. A light-skinned gunman had Miles by the collar of his coat with a pistol to the back f his head. The gunman forced his way inside the apartment with the quickness followed by a dark-skinned gunman that had Gee by the collar at gunpoint as well. Bam was caught slippin', the Uzi that Serio gave him was sitting on the coffee table with the coke.

"Get the fuck n the floor, nigga!" the light-skinned gunman told Bam as he slammed Miles to the floor and put his foot on his back. The dark-skinned gunman did the same to Gee. "Watch them niggaz!" the light-skinned gunman told his comrade. "If they move pop they muthafuckin' ass, son."

The light skinned gunman began to search the apartment. He quickly collected the coke, money, and the Uzi. With all the goods stuffed inside a shopping bag that was sitting on the coffee table, the gunman pointed his .357 magnum at Bam's head and said, "Where's the Panamanian?!" Bam swore he didn't know where Serio was. The light-skinned gunman began to pistol whip Bam viciously. "I should kill your dumb ass for bringin' a fuckin' Panamanian around here!" The light-skinned gunman continued to beat Bam with the huge revolver. Blood was all over Bam's face and shirt as well as all over the living room floor. "If I catch you or that fuckin' Panamanian back around here y'all gon' leave in body bags. Think I'm playin' if you want to, son."

Both gunmen left the apartment.

A short while later, Serio was back in Red Hook and he was heated. He'd brought an M-16 assault rifle along with him. Inside Lisa's living room, Serio questioned Bam, Miles and Gee about the robbery as if he were an FBI agent. With an ice pack to his head, Bam explained everything that went down. Looking around the room, Serio shouted, "So y'all don't got no fuckin' idea who the raas did this shit?!" his accent was thick and volatile. "Somebody better know something."

"It was Terrance and BK." Miles said. "They on stick-up time."

"Where can I find them?" Serio asked.

"They hang out two courts over." Bam said. "They fuck wit' the kid Justice I was tellin' you about." Justice was a Red Hook hustler with a lot of pull in the projects. "Terrance and BK are somewhat like hired guns on Justice's team."

"Yeah, well they better have a lotta guns if they wanna fuck wit' me." Serio said. He stood up and looked at Bam. "We still gon' open up the spot in the mornin'. Are y'all still on board? Let me know right now?"

After a little thought, Bam said, "I'm still on board." Serio was putting money in his pocket and that's all that mattered as far as Bam was concerned. "I'll be ready in the mornin'."

Miles and Gee were still on board as well.

"When I come around here in the mornin' I'ma bring firepower for everybody." Serio said. He let them out and went back into Lisa's bedroom. She was sitting on the bed

watching TV. "Come on, let's get out of here. I'ma put you in a hotel until I can get you another apartment." Serio said. "Things around here are about to get real ugly."

"Serio, I don't have to go nowhere. Ain't nothin' gon' happen to me." Lisa wasn't afraid. She'd lived in the projects her whole life.

"Come on now, I don't want to fuss wit' you. Just for a few days until I get everything in order." Serio said, softly grabbing her hand.

"Okay, but only for a few days." Lisa said, sucking her teeth.

After putting Lisa up in a hotel, Serio hooked back up with Bam. Bam showed him where to find Terrance and BK. After putting a face to each name, Serio dropped Bam off at his people's spot in Crown Heights. He then headed back to Red Hook as darkness fell. Serio was a man on a mission. Riding down Columbia Road, Serio saw Terrance standing beside a white Benz talking to a West Indian-looking dude that was wearing a lot of gold. Serio passed the Benz and turned around at the end of the block. Coming back up the block, he pulled along the Benz and jumped out with the M-16. Terrance was so used to being the one pulling the trigger that he didn't even try to run, he went for his pistol. Serio sprayed the M-16 sending scores of bullets in Terrance's direction. Shell flew everywhere as the M-16 lit up with a burst of fire. The Benz pulled off with screaming tires as Terrance's bullet riddled body fell to the cold ground. Running around his car, Serio stood over Terrance's body and sprayed his lifeless body with another blast of fully automatic gunfire. Then looking around at the scattering crowd Serio walked back to his car and got behind the wheel like nothing happened. He pulled off nice and slow and headed to Yasmin's Apartment.

CHAPTER 5

R ed Hook projects were already one of the most violent projects in Brooklyn, but after Terrance's murder it became a real live war zone. Serio had recruited a team of young Panamanians to help him fortify the building that his coke spot was in. They held the building down as if it was a foreign embassy on enemy soil. Men were in front of the building, one was on the roof and two were in the back and they were all armed with Uzi machine guns. Miles and Gee worked as lookouts. Bam worked the gate, pushing the caps through the hole in the door. Serio stayed on the scene at all times. For days, money came in bits and pieces. The frequent shootings always slowed money down, but Serio would not leave Red Hook. He swore that the only way he would leave was in a body bag. Justice and his crew were throwing everything they had at Serio and the Panamanians in retaliation for Terrance's murder. Terrance's man, BK, was on a kamikaze missions to avenge Terrance's death. He'd personally killed three Panamanians, but more always came. Whenever a body would drop on Serio's side he'd make sure a body or two would drop on Justice's side the same day. That's how it was going to be, and nobody was going to give an inch.

Lying in the bed with Yasmin, Serio was thinking about all of the drama that came with the drug trade. It was tons of money to be made, but the risks were unlimited. Fuck it, he thought. He was going to get paid regardless. The phone on the nightstand rang and grabbed his attention.

"Yeah." Serio answered.

"I need to see you, Serio."

"Reego?"

"Yeah, it's me, laope. I got some important shit to tell you. I need to see like right now. Stop whatever you doin' and let me talk to you in person real quick."

Serio's mind began to race. He looked at every situation as a possible move to trick him and he wasn't going for that at all. "Man, it's two in the mornin'. What's so important?" Serio spoke in a hushed tone, trying not to wake Yasmin.

"You need to hear this, mena."

Serio could tell that something was seriously wrong. "You want me to meet you somewhere, Reego?"

"Nah, I'm on my way over there."

"Okay." Serio hung up the phone and put on some clothes. All kinds of thoughts continued to run through his mind.

"Where you goin', papi?" Yasmin asked.

"Nowhere. Reego said he needs to talk to me. He's on his way over here. Go back to sleep, baby." Serio put on his pants and went into the living room to wait on Reego. He sat on the sofa and smoked a cigarette. He was stressing heavy. With his .45 in hand, Serio walked over to the window to see how things looked outside. Something didn't feel right. He threw on his coat and hat and went outside to sit in his car, behind the dark tinted windows. He wanted to see how Reego came. He hated to think that Reego could be up to no good, but in the game Serio knew that he could trust no one 100%. He had to stay on his toes and two steps ahead of the next man if he planned to survive.

A few minutes later he saw Reego pull up and park his little Nissan on the other side of the street. As Reego got out the car, Serio rolled down his window and called out, "Reego!"

Walking over to Serio's car, Reego got in and said, "What the raas you doin' out here in the cold?"

"Needed a place to think." Serio studied Reego's eyes and body language for any signs of treachery or double-crossing. He didn't see any. "What's so important, Reego?"

"Man ..." Reego sighed. He had a heavy load on his shoulders. He didn't know how to break the news to Serio. "I don't know how to tell you this shit."

A car rolled by slowly. Serio and Reego both looked to the right. Serio had his finger on the trigger of his .45; there had already been two attempts on his life since he killed Terrance. As the car bent the corner at the end of the block, Serio looked at Reego and said, "Just say it, Reego."

"You know Rico, right?" Reego asked, looking out the side mirror as he spoke.

Rico was a Panamanian triggerman that Polee used from time to time to take care of business. Serio and Rico had taken care of a few jobs for Polee together. Serio knew that Rico was a killer.

"Yeah, I know Rico, why?" Serio asked.

"I overheard Polee talkin' to him about hittin' you." Reego looked Serio in the eyes and could tell that the news hurt him. "Polee said that you done got beside yourself and that you went behind his back and got a connect wit' Vick. He thinkin' that you are goin' to be a problem for him later on down the line so he wants you out of the way."

Serio frowned. "Choocha de su madre." He couldn't believe it.

"I couldn't believe it either, Serio." Reego shook his head in disgust. "Polee crossed the line, I had to warn you. I couldn't have it on my heart and not tell you about it."

"Now you see what I was talkin' about when I told you that he let all this money go to his head."

Reego nodded in agreement.

"Polee thought I was gon' crawlin' back to him, but I didn't so now he wants to take me out. He thinks it's gonna be easy since I got my hands full in Red Hook." Serio lit another cigarette and nodded his head as he said, "I'ma give his ass what he wants." He took a long look at Reego and said, "You know what's next, right?"

"Yeah." Reego nodded. "Polee done lost his fuckin' mind."

"I gotta move first." Serio took a deep pull of his cigarette. "Are you wit' me, Reego?"

Reego sighed. He had already picked his side when he decided to warn Serio about the hit. "Yeah, I'm wit' you, Serio."

"We outnumbered, niggaz gon' be comin' at us from all sides, you know this right? I want that clear in your head."

"I don't give a fuck. We family, I got your back. Don't nothin' else need to be said."

Serio shook Reego's hand firmly and said, "I respect that."

The next day, Serio and Reego were riding down Franklin Avenue in a beat up blue Pontiac GTO. They were discussing plans to bring some more of their homies up from Panama. They needed more numbers to survive.

"We need more loyal homies up here, ones that ain't gon' let this money change them. Vicioso and Pete gon' be the first two I bring up."

"I like that idea there. They are family." Reego said, looking out the window.

Something caught Serio's eye. "Ain't that Rico right there on the pay phone?" He pointed across the street.

"Hell yeah." Reego said.

Serio pulled over at the end of the block. "I'ma send Polee a little message." Serio said as he pulled the hood of his coat over his head. "Get behind the wheel, Reego, I gotta take care of this myself."

Serio got out of the car smoothly and crossed the street with his Uzi hidden inside his huge coat. Walking up the block he paid no attention to the many people that were walking up and down the street. He had one thing on his mind: MURDER! As Serio approached Rico he smiled when he saw Rico hang up the phone and look his way. Rico looked Serio right in the eyes and had no reason to be apprehensive of him; he was sure that Serio had no idea about the hit on his life.

"Yo, mena ..." Rico extended his hand.

"Nothin' much" Serio shook his head, wanting to laugh at Rico's cockiness, but instead, he whipped the Uzi out and fired shots. The slugs hit Rico in the chest and everybody outside began to scatter and scream. Rico's face showed his surprise as he staggered backward and fell to the ground, struggling to pull his pistol. Serio looked down into Rico's eyes. "You was draggin' your feet, motherfucker. You know I don't know fuckin' games." Serio then sprayed Rico's body with everything left in the clip.

Reego pulled up in the GTO and yelled, "Let's go!"

Serio looked around and walked back to the car. As Reego pulled off, Serio looked at him from the passenger seat and said, "I'm playin' for keeps from here on out. No talking at all."

Amongst the Panamanians in Brooklyn, Rico's murder was big news. Everyone had seemed to know that Serio killed him and that Reego was with him. Lines were clearly drawn and there was no turning back. Polee smiled and shook his head when he got the news; he knew that he had underestimated Serio. Polee was pleased to know that Serio was on to him, he knew that it could have been him on the other end of Serio's

52

Uzi instead of Rico, but now everything was out in the open. Polee didn't think Reego would side against him. Nevertheless, he had to deal with the situation at hand. Polee moved his wife to New Jersey so that she would be out of the way. He tried to get his mother to move, but she wouldn't leave the beautiful house that Polee had bought for her when he first moved her to New York.

Sitting in a Bronx apartment with two of his soldiers, Polee waited for Serio to call him back. He'd beeped him about five minutes earlier. The phone rang a few moments later and Polee answered it, "Yeah." Polee said.

"What do you want?" Serio said flatly.

Knowing Serio's voice, Polee said, "I didn't think you had it in you, laope. I see you can play for keeps."

"We learn somethin' new every day, don't we? Anyway, what the fuck do you want? We don't have shit to talk about." Serio shot back, coldly.

"Serio, you know you can't win. Your days here in Brooklyn are numbered. This ain't Panama, you don't know what you're getting' yourself into up here. You do know this, don't you?"

"It looks like I'm catchin' on just fine don't you think?" Serio laughed a little bit. "I think you done forgot who the raas you talkin' to. I'll kill everything close to you if I have to, you know me Polee. I know all that money you makin' ain't messin' wit' your memory, is it?" Serio smiled and shook his head.

"Serio, we'll see what you're really made of, but be assured that when this is all said and done that you and that raas, Reego, gon' be goin' back home in a box. The bill's on me, I'll see to it that the funerals are beautiful."

Serio laughed. "You done really let this shit go to your head. I hope it's worth it when your days come to an end."

Serio hung up the phone and turned to Reego, who was sitting across from him in Lisa's apartment. "Polee done really lost his mind. He talkin' that Godfather shit again, like he can't be touched for some reason."

"Damn, you told him that you would kill everything close to him." Reego had a look of concern on his face.

Serio instantly understood Reego's concerned look. Reego was in love with Polee's sister, their relationship went all the way back to Santa Cruz; the two of them had plans to get married.

"You and I both know that I ain't gon' do nothin' to Mary. She's family to me, I was talkin' about everything close to him in the streets."

Reego sighed and shook his head.

"This shit is ugly. It's out of control, mena."

"We didn't make it this way." Serio stood up and lit a cigarette. "Polee made it like this and he gon' pay for it."

The next day, Serio and Reego were well armed as they headed for the Red Hook spot. They were working on almost no sleep, the night before they were out close to five in the morning trying to track Polee down. They had no such luck. Now, they had just returned from Queens where they copped five kilos from Vick for the coke spot. Even at war from all sides they were still pulling in close to $7,000 a day. With Reego on the team, Serio had a right hand man that he could trust. Since the Red Hook projects were so big they moved the coke spot to another building a few courts over by Columbia Road by the flagpole. From the new spot they could protect themselves better from attack, but the shootings and murders continued. Justice and his crew were doing all in their power to run the Panamanians out of Red Hook.

"Polee think he just gon' sit back and have somebody else do his dirty work while he keep gettin' rich." Serio said,

cruising through the Brooklyn streets behind the wheel of his Corvette. "He got another thing comin', compa. I know how to hit him where it hurts."

Serio and Reego had learned that Polee had paid some Haitians to murder them.

"I'ma start robbin' all of Polee's spots." Serio said. "That'll let him know that I ain't playin' no games wit' his ass. Since he want to hide out I'ma fuck wit' his money and clientele. That'll make him show his face. For sure."

As Serio turned onto Columbia Road, Reego pointed across the street and said, "That's that raas, Justice, right there!"

Before Serio or Reego could react, Justice, BK and a few other dudes that ran with Justice opened fire on the Corvette with all kinds of firepower. Bullets crashed through the windows as Serio stomped the gas and took the car flying onto the sidewalk and crashing into a telephone pole. Serio and Reego jumped out spraying their Uzis, trying to fend off Justice and his shooters. The broad daylight shoot out was like something out of a movie. People were running and screaming, trying to get out of the way; mothers were doing their best to cover up their kids as the bullets continued to fly with no names on them. Serio and Reego used the Corvette for cover as they sprayed at the gunmen that seemed to flood the middle of Columbia Road. Serio's crew saw the gunfight from their position in front of the building and joined in, spraying their machine guns at Justice's crew. Red Hook turned into Vietnam in seconds. Serio dropped one of Justice's gunmen with shots to the head and continued spraying.

Justice dropped two of Serio's men as he tried to hit Serio. He then locked eyes with Serio and they both let the bullets fly at each other not caring about getting hit. As bullets flew by

Justice's head, he ran out of ammo and had to take cover behind a car.

Reego caught BK running for cover and cut him down with the Uzi. BK lay in the middle of the street motionless after he hit the ground. Risking being cut down by gunfire, Reego ran down on BK and put slugs in the back of his head.

The shooting seemed to go on for hours, but only lasted for under two long minutes. Serio, Reego and their crew took heavy fire as they retreated to the building that they worked out of. Police sirens hit the air as both crews disappeared into the woodwork of the projects. When the smoke cleared three Panamanians lay dead on the sidewalk with machine guns in their hands. Two of Justice's men lay dead in the middle of the street. BK was one of them.

The Red Hook shooting made the news and was on all channels by 6 p.m. Serio and Reego sat in Serio's apartment watching the whole thing on TV in the living room while Yasmin cooked them something to eat. They'd taken a big loss this go round: Three men and five kilos of cocaine.

"This raas, Justice, got balls. I'll give him that much." Serio said, sitting on the sofa, pissed off. "But we ain't leavin' Red Hook. If they kill two, we gon' kill three. That's the way it's gonna be from here on out, Reego. Fuck it!"

"I'm wit' you to the end, you know that." Reego said. He'd been grazed by a bullet in the shoot out but didn't go to the hospital. "When the smoke clears we still gon' be around, Serio."

Serio smiled and nodded his head in agreement. Reego was everything he could ask for in a "brother." "We gotta strike back tonight; we gotta let them know that we here to stay. I'ma get us some men and we gon' hit they ass as hard as we can."

56

MONEY AIN'T EVERYTHING

Serio went to the closet and pulled out an M-16, he tossed it to Reego who caught it with two hands. Pulling out anther M-16 for himself, Serio said, "We gon' show them what this shit is all about, laope."

Polee was growing increasingly concerned about his mother not wanting to leave her house. He had damn near begged her to move and she still didn't want t hear any of it.

"Ma, I don't want to go into it right now. I need for you to go stay wit' Guy for a little while. Why is that so hard to understand? I don't want you to stay in Brooklyn, it's not safe here right now." Polee sat in his mother's kitchen trying his best to get her to leave for a while.

"I said no, Polee!" She said firmly. "Just because you and Julio are acting like fools don't mean that I have to leave my home. No one is going to do anything to me." She was no fool; she knew exactly what was going on with her son and Serio.

Polee sighed. "Ma, why won't you listen to me? Things are different now. People will come after you to get me. I can't let that happen. I have to protect you."

"The Lord will protect me." His mother rolled her eyes. "If you want to protect me, protect me from the pain you'll cause me if something happen to you out there. Stop the foolishness, Polee! I raised you better than that. Julio and Reego are like sons to me. They would never hurt me. I really can't believe how you boys are acting like enemies. What is going on?"

Polee shook his head. He had no answer. "I don't know what to say, Ma. I don't know what went wrong; I don't know how we got to this point."

"I know what went wrong." The older Panamanian woman said. "You all let the money come between friendship, money is the root of all evil. You boys have come up here and got into all this drug stuff and crime and now ya'll at each other's throat because of the lust for money and power. You all should be ashamed of yourselves. As a matter of fact, I want you all over here to have dinner. I have some things to get off my chest. I don't want to hear no for an answer."

"Ma, are you crazy? You don't understand. Julio and Reego don't want to sit down and have dinner wit' me."

"I don't care what they want to do. I'm going to call them and tell them that I want to see them."

"Ma, you can't do that."

"I've been on this earth almost sixty years, don't tell me what I can't do, child." She said.

Polee tried to protest, but his mother was the real boss and her mind was made up.

Inside the apartment that Serio shared with Yasmin, he and Reego were capping coke for the Red Hook spot. Yasmin was out of town; Serio had taken her down to her cousin Nessy's in D.C., he wanted her there until the situation with Polee was under control.

"What you wanna do about this thing wit' Polee's mother?" Reego asked. Polee's mother had gotten in touch with Serio and Reego and told them that she wanted them to come over for dinner. She told them that Polee would be present and that she had some things to address to them all. It was no secrets why she wanted them to meet. Out of respect for the woman that was like a mother to them all, Serio and Reego agreed to the dinner. Serio had second guesses about the whole thing but he rolled with it.

"It's cool." Serio said.

"Yeah, it's a risky move, but like you said, Polee's mother would never play games. She's like a mother. I trust her. I know where her mind's at."

"You're right, she's like a mother to us. We gotta see what she want to say." Serio said as he finished capping up the last of the kilo they had on the table.

CHAPTER 6

The next day, Serio and Reego were fully alert as they walked to the dining table behind Polee's mother. They could smell the enticing aroma of fried fish and other foods. When they walked into the dining room they saw Polee sitting at the table with his hands folded in deep thought. Serio and Polee locked eyes for a very intense moment and then nodded at one another as Polee's mother told Serio and Reego to take their seats. Polee's mother, Ms. Shippings, took a seat at the head of the table. The table was laid out with food. Ms. Shippings blessed the food and then said, "So, Julio, what's the problem between you and Polee? Why are you boys acting like you have no sense?" her tone was casual as she gave Serio a questioning look. Serio cut his eyes at Polee, not knowing how to answer such question. "Don't be shy, Julio." Ms. Shippings said. "I'm a big girl. I know what you boys are into."

Serio took a deep breath and looked around the table. "Ms. Shippings... you have known me since I was child, all my life to be exact ..."

"Yes, I have." She nodded, looking at Reego.

"I could never lie to you." Serio took a sip of water. "There have been some things goin' on out in the streets ..." He cut his eyes at Polee again. "Somehow, me and Polee got away from what we know is right and got off track. I take my share of the blame. At the same time, I would never cross the line with someone that I consider family. Me and Polee have

60

been brothers since we were kids." Serio was picking his words carefully.

"I see." Ms. Shipping nodded and looked at her son. Polee looked like he was holding something in. "You have something to say, Polee?"

"Ma, it's like this," Polee looked around the table and into Reego's and Serio's eyes. "I don't like how things are. Reego and Serio crossed me as far as I'm concerned--"

"Crossed you how?!" Reego blurted out. "You the one that changed! Let's be straight up. We all came up here together, as family. You forget about that. You let your head get big and then it became all about you. That's how I see it, and I'm sure Serio sees it that way as well."

"Look," Serio waved his hand and cut in. "We ain't here to point fingers." Tension was growing. Serio didn't want things to get out of hand in Ms. Shippings house. He knew that there were at least three pistols in the house. "We here to put an end to this mess. So let's find a way to do that, at least find a way to come to terms because we are all family."

Polee and Reego gave each other hard looks. Then Polee said, "I take blame for my part. I was wrong. We are family, at least we were."

"All that changed when your mind-set changed and it became all about things bein' your way or no way." Serio said. "That's where we all went wrong. We didn't come up here for that. We came up here to make things better. For all of us. That was the game plan and we should have never gotten away from that."

Ms. Shippings cut in. "I believe the bottom line is that you all got off track and need to slow down and remember where you all come from. Remember the times when our family shared everything; remember when there would only be one banana in the whole house and everyone got a piece of that one banana. Money doesn't make you who you are, what you stand for makes you who you are. Money is not everything, don't forget that. When you are all dead and gone what will all this mean? Family and friends are always more important than anything else." All eyes were on Ms. Shippings. "I want you boys to work things out the best way you can. Leave the blame out of it. Just make amends." She stuck a fork full of food in her mouth and chewed it before continuing. "Let's eat in peace and when we are done I will let you boys talk things out."

After dinner, Serio, Reego and Polee went into the living room to talk. There was still tension in the air but they seemed to be getting along.

"Let's lay it all out on the table now that we are alone." Serio said, sitting on the sofa next to Polee. Reego was sitting in the chair across from them. "Can we really put this shit behind us? Can we repair what we have broken or are we just wasting time right now?"

Looking from Serio to Reego and back, Polee said, "We have crossed many lines, as you said. Nevertheless, we all know that if one is not wit' you he is against you." Polee paused and looked into Serio's eyes. "The day you walked out on me you were on your own, and against me. You knew that. I couldn't wait for you to make a move against me." Polee then looked at Reego, pointing his finger at him. "And you ... I asked you, as a man, what side you were on and you told me that you were wit' me, laope—"

"That was before you wanted to have Serio killed. I wasn't goin' to sit back and let some shit like that go on."

Serio cut in. "Look, let's put this shit behind us. It's money to be made. Besides that, I got too much goin' on in Red Hook to be goin' to war wit' my own kind. Can we put this shit behind us or not? That's all I want to know."

"Y'all got the Red Hook thing goin' on, I'm doin' my thing in Crown Heights, we can stay out of each other way. How does that sound?" Polee asked.

"I can live wit' that." Serio said.

"Me too." Reego said.

The three Panamanians ironed things out the best way they could, considering what had already taken place between them.

With the Polee situation supposedly behind him, Serio focused all his attention on the Red Hook spot. Even with nonstop gunplay, the money still rolled in by the thousands everyday'. Serio, Reego and their crew did what they had to do in order to maintain their coke spot in the projects. Every attack on them was answered swiftly, ruthlessly, and with equal intensity.

At the same time, Serio was starting to make connections outside of New York. He had met Yasmin's cousin-in-law, Cortez, who lived in D.C. Cortez was at the top of his game in the drug trade down in D.C. Serio and Cortez got along well the few times that Serio had taken Yasmin to D.C. to spend time with her cousin Nessy. Cortez would ride Serio around D.C. and show him the city during his stays in town. It was the summer of 1985 and the city was a gold mine, according to Cortez. Things were far different in D.C. then they were in Brooklyn, as far as Serio could see. He had to go to war for every dime he made, but Cortez was lying back making a killing selling weight with no problems. That had Serio's attention. It made Serio think about testing the water

Sitting in Cortez's basement having a drink and watching a soccer game, Serio relaxed with Cortez. It was good to get a break from Brooklyn. Cortez was a brown-skinned man in his mid-thirties; he stood six feet tall and carried 200-plus pounds. He wore a small afro and a gold front tooth, along with a lot of gold and diamonds. Cortez had connects that went all the way back to Panama; he also had a network of workers in D.C. that distributed cocaine on the street level. Turning down the TV with the remote, Cortez looked at Serio and said, "Serio, I need to take you up on your offer. I've been thinking about it for a while now."

"Oh yeah?" Serio said, raising his eyebrow. He had given Cortez his word that if he ever had any problems that he could call on him. Cortez had looked out for Serio a few times and Serio respected that.

"I'm havin' a few issues wit' these Jamaicans. They are really testing me left and right. I have been trying to overlook their bullshit, but it's getting' out of hand." Cortez spoke in a hushed tone. "'I've tried to reason with' them but they continue t step on my toes. The shit is becomin' disrespectful, Serio."

"How do you want the situation dealt wit'? I can get the job done with no problem. Just let me know how you want it done."

"I want you to take care of it in the quickest way. It's fifty thousand in it for you, however you get it done. I just don't want the shit to come back to me. I can't be connected to the hit. I'm getting' too much money right now and I don't need the heat. I want you to make the situation look like it came from another direction. You know what I mean, just be creative so to speak."

"Say no more. I can take care of it wit' no problem ... All you have to do is point them out to me and consider it done." Serio said, it was nothing to talk about. Serio knew that Cortez was a good friend to have in his corner. He also knew success was greatly enhanced by good connections and bonds of friendship with the right people. If he could make Cortez's issues go away he was sure that Cortez would make shit very

easy for him to get his hands on anything he wanted or needed. "I'll take care of the situation before the weekend is out. Don't even worry about it."

Cortez smiled. "I like you, Serio. You are all about business, loco. Guys like you always make far in this game. You know how to play your cards right. I noticed that in your character the first time I met you."

"We all have a role to play, I just know how to play mine. Coming from where we come from, we have to know how to play our cards right."

Serio and Cortez went over a few things and then Cortez went to the closet and came back with a shopping bag. He handed Serio the shopping bag and said, "That's fifty grand. I'll slide you a little extra once the job is done." Serio shook hands with Cortez. It was a deal.

The next day, which was a Sunday night, Serio walked into a Jamaicans club in Northwest, D.C. The club was dark and crowded. Weed smoke filled the air in thick gray clouds. Thumping reggae music blasted from the speakers that lined the walls of the club. Serio made his way through the crowd wearing a pair of dark shades. He was armed with a MAC-11 sub- machine gun. He already knew who he was supposed to hit and he had his eyes on him. Now it was all about perfect timing. When the time was right Serio planned to strike fast.

Two Jamaicans' were at the bar smoking weed and having a few drinks. One was tall with thick dreadlocks; the other one had a low haircut with a mouthful of gold teeth. They saw Serio coming their way but had no idea who he was nor what he planned to do. Serio had a sly smile on his face. He had the whole move mapped out in his head. In a flash, Serio pulled the MAC- 11 from under his shirt and opened fire, spraying both men with 9mm bullets. The crowd began to panic and run for the door. Serio stood over the two bodies and sprayed them one last time before running for the back door of the club. Cortez had already told him the best way in and out. Once in the alley behind the club, Serio jumped into a black Buick and headed straight for I-95.

Days later, Serio was back in New York overseeing the operation of his Red Hook spot. With Cortez in his corner and the Colombian connect in Queens, Serio was in the position that he wanted to be in. He didn't care about the war that was going on between him and Justice; it was all in the game as far as Serio was concerned. Aside from the money that he was getting in Red Hook, Serio also had his extortion game down on a few Panamanians that played dirty with him when he was going through the situation with Polee. Serio had a Panamanian by the name of Fredrico that he was leaning on the most; he felt like Fredrico was siding with Polee the most while playing both ends against the middle. Serio was hitting Fredrico for five kilos a week, just for the hell of it. As far as he was concerned, he was taxing Fridrico.

Walking out of Fredrico's salon on Franklin Avenue with five kilos in a brown shopping bag, Serio jumped into his brand new BMW and pulled off. Taking in the sights of Brooklyn as he kept his eyes on everything going on around him, he was always on point as he made his way to the stash house. His beeper went off, Serio didn't recognize the number. He grabbed the car phone and called the number back. An unknown voice answered. "Who is this?" Serio asked.

"Justice."

"How did you get my beeper number?!" Serio snapped.

"Let's just say that I know a few people."

"Oh yeah ...is that right?"

"Well, what do we have to talk about?"

"We got a lot to talk about. Losin' money for one, thousands of dollars a day at that." Justice said.

"Tell me about it."

"It's clear that neither one of us is gonna give in so we might as well come to some kind of understanding. This shit we got goin' on is bringin' too much heat from Babylon. We need to have a sit down."

Serio raised his eyebrow. He smelled a set-up. "So what do you suggest?"

"Let's meet somewhere and iron things out. A public place should be fine. We can meet out in the open, in a park somewhere. You bring two of your men and I'll bring two of mine. We can talk face-to-face, just me and you."

Serio thought about what Justice was saying. The police heat was at an all-time high due to all of the shootings that were going down in the projects. Both men had been having their coke spots raided on the regular. That meant that money and product were being lost every time around. That was bad for business, to say the least.

"I smell a set-up. You gotta get real early in the morning to pull one over on me like that." Serio said.

"I'm not playin' games. I'm serious."

"I'ma take you up on that offer. Let's do it. I'm all for anything that's gon' make me more money."

Just after 4:00 P.M., Serio and Justice were in the middle of the park in the projects talking things out. Serio came to the meeting with Reego and one of their younger Panamanian gunmen. Justice came with his man Kwan and a young triggerman by the name of Cruz. Serio and Justice stood alone close to the benches while their men watched them closely.

"It's more than enough money for both of us," Justice said, "you and your people stay down there by Columbia Road and

I'll do my thing in the back. You respect those lines and I'll do the same. I think that's more than fair."

"You sure that your people gon' respect those lines?" Serio asked.

"You have my word."

Serio and Justice shook hands. Only time would tell how long the truce would last.

CHAPTER 7

High above the clouds, looking down at the world from his window seat, Vicioso couldn't believe that he was finally on a plane making his journey to New York, by way of Canada. Serio had it all set up. It was 1986, and as far as Vicioso was concerned, it was time to take things to another level. This was his shot at the title. He had to make it count. He had plans to send back home for Pimpo and Pete as soon as he was on his feet, after that he planned to send for Niecy--he had to send for the love of his life.

Vicioso couldn't contain the feelings of aspiration and excitement that he felt. His love and respect for Serio were at an all time high. He swore to himself that he would prove his loyalty to Serio for the simple fact that Serio had always been a man of his word when he came to Vicioso. There was no bigger favor one could for Vicioso than to get him to New York and put him in a position to make some real money. All kinds of thoughts went through his mind as the plane flew through the sky.

Vicioso had only been home from prison for a few weeks when Serio called and let him know that it was his time to join the crew in Brooklyn. There was nothing to talk about. Vicioso was ready to go. He'd just done eighteen months at the notorious Coiba, a prison island where he and Pete had been sent after being shot in the back by the police for an $80 robbery. During their eighteen months at Coiba they spent their days cutting down bushes to plant sugarcane, doing farm work and so on. They had to ward off poisonous snakes along the way. It was hard time. Vicioso promised himself that he would never return to prison. All of his plans for the future involved New York City.

"I can't wait to get to New York." Dwight said, sitting next to Vicioso on the plane. Dwight was from Santa Cruz as well. He had a cousin in New York that made it possible for him to make the trip to the U.S.

"Who you tellin'?" Vicioso said, sipping a cup of water. At 21, all he could think about was all the money Serio said there was in New York. Nothing else mattered.

"I got big plans, Vicioso. I'ma be sendin' most of my money back home. I gotta make sure my mom is taken care of. That's my first order of business, you know?"

"Me too, I'ma make sure my mother wants for nothin'. As long as I'm breathin', she gone be well taken care of."

Vicioso and Dwight spoke about their plans the whole flight. The excitement of the journey was so strong that Vicioso felt nervous the whole flight. Around two in the morning, the plane touched down. A short while later the passengers began to exit. Vicioso and Dwight were amongst the crowd. For the two youth it was like stepping into another world. They didn't look suspicious at all, although they both had plans on sneaking into the U.S. Playing it smooth, Vicioso looked around for Serio's contact person, but he saw no one that looked like the man in the picture that Serio sent him. His nerves began to get the best of him. Out of the blue, two white men approached Vicioso and Dwight.

"You two, come with us." The one with the blue eyes said. Vicioso's heart began pounding. He wanted to take off running but there was nowhere to go, plus he had no idea where he was.

"What's wrong?" Dwight asked the customs agent.

"Just come with us." Blue Eyes said.

Nervously, Vicioso and Dwight followed the customs agent.

Vicioso and Dwight were split up and taken into two different rooms where their passports and other credentials were checked thoroughly. Vicioso found himself alone in a small office with the agent with the blue eyes. He didn't know what to expect and began to worry that his New York plans were in danger. However things were to go Vicioso was prepared to deal with them.

"So you're a Panamanian kid, eh?" the agent asked in his thick French accent as he studied Vicioso's passport from his seat behind a messy desk.

"Yes sir." Vicioso said staying focused. He could hear Dwight in the office next door going through the same thing. The agents were putting the press on.

"Why have you come to Canada?" The agent asked in his arrogant tone. It was clear that he didn't believe a word of what Vicioso had told him so far. "Make it believable."

"Sir, I'm here on vacation. I just finished school this year and I saved up to visit Canada." Vicioso could still past for 18. "Is there something wrong, or illegal with this?"

"You bring any cash with you?"

"I have $1,200." Vicioso's mother told him that he had to have cash on him to make it into the country.

"Let me see it."

Vicioso pulled the money from his pocket and handed it to the agent.

"How long do you plan to stay here?" the agent asked as he counted the money.

"A week or two."

The agent laughed. "Not with $1,200. You expect me to believe that crap? Do I look like I was born yesterday?" He leaned forward and slid the money across the desk. "You think we don't know that you Panamanians and Jamaicans are sneaking into the U.S. through Canada? Just tell the truth. You two Panamanians are trying to sneak into the U.S. aren't you? Spit it out!"

"Sir, I told you that I'm here on vacation. I don't know anything about sneakin' into the U.S. I have no reason to do that. If I wanted to go to the U.S. that's where I would be going. I'm here because this is where I want to spend my vacation."

The agent continued to drill Vicioso with questions. Vicioso began to feel like the agent was going to put him back on a plane to Panama.

"Where'd you get that money from again? I don't buy your story," the agent said.

"I saved it workin' after school."

The agent laughed loudly. "Well, $1,200 won't last you a week or two in Canada."

Vicioso knew he had to improvise; he'd always been quick on his feet. "My mother has a nice job, she can send me more when I run out. That was her plan anyway. So that shouldn't be a problem at all."

The agent smiled. He was amused by the young Panamanian's wit. "You're a good kid. You've got your story all together, don't you? Like I haven't heard it all before."

Vicioso shrugged and raised his eyebrows. "I'm tellin' you the truth."

Another agent came into the room and said, "How does the kid's story sound?"

72

MONEY AIN'T EVERYTHING

The agent with the blue eyes smiled. "This kid is good. He has his story all together. I'll give him that much, it's no gaps in the story. The only thing I have against him is the fact that he doesn't have enough money to stay here for the amount of time that he says he plans to stay. Other than that everything sounds good."

The agent in the doorway looked at Vicioso and said, "Your friend is going back to Panama on the next flight. It's not too late for you to come clean and it'll be no problems. No harm no foul. We already know that you're trying to sneak into the U.S. That's what all of you set out to do, right?"

"I don't know anything about that. I'm here on vacation." Vicioso said.

The agents looked at one another and smiled. The one sitting behind the desk said, "Well, let's call your mother and see if she'll send you some more money for your stay here. If everything sounds good we'll let you go. That's the best we can do." The agent was sure he had the young Panamanian now.

Vicioso felt concerned but he wasn't giving up yet. "It's almost three in the mornin'." he said.

"I know." The agent smiled. "I'm calling your bluff. Let's get your mother on the phone and see if she can send you some more money, right now."

Vicioso rolled the dice and gave the agent his mother's phone number, knowing full well that she didn't have any extra money to send him. He had to wing it.

The agent looked Vicioso in the eyes and said, "I speak Spanish." He handed Vicioso the phone. "Don't even try to slide me a curve ball. I just want you to know that."

Melly answered the phone sounding dead tired. Vicioso explained to her what was going on. Melly caught right on.

"Customs say that I don't have enough money to stay here for two weeks." Vicioso said.

"So what needs to be done?" Melly asked.

"I told them that you have a nice job and can send me more money when I run out. They don't believe me."

"Do they want me to send you more money right now?"

"Hold on, let me see." Vicioso looked at the agent and asked him what he wanted to be done.

"The agent snatched the phone, pissed off. "Hello."

"Yes." Melly said playing along. The agent explained the situation to her all over again. He then told her how she had to send Vicioso the money. "Well," Melly said, "It's very late and I'm a working person, I won't be able to just get up out of bed and send the money right now, but I'll send whatever my son needs first thing in the morning, if that's okay."

Vicioso watched the agents face turn red as he spoke on the phone. He knew his mother was playing her role perfectly. When the agent was done talking to Melly he gave the phone back to Vicioso, who wrapped up the call.

"So can I leave?" Vicioso knew he had played his cards right. "You have two weeks to get out of this country." The agent behind the desk said, making his threat clear. "If you don't come back through customs within two weeks we're going to come find you and lock you up. Then we'll see how much you really want to be in this country on vacation."

The other agent added his two cents. "You can still take our offer and get back on the plane with your friend, but once you walk out that door it's on you. Think about it."

Vicioso stood up. "Can I leave now?" He sighed. "It's real late and I need to get some rest."

"Sure, kid."

With his suitcase in hand, Vicioso walked out of the airport headed for the unknown, into a completely different world.

He paused and looked back at the airport. Fate was on his side. He thought about the contact he was supposed to hook up with, he hadn't seen him yet. He was really on his own in an unknown land. Vicioso also thought about Dwight and that was a strong reminder of how close he had come to being on his way back to Santa Cruz. Putting the thought behind him, Vicioso made his way to a pay phone and called the number that Serio had told him to memorize. Looking at the bright lights all around him, he waited for someone to answer the phone. A smile crossed his face. He was on his way to better things and he could taste it. A male answered the phone and Vicioso asked to speak to Albert. Albert got on the phone and told Vicioso that he was on his way to pick him up from the airport. Things were falling into place after all.

Albert was a Pakistani man that Serio had met through his Colombian connect. Albert and Serio had a deal hooked up where Albert would make sure that Serio's homies got across the Canadian border into the U.S. safely. Living up to his end of the deal, Albert picked Vicioso up from the airport and took him to a safe house.

The next morning, after taking a shower and getting himself together, Vicioso found Albert in the kitchen having breakfast with his nephew, Tirek. Albert introduced Vicioso to Tirek, who was Vicioso's age. They all had fried eggs and bacon while getting to know one another better. After breakfast, Albert had to make a few runs so he left Vicioso with Tirek and told the two young men to keep each other company.

"I'll show Harvey around." Tirek said as Albert left the house. Looking at Vicioso, Tirek said, "I'll take you shopping and show you around. How's that sound? Help you get comfortable."

"Sounds good to me. Can I use the phone first?" Vicioso said.

"Sure it's in the living room." Tirek said.

Vicioso called his mother and let her know everything was cool so far. "I should be in New York soon." He said.

"Be careful, Harvey." Melly said.

After talking to his mother, Vicioso called Niecy and let her know that all was well so far. "I should be in New York in no time." He said.

"I miss you already, Harvey." Niecy said. "I can't wait to be in your arms."

"I miss you too, mami, but don't worry. Things are about to change for the better. Believe that. I'm goin' to make things the way they should be for us. I have big plans. Everything will work out just fine."

"I believe you. I just can't wait for you to get New York and send for me. That's all I can think about." Niecy said.

Vicioso spoke to Niecy for a while and assured her that everything was going to work out just fine. "I gotta go, I love you, okay?"

"I love you, too. Make sure you call me every day until you get to New York."

"I will."

Vicioso and Tirek hit the streets of Toronto and Tirek treated Vicioso like family. Tirek took him shopping and bought him a few outfits. He then showed him around town. In the process, Tirek stopped at few restaurants and collected stacks of money from the owners. Vicioso paid close attention, but asked no questions; he could tell that Tirek had his hand into some kind of crime.

Later on, Tirek took Vicioso to a few nightclubs where he again collected money and got free drinks and food. Tirek gave Vicioso a few hundred dollars to spend and keep in his

pocket. Vicioso wondered what it was going to be like when he got to New York. If things were this sweet in Canada, he knew that he would be living like a king in New York as a part of Serio's crew. Money would make all things better as far as he could see.

Days later, Vicioso and Tirek were sitting in the basement of the safe house watching TV while waiting for Albert to bring back some pizza. Vicioso couldn't contain his excitement: Albert had told him that he would be taking him to New York by nightfall. He was so close to getting where he wanted to be that he could taste it. All he could think about was how things would be when he hooked up with Serio. He was sure that Serio would have things laid out for him. Knowing how fast he caught on to things, Vicioso knew he would get the hang of the way things went in New York in no time.

"You're on your way to New York now, eh?" Tirek smiled, loading a .357 magnum.

"Yeah." Vicioso nodded as he gazed at the huge revolver.

Tirek noticed the way Vicioso looked at the pistol. "You look like you never seen a gun before?"

"We don't see them often back home, unless the police shootin' one at us."

"Are you serious?" Tirek picked the gun up. "You never fired a gun before?

Vicioso laughed. "I've never even held one before."

"Get the fuck outta here." Tirek laughed, he couldn't believe his ears. "Here," he handed Vicioso the pistol. "You gonna see a whole lot of these where you going. Get used to it. If I was you I'd get me one of these motherfuckers as soon as I get where I'm going."

Holding the pistol, Vicioso said, "A knife is all I ever needed back home."

Tirek laughed again. "Trust me, you gon' need more than a knife in New York, you can bet that."

Later on, darkness surrounded Vicioso. The ride was bumpy and a little claustrophobic, but it was worth it. Vicioso was finally on his way to New York. He thought about Pimpo and his other homies, if all went well for him they would surely be making the trip soon. All kind of thoughts went through Vicioso's mind as he rode in the trunk of Albert's Buick. For what seemed like hours, Vicioso mind raced until the car stopped. He heard the engine cut off, and then a door opened and shut. For some reason, Vicioso's heart began to beat faster, he felt like something was wrong. The trunk opened and the bright lights of the bus station made Vicioso squint his eyes as Albert helped him out of the trunk. Dusting himself off, Vicioso put his hand on his waist and looked around with a smile on his face. "I'm finally here, New York, New York, big city of dreams. This is what I been waiting for." He had arrived and the what he felt inside was beyond words.

Albert smiled and patted Vicioso on the back. "You're not all the way there yet. This is Buffalo. Here," Albert handed him a bus ticket. "That'll get you to New York City, you're on your own from here. Serio will be waiting for you at the station there. I wish you the best. Be safe. And whatever you do when you get where you going, don't forget where you came from. Don't let the money change you."

Vicioso shook Albert's hand. "Thanks for everything. You helped me out a lot, I'll never forget that."

"Don't mention it. Just make something of yourself now that you have a shot at a better life. Make every step count. Never forget who you are and where you come from. Most importantly, don't let this country change you, kid. I can't say that enough."

78

MONEY AIN'T EVERYTHING

July 5, 1986 was the day that Vicioso's life would change forever.

CHAPTER 8

Vicioso hit New York City just after 1:00 A.M. As he stepped out of the bus station into the cool air of the early morning hours he took in the sights of the city. He could tell that he was in a totally different world by the lights, tall buildings and the people that were still walking the streets as if it was one in the afternoon. He took it all in as he looked around for Serio. Vicioso felt like Tony in Scarface and as far as he was concerned New York was one big pussy waiting to get fucked. Looking around at all the people that were still walking the streets he thought to himself that the city really never did sleep.

A car horn blared grabbed Vicioso's attention. He looked around and saw Serio sitting behind the wheel of a brand new white BMW. A smile crossed Vicioso's face as he walked to the car; he got in the passenger seat and gave Serio five. "Que sopa, mena?"

Serio smiled. He had that getting money look. The gold Cuban link with the diamond-covered Jesus piece was making a big statement. "Look at you," Serio looked Vicioso up and down. "You all grown up." He reached over and hugged Vicioso firmly, like a little brother he hadn't seen in years. "You still got that baby face, but you done got a little taller, a little hair on your face too."

Vicioso smiled. "I'm ready for the world. You know what time it is. I'm tryin' to get paid."

80

"I hear that. That's the attitude." Serio started the car up and pulled into the light traffic. "We got a lot of catchin' up to do. A lot to talk about."

"I'm here now, we ain't got nothin' but time, Serio." Vicioso said as he looked out the window like a tourist. He couldn't hide his excitement.

"How was your trip? Everything went well?"

"Not bad at all. I ran into a little trouble at the airport, but once I got through that everything else was okay. Albert and his nephew treated me real good in Canada."

"They're good people, they understand how it is to want something better out of life." Serio lit a cigarette. "But now that you're here, shit's a whole lot different and you gon' have to catch on fast if you plan to survive. All odds are against us. We are outsiders in this country. Don't ever forget that. We gotta fight for everything we get and any day could be our last so every step we make gotta count. This is not a game at all. It's play for keeps over everything." Serio glanced at Vicioso who was paying close attention. "It's about playin' to win, playin' for keeps."

"I understand." Vicioso nodded.

"One slip and you goin' back home in a box. It's not a game I want you to always remember that." Serio took a long pull on his Newport and blew the smoke out the window. "On the other hand, you gon' see your share of the money... it's a whole lot of that up here. As long as you stay sharp everything you got comin' you gon' get. I'ma show you the ropes. Everywhere I got, you got."

Vicioso was all ears. Serio was talking his kind of talk. For as long as Vicioso had known Serio the older homie was always about his business. Vicioso truly believed that Serio would lead him in the right direction.

"This spot I got in the projects is real rough. I'm talkin' bout murders in broad daylight rough. It ain't like Santa Cruz, they comin' wit' machine guns like it's a movie or somethin'. Billy the kid shit, compa. You gotta keep your eyes open at all times. One slip and these niggaz gon' put your raas in the dirt and they ain't gon' think twice about it. It's no talkin', the only talkin' you gon' hear if there is a problem is the talkin' of firepower." Serio explained the Red Hook situation to Vicioso, putting him on point about everything; he told him who was who and about the truce with Justice and his crew. Vicioso took it all in as if he were studying for a test in school. He knew his life and success depended on how fast he could catch on to the way of life in the big city.

"We're the only Panamanians in Red Hook, I had to earn that wit' blood sweat and tears. I ain't gon' give it up without a fight to the death either. This is all we got Vicioso." Serio spoke with firm conviction.

A short while later Serio pulled up in front of a tall building and parked. "We're in Brooklyn now, I got a stash spot in that buildin' right there where I keep most of the product." Serio looked around at the few people that were walking outside. "Are you sure you ready for this shit?" he joked with Vicioso. "Let me know now or forever hold your peace."

"I'm ready for whatever, you ain't gotta say nothin' twice." Vicioso said.

Serio took Vicioso inside the Brooklyn apartment where Reego was in the kitchen cooking cocaine into crack. Seeing Vicioso come through the door, Reego smiled and said, "Hey, compa. You made it, eh? We been waitin' for you."

Yeah, I'm here, ready for the world." Vicioso said, looking around the small apartment.

"You in the big leagues now." Reego winked at Vicioso.

MONEY AIN'T EVERYTHING

Serio cut in. "We gotta take some more coke to the Red Hook spot tonight. How long you gon' be?" he asked Reego.

"This is the last brick right here. The rest are in that shoppin' bag on the table."

"Cool." Serio then looked at Vicioso. "Follow me." He took Vicioso to the back room where there was a green duffel bag on the bed. Serio grabbed the bag and said, "Me and Reego gotta shoot over to the projects, we'll be right back. I want you to count the money in this bag to save me sometime. You can handle that right?"

"I got it, chief." Vicioso grabbed the bag and looked inside; he'd never seen so much money at one time. His mind began to race. He knew for sure he was where he wanted to be. He couldn't wait his turn to roll in the dough. Just a fraction of the money inside would be enough to set him straight for the moment.

"See you when I get back." Serio left the room.

Vicioso got down to business. It seemed like it took hours, but he got the job done. Vicioso counted up $500,000. He sat on the bed and played with the money for a second when he was done. He told himself that he would soon have duffel bags full of cash as well. When that day came his family would want for nothing. Putting the money back in the duffel bag, Vicioso sat the bag on the floor and went out to the living room where he took a seat on the sofa and watched a little TV.

A short while later, Serio returned without Reego and found Vicioso playing with an Uzi that he'd left in the kitchen. "That's a deadly toy there. You don't know nothing bout that there." Serio said.

"If this is a toy you gotta show me the real thing." Vicioso joked as he sat the machine gun on the table.

"How much was in the duffel bag?" Serio said, taking a seat beside Vicioso.

"Five-hundred grand on the nose."

Serio smiled and patted Vicioso on the back. "I already knew that. I was just testing you a little bit. I always want to see how my men act around money when no one is lookin'. Money has a way of making people act in a different way."

"You don't have to worry about me, Serio. You can trust me wit' your life. Loyalty means more to me than any of this other shit. I mean that with all my heart."

"I know, I know, Vicioso." Serio smiled. "It won't be long before you have money like that. All you gotta do is play your cards right. It's all coming."

The next day, Serio took Vicioso shopping and bought him all the top-of-the-line clothes that were out. He also bought him a big, gold Cuban link with the diamond-covered Jesus piece. Vicioso felt like a super star. After they finished shopping, Serio drove around New York City showing Vicioso the city while schooling him to the game. Vicioso sucked the game up like a young and eager apprentice taking notes about his new craft. Serio made it clear that Vicioso was family and that he didn't have to work his way up in the ranks of the crew. After all, Vicioso played a role in the whole move to New York by stealing the diamonds back in Panama. However, Vicioso wanted to earn his keep in the U.S., he wanted to learn the game every step of the way and had no problem getting his hands dirty.

"Believe me, you gon' get your hands dirty." Serio said as he drove across the Brooklyn Bridge. "You can count on that, sooner or later you gon' have to murder one of these mada raas that get in the way."

Looking out the window at the East River, Vicioso said, "I don't have a problem wit' that. Whatever needs to be done, I'm willing to do it. If you need somebody murdered, just

84

give me the word and it's done. It's no sweat to me, I can handle it, Serio."

Serio smiled. "You're somethin' special. Way before your time."

"Let me ask you somethin'." Vicioso said.

"What is it?"

"What really went down between you and Polee? I been meaning to ask you that. It don't make sense to me."

Serio sighed. "It's a long story, but to make it short, we let the money come between us and got off track." Serio explained the situation as they headed down Atlantic Avenue. "Me and you ain't gon' never go through no shit like that though. That shit was some bullshit that should have never went down. It fucked my head up, too."

"No doubt. I understand." Vicioso said.

"Look here, whatever you need, just let me know. I'ma make sure you got money to send back home and whatever else you need until you get on your feet. I got my woman to get you a little apartment on Flatbush Avenue. You'll be ok there. It'll be a nice little something that you can call your own." Serio said. His car phone rang and he answered it. It was the Colombian connect, Vick. He spoke to Vick for a few seconds and hung up the phone. "We gotta go pick some money up from the other apartment."

A short while later, Serio parked in front of the building that Yasmin lived in. He looked at Vicioso and said, "I'll be right back, keep your eyes open." Serio went inside the building and returned a couple minutes later carrying a shopping bag. He got back in the car and handed Vicioso the shopping bag and a .45 automatic. "We gotta go drop the money off in Queens. You need to pay close attention to every move we make so you know what's going on around you."

Vicioso looked down at the .45 and nodded. "Say no more."

"All you gotta do is point and squeeze if anything ever goes wrong." Serio smiled and nodded at the pistol.

Looking in the shopping bag, Vicioso said, "How much money is this?"

"Two-hundred grand. We cop with about that much every time now." When they got to Queens, Serio told Vicioso to follow him into a small corner store where they met Vick. Serio introduced Vick to Vicioso.

"I'll have the keys tomorrow." Vick said as Serio handed him the shopping bag.

"I'll see you tomorrow then." Serio said as he shook Vick's hand.

Serio and Vicioso left and headed back to Brooklyn. Along the way Vicioso looked like he had something on his mind so Serio said, "What you thinking about?"

"You trust that guy with that much money?"

Serio laughed. "I been doing business wit' him for a while. We do business like that sometimes, he's always been straight up wit' me. He good for the money Vicioso, don't worry about it. Aside from that, we always take certain risk in the game. Don't get that confused wit' trust. Trust no one."

"I understand." Vicioso said.

Their next stop was Red Hook projects where Serio introduced Vicioso to the rest of his crew.

The next afternoon, Vicioso was sitting in the living room of the apartment that Serio had got for him. He was watching TV and talking to Niecy on the phone. "Yeah, Serio got me up in a little apartment already. Things looking real good." Vicioso said, smoking weed with his feet up on the coffee table.

"You be careful up there, Harvey." Niecy said. "I hear so many things about New York."

"Don't you worry about nothin'. I'm okay. Pretty soon, I'ma have you up here wit' me. I miss you already. Mark my words."

Niecy blushed. "I miss you, too. How long do you think it will be before you can send for me?"

"Serio said it shouldn't take but a few weeks. So just give me a minute. I'm on top of everything."

"Harvey, Pimpo just walked through the door, looking just like you."

"Let me speak to him."

Pimpo got on the phone. "Heyyyy, que sopa, laope?"

Vicioso laughed, he missed his missed his little brother. "Everything is workin' out just fine. You gon' love it up here." Vicioso told Pimpo how things were going so far. "Serio really got shit under control up here. You gon' love it."

"Do they really run around wit' machine guns and shit up there in broad daylight?" Pimpo asked.

Vicioso laughed. "I ain't seen that yet, but Serio said it's like that when shit gets out of hand, but one thing I have seen is a lot of money. More money than I ever seen. Niggaz make a lot of money up here. I never seen so much money in my life, I'm telling you. This shit up here is a dream come true."

"I can't wait to get up there. But look, let me give the phone back to Niecy before she chops my head off. I love you. See you soon, I gotta run. You know how shit is down here."

"I love you, too. I'ma send you and Ma some money as soon as Serio come pick me up. I really don't know my way around yet."

"Cool." Pimpo gave the phone back to Niecy.

Serio walked into the apartment while Vicioso was on the phone with Niecy. The look on Serio's face made it clear that he was pissed off. Looking at Vicioso, Serio said, "I need to talk to you."

Vicioso nodded. "Niecy, I gotta go, mami. I'll call you a little later. You'll have that money before the day is out. I promise."

"What's wrong?" Vicioso asked Serio once he hung the phone up.

"Vick was supposed to meet me wit' the coke and he ain't show. When I called his spot they say they ain't seen him since last night. Polee said he ain't seen him neither. I'm thinkin' he ran off wit' my money. I hope that ain't the case, but if it is shit is about to get real heated." Serio said, smoking a Newport.

"You don't got no idea where he might be?" Vicioso asked.

"We bout to find out. Get your pistol." Serio headed for the door.

There wasn't much talking inside the car as Serio headed for Queens. Polee had given him some information about where Vick might be. Reego sat in the passenger seat while Vicioso rode in the back seat wondering what was in store. From the look on Serio's face, Vicioso could tell that they were about to murder shit. He was ready. Whatever he had to do for the team, he was down for it.

The first two locations that they checked in Queens turned up nothing, both apartments were empty. They then headed to another spot in Staten Island. Pulling up on a tree-lined street in a section of town that was far from Brooklyn-like, Serio parked in front of a big white house with a well-cut lawn. A gold Benz sat in the driveway. "Let's go." Serio said as he headed for the house. Reego and Vicioso followed behind

with their pistols concealed. "Follow my lead." Serio said as he rang the doorbell.

The door slowly opened and in the doorway stood a beautiful Colombian woman with light-brown skin and long black hair tucked behind her ears; she couldn't have been older than 22. "Yes," she said with a smile and a heavy Colombian accent.

Serio carefully looked over his shoulder, pulled his pistol and grabbed the young woman by her T-shirt, placing the pistol to her head. "Don't scream." He hissed as he and his two comrades eased into the house and shut the door behind them.

"Where's Vick?" Serio shouted, shoving the Colombian woman down on the sofa in the living room.

"I don't know!" she screamed. A mask of fear covered her face. She began to shake as her eyes darted back and forth. Frozen with fear she balled up into a protective knot.

"Vick left town! He had to go back home for some reason! That's all I know. I swear to God!" she cried.

"What the hell is goin' on?" An old Colombian lady said as she came out of the kitchen. Reego grabbed her and made her take a seat on the sofa beside the other woman. Serio then told Vicioso and Reego to search the house.

They got right down to business. While Vicioso and Reego went to search the house, Serio turned his attention to the crying women. "Vick owes me a lot of money and I want my money. I don't want to hurt you two, but I will if somebody don't tell me where I can find Vick. I'm only going to say this once nicely."

Hugging the younger woman, the older one said, "Vick is not here! I told you they already."

"Where is he?" Serio shouted, pointing his pistol in the girl's face. "Don't fuckin' play with me. I'm not the one. I will make you wish that you were already dead. Take my word for it."

"I think he's gone back to Colombia." The old lady screamed through her sobs. "We don't have anything to do with what he has done. Please believe me."

"The house is empty, they're the only ones here." Reego said as he came down the steps followed by Vicioso.

Serio sighed. Anger was clouding his judgment. He looked at the two Colombian women as he thought about his next move. He was going to make sure Vick paid dearly for crossing him. Looking at the women on the sofa, Serio nodded at Reego and said, "Go start the car."

Reego hit the door and headed for the car.

Vicioso waited for the word. He gave Serio a look like: What's next?

"We takin' them wit' us, laope. Tie them up."

CHAPTER 9

Please don't hurt my family. Please, I'm sorry, I will fix this, I just need some time." Vick pleaded over the phone, he was in his mother's house back in Colombia. He'd learned that Serio had kidnapped his aunt and niece a little over a week ago. They were being held somewhere in Brooklyn. As soon as Vick learned about the kidnapping he sent word for Serio to contact him. "I never meant to fuck you over, Serio. I got in over my head with some serious people back home. I fucked up their money and they threatened to kill my mother and sister. I swear to you, I'll get you all of your money back. Just ... please don't hurt my family. Please, Serio!"

On a Brooklyn pay phone down the street from one of his stash houses, Serio said, "I want five-hundred thousand. You got a week to get it. I don't care how you get it, but if you don't get it you gon' hear about your family in the fuckin' papers. I swear to God you piece of shit."

"I can't get that kind of money in one week, not right now... please ... give me a little longer. I'll have the whole five---"

"You got until nine tonight to get me the first two-hundred grand. Call this number at eight on the nose to set it up. Tell whoever answers the phone where to pick the money up. Play games if you wanna." Serio hung up and jumped back in his BMW.

Vicioso sat in an old metal fold-up chair in the hallway of the apartment where the Colombian women were being held hostage. He was watching them closely. It was his job. He had mixed feelings about the whole situation, but chalked it up as part of the job. Serio told him off the top that there was always a price to pay for everything. Vicioso was relieved that Serio didn't make the call to kill the women. At least for the time being because Vicioso was sure that if it came down to it that Serio wouldn't think twice about killing the women himself. It was all in the game.

The door to the apartment opened. Vicioso had his finger on the trigger of the Uzi, ready to work, but it was only Serio coming in. "What's up?" Serio asked, seeing Vicioso watching TV outside the bedroom that the women were in. Serio took a quick look inside the bedroom; the women were sleeping. They weren't tied up but Serio made it clear that they would be shot on the spot if they didn't go along with the program. "Everything cool?" he said as he gave Vicioso five.

"Yeah, everything is cool." Vicioso said.

"I just spoke to Vick." Serio took a seat beside Vicioso and told him about the conversation he'd had with Vick. "I let him know that I ain't playin' no games. I'd hate to do it, but I'll kill his people without a second thought if he don't get that money together. That's just the way it is."

Vicioso nodded, but had something else on his mind. "Let's say that Vick does get the money together, what do we do with the women after that? They seen our faces. They can tell the cops what we look like and all that shit."

"Don't worry about that. New York is a big city, the police won't get involved. Besides that, Vick won't let his family bring the police into it. Most likely, Vick gon' find a way to get the money together and then we gon' let his family go."

"I understand." Vicioso was catching on quickly.

Serio lit a Newport and smiled at Vicioso.

"Que sopa?" Vicioso asked.

"You know you are officially in the game now, right?"

"Why you say that?" Vicioso raised his eyebrows.

"You done kidnapped somebody. They give out a lot of time for that kind of shit up here. I want you to know how serious this shit is. Aside from that, you already know how them Colombians are. They never forget a wrong done to them."

"Me neither." Vicioso said with a shrug.

"That's right." Serio smiled. He looked at his watch and said, "Marcus gon' be here in a minute. You can leave when he gets here."

"Cool."

Serio got up to leave. "I'll catch you later, I gotta get on top of this money."

Three weeks later, Reego pulled over and parked an old Toyota behind a blue late-model Cadillac on Myrtle Avenue just after eight P.M. The Fort Greene section of Brooklyn was alive and moving fast. Reego nodded down the street and told Bam, "Check the Pontiac." Bam got out of the car and walked a few cars down where he got into a red Pontiac. Reego watched Bam carefully, making sure there was no foul play. One wrong move and somebody could lose their life. One could never be too careful when dealing with Colombians. Vicioso was in the back seat of the Toyota with an Uzi, he was keeping an eye on everything as well. This was the third cash pick up from Vick. Every pick-up was in a different location. Vicioso was learning well on the job.

Bam found the keys to the Pontiac under the floor mat and started the car. He pulled up alongside the Toyota and lowered the window on the passenger side. "Ay, all the money's in here. We good to go."

"Let's get out of here then," Reego said.

Both cars headed for Red Hook.

The whole move with Vick had taught Vicioso a good lesson: Don't play with people's money.

Panamanian Greg walked through the light crowd inside the Panamanian club on Flatbush Avenue. It'd been awhile since he'd been on the scene. He'd spent a few years out of town, so to speak. The reggae music was loud and thumping as he made his way to the bar. A few people looked pleased to see him, but others looked fearful. Greg had that kind of effect on people. He took it all in and made a mental note of who was who. Things in the streets seemed to change overnight. Greg saw the man he was looking for and stepped to him.

"Freddie," Greg patted Fredrico on the back as he took a seat beside him at the bar. Fredrico looked surprised and fearful, as if he'd seen a ghost. He flashed a fake smile. Greg caught the vibe and said, "Good to see you, old friend. Been a minute since I saw you last."

"When did you get out?" Fredrico asked. He already had Serio squeezing him, so Greg was the last person Fredrico wanted to see. Greg was known to put the squeeze on anybody that was getting real money in the streets.

"Just hit the streets today. Feels good to be out. It's nothing like being free and being able to go wherever you want and do whatever you want to do." Greg looked around the club, taking it all in. "I got big plans, too. I hear a lot of shit has changed. I want what's mine. You know?" he smiled. Wasting no time, Greg went straight into his plans to get back on his feet. Fredrico listened carefully, knowing some extortion was coming, sooner or later. Greg had a history of that kind of thing, just like Serio; they were both strong-arm niggaz dating back to their youth in Panama.

94

Unlike Serio, who was from Santa Cruz, Greg was from Colon, Panama. "Look here, though," Greg said, rubbing his trimmed goatee. "I been hearing that Serio done came up here and set up shop." Greg and Serio had bad blood between them. "I hear that he been leanin' on you real hard too. Is that true?"

Fredrico shrugged. He knew he was a coward---everybody did--- but he didn't like it thrown in his face. "Yeah, Serio keeps his hand out, if that's what you mean. You know how it goes. Everybody wants something."

Greg laughed. "Yeah, that's what the raas I mean. You know damn well that's what I mean. Don't play dumb, Freddie. I hear he been leanin' on a few different guys from back home. I really don't understand how everybody can be so fuckin' scared of one man. He bleeds like us. Nevertheless, I plan to put an end to his shit. However, I gotta get on my feet first." Greg raised his eyebrows. "I need a good four or five keys to get things movin' for me. You can handle that right?"

With a slight sigh, Fredrico killed his drink. "Yeah, I can do that for you."

Greg smiled. "That's what friends are for." He patted Fredrico on the back and added, "Don't you worry about Serio, I'ma take care of him for you. I promise you."

Bam was on the clock this time around, watching the hostages. He sat on the sofa watching Sanford and Son with a .45 at his side. He was getting a nice piece of money fucking with the Panamanians. He was also doing a little bit of stealing from Serio to make a little extra money on the side. He knew he was risking his life but he was willing to take the chance being as though Serio had so many other things on his hands at the time. Besides, so much money was being made in Red Hook that Serio would never miss the little bit that Bam was stealing.

Bam got up to check on the hostages. He saw the young one in the mirror brushing her long hair. She was wearing nothing but her bra and panties. The older woman was sleeping. Bam had lusted after the young Colombian from the first time Serio had him watch over them. She had a body that was out of this world. She looked at Bam and smiled. "Can I have some juice?" she asked, not trying to hide her body from his lustful gaze.

"Throw on a T-shirt and I'll get you some juice." Bam said. The young woman threw on a T-shirt and followed Bam to the kitchen where he got her a big glass of orange juice. She smiled and thanked him as she sipped her juice.

"Can I sit out here and watch TV with you for a little while? I'm sick of being stuck in that room all day." The young woman said. By this time the young woman had a feeling that they weren't going to be harmed; she knew that Vick was getting the money together to have them returned safely.

Bam had let her sit in the living room with him and watch TV a few times. He felt strongly that she wouldn't try anything dumb. "Yeah, you can hang out for a little while."

Bam allowed her to sit on the sofa with him and watch TV for a while. He then lit up a little weed. "Can I have some of that?" she asked.

Bam laughed. "You want some of this?"

She nodded with a cute smile. "I smoke, you not the only one that smokes."

"What the hell, you can have some." He let her hit the weed. She took a light pull and almost gagged. Bam had to laugh. "Take it easy." He said.

She laughed. "I'm okay." She smiled and then took another pull. Minutes later everything became funny to her.

"You okay?" Bam asked with a smile as he lit a Newport.

"Yeah." She nodded.

They sat and watched TV for a few minutes and then she shocked Bam: She kissed his lips out of the blue. "Hold up!" He jerked away giving her a light push.

"You don't want me, you don't like me?" her eyes were sexy and slanted from the weed.

"That's not what we here for. It don't have nothin' to do wit' me liking' you." Bam was high as shit wondering what harm could come from a little fun with the sexy young Colombian woman. After all, he wasn't taking the pussy, he thought. He knew Serio would have a fit if he found out about somebody fucking the young woman, but fuck it, Bam told himself.

"You know you want Me.," she said, standing up for Bam to see her body. She could feel the wetness between her thighs as she pulled her T-shirt over her head and let it fall to the floor. "Let me please you." She got down on her knees and undid Bam's shorts. He didn't protest. She looked into his eyes as she pulled his manhood out of his boxers and began to stroke and lick it. "You like that?" she asked. Bam nodded as he rolled up some more weed. She then slid him inside her warm, wet mouth with affection. Wet sounds and slurps were the only sounds in the room aside from the TV. Bam let out a few low moans as he watched her bob her head up and down, taking him deep into her throat.

She came up for a second and said, "I want to feel you inside me." Standing up she slid her panties off and straddled Bam. She cased down on him, taking him deep inside her with soft moans as she held onto his shoulders. Her eyes rolled back into her head. "Aaaahhhhh ..." she enjoyed the fullness that she felt inside, she'd never had a black dude inside her tight wetness. She slid up and down with long strides as she began to speak in Spanish, expressing her deepest, nasty fantasies. Bam had one hand on his .45 while letting her do her thing. She rode him like a long lost lover as she tried to keep her moans under control. She didn't want her aunt to hear what was going on.

"Oh my God!" a voice gasped.

Bam looked up as the young woman continued to ride him. They both saw the older woman cover her mouth in shock. The look on her face was pure surprise. She ran back into the bedroom and slammed the door. Bam smiled and shook his head as he kept digging up in the pussy.

Two days late, Serio and Vicioso were standing in front of the building in Red Hook on a cool summer night talking about business. Serio had let the Colombian women go after collection of $500,000. He wasn't worried about the police, he and his crew really didn't exist in the U.S. ---they were illegals.

"You think we will run into Vick again?" Vicioso asked, blowing cigarette smoke into the air, watching everything that was going on around them.

"I don't think so, but if we do I got somethin' for his raas. He lucky I let his people go; I shoulda put them in the dirt just for him playin' wit' my money."

"I see where you comin' from with that one, but I think you did it the right way."

Serio watched the traffic going into his coke spot, business was picking up. "Did you make sure the apartment was clean?"

"Yeah, I did it myself."

"I like how you stay on top of business, Vicioso. I got twenty thousand for you out of the money I got from Vick. I'll give it to you when we stop by Yasmin's."

Twenty thousand dollars! Vicioso felt rich already, and all he had to do was kidnap some Colombian women with Serio. He loved America. To him it was nothing like it.

"There are good times and bad times in the game, Vicioso. Make sure you save your money. Keep your cash for a rainy day."

Vicioso nodded. "As long as I got enough cash to send back home I'm okay; I'ma make sure I take care of myself."

Serio smiled. "Keep that mind set and you'll be rich before you know it, Vicioso." Serio lit a Newport and changed the subject. "Look here, I gotta take a trip down to Washington. I need a new connect and I got a man down there that loves me. He'll make sure we eat good up here. I want you to take the ride wit' me. I want you to meet him, he'll love you. He's a good friend to have, too."

"Cool wit' me, whatever you say Serio. When we supposed to take the trip?"

"This weekend, but I need to take care of a few things first. Come on, let's get out of here. I wanna take care of a few things before it gets too late." Serio threw Vicioso the car keys. "You drivin' too. Don't crash my shit." He'd taught Vicioso how to drive a few days ago.

Vicioso laughed. "I learn fast at everything I do! I got you, compa."

On the phone with Niecy, Vicioso sat on the sofa watching TV in his little apartment eating pizza. Thirty five thousand dollars sat on the table that his feet rested on. His stash was growing fast. Serio slid him cash for every little thing he did. One minute he was picking up money, since he knew how to drive now, the next minute he was dropping off kilos to Bam and Reego in Red Hook. He was in the mix all the way and he'd only been in the U.S. for three months.

"You drivin'?" Niecy asked.

"Yeah, Serio be lettin' me keep his car all the time. I'm up here ridin' around in a BMW and shit."

"Don't forget where you come from boy." Niecy joked.

"You know I'd never do that, baby."

"So I guess you on top of the world up there." Niecy said.

"Nah, not yet." He laughed. "You remember how Tony came up in Scarface? I'm movin' like that now, I'm just getting started. I gotta crawl before I walk."

"Yeah, I hear that. You better not forget about me, I know that much, Harvey."

"How could I forget about you? Huh?"

"I'm just sayin'."

"Say no more, baby. I'm already on top of getting you up here. Serio got a man in Washington that told him he could get you up here through Miami. Let me take care of this. Things just been movin' real fast for me, I'm still gettin' used to this place."

"Serio is really takin' good care of you up there I see."

"We are brothers up here; we take care of each other. We trust each other wit' our lives."

"That's good, because if somethin' happens to you up there somebody gon' have to answer to me."

Vicioso laughed. He loved Niecy; she had that fire in her that turned him on. "Don't worry baby, I'ma be fine. I just can't wait to get my hands on you again. I miss your sexy-ass so much; I can't wait to make love to you again."

Niecy blushed. "I can't wait either. I'm really missin' you a lot. These days are gettin' longer with you gone, Harvey."

"Don't you worry. You'll be up here soon." Vicioso said. "Don't you ever forget that you mean the world to me, Niecy."

The sound of Eric B. and Rakim was pumping through the speakers of the new BMW as Vicioso drove through Brooklyn headed for Red Hook. He was riding with an Uzi and two kilos of cocaine. Serio had let him know how careful he had to be riding through Brooklyn dirty. Vicioso kept his eyes open. All he had to do was drop the kilos off with Bam and pick up the money and his job was done. Things were beginning to move a little faster now. He'd taken the trip to D.C. with Serio and met Cortez. Serio introduced Vicioso to Cortez and a few of his men in D.C. For starters, Cortez sent them back to New York with twenty kilos. Payment didn't have to be made until the bricks were sold. Serio couldn't beat that! Cortez was a good friend to have. On top of that, Cortez was only charging Serio $10,000 a kilo.

Vicioso pulled up and parked Serio's BMW on Columbia Road by the flagpole. He looked around as he grabbed the shopping bag on the floor with the keys in it; he checked the Uzi and slid it in the shopping bag as well. Getting out of the car, Vicioso kept his eyes on everything moving. Reego, Marcus and a few other Panamanians were hanging out in front of the building as Vicioso headed for the door. "What's up, Vicioso?" Reego said giving Vicioso five.

"Just playin' my part." Vicioso said. He spoke to Reego and the crew for a second, and then he took the coke up to the spot where Bam was waiting.

Inside the apartment with Bam, Vicioso sat the coke on the dining room table. "This is enough coke for today and tomorrow. Serio said for you to call me if you need some more before then."

"Okay." Bam said, handing Vicioso a brown paper bag. "That's fifteen Gs right there."

"You a few dollars short ain't you?" Vicioso said.

"The coke was a little short last time." Bam said.

Vicioso raised his eyebrows. "Nah, I capped that shit up myself, Bam. You must've miscounted somethin'. I know what I gave you. I counted it twice."

"Son, I'm telling you the shit was short last time. I ant gon' play no games. But, for the sake of what you sayin', I'll make up whatever's short out of my pocket."

"Yeah, okay. I'll let Serio know what you said." Vicioso left Red Hook and went to pick Serio up from his apartment. For the whole ride Vicioso was thinking about the short money. It was no way that anybody could tell him that the coke was short when he was the one that was on top of that part of the operation.

Later on, Reego decided to take Vicioso out to Dynamite, a club that Reego and Serio had slid through every now and then. By now, Serio's crew was known as La Banda and their name was ringing. The music was loud and the club was dark and humid with a thick crowd. Vicioso enjoyed the music while smoking weed in the back, watching everything. He didn't really like the club scene, but it was nice to get out and meet new people in New York. A number of people even knew who he was since he ran with La Banda.

After an hour or so inside the hot club, Vicioso was ready to go. He wanted to get back to his apartment so he could get some rest. He had to get up early in the morning to take care of a few things for Serio; Vicioso dealt with his duties like a real job. Walking up on Reego, who was dancing with a badass Panamanian girl, Vicioso yelled into his ear, "I'm ready to go! My head is startin' to hurt."

"Okay." Reego said. "Let me use the bathroom first." Reego headed for the bathroom.

The Panamanian girl that was dancing with Reego looked at Vicioso and said, "You're Vicioso?" she looked him up and

down as if she couldn't believe he was the young Panamanian that she'd been hearing about.

Vicioso nodded. "Yeah, I'm Vicioso, why?" He said, looking around the club. It was too many people jammed in one place for him.

"You look so young. I been hearin' about you, though."

"Is that so?" Vicioso wasn't in the mood.

"Yeah, I'd like to get to know you, too." The girl licked her lips.

"No disrespect, but I got a woman." Vicioso stepped off heading for the bathroom.

Reego bumped into Vicioso as he came out of the bathroom. "You ready?"

"Yeah, let's go."

Reego and Vicioso left the club, heading down Flatbush to Reego's car. People were walking up and down the street on both sides of Flatbush, heading for the club. A dude with a black hat on caught Vicioso's attention; the dude was crossing the street far too fast. Something told Vicioso that danger was coming. "Ay, Reego—" Vicioso began, but his words were cut short when the dude in the black hat pulled out a pistol from under his shirt and opened fire. It all happened in seconds. The loud thunder of the shots sent people scattering and screaming in all directions. Vicioso and Reego went for their heat, but the first shot dropped Reego as the gunman in the black hat advanced on the two Panamanians. Automatic gunfire ripped through the night as Vicioso let his Uzi pistol fire; the fully automatic machine gun made the gunman take flight, although he was still shooting over his shoulder. Vicioso gave chase, stepping out into the middle of the street, trying to gun down the gunman.

The Uzi in Vicioso's hands was roaring like it would never stop. He chased the gunman for half a block, tearing up parked cars along the way. The gunman disappeared into a dark alley. Vicioso ran into the dark alley behind him, but the gunman was nowhere to be found. Vicioso returned to the scene of the shooting to check on Reego. Almost instantly, sirens filled the air. A small crowd began to form outside the club.

Smoking Uzi still in hand, Vicioso kneeled down beside Reego and said "Reego! Reego! You okay?" Vicioso held Reego's bloody body in his arms. "I'ma get you out of here. I'ma get you to a hospital."

Reego groaned in anguish as Vicioso helped him up. His shirt was covered in thick, dark blood. "We gotta ... get outta here before the beast come, Vicioso."

"I'ma get us outta here." Vicioso helped Reego into the car and laid him across the back seat. Police sirens were getting closer. Vicioso jumped behind the wheel and took off like he was in a racecar.

CHAPTER 10

Serio, Vicioso, Bam and two of Serio's men were huddled up in the lobby of the hospital talking about what had gone down outside of the club. Murder was the next move, without a doubt. Polee showed up a little later to show his support and to let Serio know that he had his back, no matter what they'd been through. After discussing a few things and getting Vicioso's side of the story, Serio had Bam take Vicioso to his apartment on Flatbush. Serio didn't want Vicioso hanging around the hospital as the cops began to show up.

Polee wanted to have a few words with Serio alone so he pulled him to the side and said, "Who do you think was behind this?"

Serio looked around and whispered, "Between me and you, I got a phone call sayin' it was Greg."

"Panamanian Greg?"

"Yeah, laope."

"I didn't even know his raas was on the streets." Polee folded his arms and rubbed his chin. He knew that shit was about to get real heated.

"I didn't know he was on the streets either." Serio puffed on a Newport. "One thing I do know is that Greg and whoever he got runnin' wit' him is gon' get what they got comin' for this shit here. It's no doubt in my mind that this hit was for me. Retaliation gon' be real swift. You can count on that, Polee. I'ma pay a few home visits tonight! Taking no names."

Polee nodded his approval. "I'ma put my ear to the streets and see if I can find out where the nigga Greg layin' his head."

"Let me know what you come up wit'. I'ma make an example out of his mada rass!"

Polee put his hand on Serio's shoulder and said, "I'm not tryin' to tell you how to run your operations, but keep in mind that you are the boss, Serio. The top man, the captain of the ship. See where I'm comin' from? You can't keep bein' that nigga that pull the trigga. You got people to do that for you now, Serio. When you the boss all you do is call the shots. You got money to make, you gotta make sure the show goes on. Vicioso showed you tonight that he can take care of business under pressure. Let him pull the trigga, Serio."

"No disrespect, Polee, I know how you handle shit, but Reego is my right-hand man, my brother. Right now, he's laid up in that hospital room wit' two bullets in his chest. I can't act like it didn't happen and just send Vicioso and some of my men to take care of it. Some things I gotta do myself. You know how I am. I like things done a certain way. You are right about me bein' the top man, but the top man also has to make sure everybody is taken care of. By the time Reego get's back on his feet I want Greg to be a dead man; that means more to me than the money I'll miss out on in the process."

Polee nodded. "I respect that, Serio.

When Serio left the hospital he headed straight for Vicioso's apartment and picked him up. They went looking for Greg off the top, checking different locations until sunrise. They came up with nothing. They finally called it quits around six in the morning and went back to Vicioso's apartment where they got a little bit of sleep.

Around noon, Vicioso was cocking his .45 automatic, he and Serio were about to head out looking for Greg again; they

also had plans to pay a visit to a few other people that may have aided him.

"We gon' make everybody pay that had somethin' to do wit' Greg, you hear me?" Serio said.

"I'm all for it." Vicioso tucked the pistol in his waistband. He had no second thoughts about taking care of business.

"Fredrico knew Greg was plannin' to hit us." Serio said.

"How did you find that out?" Vicioso asked.

"Made a few calls before you woke up. Fredrico gon' have to pay for that in blood." Serio walked over to the window and looked down onto a busy Flatbush Avenue. "Call Bam and tell him to make sure he keep shit runnin' smooth around Red Hook, tell 'em we gon' have to take care of a few things so he need to tighten up security."

Vicioso got Bam on the phone and told him what Serio said. Bam was cool with the game plan. He had the know-how to run the operation; he knew where one stash of kilos was so he could stay on top of business.

Serio's beeper went off just as he and Vicioso were about to leave out the door. Serio didn't recognize the number, but called it back anyway.

"I knew you would call back." The voice had a thick West Indian accent. "I guess you know it was me that popped your man, Reego."

"You think this shit is a game or somethin'? You think I ain't gon' bury your raas?!" Serio snapped, raising his voice. "You're a walkin' dead man!"

"I feel the same way about you. Reego lucky he had that youngster wit' him. What's his name? Vicioso? He got balls, I'll give him that much. He saved Reego's life, but he only bought y'all some time. Your run is up. If you as smart as I think you are you'll pack your shit and go on back home before I put you in the dirt, payaseto."

Serio burst out laughing. "Fuck you!!!" He hung up the phone and looked at Vicioso. "That raas must think we playin' games wit' his ass." Serio told Vicioso what Greg had said on the phone.

Vicioso laughed. "I had his ass runnin' for his life. Fuck what he talkin' 'bout. Let's go find them niggaz!"

Fredrico stacked $110,000 into the safe in the back office of his salon after selling ten kilos. His hands shook badly. Something clearly had scared him to death. The hit on Reego was a dumb move as far as Fredrico was concerned. He knew that Serio was about to move hard and fast. In Fredrico's mind, it was a good time to head south to Miami. He'd been thinking about relocating there anyway. His sister's husband had been telling him how much money there was in Miami.

"Freddy." A sexy voice called from the doorway. It spooked Fredrico. It was one of his stylists. "I didn't mean to startle you."

"Don't sneak up on me like that then!" he wiped sweat from his forehead. "What do you want?!" his tone was cold and nasty. It was a cover-up for the embarrassment he felt for showing his cowardly colors.

"I just wanted to tell you I'm leavin'. I'm goin' to lock up since you said we closed for the day."

"Good, see you later." He dismissed her just like that, with an arrogant wave of the hand. She rolled her eyes and left, tired of the way he treated her. Once he was alone, Fredrico made his way to the bathroom. He took a seat on the toilet. His bowels were in a nervous uproar. Emptying his bowels he lit a cigarette and wondered what Serio's next move would be and what he would do if he knew that Fredrico had known about Greg's plan to kill Serio. It would have been great if Greg had killed Serio, but he went and shot Reego first since he couldn't find Serio. Now a monster had been awakened.

The more Fredrico thought about Serio the more terrified he became.

The bathroom door was kicked open with a loud cracking sound. It scared Fredrico so bad that he fell off the toilet and was in the corner trembling with his pants around his ankles. Serio towered above him with an Uzi in hand. "Caught you wit' your pants down, huh?" Serio said as he reached down and slapped the shit out of Fredrico like a renegade whore. Fredrico began to beg for his life. "Shut the fuck up!" Serio then grabbed Fredrico by the collar and dragged him out into the office area where Vicioso was standing in the doorway. Serio threw Fredrico to the floor and then sat on the sofa and crossed his legs as if he was on a job interview. Fredrico whimpered as he pulled his pants up. "So," Serio began. "You knew about Greg's plan for me and you didn't warn me, huh? That's how we play things out now?"

"I swear to God I didn't know a thing." Fredrico lied.

Vicioso gave him a hard kick to the gut and Fredrico cried out in pain. "Lyin' choo cha de tu madre!" Vicioso hissed, pointing his weapon at Fredricio's head.

"What do you take me for?" Serio asked calmly.

"You must think I'm one of these clowns that you deal with."

Struggling to catch his breath, Fredrico said, "I swear ... look, it's over a hundred grand in my safe and about six or seven bricks. You can have it, just don't kill me. Please don't kill me, Serio! Please!" He put his hands together like he was praying to Serio.

Serio laughed. "Where can I find Greg, you coward?" Serio's voice was almost a whisper.

"He got a spot on the Lower East Side. He staying wit' some Puerto Rican bitch down there."

"You think you can buy your way out of everything, don't you? I hate that about you spineless cowards." Serio asked as he stood up. Vicioso was waiting for the call.

"Open the fuckin' safe." Serio walked Fredrico over to the safe and told Vicioso to grab a trash bag to put the goods in. When Fredrico had the safe open, Vicioso cleaned it out and set the trash bag on the floor. Serio sat back on the sofa as if he was thinking about his next move. Vicioso was standing behind Fredrico. "If I thought you was a threat I'd kill you myself, but I'ma let you live---"

"Thank you! Oh my God, thank you, Serio! Thank you! Thank you so much, familia!"

"You'll get what you got comin' sooner or later. Cowards die a thousand deaths." Serio gave Vicioso the signal.

BANG! BANG!

Reego stayed in the hospital for just over a week. He recovered well. Once he was out of the hospital, Serio wanted him to lay low for a while and chill. Things were heated between Serio and Greg. Greg had a nice crew of killers running with him that were from Colon, Panama. The Colon Panamanians and Serio's La Banda crew were warring like Medellin mercenaries in the streets of Brooklyn. A rash of dramatic shootings and murders exploded and they were all connected to Serio and Greg. Most of the action took place around Franklin Avenue and Flatbush Avenue. Through it all, Vicioso was making a name for himself behind the trigger; he was on the scene almost every time gunplay went down. It seemed like he was on a mission every day. After the first body, it was nothing to it. He had no problem with pulling the trigger, it was easy. He would put the work in anywhere at any time. After a few broad daylight shootings on Franklin

MONEY AIN'T EVERYTHING

Avenue, Vicioso's name started ringing more than ever. Serio was right by his side every step of the way. Seeing Vicioso in action on the front line gave Serio a newfound respect for the youngster. Vicioso was fearless. As the hunt for Greg continued, they seemed to miss him by minutes; every spot they checked for him was a spot that he'd just left.

At that same time, with all that was going on, Serio never lost track of what was going on with his Red Hook spot, even though Bam was damn near running the drug operation.

Cigarette smoke filled the inside of the old Monte Carlo that Serio was driving through Brooklyn. Bam was riding shotgun. Vicioso sat in the back seat, in deep thought about how things were going. Serio had hit him off real nice after they hit Fredrico. Vicioso sent $50,000 home. Pimpo was to use some of the money to make the trip to New York. However, Vicioso was having second thoughts about bringing Niecy to New York with all of the bloodshed and murder that he was knee deep in now. There was a price to pay for everything.

As Serio drove down Atlantic Avenue, he and Bam discussed business. Money and coke was still coming up short. "Money keep comin' up short, what's the deal, Bam?" Serio asked.

"Shit been real hot. The cops been all over the place. You know how that shit goes. They chased me the other day when I was comin' out the stash spot. I had to throw the coke. All the bodies around Red Hook got the cops campin' out damn near." Bam smoked a cigarette as he looked out the window. "Plus them Jamaicans done opened up a new spot behind Lisa's building and shit."

"Yeah, I heard about that. But anyway, you been keepin' shit movin' other than that." Serio said, with a smile.

"You my nigga, son. You know that. We gon' get this money together." Bam said, with his lying-ass.

"I been thinking this whole thing wit' Greg should be over wit' real soon. As far as the coke shit goes, the crack shit is movin' faster than anything I've ever seen. It seems like the faster Vicioso drops bricks off at the spot the faster they move. I'm thinkin' 'bout openin' a new spot wit' my new connect. I'ma let you run the spot and let Vicioso run the Red Hook spot. What you think about that?"

"I don't know Serio. The Red Hook spot runnin' nice and smooth. If we open a new spot we gon' have to go through all the bullshit over again. You know? I'm so sure that's good move right there."

"That makes sense." Serio nodded as he pulled into a dark alley just off Flatbush Avenue. The whole car was covered with darkness. Serio cut the car off, looked at Vicioso through the rearview mirror and raised his eyebrows.

BOOM!

A single gunshot rocked the car from the backseat. Blood and brains flew all over the windshield as Bam's body slumped forward against the dashboard. Serio glanced at the body with disdain. After all that Serio had done for Bam he couldn't believe that the nigga had started stealing.

Shaking his head, Serio said, "You can't be nice to these bastards these days, Vicioso. They always take your kindness for weakness until they laying somewhere with they brains blown out. All over a few dollars."

"That's crazy. Don't make no sense to me. I knew something funny was up wit' Bam's ass."

"He must've thought I was going to miss what was going on since I was so busy dealing with all this other bullshit."

"Well, we won't have to worry about his raas no more."

"Let's get rid of his body." Serio said to Vicioso.

Vicioso stepped outside the Red Hook apartment building into the hot summer air. People were everywhere; the projects were always alive. Always on point, Vicioso spotted a stranger in a trench coat and knew something was wrong. It was too damn hot for a trench coat. Vicioso locked eyes with the stranger and pulled his .45 automatic. The stranger opened his coat and whipped out an AR-15 assault rifle in broad daylight and sprayed a burst of rounds at Vicioso. Vicioso fired back and tried to run back inside the building but the bullets were crashing into the door so Vicioso dashed across the court, still firing his pistol. He was trying to make it behind the building.

People scattered in every direction, running and screaming as gunfire tore through the projects. Greg gave chase, firing small burst of fire at Vicioso, who was running top-speed like an Olympic sprinter. Bullets flew by his head on both sides as thoughts of death crossed his mind. He knew he didn't stand a chance shooting it out against an AR-15 with his pistol so he kept running, firing a few shots here and there. Vicioso was trying to make it back to Columbia Road were Serio's spot was. Greg kept firing, it seemed like he had countless bullets in the AR-15. Cutting through the back of a building, Vicioso lost Greg for a second. He ran up the steps and shot to the roof. Once on the roof he ran and jumped over to the next building.

He looked down from the roof and saw Greg running across the court. Vicioso fired shots at Greg from the roof, making Greg take cover. Greg aimed at Vicioso and sprayed a burst of bullets. Vicioso jumped out the way.

Out of the blue, two cops bent the corner down below and yelled, "Drop the weapon!" Greg took one look at the cops and sprayed in their direction. One of the cops took slugs right in the face. Greg took flight. With one cop on his back shooting at him, Greg tried to run across the street but ran into more cops that were jumping out of a patrol car. Knowing that his time had come, Greg took a deep breath and sprayed at the cops, dropping one, but the other two took him down with bullets to the head. Vicioso watched the whole thing from the rooftop. Once he saw Greg go down Vicioso made his way back inside the building.

Greg's murder at the hands of the NYPD was all over the news later on in the evening. The top story was about the violence in the Red Hook projects. Most of the violence in the projects was blamed on the explosion of the drug trade and foreign elements that were adding to the already deadly mixture of urban life and poverty in American streets. Foreigners were said to be moving in on the lucrative drug markets of New York and Miami in an attempt to cash in on the fast cash. The feds were promising to put a stop to the violence and to clean up not only Red Hook, but also drug-infested areas all over New York City.

Serio and Vicioso sat on the leather sofa in Serio's living room smoking weed as they watched the news. Serio pointed at the TV and said, "If the feds really step in things gon' start gettin' real tight around Red Hook. They gon' make it real hard for us to eat. Real hard." He shook his head and sighed. "We gon' have to be ready for that."

"They can't stop what's goin' on in the projects." Vicioso said. "If they close down one spot we just open another one. Ain't that how you said shit go up here?"

"Yeah that's how shit go, but the feds can make shit real hard for us to get money. When they get their hands on you they make sure they hit you wit' somethin' that sticks, or fucks your whole operation up. We need to start lookin' for a

new spot. Just in case. The Red Hook spot is gettin' too hot for business."

"I like the Red Hook spot, though." Vicioso blew smoke into the air. "It's a gold mine."

"It's a gold mine all over this country. Don't ever forget that. Wherever you go you can get paper." Serio lit a Newport. "All you gotta do is find a spot that looks nice and set up shop. Simple as that Vicioso." Serio schooled him to the science of setting up shop in new places and towns. Philly, Jersey, Baltimore, D.C., VA and Miami were just a few spots where Serio knew the drug trade was booming. Crack was taking over. If a nigga had the balls to take his piece of the pie he could get paid in full. Serio understood this well and it was always on his mind.

Changing the subject, Vicioso said, "So what we gon' do about the rest of them Colon boys? It ain't over just 'cause Greg got killed. We need to deal wit' they ass too."

"We gon' wipe them out. You know how it goes." Serio winked at Vicioso.

CHAPTER 11

arvey, I've been hearing things about you. Word travels. You know that. You stay in my prayers, but I worry about you." Melly said, on the phone with her son from her bedroom in Santa Cruz. "I want you to cool down up there."

"Ma, who keeps tellin' you these things? Worryin' you like that?" Vicioso asked.

"I wasn't born yesterday, Harvey! I know what you and Pimpo are doing up there. All I want you to do is be safe and look after Pimpo. Understand me?"

"Yes."

"Are you saving your money?"

"I'm trying to. Aside from the money I send you I gotta take care of myself too. I got bills and all that also. I'm tryin' to get a new apartment for me and Niecy. The one I got right now is too small for me, her, and Pimpo." Vicioso lit a Newport. "Serio still be lookin' out for me though. So things are alright."

"Stop depending on Serio and start saving your money. You're not up there to party and have fun, spending your money on nothing. You are risking your life. At the end of the day what do you have to show for it? Don't forget what you went up there for. I don't want you spending your whole life looking over your shoulder. You went up there to make a way for you and your family. You can't do that if you come home in a box, you hear me?" Melly went on admonishing her son for a few minutes. She knew that Vicioso and Pimpo

were deeply involved in the drug trade in New York. She had a number of friends and family in New York, it wasn't hard to get word back to Panama. Vicioso and Pimpo's names were ringing all the way back home. They'd been laying shit down strong in the streets of Brooklyn. The war with the Colon boys was reduced to a minor conflict after La Banda tore into what was left of them following Greg's death.

"Ma, I understand what you are sayin'. I'ma be safe. Okay?" Vicioso said.

"I'm serious, Harvey."

"Ma, I understand, but let me ask you this: Did you go look at homes like I asked you to?"

"Yeah, but I don't know what you want to do yet. I don't want nothing too big. It has to be just right."

Vicioso laughed. "Ma, get whatever you want. Don't worry about the size or the price. Whatever you want you can afford now. Okay?"

"I'll take care of that you just be safe up there. That's all I care about."

"I will. I love you." Vicioso said.

"I love you, too."

When Vicioso got off the phone with his mother he looked over at Niecy's sexy body under the sheets in their Atlantic City hotel room and smiled; his plans were coming together well. They had spent the last few days enjoying a getaway from Brooklyn. Vicioso needed the down time. Life was moving 100 miles per hour for him in Brooklyn. However, with Niecy in New York with him now, things were coming together for Vicioso. In no time he would have his own operation up and running and then the real money would begin rolling in.

"Your mother's right, Harvey." Niecy said. She wasn't sleep; she'd heard the whole conversation. "You need to start thinkin' about yourself sometimes. I know that Serio has done a lot for you, but you're riskin' just as much as he is up here. You should have just as much as he does. You come first at the end of the day."

"What you mean?" Vicioso gave Niecy a sharp look. A look that she rarely saw at that. In his mind she was focused on the wrong thing.

"Papi, you do so much for Serio and we still livin' in an apartment on Flatbush. Don't get me wrong, I'm happy because I'm wit' you, but I got eyes. I see how Serio and Yasmin livin' and I see how we are livin'. Serio done bought a house. Don't you think we should be livin' like that too? You deserve that much?"

Vicioso was rubbed the wrong way, but his baby was right. He'd been running the Red Hook spot since Bam's murder. He'd also been making Serio a lot of money. On some days he pulled in $25,000 to $30,000 running the Red Hook spot and then turned the money over to Serio, only seeing a portion of the cash. In Vicioso's eyes he was playing his role. He was a team player. However, as he thought about what Niecy and his mother were saying it made him think about how other people were moving up in the world. Serio had just bought a huge house for himself and his woman. They were living the American dream. Reego had his own operation in Crown Heights and Serio hit him off with the bricks to open the spot. Maybe it was time for Vicioso to get a bigger piece of the pie.

"You see what I'm sayin', baby?" Niecy asked as she kissed Vicioso's lips.

"Yeah, I see what you sayin', but let's worry about all that later. Right now I'm tryin' to think about you, pleasing you in all the right ways." He rolled on top of her. "Okay?"

She laughed. "Whatever you say, baby."

Snow was falling in New York. Vicioso hated the cold winters, but nothing could stop the money from coming in. Business came first. Vicioso, Pimpo, and a few other Panamanians were in the hallway of Serio's Red Hook coke spot smoking weed and talking about Panama. Vicioso had Miles working the gate and had just given him $20,000 worth of caps. Miles had been kept on after Bam's murder because he was loyal. Aside from that, Vicioso was sure that Miles understood what happened to Bam and why it went down in such a way.

Outside a dark green BMW 320i with gold BBS rims pulled up on Columbia Road with L.L. Cool J. blasting from the speakers. Vicioso saw the car and stepped out into the cold air to holla at Savior, who was behind the wheel. Vicioso had met Savior and his younger brother, Calvin Klein, through Serio. Their names were ringing. Vicioso jumped in the passenger seat and gave Savior five. "What's up, Savior? Man, I'm telling you, you always looking good. You the man. I give it to you. Let me get this car up off you."

Savior laughed. "You know me. Getting' money, you know how it goes." Savior turned the music down. "You really wanna buy this Beamer, kid?"

"Yeah, what you want for it?" Vicioso loved the BMW that Savior had. The car was a year old, but it was still a 1986 model with thousands of dollars of work done to it.

"Give me twenty-five." Savior was damn near giving the car away, but he liked Vicioso.

"I got that right now. Wait here." Vicioso jumped out the car and ran back inside the building. He returned with a brown paper bag containing the cash. "There you go right there."

"Cool. It's yours, just drop me off in front of my building." Savior said as he looked inside the paper bag, flipping through the cash. He knew Vicioso's money was good.

Vicioso and savior switched seats. Once behind the wheel, Vicioso dropped Savior off in front of his building. A brand new black 1987 BMW was parked in front of the building. "That's me right there, kid." Savior smiled, pointing at the BMW. Calvin Klein and a few other dudes were standing in front of the building.

"You doin' big things." Vicioso gave Savior five.

Heading back around Columbia Road, Vicioso turned the radio up, pumping L.L. Cool J. He now owned his first car, a BMW at that. He told himself it was time to start doing some things for him. Pulling up by the flagpole, Vicioso blew the horn for Pimpo.

Pimpo came running to the car in his huge winter coat. "You bought this?" he said as he jumped in the car. "You gotta teach me how to drive! You know I want one of these right here."

"I got you." Vicioso smiled and rubbed Pimpo's head as they pulled off. "We gon' do that later on. Right now we gotta pick that coke up from Serio. He want us to meet him at the spot."

Vicioso and Pimpo met Serio at a New Jersey hotel and picked up twenty kilos. They took the cocaine to the Brooklyn stash house and put it up. Vicioso would coke it up later on. After putting the coke up, Vicioso and Pimpo cruised around in the BMW. Pimpo was looking out the window with an Uzi lying across his lap.

"Did Niecy find another apartment yet?" Pimpo asked.

"She on top of that right now." Vicioso said, smoking a Newport.

"You can keep the spot on Flatbush. Until you ready to get another spot anyway."

As they cruised down Franklin Avenue, Pimpo said, "Ain't that one of them Colon niggaz?!" He pointed out the window as he gripped the Uzi. Vicioso took a look. The dude was one of the Colon dudes that had shot at Pimpo a few days ago. Pimpo was ready to jump out the car and gun the nigga down. In broad daylight! "Hold fast!" Vicioso said as he grabbed Pimpo's shoulder. "We can't do it like that. Let me pull around the corner." Vicioso bent the corner at the end of the block and said, "Go ahead, hurry up. I'll be waitin' right here. Spray and get out of there."

Pimpo jumped out and ran around the corner with the machinegun in hand. A few seconds later, all hell broke loose as fully automatic gunfire hit the air followed by the sound of crashing cars. Pimpo came flying back around the corner with the smoking Uzi in hand and jumped back in the car. "I got his ass!" he said as Vicioso pulled off.

Time began to fly and 1987 came in with money falling from the sky. Money was coming in faster than it could be spent for Vicioso and Pimpo. Gunplay was just another day at the office as far as they were concerned. They were engulfed in the fast life and had developed a serious habit of spending money by the tens of thousands of dollars. Aside from the money that they sent back home to their mother, the brothers splurged like heavyweights. What the fuck? Life was short, that was their outlook.

Vicioso spoiled Niecy with diamonds and gold. He taught her how to drive and gave her the BMW that he bought from Savior a short while after he bought it. He decided to step it up and bought himself a brand-new black 1988 BMW 535 and put chrome BBS rims on it. Pimpo wouldn't be out done: He copped a white 1988 BMW 535 with chrome BBS rims.

Vicioso and Niecy moved into a nice Brooklyn apartment off of Flatbush Avenue and had it laid out as if royalty lived inside. Pimpo was fine in the little apartment Vicioso had when he first got to New York, Pimpo didn't feel the need to move as long as he was sitting on a load of cash. Life was looking up by all means.

A long with all the money making came a lot of heat. The NYPD started hearing more and more about the Panamanians that were getting money and dropping bodies in connection with the drug trade in Red Hook. Serio and Vicioso were two of the names that kept coming up. Vicioso had even been questioned about a few different shootings that had taken place in the projects and around Franklin Avenue, but nothing ever came of it. As far as the NYPD knew, Vicioso was John Wilson of Brooklyn, New York; that's what his ID read. Nevertheless, Vicioso was on top of his game and had big plans for the future. Every move he made was in step with his main to goal: to get rich.

Walking down the steps into Serio's basement, Vicioso carried a shopping bag full of Serio's money. From the look on his face, it was clear that Vicioso had something on his mind. Serio was sitting in a deep black leather chair watching a big-screen TV. He was watching a videotape of his mother's birthday party back home in Panama. Vicioso's mother was at the party. Serio had paid for the whole thing. Serio looked up and saw Vicioso sitting the shopping bag on the pool table.

"That's eighty-five G's." Vicioso said.

Serio smiled and paused the tape with the remote. "You run a tight ship, Vicioso. I like that." Serio was still very much on top of his game, but he didn't really have to do much dirty work anymore. Vicioso made sure that things in the streets ran smoothly. Serio only showed up about the money

or the connection with Cortez. Other than that, Serio ran his business from behind the scenes and tried his best to stay off the radar.

Vicioso took a seat across from Serio and said, "That crack shit be movin' like it's no tomorrow. They can't get enough."

"Yeah, I see." Serio lit a cigarette. "Did Yasmin tell you that she and Niecy are plannin' to take a trip back to Panama for her mother's birthday?"

"Yeah, Niecy said somethin' to me today. I think they just want to get away from all this for a second. I can't blame them." Vicioso joked.

Serio laughed. "I don't blame them either. There's a price to pay for everything, but I wouldn't trade it for anything in the world."

"Me either. We done came a long way from back home, and I ain't even been here for a whole year yet. I must admit that everything you said about this shit up here was true."

"I see Pimpo's comin' along real well. He got that same drive you had when you first came. He likes that gunplay a little more though." Serio laughed. "It seems like he gets a trill from the shit."

"Yeah, he do." Vicioso smiled as he kicked back in the chair. His diamond-covered Jesus-piece was glistening in the light.

"On another note, I need to holla at you about somethin', Serio."

"What's on your mind? You okay?" Serio blew smoke in the air.

Vicioso rubbed his chin and said, "When I first got here you said that I could get rich up here … and don't get me wrong, I been seein' a bunch of money, I'm grateful for that, but I was thinking that it's time for me to start my own thing. Spread my wings. You know?"

Serio gave Vicioso a look that made it very clear that he was not ready for this conversation. However, he had to hear Vicioso out; he'd given him his word that they would never go through what he and Polee went through a while back, he'd also given him his word that he'd let him fly when he was ready.

"You not seein' enough money, Vicioso? What's the problem?"

"Nah, it's not really that. I'm just ready to lay back like you and Reego. It's time for me to get money from behind the scenes. Maybe even sell some weight. I was even thinkin' about the store idea we talked about. You know? Like you was telling me, I need to stay off the radar. You understand?"

Serio nodded. It was a sad nod, like he was sending his only son off to fight in a war. "You deserve that much, Vicioso. I understand. We all have to do our own thing sooner or later."

"One more thing."

"What's that?"

"Pimpo's comin' wit' me."

"Nah, I can't do that. I need somebody strong like him on the team if you gon' go do your own thing. At least until you get your thing up and runnin'."

"Can't do that, Serio. Pimpo's comin' wit' me. Me and him gon' start our thing together. That's my baby brother; I gotta keep an eye on him and make sure he's taken care of. It's a joint thing so to speak."

Serio looked irritated and a little confused. "What you mean you can't do that?! Pimpo works for me! Not you, Vicioso, don't get beside yourself." his voice was full of authority. It was clear that he was pulling rank.

"Yeah, he does work for you, but he's my brother and we're a package deal. It ain't in the talk. I need him by my

124

side. Nobody can answer to my mother about my brother but me. That's just the way it is."

Serio leaned back and took a deep pull on his Newport. After a few seconds of thought he said, "What you plan on doin'?"

"You know Justice and them Jamaican boys been goin' at it about that spot back there by Lisa's building. Me and Pimpo gon' take the spot and get rid of them. That'll stop some of the shootin' around there and it'll give us our own spot. It should be easy to do it that way."

"Them Jamaican's got a team of ten or fifteen strong. How you and Pimpo gon' just take the spot?" Serio smiled. "You think they gon' just roll over and hand you the keys?"

"You always told me if you crush the head the body will fall so that's what we plan to do. I know where the Jamaican dude Pasquale lay his head. We gon' hit him at his spot and take him out. Justice won't mind, we'll be doing him a favor. Once the heat dies down everything will be fine. Ain't nothing else to it."

Serio laughed. "You got balls. If you don't get yourself an early grave you gon' get a lot of money." Serio stood up and plucked his ashes in the tray. "Here's the deal, I'ma give you five bricks to start off with, but you give me your word that you gon' buy your coke from me. Keep it in the family, you know?"

"Deal."

"Remember this, Vicioso: Only the strong survive." Serio shook his hand.

CHAPTER 12

Two weeks later, Vicioso and Pimpo caught Pasquale coming out of his Brooklyn apartment late at night and kidnapped him. They ended up leaving him handcuffed and shot in the back of the head in his bed. His right-hand man met the same fate. The head of the operation had been crushed. Vicioso and Pimpo then laid claim to Pasquale's Red Hook coke spot after a full week of gunplay with his old workers. The backbone of resistance was crushed when Vicioso and Pimpo came through with a five-man crew of Panamanian gunmen with Uzis and sprayed shit like the Saint Valentine's Day Massacre. The broad daylight slaughter was all over the news for days.

After the heat died down, Vicioso and Pimpo opened up shop and ran it with one lookout, a teenager that lived in the building. For the first few weeks things were tense in the projects. Slowly, Vicioso began to hire a few workers. He'd met one dude by the name of Rufus, who used to buy a little weight from him. Rufus had fallen on hard times so Vicioso gave him a job working the gate. The new spot started off pulling in close to $8,000 a day. Vicioso kept the spot open from 8 A.M. to 4 P.M.; his plan was to keep it that way until business picked up. He and Pimpo were officially running their own spot.

Pimpo stepped outside and fixed his jacket so that his Uzi couldn't be seen. He'd just collected $7,000 from Rufus and was now on his way to his apartment to put the money up. As

he headed for his car he kept his eyes on everything moving. People were all over the place. Spring was back in town. As Pimpo walked through the projects he thought back to how things were in Santa Cruz. Things had really changed for the better, as far as he was concerned. He loved Brooklyn. Out of the blue, somewhere nearby, automatic gunfire tore through the air. It was nothing new or out of place in Brooklyn. Pimpo wasn't even concerned; the gunfire wasn't close enough to merit his attention. He looked around carefully and kept stepping. As he approached his car he became angered. His BMW was his pride and joy. He couldn't believe someone had the audacity to be sitting on it and to have cold beer in a paper bag sitting on the hood as well.

On top of that, the violator was someone he knew: Panamanian Marcus, one of Serio's workers. Marcus was in deep conversation with a sexy, young Panamanian girl. Marcus was older than Pimpo by a few years and had watched Pimpo grow up back home. Pimpo walked up and smacked the beer off the hood of his car. Marcus and the young girl looked surprised, a few other people walking by looked surprised as well. "My shit look like a fuckin' park bench to you?!" Pimpo snapped, glaring at Marcus.

Tension was thick and everyone around seemed to know that something was about to go down.

"The fuck wrong wit' your raas?" Marcus stood up, pissed off. The young girl began to back away, sensing danger. Two other Panamanians that were hanging out with Marcus began to cross the street to see what was going on. From a far, it looked like they were going to aid Marcus against Pimpo.

Seeing the two Panamanians coming his way Pimpo whipped out his Uzi in a flash, pointing at the two approaching Panamanians. "What the fuck y'all comin' over here for? You want to make something out of this?" Pimpo hissed.

Marcus and his comrades began to back away from Pimpo slowly. They knew Pimpo would spray without warning.

"Y'all act like y'all gon' do somethin'! Y'all ain't gon' do shit!" Pimpo spit.

"Damn, we family, Pimpo!" one of the dudes said with his hands up in the air. "Put the gun up."

Pimpo looked at Marcus with a frown and said, "If I catch you sitting on my shit again I'ma act like I don't know you." He kept his Uzi in his hand as he got in his car, watching Marcus and his cohorts. He pulled off with the music blasting, still pissed off.

"You not goin' nowhere!" Niecy pulled Vicioso back into the bed as he tried to get up. "You said you was spendin' the day wit' me."

Vicioso smiled. "I'm just goin' to the bathroom, mami."

She let him go and smiled. Vicioso was putting so much energy into his Red Hook spot that he was spending little time at home. Niecy had started demanding that he spend more time with her. Out of love, he did just that. He made it his business to try to put family first at all times.

Vicioso returned from the bathroom and said, "Are you and Yasmin still goin' to Washington to see her cousin this weekend?"

"Yeah, I want to go shoppin' down there. She keeps tellin' me about Georgetown."

"I might make the trip wit' you." Vicioso said as he climbed back into bed in nothing but his boxers. "I wanna get away from Brooklyn for a minute. I could use a vacation."

Niecy smiled. "Yeah, it'll be nice. We can spend the weekend together in one of those nice hotels. Go shopping, go

around and see all the different sights in Washington. That would be fun and peaceful."

Before Vicioso could say anything he was cut off by the phone.

He reached over and picked the phone up off the nightstand. "Hello?"

"Get over here!" Pimpo said sounding pissed off.

"What's wrong?!" Vicioso said, sitting up, fully alert.

"Just meet me at my apartment. Bring your heat, too!" Pimpo hung up.

Vicioso sat in the bed next to Niecy still holding the phone to his ear. A concerned looked covered his face. His mood had clearly changed. He wondered what was up with his little brother. With all the drama that came their way on the regular, Vicioso began to think the worst.

"What's wrong, Harvey?" Niecy asked. "Is he okay, Harvey? Is everything okay?"

"I don't know. He wouldn't say." Vicioso got dressed and grabbed his Uzi. He gave Niecy a kiss on the lips and said, "I'll be back as soon as I find out what's goin' on."

Niecy sighed. "Okay." She knew there was nothing she could say to keep Vicioso from going to check on his little brother. As Vicioso left the apartment Niecy wondered if she would ever see him again. Every time he left out she wondered if she would ever see him again.

Inside Pimpo's apartment on Flatbush Avenue, Pimpo and Vicioso sat on the sofa while Pimpo told Vicioso what had just went down: Pimpo was about to leave out to head back around Red Hook when he saw Marcus and two other dudes parked across the street from his apartment. Since he'd just had words with them and pulled a gun on them he knew what was up. Pimpo asked no questions. He snuck out the back of his building and crept around the front in an attempt to catch them from the blind side and air the car out. However, when he got around front Marcus was bending the corner at the end of the block leaving the scene. Now Pimpo was ready to murder shit. It was wartime all over again. "They were comin' to hit me, Vicioso! I know it! I'm not playin' that raas at all. It's time to pay they ass a real visit, playin' for keeps."

Vicioso knew Pimpo was right. He was boiling with anger at the fact that they had come to kill his brother. No matter what the cause. That was crossing the line. Vicioso didn't care if Pimpo did pull a gun on them. Right or wrong, his brother was his brother and planned to stand with him till death.

"They gotta answer for that, Vicioso. I don't play that raas." Pimpo's West Indian accent was full of anger and venom.

"You wit' me or what?"

"Fuck you mean am I wit' you or what?" Vicioso frowned as he raised his voice. "You know better than to ask me some shit like that! We blood! I'm wit' you against whoever! Anybody!" Vicioso sighed. "At the same time, you know Marcus works for Serio. We need to holla at Serio before we move. We can't just disrespect him and kill one of his workers without sayin' somethin' to him. I'm sure Serio don't know about this shit. Serio is still family, laope. It's rules to this shit."

"Honestly, Serio is the last thing on my mind right now. I don't give a fuck who Marcus works for. He came to kill me! The only rules that matter right now is my rules, and rule number one is for me to put these niggaz in the dirt. Fuck all that other shit."

"Serio is still family. Even wit' all that said, Pimpo."

After a few moments of thought, Pimpo sighed and said, "Yeah, you right. So what you sayin'?"

130

"Let me call Serio." Vicioso said.

Vicioso called Serio and explained the situation to him. Serio wanted to get to the bottom of the matter off the top. He told Vicioso to meet him on Columbia Road and to bring Pimpo along. After Vicioso got off the phone he looked at Pimpo and said, "Let's go."

Vicioso and Pimpo met Serio and Marcus in the courtyard of Serio's coke spot by Columbia Road. It was dark and cold outside with a lot of foot-traffic throughout the projects. Pimpo was itching to smoke Marcus on the spot, but he didn't want to disrespect Serio. It was burning him up inside.

Nevertheless, Pimpo was not feeling what Serio was talking about. He didn't want to hear shit at the moment. Serio wanted to make peace between Pimpo and Marcus. That peace was looking extremely remote being as though Pimpo and Marcus kept exchanging angry and threatening words. Marcus was fucked up that Pimpo had pulled a gun on him. Serio and Vicioso both knew that Pimpo was wrong, but he was still young and had a lot to learn. At the same time Marcus was wrong for taking it upon himself to make a move on Pimpo without talking to Serio about it. The whole situation was a time bomb waiting to blow.

Becoming frustrated Serio snapped. "Fuck all this back and forth shit!" He waived his hands in the air. "We gon' end this bullshit right here!"

Vicioso was staring at Marcus with a hard glare but spoke to Serio. "Serio, it don't look like this raas wanna end this shit. Marcus act like he still wanna do somethin' to my brother and we all know that ain't going down like that." Vicioso was thinking about smoking Marcus himself. One wrong move would be all it took.

"Who the fuck you think you is, Vicioso?" Marcus snapped. "You don't call no fuckin' shots! You must think you the boos or something now that Serio done gave you your own spot. You ain't no boss."

"Let me murder this nigga, Vicioso." Pimpo said, with his finger on the trigger.

"Hold on!" Serio shouted.

"You better stay in your fuckin' place!" Vicioso snapped at Marcus as the tension grew thicker.

"Fuck you!" Marcus shouted.

No sooner than the words left his mouth Vicioso was pulling his Uzi. Serio grabbed Vicioso, trying to stop him from killing Marcus as he took off running for the apartment building.

Vicioso gave Serio a crazy look. Pimpo did the same. "Why the fuck you grabbin' me? You heard what the fuck he said." Vicioso snatched away from Serio. Pimpo pulled out his Uzi and ran after Marcus, spraying the machine gun. Vicioso followed right behind his brother, spraying the Uzi with shells flying everywhere. People began to take cover as gunfire tore through the courtyard. A loud cannon-like gunshot went off behind Vicioso and Pimpo just as Marcus made it inside the building. Vicioso and Pimpo stopped shooting and turned around to see Serio holding a smoking chrome revolver. He had fired into the air to get their attention.

"Who the fuck do you two think you are?!" Serio shouted. He was pissed off that Vicioso and Pimpo were firing machine guns outside his coke spot making shit hotter than it already was.

Vicioso looked at the gun in Serio's hand and was shocked. "What the fuck you gon' do with that?" Vicioso said. Pimpo's eyes went back and forth between Serio and Vicioso. He understood what was coming but never wanted the situation to go down in such a way. Nevertheless, Pimpo was

with his brother all the way, against whomever. He hoped Serio wouldn't push the situation further than it had already gone, surely Serio knew he had no win. His revolver was no match for two Uzis.

"I said leave that raas alone, laope!" Serio shouted.

"You ain't gon' shoot me. I know you ain't crazy." Vicioso turned his back and begin walking towards the building. Serio wasted no time, he shot at Vicioso twice. Two bullets slammed into the brick wall. Pimpo was the first to fire at Serio, but after a quick burst of gunfire his Uzi jammed. He began vigorously working to unjam his machine gun as Vicioso began spraying at Serio. Loud and frightening fully automatic gunfire roared nonstop through the projects like a tornado. Running backwards, Serio fired his last shots at Vicioso and then broke into a full sprint. Vicioso gave chase with the Uzi blazing as they ran across Columbia Road.

Just as Marcus and two other guys came running out of the building, Pimpo got his Uzi working again. He sprayed at Marcus and his two comrades. They exchanged fire like a scene out of a gangster movie from the old days. Moments later, Vicioso returned to the scene firing at Marcus and his comrades with Pimpo. Vicioso and Pimpo held the fort down long enough to disappear into the night.

Once inside Vicioso's BMW, he and Pimpo went flying down the street as if the police were on their backs. Shit was now on another level and they both knew it.

Pimpo looked at Vicioso and said, "Did you get him, compa?"

Vicioso lit a cigarette and sighed with regret.

CHAPTER 13

Niecy tried to wait up for Vicioso to return but ended up falling asleep a short while after he left the apartment. As she enjoyed her peaceful sleep her bedroom door opened slowly, without waking her. "Niecy, wake up." A hand shook her gently. "Wake up."

"Huh?" Niecy slowly opened her eyes and saw Vicioso standing over her. "What's wrong, Harvey?"

"You gotta get up, I need you to go wit' me. Get dressed, it's very important." Vicioso said in a tone that made it clear he was serious.

Rubbing her eyes, Niecy looked at the clock and said, "It's almost two in the morning, what's goin' on?!"

"I'll tell you about it in the car, just hurry up and get dressed." Vicioso said. He knew shit was about to blow and he wanted to get Niecy out of their apartment and into a hotel somewhere. He had to keep her safe by all means.

Niecy got up and went to the bathroom to get herself together. Minutes later she was ready to go.

"What's goin' on, Harvey? Tell me somethin'." She said as they headed out the door.

"Me and Serio fell out. Shit got way out of hand." Vicioso said, opening the front door.

Niecy stopped in her tracks and said, "Fell out how?"

"It's a long story, baby. I'll tell you all about it but right now I need to get you out of here."

Niecy sighed and shook her head. The look in Vicioso's eyes worried her. It was a look she'd never seen before.

Vicioso woke up in a small New Jersey hotel room a few hours later. The weight of the Uzi on his lap reminded him of what was going on in his life and assured him that his dream was very much a reality. He looked at his Rolex and saw that it was a little after six in the morning. He had so much shit on his mind that he had dozed off. Looking across the room he saw Pimpo knocked out on one bed with his Uzi by his side; Niecy was in the other bed, knocked out as well.

Vicioso still needed time to think. Sitting in the chair looking out the window into the parking lot, Vicioso lit a Newport and took a long hard pull. He was fucked up mentally about what had gone down between him and Serio. He loved Serio and looked up to him. He couldn't pretend that wasn't true. Serio was his brother, they were family. Nevertheless, he couldn't believe Serio had shot at him. Tried to kill him. Why would Serio force his hand? Vicioso's mind was racing in a thousand different directions. Guilt and regret was weighing heavy on his shoulders and he couldn't shake those feelings. All he could think about was the dream he'd just had.

In his dream, Vicioso had wounded Serio with slugs to his back and then ran him down like a lion on the heels of its prey. Serio fell helplessly to the ground in the dark alley that they ran through. As he struggled to get up, Vicioso shot him a few more times in the back and knocked him back to the ground. Serio slowly turned over, covered in blood, and looked up at Vicioso who was standing over him with a smoking machine gun in hand. There was nothing but rage in Vicioso's eyes, pain and rage. Serio smiled and said, "This is what it comes down to, huh?" He coughed painfully as his breath grew short. "I bring you up here, teach you everything you know, and you gun me down in the streets like a dog? This is the thanks I get? You the man now—"

With tears in his eyes, Vicioso opened fire, cutting Serio's words short. Serio's body jumped up and down with violent convulsions as the Uzi tore into him with no mercy. In seconds, years of brotherhood and friendship vanished in a hail of gunfire.

Pimpo snapped Vicioso out of his deep thought when he got up to use the bathroom. Vicioso couldn't get the dream out of his head. When Pimpo returned from the bathroom he looked at Vicioso and said, "So what we gon' do, sit back and wait for the heat to come?" He wanted to get the shit out of the way; however it was going to be. "I say we go on the attack."

"It ain't that easy, Pimpo." Vicioso said. In reality, Serio wasn't dead. He got away from Vicioso when they ran into the dark alley. Vicioso was sure that Serio was now somewhere plotting his murder as well as Pimpo's.

"We can't second guess this shit now, Vicioso. You know how Serio gon' come at us. He gon' come full force, with everything he's got, all guns smoking. I say we go find his ass first and get it over wit'. The only way we gon' have a chance is to go straight at him, guns blazin'."

"This ain't no regular nigga, Pimpo. We can't just go to his house and kill him in front of his wife and kids, they family, you know that." Vicioso couldn't bring himself to go after Serio at his home. That was going too far in Vicioso's book; his heart wouldn't let him; his principles wouldn't let him.

"We gotta take care of Serio in the streets."

Pimpo sighed. "I don't give a fuck about all that shit. Once it's war, it's war."

"That's how we gotta do it, Pimpo. That's how it's gotta be."

136

Just after 1:00 P.M. the next day, Vicioso and Pimpo left Niecy in the hotel room and headed to Pimpo's Flatbush apartment to strap up. They were going to take the drama to Serio by hitting his Red Hook coke spot. Niecy tried to talk Vicioso into talking things out with Serio. "Serio's family!" She said. Reego also beeped Vicioso and tried to make peace between him and Serio. It seemed like everybody knew what was going on in only a few hours. Vicioso wasn't trying to hear shit from anybody. He knew he couldn't take any chances when it came to Serio so he planned to take it all the way.

Inside Pimpo's apartment, Pimpo sat on the sofa loading clips for the machine guns. "So we just gon' go through there sprayin'?"

"We might as well." Vicioso said, smoking a Newport. "We already know Serio's workers are out to get us just as much as he's out to get us so we might as well let them muthafuckas know we serious."

"Cool." Pimpo shrugged. "Fuck it! I want to do it that way anyway."

Vicioso looked at his little brother and smiled. Pimpo was one of a kind. With that being said, Vicioso worried about how long his brother would last considering the way he looked at life in the drug game.

The phone rang as they were talking about how they planned to go through Red Hook. "Yeah." Vicioso answered.

"You think you gon' get away wit' that little shit you did last night?" Serio's voice was calm, almost a whisper.

"I'm ready for whatever! Your days are numbered." Vicioso snapped.

"You done crossed the line, Vicioso. You and Pimpo. Y'all ain't ready for what comes wit' me, you know that. It's no holds barred."

"I don't care nothin' about your shit. You crossed the line. You gon' shoot at me and Pimpo over that raas. I'm the one that been loyal to you since day one. I'm the one that risked my life for you. What the fuck Marcus done? He ain't even paid no dues. That nigga ain't even family for real. How the fuck you gon' pick his side over me and Pimpo?! Have you lost your damn mind?"

"You done took the game and ran wit' it; you don't listen no more or nothin'. People don't last long when they start actin' like that. At least Marcus knows how to listen. He knows how to play his position." Serio said.

"Fuck that! I'm my own man. I call my own shots."

"You think you got what it takes to fuck wit' me, Vicioso?" Serio sounded amused, like he didn't take Vicioso serious. "You got another thing coming youngster."

"You'll see ..."

Serio laughed a little bit. "Nigga, I made you. You hear me? I taught you everything you know. If I wanted to kill you, you would be dead by now. Don't forget that. You disrespected me. You and Pimpo gon' come up in my spot and start shootin' and I'm supposed to look the other way. You know better, you know damn well I ain't gon' stand for no shit like that."

Vicioso didn't say anything for a second. He was still pissed off and wanted to murder his brother/mentor. "How the fuck you gon' pick that mada raas over me and Pimpo? He'll never stand wit' you like us. You know better."

"That's not what it's about, Vicioso. I told you let me take care of it. You was supposed to listen to me, out of respect. You know damn well that I'da murdered the nigga if he tried to do somethin' to Pimpo or you. If I say let me take care of it then you should have let me do that. You know my word is good as gold."

"So I was supposed to let that nigga run in the building and come back and kill my brother, right?"

"Are you payin' attention to what I am sayin', Vicioso? I would never let that happen. I would've killed him myself if he didn't listen. It would have never been a warning shot. I run the show. What I say is law. You know that."

Vicioso thought about what Serio was saying. He had to make sure Serio wasn't trying to get him to put his guard down. Serio was a shrewd motherfucker; he could trick a nigga out of his life like taking candy from a baby. Vicioso had learned from the best so he knew what he was dealing with.

"Look here, Vicioso." Serio said, "Men lose their tempers sometimes. We both overreacted last night. I'ma give you your space. I won't come after you and I trust that you will do the same. Let's cool off and let this shit blow over. I'll take care of Marcus today. Myself. Besides, I could never face your mother if we went to war. No one would come out on top, it would cause too much pain."

"You want me to just forget that you shot at me? You want me to forget that you picked sides against me?" Vicioso asked in disbelief.

"You shot at me in return. No blood was spilt. Let's stop it right now before it gets too ugly and people die."

Vicioso thought about it for a minute and said, "Cool."

"We'll talk when you cool off. Talk to Pimpo for me, let him know that there's no love lost." Serio hung up.

After Vicioso hung up the phone he was still fucked up and wasn't going to put his guard down. Nevertheless, he was going to honor the agreement he had with Serio.

"What's up?" Pimpo asked, slapping a clip in his Uzi. "I know we ain't gon' just overlook that shit and pretend that it never happened."

"Nah, but we gon' try to let this shit blow over." Vicioso said. He told Pimpo what Serio had said. "We gon' honor that. He's still family."

"I don't know about that." Pimpo said. "I done seen what Serio can do to a nigga. I ain't tryin' to get the short end of the stick."

We just gon' stay on high alert for a while. I don't think Serio would try to cross us like that." Vicioso said. "Some things he just not gon' do."

It took a little more talking, but Vicioso convinced Pimpo to honor the agreement with Serio.

They still strapped up and headed for their Red Hook spot. There was money to be made.

CHAPTER 14

t took some time but Vicioso and Serio honestly put their issues behind them and moved on with no animosity. Pimpo was in accord as well. By the summer of 1987 Vicioso was buying kilos from Serio for $11,000 apiece. The coke spot that Vicioso and Pimpo had in Red Hook was bringing in close to $15,000 a day. Vicioso had even brought a few homies of his own up from Panama to put on the team. His man Pete was now in Brooklyn; Pimpo's man, Leo, was in Brooklyn as well. They had another homie by the name of Andrew on the team as well. They were eating like one big family. Money was coming in so fast that Vicioso and Pimpo would sometimes lose count. They were spending it just as fast as it came in. They both made sure they sent money back home, that never changed. Vicioso had planned to bring his mother to the U.S. but changed his mind once things started to get violent. Niecy was cool with the program as long as she had her man by her side she couldn't care less.

Pulling up around Red Hook in his BMW, Vicioso parked and waited for Andrew to come out and meet him. People were everywhere. Vicioso felt at home in the projects by this time. He saw Andrew come out of the building and head for the car.

"What's up, Vicioso?" Andrew gave him five as he got in the car.

"I'm cool, just came through to take care of you." Vicioso handed Andrew a brown paper bag with a half of kilo in it. "I'll see you when you finish."

"Thanks, man. You really been lookin' out for me real nice." Andrew said. He was seeing a nice piece of money fucking with Vicioso.

"We family. I wanna see you get where you need to be. I'm only doing for you what was done for me when I got up here. That's how it works. When you get on you gotta do the same for the next man that comes up. We gotta look out for each other out here. That's how this shit works."

"Always." Andrew said. He then gave Vicioso five and got out the car.

Vicioso pulled off and went to pick Niecy up. He planned to spend the day with her.

A few days later, Vicioso was sitting on the sofa in Pimpo's living room counting money for their re-up. He sat $10,000 aside to send home to his mother just as Pimpo walked through the door carrying a shopping bag.

"What's up?" Pimpo said, sitting the shopping bag on the floor beside Vicioso. "That's thirty G's right there. Andrew gave me eight for you."

"Okay." Vicioso said, focused on the handful of money he was counting. "How shit look around Red Hook?"

"Everything's cool." Pimpo sat down and lit a Newport. "Money comin' like it's supposed to."

Vicioso and Pimpo talked about business for a second until the phone rang. Vicioso answered it. It was Serio.

"You busy?" Serio asked.

"Nah, not really, just countin' a little money. I was about to come your way. What's up?" Vicioso said.

"Put that on hold. Somethin' just came up. I need you."

"You okay?"

"I'm cool, but Cortez needs a favor. Can you leave town for a day or two?"

"For you I can. What's wrong?"

"I'll tell you when I see you. Can Pimpo come along? I need two men I can trust and depend on."

"Yeah, you know Pimpo cool wit' whatever." Vicioso said, looking at Pimpo.

"I'll be over there in thirty minutes." Serio hung up.

"What's up, Vicioso?" Pimpo said.

"Serio said he need us to go take care of somethin' in Washington wit' him for Cortez."

"Oh yeah?" Pimpo knew Cortez was at top of the food chain as far as their coke supply was concerned, he was down with no questions asked.

Serio picked Vicioso and Pimpo up and they hit I-95 South in his BMW. Along the way Serio explained to them that Cortez was having a few problems that he needed taken care of. Since Serio and his crew weren't from D.C. Cortez felt that they were perfect for the job. They could take care of it and get out of town before the police even knew who they were. They would be in and out of town like ghost.

When Serio, Vicioso and Pimpo arrived in D.C. they met Cortez at one of his stash-houses on Longfellow Street, Northwest. While Serio and Cortez sat at the dining room table discussing the situation, Vicioso and Pimpo sat on the sofa in the living room smoking weed and watching TV. All they needed to know was who had to be hit and where they were, simple as that.

Smoking a Newport, Cortez looked Serio in the eyes and said, "I called you because somebody on my team is working with the enemy. That's between us. Nobody knows why I called you down here and I want to keep it like that. As far as you are concerned, you came down to talk business. Even my people that you know, don't tell them why you are here."

"I understand. Say no more." Serio nodded.

"Here's the deal: I got this Panamanian that came up here from Miami this summer. They call him Disco. He been steppin' on my toes, undercuttin' my prices and some more shit. I been sellin' bricks down here for twenty, he done started sellin' them for sixteen. We had a few words a few times, but last night in the club we had words again and the raas tells me that my days are numbered. I laughed it off like it was nothin', but he has to go. I need this taken care of nice and smooth. It can't have my name on it at all. I don't need the police on me down here."

"I can do that, but let me ask you this: Why do you think that somebody on your team workin' wit' the enemy?" Serio asked.

"I put some money on Disco's head two weeks ago, the same night I did it the same dude that took the hit turned up dead. Somebody on my team tipped Disco off. I'm sure of it. That's how shit is going right now."

"I understand." Serio nodded. "All I need is a ride and a few weapons for me and the youngsters." He nodded toward Vicioso and Pimpo.

"I'll take care of that." Cortez said.

Later on, Cortez was sitting in his basement thinking things over. The drug trade was getting to violent for him. Sure he made tons of money moving cocaine, but if it was going to cut his life short he was thinking that it might be time to call it quits. He'd made enough money--more than enough! He didn't like to be connected to any violence. However, he couldn't let somebody run over him. He was not the average kingpin so one would think that they could get away with trying him. He appeared to be a regular workingman to those

who didn't know him. He wasn't flashy; he even drove around in a beat-up pickup truck and was often seen taking his kids to school.

"Cortez." Manuel said as he came down the basement step wearing gold and diamonds. "What's up, bro?"

Manuel was Cortez's right-hand man as well as his brother-in-law. They had a bond that went all the way back to Panama when they were teenagers.

"I was just sitting down here doin' a little thinkin' and watchin' the news." Cortez said, smoking a cigarette.

Manuel looked at the news and saw that Manuel Noriega was the topic. The news was talking about how the Panamanian general was really the power behind the civilian president.

"They talkin' about ole Noriega, eh?" Manuel said as he took a seat beside Cortez.

"Yeah, the U.S. don't like how he running things down there, they always in somebody's business. Power is a dangerous thing. When one is in power there's always somebody that wants to take it."

"Yeah I know." Manuel said.

"Did you make sure that everything went well wit' that situation?" Cortez asked.

"Yeah, it's fifty kilos at the spot. I made sure everything went smooth."

"Good." Cortez said.

"I just saw Disco's boys up Georgia Avenue. They're gettin' bolder every day. They were up there sellin' weight. We really need to do somethin' about that shit real quick."

"Don't worry about that. I'm on top of it. It'll be taken care of soon. I need for you to make sure that everything continues to run smoothly until I get to the bottom of this situation. Okay?"

"That's no problem. You know that!" Manuel looked at his watch and said, "I gotta run. I'll be back after I take care of a few things across town." He got up and shook Cortez's hand.

"Keep your eyes open."

"Always." Manuel said before leaving.

Cortez left the house a short while after Manuel. He had to hit the streets and check on a few things. He had a few things in the making. His first stop was a Panamanian club on Georgia Avenue. He went inside and headed straight to the back where he found a dude by the name of Jerome. "Did you take care of that for me yet?" Cortez asked Jerome while they were alone in the back office.

"Yeah, I did and you ain't gon' believe this shit here." Jerome said as he shut the door to his office.

"Manuel crossed you." Jerome said.

Cortez nodded. He was crushed. He had a feeling that Manuel was the one that was working with Disco so he had Jerome cut into Disco's crew and act as if he was really on their side in order to find out what was going on. No one knew of Jerome's relationship with Cortez, not even Manuel. "Are you sure?" Cortez asked.

"I'm more than sure. You got a one-hundred kilo shipment comin' in this week from Miami, right?"

"Yeah."

"Comin in through Baltimore?"

"Disco knows all about it and he plans to hit you for the whole shipment. Manuel gave him the 411."

"Thanks, Jerome. You've been a good friend. You will be rewarded well for your loyalty when this is all over." Cortez got up and left.

Inside Serio's hotel room, Cortez told Serio what was going on. Serio had seen a lot over the years, but even he was spent

when he learned that it was Manuel that had switched sides. Manuel was family for real; his sister was Cortez's wife.

"No one can be trusted when money is involved." Cortez shook his head in disgust; he was deeply hurt.

"Are you positive Manuel did this?" Serio asked. Not only was Manuel's sister Cortez's wife, Manuel's sister was also Serio's wife's cousin. A lot of shit was on the line. Too many people were intertwined.

"I'm positive. Manuel is the only one that knows about the location of my next shipment!" Cortez sighed. The whole situation put a deadly twist on things. Cortez was putting a death sentence on his lifelong friend and brother-in-law.

Serio sighed. "Well ... it's really nothin' else to talk about. Manuel picked his side. I'll take care of it for you. Startin' wit' Manuel."

Cortez looked Serio in the eyes and said, "No one can ever know about this, especially my wife. No one can ever know what we've done. Understand?"

"This will go to my grave wit' me, Cortez." Serio nodded.

A blue Grand Marquis pulled into a dark alley off of Georgia Avenue in a drug-infested section of Northwest. The car parked and the lights went out. Serio was behind the wheel; Vicioso was riding shotgun and Pimpo was in the back. They looked around to make sure everything was everything.

Serio looked at Vicioso and Pimpo and said, "I'm goin' in first. I don't want to spook this raas. If it gets out of hand inside I'ma kill 'em on the spot. You two just stay ready. Shit can get out of hand real fast." Serio noticed that Vicioso looked uncertain. "What's wrong?"

"I don't think you should go in alone. Anything could happen. What if Manuel gets spooked when he sees you and thinks something's wrong?" Vicioso knew how dangerous the club was that Serio was going in. The Panaroyal was a club that a man could walk in alive and come out dead under a white sheet.

"Don't worry." Serio said. "Manuel don't even know that Cortez is onto him. If I don't come out in…uh… ten minutes, you and Pimpo come in sprayin'. Cool?"

"Whatever you say." Vicioso said as he checked his Uzi again.

Serio got out of the car and went inside the club. A few minutes later, Serio and Manuel came out the back of the club as if nothing was wrong. After all, they were family. Serio was good at what he did. He was walking Manuel to his death as if they were going out for a few drinks. Vicioso smiled and shook his head as he watched the two men approach the car. Serio was deadly.

"Is Cortez okay?" Manuel said as he and Serio walked down the alley. Serio had told Manuel that Cortez needed to see him.

"Yeah, Cortez is okay." Serio eased his pistol out and smacked Manuel in the face.

"Ahhhhhgggrrrhhh!" Manuel grabbed his eye and took a knee. "What the fuck is goin' on, Serio?"

"You fuckin' snake!" Serio smacked him in the face with the pistol again. Manuel fell flat on his back in the dirty alley. Serio stood over him and pointed the pistol in his face. "How could you cross family like that, you piece of shit? Huh? You think some stranger will treat you better than family?"

Vicioso and Pimpo got out and walked up beside Serio with their Uzis in hand.

"What the fuck are you talkin' about, Serio?!" Manuel said in agony as Serio put his foot on his chest and pressed down.

"You know what the raas I'm talking about." Serio looked at Vicioso and said, "Handcuff 'em and put him in the trunk. Let's get out of here."

Vicioso and Pimpo handcuffed Manuel and stuffed him in the trunk. They jumped back in the car and Serio pulled off.

Manuel was taken to a house in Silver Spring, MD where he was dragged from the trunk of the car into a dark and dirty basement. Serio questioned him and pistol-whipped him for close to twenty minutes before Manuel admitted to working with Disco. He also told Serio that Disco had promised him his own operation and a connect once Cortez was out of the way. Manuel longed to be the number one man and as long as Cortez was around he would always be number two. Manuel also told Serio where he could find Disco.

"You picked the wrong side, you know that right?" Serio asked Manuel as he placed his pistol to his forehead.

Sobbing, Manual said, "Please, Serio. We're family! Please don't kill me."

"That's where you wrong, Manuel. We ain't family; we ain't nothin', now you gotta pay the price. Make sure you pick the right side next time." Serio pulled the trigger and shot Manuel five times in the head without blinking. Looking back at Vicioso and Pimpo when he was done, Serio said, "Let's go. Cortez got somebody to clean this shit up. We can finish the job tonight if we move quick and get back to Brooklyn before the weekend is over."

Inside the Days Inn on Eastern Avenue, Disco was ass-naked bent over the table by the window sniffing a line of cocaine with a one-hundred-dollar bill. Coke was his thing and he had a Tony Montana habit. A badass, brown-skinned Jamaican broad was lying across the bed ass-naked as well. She was high off the coke as well and feeling freaky. They'd just finished fucking and she was ready for more already.

"C'mon, Disco." The broad said in her thick accent. "Let me clean ya' rifle."

Disco smiled and walked toward the bed. He was already hard. He stood in front of her as she took a seat at the front of the bed and grabbed his dick in her soft hands. He rubbed his hand through her long, silky hair as she licked him up and down. She played with the tip of his dick with her tongue and the slid him all the way in her warm mouth. Disco put both hands behind her head and leaned his head back with his eyes closed. All he could hear was wet and popping sounds as she went to work. She took him all the way inside her throat and held him there for a second. She came up for air and said, "Fuck me, Disco."

"Turn around." Disco said.

She turned around and bent over the bed with her ass up in the air. "Fuck me hard, Disco." She looked over her shoulder and licked her lips. Disco smacked her on the ass and grabbed her hips as he slid inside her wet pussy from the back. "Aaaaahhhh, yeah." She moaned as she pushed her ass back at him. "Deeper ... deeper." Disco began pulling her to him, digging up in her harder. "Oh yes, like that! I feel it in my stomach!"

Serio kicked the door to the hotel room open and caught Disco fucking the shit out of the broad. With no questions asked he opened fire with his Uzi, spraying Disco in the back causing him to fall on top of the broad. She screamed at the top of her lungs. Serio sprayed her as well, with no remorse, turning the white sheets red.

Meanwhile, right across the hall, Vicioso and Pimpo kicked in the door of another hotel room where Disco's two gunmen were. Automatic gunfire was traded for a second, but Vicioso and Pimpo had the ups. They sprayed the whole room in seconds and left the bloody bodies on the floor. Vicioso and Pimpo ran into Serio at the end of the hallway, they all ran down the back stairs and out the back door. They jumped into

the getaway car and headed back to D.C to let Cortez know that the job was done.

Cortez paid Serio, Vicioso and Pimpo $50,000 each for the work they put in. Serio wanted to get out of D.C. as soon as possible; however, Cortez wanted them to hang around for a few days to make sure things fell back in place as smoothly as possible. Serio had a few things to take care of back in Brooklyn, he couldn't stay. Vicioso liked Cortez and saw an opportunity in hanging around for a few days, he volunteered to stay behind for a few days to watch Cortez's back on a personal tip. Cortez felt comfortable with that. Vicioso gave Pimpo instructions on how to carry things with their Red Hook spot and left it at that, he knew Pimpo could hold things down for a few days. He called Niecy to let her know what was going on.

"Mami, I'ma be out of town for a few days. I gotta take care of a little business, okay?"

Niecy sighed. "Harvey I'm gettin' tired of sittin' up in here by myself. I need you up here wit' me. I didn't come over here to be by myself. I came over here to be wit' you. Don't you understand that?"

"Niecy you know how it goes. I'm on top of business. I told you how shit goes, work wit' me, baby. I'll be up there in a few, Pimpo gon' bring you some money for me."

"Okay, Harvey. Just be careful." Niecy hung up. She loved Vicioso to death.

For the next few days, Cortez kept Vicioso with him at all times while he took care of business in the streets. People knew that Cortez had taken care of Disco; it was common sense for those who knew where their ass was in the streets. Vicioso was looked at as Cortez's new muscle, he was always riding shotgun with an Uzi.

Riding down Georgia Avenue in Cortez's Saab, Vicioso was leaning way back in the passenger's seat nodding his head to the sounds of Panamanian artist EL General. It was already after 11:00P.M., but the Avenue was still alive with action; it reminded Vicioso of Flatbush. Cortez turned the music down as he crossed Rittenhouse Street and said, "So you still in a rush to get back to Brooklyn?" Cortez knew Vicioso was paying close attention to how sweet the weight game was in D.C. Vicioso had seen Cortez collect thousands of dollars a day. Cortez was also teaching Vicioso how to sell weight on D.C. terms. He offered to set Vicioso up with his own D.C. operation. "You know its more money to be made down here than it is in Brooklyn, less drama, too."

Vicioso smiled. "Less drama?"

"Well, every now and then somethin' comes up, but that's a part of the game."

"I'd love to do some things down here, but I gotta get back to Brooklyn. I got too much goin' on up there right now."

"You could have things goin' on in D.C. and Brooklyn." Cortez said. "Yeah, but my woman is in Brooklyn, plus me and Pimpo got our own spot in Red Hook and I gotta be around to watch over that, shit can get out of control in the blink of an eye."

"Come on, Vicioso, I like you and I know you could do big things down here. I need a good man that I can count on down here. Pimpo can hold down the Red Hook spot. Shit, I can even hit you off wit' coke for the spot, compa."

Vicioso thought about it for a second.

"Check this out," Cortez smiled, "I'ma introduce you to a few people that I deal wit' down here so you can have a few connections in the city. You can see for yourself how fast you get paid down here; I bet you that if you spend one summer down here you won't want to go back to Brooklyn. You can

bring your woman down here. I'll set you up in a house and everything. What you say about that?"

Vicioso smiled, he admired the older dude. "You serious? Don't be jokin', you talkin my kind of talk now."

"I don't play no games about money. I offered Serio the same thing but he didn't want to leave New York either, but I can tell that you think big."

"Let's do it." Vicioso laughed. "It's time to get paid!"

CHAPTER 15

Vicioso talked Niecy into spending the summer in D.C. with him while he put a few things together. Cortez let him stay in one of his Northwest homes on Peabody Street. It was a nice three-bedroom house with a small front yard and back yard; it was already furnished with great taste. Niecy loved it. It was in a nice neighborhood, which allowed Niecy to spend time out on the front porch enjoying the summer. She never got to chill like that in Brooklyn. The whole move to D.C. was something she could really get used to. Aside from that, she got to spend more time with Vicioso since he was moving weight. It was like it all happened overnight. Cortez plugged him in with D.C. dudes that were buying five and ten kilos at a time for $23,000. Cortez gave Vicioso the bricks for $11,000 apiece so he was seeing $12,000 profit just for serving the weight. It was sweet money and drama-free for the most part. One of Vicioso's best customers was a dude by the name of Barry that was from Southeast. Barry was spending close to $100,000 a week with Vicioso; he also brought more Southeast clientele. In just two months Vicioso had a strong thirty customers spending with him. All he had to do was go meet them, give them the coke, and get the money that was it. The rest of his time was spent with Niecy. It was just the way he wanted it to be. Vicioso wasn't big on hanging out at all. Family and business was the order of the day.

MONEY AIN'T EVERYTHING

In New York it was BK all day for Pimpo. He loved the fast life, the gun bussin' and brick flipping. With Vicioso in D.C. for the summer he was running the Red Hook operation, although Vicioso still had a say-so in the shot calling. Pimpo was seeing so much money that he had to buy a money machine to count it. Things couldn't get any better as far as he was concerned.

With things under control in D.C., Vicioso and Niecy were in his BMW on their way up I-95 headed to Atlantic City for a few days. This was the life they wanted when they came to the U.S., a life where money wasn't a worry and they could enjoy the finer things in life without a care.

Behind the wheel, Vicioso looked at Niecy and said, "You know Cortez offered to sell me the house."

"He did?" she smiled. She loved the house. "What did you say?"

"I told him that I'd think about it, 'cause if we goin' back to Brooklyn we might as well buy a house there. We got enough money. You see what I'm saying?"

Niecy wasn't in a rush to get back to New York. Vicioso was always in some shit up there. She liked D.C. much better. "I think you should buy the house. I'm not in a rush to go back to Brooklyn. Things are nice down here. Besides that, even if we go back to New York to stay it would be good to still own a house in Washington."

Vicioso cut his eyes at her and smiled. "I like that. I guess you like D.C. now. At first I didn't think you were going to like it in Washington."

"I didn't. Nessy's brother had just got killed and I thought you would be caught up in that so I thought Brooklyn would be a better place for us. I understood what was goin' on in Brooklyn, I didn't know what to expect in Washington. But I like it in Washington much better, plus I get to spend more time wit' you." She smiled.

"Yeah, I like it much better down here, too. I'ma go ahead and buy the house."

"How much Cortez want for it?" Niecy asked looking out the window.

"A hundred and fifty thousand. I can handle that. I'ma put it in your name."

Niecy smiled.

"You like that don't you, sexy?" Vicioso smiled and rubbed her smooth face with the back of his hand. "We gon' be alright, baby. I told you. It'"

"I know, Harvey." Niecy leaned back in her seat. Life was good, far better than it was in Panama money-wise.

A short while later they checked into an Atlantic City hotel. Their plush suite overlooked the Atlantic Ocean. While Niecy took a hot shower, Vicioso stood on the balcony looking out at the ocean. The wind off the water brought the smell of the ocean into his face. He took a deep breath. It was refreshing. He was at the top of his game, but there was still room for growth. In time he would be the man, just like Serio, just like Cortez. Everything took time. All he had to do was play his cards right. Nothing was more important and nothing would stand in his way.

Vicioso walked back into the suite and took a seat on the sofa in the living room. It felt good to be able to relax for a second. He picked up the phone and called Pimpo. He told him he was in Atlantic City. Pimpo said that he was going to come through before the weekend was over so they could catch up on a few things.

"Be safe, see you when you get here, bro." Vicioso said as he got off the phone.

Just as Vicioso hung up the phone, Niecy came out of the shower with a towel wrapped around her. Vicioso looked at the sexy shape of her body and her wet hair. He was instantly turned on. "You the sexiest black woman I ever seen." She blushed.

"No lie, baby."

He got up and walked over to her with a devious smile on his face. Taking her in his arms, squeezing her body against his, he rubbed and squeezed her ass saying, "I take that back. You the sexiest woman I ever seen period."

Niecy wrapped her arms around his neck and kissed his lips. "I don't believe you. Prove it to me."

Vicioso guided her to the huge bed and laid her down. He climbed on top of her and began to kiss her passionately as he caressed her wet body with the smoothness of a masseuse. She let out a soft, sensual moan as he undid the towel that was wrapped around her. He rose up and licked his lips as he took in the sight of her sexy, wet, brown body. She rubbed his chest and helped him take off his clothes. After he came out of his clothes he kissed her again. He kissed her all over her face, sucked on her ear, licked down her neck, caressed her breasts and kissed all over them, sucking on them. He continued to kiss and suck on her body, pleasing her nice and slow. "Um ... baby." She moaned. "Don't stop." After a little foreplay, Vicioso took her to the next level with strong lovemaking that took them well into the early hours of the next day.

Two days later, Pimpo showed up in Atlantic City. He met Vicioso in the hotel restaurant and they had lunch while Niecy was upstairs taking a nap. Vicioso told Pimpo how sweet things were in D.C. and how much money there was to be made. Pimpo was impressed, but there was nowhere in the world like Brooklyn as far as he was concerned. He loved

BK. The fast pace of New York along with the gunplay kept him going, it was a driving force in his life.

"Don't get me wrong, Brooklyn is a gold mine and I know you love the fast life, but D.C. is a better business move for us, Pimpo." Vicioso said. "You need to think about comin' to D.C. We got to start thinking about the future if we are going to survive."

"But we gettin' more money wit' you in D.C. wit' Cortez and me up in Brooklyn. It's like the best of both worlds. What more can we ask for? It's a two headed monster." Pimpo sipped his soda.

Vicioso leaned forward as if he was about to tell a secret and said, "Between me and you, Cortez is getting' old. He wants out of the game for real. He wanted to hand his whole operation over to Serio, but Serio didn't want it. I guess Serio thinks D.C. is too slow or somethin', but I see the big picture. Me and you can do real big things in D.C. once Cortez is gone. Right now, Cortez is showing me the ropes. It's only a few big niggaz in D.C. that's movin' a lot of weight. If I can talk Cortez into turnin' me on to his connect before he gets out the game we can take shit to another level in no time."

Pimpo thought about what Vicioso was talking about for a second. "I like the sound of that." He nodded with a smile on his face.

"Let me work it all out and we gon' be set in a few months." Vicioso bit into his cheeseburger. With food in his mouth, he said, "So what's goin' on wit' the Red Hook spot?"

"Everything's cool. Money comin' in like it's supposed to. The spot pulled in like twenty-three-thousand in one day last Sunday."

"You savin' the money, right?" Vicioso raised his eyebrows.

"Yeah," Pimpo smiled. "I'm doin' the best I can. I spend a little bit on myself, but we got a nice stash."

"Cool, make sure you keep a nice stash. Shit ain't gon' always be sweet like this. Hard times gon' come. That's part of the game. Never forget that. As long as we are always on point can't nothing hold us back."

"I know, I know." Pimpo nodded.

"What's up wit' Andrew?"

"He makin' a lot of moves on his own. He got some Colombians from Queens he fuckin' wit'. Me and him got into it the other day. Shit got a little heated."

"Heated like what? What was said?"

"I told him that if he gon' make money around Red Hook that he gotta buy his shit from us or Serio. He ain't gon' be takin' the money to Queens and shit. He acts like I'm sayin' somethin' wrong. But you told him from the start how shit go. I guess he think since you in D.C. that shit done changed. I ain't havin' that."

"Yeah, I see what you sayin'. You think that's gon' be a problem?"

"Hell no!"

Vicioso laughed. At 19, Pimpo was way before his time.

"Aside from that, it's the same ole shit. The police bringin' the heat. I can't even take a piss without havin' the police on my back when I'm around Red Hook."

"Perfect example about what I was tellin' you about D.C. The cops ain't even a problem. I ain't had a run-in wit' them yet." Vicioso said. "But, anyway, just stay on your toes. Shit 'bout to fall in place for us, real big, too. I promise you."

Back in D.C., days later, Vicioso pulled up in the parking lot of the Safeway on Georgia Avenue in his BMW 528e. It was a little after eight in the evening and the parking lot was busy; it was good cover for a drug transaction. Vicioso drove around the parking lot one time to make sure everything was cool then he parked in the back corner and waited for Barry. A few minutes later, Barry pulled up in a Gold Nissan 300ZX and parked beside Vicioso's BMW. He got out of his car and got in Vicioso's with a shopping bag in hand.

"What's up Panama?" Barry gave Vicioso five. Most D.C. dudes that bought coke from Vicioso called him Panama.

"Everything's cool." Vicioso said, with a chrome .45 on his lap and a brown shopping bag on the floor by his feet with four bricks of powder coke inside. "What's up wit' you? How's things going for you?"

"Getting' this money, you know how shit go wit' me, joe. Shit lookin' real good, my nigga. I'm movin' this shit faster than I can cook it."

Vicioso handed Barry the shopping bag he had on the floor. "That's five right there. You just hit me wit' twenty next go-round."

Barry looked in the shopping bag and said, "Good lookin'' out, P." He then looked down at the shopping bag he'd brought and said, "You know my money good, it's all there."

"Yeah, I know." Vicioso nodded.

Barry gave him five again and said, "I'ma get wit' you in a few days." He then got out of the car.

Vicioso pulled off and headed towards Cortez's house. As he drove down Tuckerman Street he checked the shopping bag that Barry left in the car. It looked like $80,000. Barry was coming at Vicioso with more and more money every time around. Vicioso never made any moves in Southeast, but from the way Barry was copping, Vicioso knew it had to be tons of cash on the south side of town. He had to get some more of that south side money. He planned to make that a priority as soon as possible.

MONEY AIN'T EVERYTHING

When Vicioso got to Cortez's house Cortez's wife let him in and told him that Cortez was down in the basement. Vicioso went downstairs and found Cortez shooting pool by himself. He looked like he was in deep thought. Cortez looked up and saw Vicioso. "What's goin' on, Vicioso?"

"Just droppin' by to drop some money off." Vicioso said as he sat the shopping bag on the floor and picked up a pool stick.

"How much you got in the bag?" Cortez said as he sank the 8 ball.

"Two-fifty."

"You makin' a lot of moves on your own, ain't' you?" Cortez smiled.

"You showed me the ropes down here. I catch on fast. This is what I do."

Cortez nodded and sat his pool stick down. "Put the pool stick down. I want to talk to you for a second." He and Vicioso took seats in front of the big screen TV.

"What's on your mind, Cortez?" Vicioso asked.

"It's no secret between me and you that I'm about to wash my hands of the game. It's gettin' too violent. It's a young man's game and I'm getting old, Vicioso. It's time for me to cash in my chips. A good businessman always knows when to cash in. You understand?"

"Yeah. I see what you're sayin'." Vicioso nodded.

"I like you, Vicioso, you're a loyal man. You don't let anything get in your way. The only thing you need to work on is your temper. You got to work on that if you want to last in this business. You got a temper like a fighting dog. Sometimes that can cloud a man's judgment, if you know what I mean."

Vicioso laughed. "Like a fightin' dog?"

"Yeah, you really need to work on that. Anyway, I see that you are makin' a lot of money down here, just like I said you would. You gotta start thinkin' about the future. This drug game is something that we use for a time to get what we need to move on to other things. You see how I got businesses and now I'm ready to leave the game alone, that was my plan from the start: To get out of Panama and make somethin' of myself for my family. That's what you need to think about. I tried to tell Serio the same thing. If you don't learn nothin' from me, learn when to call it quits, Vicioso. How much money is enough? You see what I'm sayin'? Money ain't everything. Don't let this stuff control you. Don't let it take you away from those that you love."

Vicioso nodded. Cortez always spoke with the wisdom of an old kingpin. A man with vision.

"All you gotta do is stay focused and you gon' go far in this country, Vicioso." Cortez lit a cigarette and continued. "I say all of that because I've been thinkin' … and I want to introduce you to my connect."

Vicioso could do nothing but smile. "You serious?"

"No doubt, I need to pass the connect on to somebody worth it."

Red Hook was alive and in full swing. People where everywhere. Loud rap music blasted from parked cars. Dice games were going on out in the open. Drug traffic was moving back and forth at full speed. Pimpo was standing outside the building where the coke spot was; he was smoking weed and talking to a few Panamanians. A bad-ass broad by the name of Tracy came out of the building across the court in a pair of tight-ass jean shorts that were so short that the bottom of her ass checks was hanging out. Her fresh hairdo, big gold earrings and thick thighs turned Pimpo on instantly. He'd been fucking Tracy for months. She was the closest thing he

had to a girlfriend. Tracy saw him and ran up to him, giving him a hug and a kiss on the lips. She then seductively licked his ear and whispered, "I just had a crazy dream about you. You wouldn't believe it."

Loving the way her tongue felt in his ear, Pimpo smiled and said, "What was I doin' in the dream?"

"Fuckin' the shit out of me from the back. I'm still wet."

"I can make all your dreams come true if you want to." He smiled.

"That's what I came to get you for." She rubbed his dick through his Fila shorts.

"Let me take care of a few things out here and then I'ma come right up to your spot. Be ready, too."

"Okay," Tracy said, licking her sexy lips before walking back to her building throwing her phat ass side to side like a stripper.

Pimpo began to make his rounds. The coke spot was pumping and running smooth. After checking on the spot Pimpo made his way to Tracy's apartment. As soon as he stepped outside he saw Andrew bending the corner from behind the building. He and Andrew had just had a fall out the night before; Pimpo told Andrew not to come back around Red Hook.

"Didn't I tell you don't come back around here no more?!" Pimpo hissed as he walked towards Andrew with his face twisted in a mask of anger. Pimpo didn't care that Andrew was strong among their circle of Panamanians.

"Who the fuck you think you are, Pimpo? You don't run shit around here!" Andrew pulled a small Uzi from under his shirt.

"What the raas you won' do?"

Pimpo didn't give a fuck about the Uzi, he looked death right in the eyes many times before. He pulled his .45

automatic and frowned his face up as he said, "What the fuck you think you gon' do wit' that piece of shit? You a dead man now!" He was still approaching Andrew; his heart and ego wouldn't allow him to back down.

Andrew was done talking. He opened fire with his machine gun, hitting Pimpo in the chest with the first murderous burst of shots. Wounded bad, Pimpo staggered backward and began to fire his .45 with a sense of urgency.

His first shots went wild and wide due to the fact that the machine gun fire was tearing through his upper body like a chainsaw. Pimpo fell to the ground still firing his pistol, but he was hit too bad to put up a real fight. Andrew knew Pimpo was finished, he took off running. Bystanders that had ran for cover when the shooting jumped off began to crowd around the body just as Pimpo's crew came running outside the building. Tracy heard the gunfire and ran outside. When she saw Pimpo on the ground bleeding she ran over to him, knelt down and took him in her arms. She didn't care about the blood getting all over her. "Pimpo! Pimpo!" She screamed. "Wake up! Wake up! Somebody help!!!!"

In D.C., it was a little past 9 P.M. and Vicioso and Niecy were just leaving the movies in Georgetown. As they walked up M Street heading for the car, Vicioso had his arm around Niecy whispering seductive words in her ear about what he was going to do to her when they got back to the house.

"You crazy." Niecy laughed as they made their way through the crowds of people walking up and down the street.

Vicioso's beeper went off when they got inside the car. He looked at the number and jumped on the car phone to call Serio. Something had to be wrong if Serio was beeping him with code #911. Serio only hit with code #911 when

something serious was going on. Vicioso's heart began to pound. Sweat even began to form on his brow all in a matter of seconds.

Niecy saw the look on Vicioso's face and said, "Is everything okay?"

"Hold up." Vicioso said to Niecy as Serio answered on the other end. "What's goin' on, Serio? Is everything okay?"

Serio sighed. "I got bad news." His voice was rough and his tone slow and stressed like a worn general in a drawn out war. Serio really didn't know how to break the news to Vicioso about Pimpo. He searched his mind for the right words.

"What's wrong?!" Vicioso shouted. He didn't like the vibe he was getting from Serio.

"It's Pimpo, Vicioso. He's dead."

Vicioso's whole body went numb. He said nothing for a moment. "I'm on my way up there right now and when I get up there I'ma tear that muthafucka up!" Vicioso hung up. He pulled off, speeding up the street with a cold expression on his face. His gaze was straight ahead like a man possessed. Niecy knew something was very wrong. Memories of his brother flooded his mind. His heart was heavy. The pain inside was tearing him apart as he tried to hold back tears.

"Harvey, what's wrong?" Niecy said. "Talk to me!"

Vicioso said nothing for a few moments. Then tears began to run down his face. Niecy knew something was gravely wrong. Her heart dropped as if she knew what had happened.

"Pimpo's dead. I gotta go up to New York for a minute and take care of a few things." Vicioso wiped tears away from his face. He knew what had to be done and he was the only person that could do it. Hard times were on the way.

"Oh my God." Niecy covered her mouth. Fear overtook her body. She knew Vicioso was about to go off. She was speechless. "Oh my, God."

Vicioso didn't speak another word for the rest of the ride home. All kinds of murderous thoughts haunted his thinking. No prisoners would be taken. He dropped Niecy off at the house, grabbed a few guns and some money, and then jumped straight on I-95 North.

CHAPTER 16

Vicioso headed up I-95 with no music, no weed, no nothing. Just his thoughts and his anger. He couldn't believe Pimpo was dead. It didn't seem real. Vicioso's thought drifted back to Santa Cruz when Pimpo was just a kid playing Ping Pong in the projects, before the street life. Life was rough then, but there was no drama. Vicioso thought about his mother's eyes filled with tears. She was going to take Pimpo's death the hardest. How was he going to tell her that her baby boy was dead? The more Vicioso thought about the situation the more he began to blame himself for Pimpo's murder. *I should have been there*, Vicioso thought; *I shouldn't have left New York.* All that was left was for Vicioso to make motherfuckers pay for what had happened to his brother. Nevertheless, that still wouldn't take away the pain nor would it bring Pimpo back.

Hours later, Vicioso's BMW pulled into Serio's driveway late at night. There was only one light on in the house. Vicioso knew Serio was up waiting for him. Vicioso got out the car slowly and walked up to the front door of the huge house. He knocked on the door and Serio answered, letting him in. Serio gave him a firm hug and said, "I got your back. I'm with you all the way." Serio then shut the door and led Vicioso down into the basement where he told Vicioso what happened to Pimpo, according to the way he'd heard it from Pimpo's crew. Vicioso couldn't believe that Andrew had killed Pimpo. For someone close to the family to kill Pimpo fucked Vicioso up a hundred times more. Vicioso had real love for Andrew and his family. Andrew and all his brothers were soldiers.

"I was good to that raas, Serio. I did everything I could for his ass. I can't believe he would do some shit like that." Vicioso said. "Pimpo was good to that raas. We let him eat wit' us; we put him on his feet. This is how he shows us thanks. He kills my brother." Vicioso rubbed his chin as he spoke.

"I need to use the phone."

Serio pointed at the phone and said, "I'ma give you a minute." He knew what Vicioso had to do. The one thing no son or brother ever wanted to do.

Vicioso got on the phone and called Panama. His heart pounded with dread. He didn't know what to say or how to say it. His mother answered the phone in a groggy voice as she was just waking up.

"Ma ..." Vicioso couldn't even get the words out. He seemed to be choking up.

"What's wrong, Harvey?" Melly could feel the vibe. She knew something was very wrong; she could feel it in her heart and it made her weak in the knees.

Vicioso said nothing for a moment. The silence seemed to last forever.

"It's Pimpo, isn't it?" Melly could feel it. "Isn't it?"

"Yeah." Vicioso said with a long sigh.

"Is he ... dead?"

"Yeah, Ma, he's dead."

There were a few awkward moments of silence. Tears began to run down Melly's face. Her baby boy was gone. The one thing she feared the most was now a harsh reality and there was nothing she could do to ward off the pain and anger. She said, "Send my baby back home, Harvey. Just send my

168

baby back home." She began to break down into sobs as she spoke. Hearing his mother cry over the phone only added to the fire that was burning inside of Vicioso. He wanted blood and nothing would be able to quench his thirst until every soul that had something to do with his brother's death was murdered.

"I'll have him sent home as soon as possible."

"What happened, Harvey? What happened to my baby? How could you let something like that happen?"

In the best way he could, Vicioso told his mother what went down. Even she couldn't believe that Andrew had killed her son. She'd watched Andrew grow up in Santa Cruz. She'd had him in her home. Fed him at her table.

"I guess you'll be comin' home in a box, too. That's what's next, isn't it, Harvey? I'm going to lose both of my sons up there to that madness that you all are caught up in. It's foolishness, pure foolishness." Melly began to vent her pain and anger as she cried over the phone. Then she fell silent for a second and took a deep breath before saying, "If I have to cry down here and drink coffee and play dominos, somebody up there better be doing the same damn thing."

"I understand. Say no more, I'm already thinking the same way." Vicioso said. After Pimpo was buried, family and friends would come together for nine days to drink coffee and play dominos to deal with the mourning. "It's gon' be a fair share of drinking coffee and playin' dominos up here. You can believe that."

"Be careful, Harvey. Whatever you, be careful up there. I don't want to get a call about you."

"I will be on my toes, Ma. I promise you that much." Vicioso took a deep breath. "I'm sorry I had to call you with news like this."

"Do what you have to do, Harvey. Make sure my baby's death doesn't go unpunished no matter what you do."

"As it should be."

After Vicioso got off the phone with his mother he called Serio back into the basement. Serio came down the steps with an Uzi in one hand and a bulletproof vest in the other. "I already know what's next." He said as he handed Vicioso what he needed. "However you wanna do this I'm with you."

Taking the Uzi and the vest, Vicioso said, "I need to take care of this one by myself. It's personal, plus I don't want to make this your beef."

"Your beef is my beef." Serio put his hand on Vicioso's shoulder. "I don't want you out here lookin' for Andrew while you are still emotional. That's dangerous. Let me go wit' you. You could use some extra eyes."

"You once told me that there are some things a man gotta do alone, right?"

"You right." Serio nodded.

"This is one of those things, Serio."

Vicioso combed the streets of Brooklyn until sunrise but had no success finding Andrew. He had a feeling that things would play out in such a way so he decided to check into a hotel to get a little rest. When he woke up a few hours later he got Niecy on the phone and told her he needed her to come to New York to take care of getting Pimpo's body back to Panama. He was in no mood to deal with that. Niecy was ready and willing to do whatever was needed to help her man.

"I'll get on the road right now. See you in a few hours." Niecy said.

"Thanks, baby." Vicioso said. Niecy was a soldier. She was always down. Vicioso gave Niecy a few instructions and got off the phone. He then jumped in the shower to wake himself up. After he'd gotten himself together, Vicioso

headed for Flatbush Avenue to check on the whereabouts of Andrew. Somebody had to know something. While riding through Flatbush he spotted Andrew's uncle walking into a barbershop. Vicioso's mind began to race. He knew that once he killed Andrew he would be at war with all of his uncles and brothers. It would be nothing to talk about; it would be on sight gunplay. He pulled around the corner and parked. It was just after 11:00 A.M. and people were everywhere. Vicioso got out of the car with no mask on and walked back to the barbershop with the Uzi out for everybody to see. He didn't give a fuck! People on the sidewalk got the hell out of his way. Vicioso opened the door to the barbershop just as Andrew's uncle, Bobby, was getting in the chair. It seemed like the whole barbershop froze in fear. Bobby went for his pistol as soon as he saw Vicioso. Vicioso opened fire, spraying the Uzi with both hands. He ate Bobby up in seconds and then walked out of the barbershop like it wasn't shit.

A few hours later, Niecy was in Vicioso's hotel room. He'd explained everything he needed her to do. She was down. "Things about to get real ugly, Niecy. I don't want you out in the streets, take care of business and go straight to Serio's house. Okay?" He grabbed her hand and squeezed it softly. "I want you to know that no matter what happens in life, I love you. You are my everything."

"I love you, too. I understand, but Harvey, please be careful." Niecy said, she knew what was going on. Her fears were unbelievable.

"I'll be okay, baby." Vicioso kissed her and pulled a stack of cash out of his pocket. It was a little over $9,000. "This is enough to take care of things, if you need more just beep me."

"Okay."

"Contact my mother once you've taken care of everything for Pimpo."

"I will." Niecy said. She hugged Vicioso and said, "I love you. Be careful."

"I love you, too."

Niecy left. Vicioso lay down for a second and got lost in his thoughts. Shit was out of control, but he had to roll with the punches. He told himself that he had to deal with the good and the bad. It was part of the game. Whatever the future was to bring would only make him stronger, if it didn't kill him.

Word of Bobby's murder spread through the streets of Brooklyn in no time. The streets were saying that Vicioso was out for blood and that meant nobody was off limits. Some people were glad that Bobby had been murdered, but others were hurt to hear about the death of a street legend.

On top of that, Vicioso's picture was on the news: He was wanted for Bobby's murder. When he saw the news all he did was shake his head; he didn't even care. Once he caught Andrew and took care of business he'd be on the highway back to D.C. With the law on his back was only going to make things harder to take care of.

While Vicioso was out looking for Andrew he ran into Pete. Pete was also out looking for Andrew. He'd gotten word of what went down with Pimpo and was fucked up about the move. Sitting in Vicioso's BMW, Pete told him that he'd heard Andrew was laying low in Harlem some other Panamanians. The catch was that Pete didn't know exactly where the spot was.

"Where you get that info from?" Vicioso asked.

"This girl I been dealin' wit'. She heard Andrew's man talking about it. Shit got back to me and I was on it." Pete said.

"Who his man? Tell me somethin' about him."

"The nigga that own the club on Flatbush. You know who I'm talkin' bout."

"I need to see him then."

Vicioso and Pete headed for Flatbush. It was a little past 11:00 P.M., and people were everywhere as they made their move. Driving had to be careful with the police looking for Vicioso. A short while later Vicioso pulled up and parked a block away from the club and looked at Pete, he said, "You know everybody know I killed Bobby. As soon as we walk in the club they gon' know what's goin' on. It ain't gon' be no talking."

"I know. Let me go inside first. I can take care of it if I see that motherfucker." Pete said.

"Nah, I gotta do it. I gotta do it myself. I don't even care who sees me." Vicioso's words were cold. He checked his Uzi and continued. "You don't have to go in wit' me."

"Fuck that. I'm wit' you all the way, ain't no tellin' who's inside. We in this together, like back in the day."

"Let's go then. I want to get it over with as fast as possible."

Vicioso and Pete headed inside the club from the back. Once inside, they were engulfed by weed smoke, darkness, loud reggae music, and a crowd of dancing people. The darkness was a good cover for Vicioso and Pete. They made their way through the crowd inconspicuously. That is until someone bumped into Vicioso. He looked to the side and saw a dude by the name of Carlton. Carlton worked for Serio.

"What the fuck are you doin' in here, Vicioso?" Carlton yelled over the music.

"I'm lookin' for somebody." Vicioso said with no further information.

"The police are lookin' for you. You can't be up in here like this, Vicioso. Somebody gon' call the police on you. You don't need to be showing your face around here."

"I'm okay, don't --"

Gunfire exploded inside the small club. Panic and dismay spread in seconds as people began to scatter. Vicioso dove to the floor and pulled out his small Uzi as the gunshots continued to ring out. He couldn't see where the shots were coming from but he could tell they were being fired in his direction. Instantly, another gun began going off. This one was a machine gun, it was popping as if it would no stop.

"Vicioso!" Pete yelled, shooting at the bright muzzle flashes across the club. "Watch your back!!"

Vicioso saw the gunman and popped up spraying his Uzi. He and the gunman fired at each other through the crowd of running people. Pete rushed in from behind and fired a number of shots into the gunman's back, dropping him. It was George, one of Andrew's brothers.

"Let's get the fuck outta here!" Pete yelled.

Vicioso and Pete hit the door with everyone else and headed straight for the car. Police were coming down the street at the same time. They jumped in Vicioso's BMW and sped away.

Niecy arranged a small wake for Pimpo before he was sent back to Panama. Only close friends attended it. Vicioso couldn't show his face. The club shooting had his face on every TV station in the New York area; even his real name was mentioned this time. An article in the paper read: "... Panamanian national, illegally in U.S., kills man in Brooklyn club hours after killing another man..." The manhunt was growing in intensity.

Wanted by the NYPD, with his face on blast on TV, Vicioso had to get out of New York. He called Niecy at Serio's and told her to meet him back in D.C. he had to get out of town. He didn't want to leave New York without killing Andrew, but he couldn't even walk down the street without people pointing at him. It was a no win situation.

174

Nevertheless, Vicioso was still dead set on dealing with Andrew.

Vicioso returned to D.C. and laid low for a week. However, the heat was on. The house that he bought from Cortez was raided early one Monday morning at 6:00A.M. The FBI was after him for the New York murders and had learned of his whereabouts. Vicioso and Niecy were in Virginia Beach at the time; they had spent the weekend at Cortez's beach house. Vicioso needed time to cool off and think about the next move. When the feds raided the house they found $750,000, and number of machine guns, but no Vicioso. Cortez was the one to break the news to Vicioso about the raid. Vicioso knew his time in the U.S. was coming to an end. Aside from the money he had in the streets, Vicioso was back at square one. He was broke damn near, broke and on the run. He felt like he had nothing to lose.

He and Niecy stayed at Cortez's beach house until Vicioso figured out what he wanted to do next. His options were slim. He couldn't go back to New York. That was out. All that was left was to take his show on the road, but where to? One wrong move and he was sure to end up in an American prison.

A phone call from Serio only added to the drama.

"I just got a call from back home." Serio said.

"What's up?" Vicioso asked, lying in the bed next to Niecy in the beach house.

"Andrew called me." Serio said.

Vicioso sat straight up. "Fuck he call you for? What does he have to say?"

"He wants to get in touch wit' you. Said it's very important."

"Me?"

"Yeah."

"We ain't got shit to talk about." Vicioso raised his voice, waking Niecy.

"From the way he was talkin', I think you to do have somethin' to talk about." Serio's tone was dead serious. Almost as a warning.

"What you mean by that?" Vicioso didn't see the point. Andrew had killed his brother. There was nothing to talk about. It was all out war.

"Think about this, Vicioso. Andrew did what he did to Pimpo and now he's back in Panama. His uncle and brother turned up dead. He's no fool. He knows who did it. Think about the situation. We all have family back home."

It all made sense. "So the nigga talkin' 'bout doin' somethin' to my family?" Vicioso felt an urge of anxiety.

"He ain't say that, but it ain't nothin' we can do to stop him." Serio said with a sigh. "I'm sure he don't want to do that. He just wants to talk to you." Serio gave Vicioso the phone number for Andrew. "Call him, Vicioso. Keep that shit between the two of you. Otherwise shit gon' get real ugly; y'all just gon' keep killin' relatives and shit like that."

Vicioso took a deep breath. "I'ma call the nigga."

"Good. On another note, I see you still in VA. What you gon' do? You can't stay down there."

"I'm 'bout to head to Philly. Niecy got some people there she knows. Can't nobody connect me to Philly. I figure I'll lay low in Philly until I can regroup and go back to the drawing board. I might even hit Miami. Wherever I go it gotta be somewhere that I can get some money and not draw too much attention."

"Cool, if you need anything just call me. I got people in Philly and Miami, they'll treat you like family." Serio said. "Keep your eyes open. Take shit slow. Now that you're on

the run everything's going to be different. It's no room for error."

"Say no more."

When Vicioso got off the phone with Serio he called Andrew.

"I'm glad you called. We really need to talk." Andrew said, answering the phone in the projects of Panama.

"What we got to talk about?" Vicioso said.

"I know I can never get you to understand what went down between me and Pimpo but--"

"But nothin'! You crossed me! You crossed family! You killed my brother!" Vicioso was heated, his emotions were getting the best of him even though he told himself that he would be calm when he made the call.

"If you were in my shoes you would have done the same thing. But that's another story. The lines have been drawn now and we have to live with that. For what it's worth, I never meant for it to go down like that. Pimpo forced the issue. Shit got out of control. Nevertheless, I wanted to talk to you so we can keep this shit between us. Your brother is dead and I know we gon' have to deal wit' that in time. At the same time, I done lost a brother and an uncle. I know how the game is played. If I keep losing family up there then it's only fair that you start losing family down here. It's no other way to look at things. That's no threat; it's just the way it is. I don't want it to go down like that, but if I'm forced to I will play the game." Andrew's voice was firm and sincere.

Vicioso was angered by what Andrew was insinuating. "You right, we need to keep this between us. We'll cross paths again, even if I have to track you all the way back to Panama. We will see each other. You got my word that I won't do anything to your family up here, but if my mother or anybody in my family even slips on a rock or catches a cold

I'ma wipe out everybody in New York that even know you, I swear to God! We clear on that?"

"Fair enough. I feel the same way. And for the record, I never meant for it to go down like that between me and Pimpo. He was family to me. Nevertheless, I want you to know that if anything happens to my peoples up there it won't be pretty down here."

"Whatever." Vicioso hung up.

"What was that all about?" Niecy asked when Vicioso got off the phone.

Vicioso explained the Andrew situation to her.

Niecy just shook her head. "This shit is crazy! There's too much going on, things are getting too out of hand."

"I know, but I have to deal with it. It's all a part of what comes with the lifestyle."

"I didn't think it was gon' to be like this up here."

"I know baby. I been doin' a lot of thinkin' and for real I think that maybe you should go back home. I could make one more run up here and send all the money back home and then come back home myself."

"Harvey, I'm all for goin' back home, but not without you. I'm wit' you until the end, baby. You know that. Whatever you go through I'm right here by your side. No matter what. There's no me without you by side."

"But the FBI is lookin' for me now. I don't want you to get caught up in this bullshit, baby."

"Harvey, I don't care. If you're on the run then I'm on the run, too. I mean that. All we have is each other."

Vicioso sighed and smiled. "That's why I love you, girl." He kissed her.

A few months later, a light snow fell on the mean streets of North Philly in February of 1988. A group of teenage hustlers were standing in front of the liquor store on the corner

MONEY AIN'T EVERYTHING

pumping coke hand-to-hand. It was bitterly cold and dark outside but the hustle didn't stop. Money had to be made. After serving a few crack heads, one of the teenagers said, "It's cold as shit out here." He blew hot air into his hands to warm them up as he watched a few cars roll by blasting rap music.

"No bullshit." Another teenager said as he served a crack head. "I'm ready to call it a night. My baby mother waitin' on me anyway. I made a few dollars so I'm cool."

In a flash, a black Camaro bent the corner smoothly and came to a quick stop. A short gunman in a black ski mask jumped out holding a huge chrome .357 revolver.

"You niggaz know what time it is! Get on the ground!" The gunman ordered. The teenagers were caught slipping. "Don't try to run or I'ma start shootin'." The gunman then grabbed one of the teenagers by his coat and smacked him in the face with the .357. The teenager groaned and cringed as the gunman slammed him to the cold ground and then aimed the .357 at the other teenagers that were already on the ground with their arms outstretched. The gunman then stood over them and robbed them of their money, coke and jewelry. Unsatisfied with what he'd taken, the gunman began to pistol-whip one of the teenagers. "Y'all been out here all night and this all y'all got?! What the fuck y'all been doin'? I should bus' your ass for bullshittin'! Get the fuck outta here!" the gunman waved his .357. The teenagers got up and ran down the street. The gunman laughed to himself as he walked back to the car, watching the teenagers run. Off of impulse the gunman fired two thunderous shots in the air for the hell of it. The teenagers dove to the ground in hopes of not being shot. One slid face-first in the snow. The gunman jumped in the car laughing. The Camaro pulled off into the night.

179

The driver of the Camaro was dying laughing as he drove by the teenagers. He looked at his partner in crime, Roni, and said, "You crazy as shit, scarin' them young boys like that."

Roni laughed. "They'll be okay. Who knows? I might have changed their lives: Scared them straight." Roni pulled off his ski mask, revealing his young, boyish features. He was no more than 5'5", light-skinned with curly black hair that he got from his Puerto Rican mother. At 18, he was what one would call a real stickup kid. After all, he was raised in Philly--the home of "get down or lay down."

The driver, Yusuf, headed for their neighborhood still laughing. Yusuf and Roni were childhood friends that had grown into crime partners. They were the same age. Yusuf was much bigger, standing a little over six feet tall. He carried 200 pounds. As he laughed, his smile made him look like the Joker. Once they hit the Logan section of Philly, Yusuf parked on Marvine Street, where they hustled. The two partners were far from big-time hustlers, but they saw a few dollars from time to time. Robbery kept them above water. They did whatever they had to do to get the job done.

Sitting in the car with the heat on, counting money from the robbery, Roni looked out the window and saw a few homies on the block pushing coke hand-to-hand. Most of them were working for their older homies, Avery and some Jamaican nigga he had brought around the way. Roni and Yusuf weren't the type to work for somebody else, plus they didn't like the fact that the Jamaican dude was in their hood getting money. They had plans of robbing him, but wanted to do it without Avery knowing about it.

"Here you go." Roni handed Yusuf $430 in cash and $200 worth of caps of coke. "That's yours."

"Let's get rid of this shit real quick and get somethin' to drink for the night." Yusuf looked at his watch. It was 11:27 P.M.

"Nah, I'ma get rid of this shit and call it a night." Roni said. "I told Cookie that I was gon' spend the night wit' her. We gon' hook up in the morning."

Yusuf laughed. "You kill me wit' that lover-boy shit."

Roni smirked. "Yeah, yeah, whatever, nigga. Just be safe."

"Come on, let's get rid of this shit." Yusuf said as he saw a few crack heads coming down the street. "It's a few dollars out here."

Roni looked around and agreed to hang for a second and see if they could get rid the coke they got from the robbery.

Roni and Yusuf hit the block and started serving crack heads. The block was pumping, too. Their homie, Shawn, walked up and gave them five. "What's up wit' y'all?" He said, looking up and down the block.

"I see y'all got some coke."

"Yeah, a little somethin'." Roni said, serving a crack head.

Shawn was Avery's nephew; he was the same age as Roni and Yusuf. Shawn was the lieutenant for Avery's drug operation on the block. He and Roni were real cool, but they were on two different kinds of time. Shawn's thing was drug dealing. Roni and Yusuf were into whatever they could do to get a dollar.

"Roni, you and Yusuf need to get down wit' the program." Shawn said. He'd been trying to get Roni and Yusuf on the team for a while. He wanted to see them get some real money. It was no secret that niggaz were getting paid fucking with Avery and the Jamaican. They were making all the real moves. "You know Avery gon' look out for the home team.

Y'all need to get some of this money. Money coming in, I'm telling you, cannon."

"Nah, that ain't for me, Shawn. You know I do my own thing." Roni said. "Plus I don't fuck wit' no Jamaicans. I ain't grow up wit' them niggaz."

Shawn laughed. "He ain't Jamaican, he Panamanian. He good peoples, too. I'm tellin' you. We gettin' money."

"Some niggaz do anything for money. I ain't one of those niggaz at all." Roni said sarcastically. "Just 'cause a nigga got coke and shit don't mean he good peoples. That Jamaican or whatever you call him ain't even from around here. I ain't fuckin' wit' him."

Shawn looked at Yusuf to see if he felt the same way as Roni, but Yusuf had his game face on. His thoughts were under wraps.

"Check this out," Shawn said, looking back at Roni. "The Panamanian is the only one around here that's bringin' in coke, but if you don't want to fuck wit' him that's cool. At the same time, it won't hurt you to buy some coke from me. We homies, I know me and you can get some money together. Fuck wit' me and let's get paid. See where I'm coming from? The faster I move what I get, the more I get. I can give you and Yusuf good deals and you two won't even have to deal wit' the Panamanian. In the end, we all blow. You can't beat that. I'm telling you, when I say this shit go from two to four I put that on everything. Your money double every time. It's nothing like it." Shawn raised his eyebrows.

Roni cut his eyes at Yusuf, he wondered what he was thinking. He looked back at Shawn and rubbed his chain with a sly look in his eyes and said, "I'll think about it." A crack head walked up and Roni stepped off to serve her. He had to admit that Shawn had him thinking. The coke game was wide open and it was just taking off around his way for real.

182

MONEY AIN'T EVERYTHING

Anybody could get paid if they had their mind in the right place.

Shawn continued to sell the idea to Yusuf, who he knew could smell opportunity faster than Roni. "I'm tellin' you, Yusuf, it's a new day in time. Niggaz gotta get some real money. We ain't gon' get no money if we don't wanna fuck wit' niggaz we ain't grow up wit. Niggaz from other places got the fuckin' plugs. That shit gon' have us sittin' in the same place while everybody else gettin' paid in full." Shawn had the talk game down to a T. He shrugged his shoulders. He couldn't force Roni and Yusuf to get money. "Just think about this: How much money y'all gon' get robbin' niggaz on the corner? Everyday you living from one move to the next. Ain't no future in that there. Wake up. Come on man, it's '88. It's time to get money."

A silver BMW with chrome rims pulled up and stopped right in front of Shawn and Yusuf. The passenger's side window slowly came down. Avery, who was a very large man, spoke to Yusuf and then told Shawn that he needed to holla at him. Shawn gave Yusuf five and told him he'd catch him later. Shawn then jumped in the back of the BMW. Yusuf watched Shawn, Avery and the Panamanian pull off. As the car cruised down the street, Yusuf thought about what Shawn was talking about. It was time to get some real money.

The phone woke Vicioso up at 10:34 A.M. He struggled to open his eyes as he answered the phone.

"Yeah." His voice was groggy and rough.

"Panama," Avery said. "We need to go shoppin', ASAP. I don't have shit to wear to the club."

Vicioso was dead tired. He'd been out all night and had just got in the house at six in the morning. Nevertheless, he was mentally alert; he understood that Avery was speaking in code, telling him that more coke was needed on the block. It was moving faster than they could cap it. The young boys were out of work. "I'ma be around there in a little while." Vicioso said. "Let me get myself together. I can't even think straight right now."

"Okay, but I'm tellin' you we need to get to the mall. Fast! Avery was standing on his front porch looking down the block at Roni, Yusuf and a few other young dudes that didn't work for him. They were making a killing while his young boys were out of product. Avery didn't like the sight of all that money being made when none of it was going into his pockets.

"Give me a minute. I'm getting' up right now." Vicioso hung up the phone and laid back down for a second. Niecy rolled over and rubbed his chest. Her soft touch felt so good. Vicioso ran a hand through her hair. "I woke you up, baby?" he asked as he kissed her forehead.

"Not you. The phone woke me up. Who was that?"

"Avery, he need to holla at me about a few things."

"I wish you would slow down a little bit. We came up here for you to cool down. Don't forget you on the run. We barely been here six months and you already knee-deep into things."

"You right, baby, but I gotta get some money. I can't lay around and act like everything is going to be cool. We lost everything in Washington. I ain't gon' get no money if I just lay low 'cause I'm on the run. I gotta make some things happen. You know how shit go." He rubbed her face and continued. "Besides, don't nobody really know me up here. I'm a new person in a way. After all, I'm illegal in this country anyway." He kissed her and climbed out of the bed. "I'm behind the scenes up here. Everything's cool. It's different than Brooklyn and Washington. Trust me, if things get out of hand we are out of here first thing smokin'."

"If you say so."

"Trust me, baby."
"You know I trust you."

Vicioso jumped in his BMW in a hurry to get out of the cold and headed to Avery's house. Philly was a nice spot for him spot for him. It was a spot where he go and start over. Things weren't moving as fast as Vicioso would have liked, but then again, he was on the run so things had to move at slower pace. Aside from that, he really didn't have a for sure connect in Philly. That was the one thing he needed. Without a solid connect in the Philly area Vicioso had to play the highway to re-up. He'd taken a few trips down I-95 to D.C. to holla at Cortez but that was too risky. Vicioso made up his mind that he would make new connections on his own in Philly; that would keep people from knowing where he was. He cut himself off from Washington and New York to keep his whereabouts low key. Nevertheless, the show had to go on.

A short while later Vicioso pulled up in front of Avery's house and blew the horn. Avery came out the front door and made his way to the car.

"What's up, P?" Avery said as he jumped in the warm car.

"I'm good. Where the grip at?" Vicioso asked.

"Shawn went to get it. He'll be out in a minute."

Moments later Shawn came out of the house with a shopping bag in hand. He walked up to the car and got in the back seat. Sitting the shopping bag on the floor, he said, "What's up, Panama?"

"Everything's cool. 'Bout to go take care of this business. Have everything ready when we get back." Vicioso said.

"I got that." Shawn said and got out the car.

Vicioso pulled off and headed to the house of a Colombian lady that he had met through some people he had dealings with when he first got to Philly. That's when he was staying around Dauphin Street, where Niecy had family. While around Dauphin Street, Vicioso met a few people that opened up doors for him in North Philly. Among them were Big Momma, Cristal, Jamie and Lloyd. Once he got down with them he got cool with a crew of dudes from 11ᵗʰ and York projects. Vicioso met Avery through the dudes from 11ᵗʰ and York and they seemed to click overnight. The dudes from 11ᵗʰ and York were serious soldiers--Tony, Kaleef, Man and Charlie were the ones Vicioso dealt with the most. They had the power to make things happen and Vicioso caught on to that off the top. Their whole crew ended up going to prison for a string of bodies and kidnappings shortly after Vicioso came to town. Once they were locked up, Vicioso and Avery started doing a few things together in Logan. So far, Logan was sweet.

Vicioso pulled up and parked down the street from the Colombian lady's house. He looked at Avery and said, "Let's see what this like.

Not too far away, Roni walked into his girlfriend's bedroom and saw her on the bed in a long white T-shirt doing her toenails. Cookie looked up, startled, and said, "Don't be sneakin' up on me like that."

Roni laughed. "I ain't sneakin' up on you. I'm checkin' up on you. Just making sure you okay." He sat down beside her rubbed her thick, light-brown thigh.

"Boy stop! Cookie blushed with a big smile on her face. "You gon' make me mess up my toes. Get off me. I'm mad at you anyway. For real."

"For what?" Roni smiled.

"You said you was comin' over last night and you ain't even show, you ain't even call. I guess you was wit' some other bitch. That's how you do anyway."

186

"Come on now." Roni kissed her cheek. "You know good and well I ain't got time for that. You know it's all about you."

"Whatever, you wasn't wit' me last night. I don't know where you were." Cookie sucked her teeth and rolled her eyes.

"Baby, it got late and I didn't want to wake your grandmother up. You know she act."

"So why didn't you call?" You coulda' done that."

"I'm sorry, baby. I didn't mean nothin' by it and I wasn't wit' no other bitch. Get that out your mind." He rubbed her back and kissed her soft lips, sliding his tongue in her mouth, making her wet. "You know I love you, girl."

Roni's love for Cookie was nothing new. There was something special between them since day one. It was the summer of 1984. Back then, Roni ran with the 11-C Boyz, hanging around 11th and Courtland and 11th and Lacomen. Things were really moving fast in his young life at the time. His cousin Idris had been murdered and that event was bringing out a dark side in Roni. It made him a mean motherfucker when he walked the streets. He needed some sunshine at the time and Cookie became that.

As Roni walked down the street in a black Gucci short set he passed a house with two girls on the porch. They were laughing and joking. One called out, "Hey, boy! Yeah you! In the black Gucci short set wit' them sexy legs."

Roni looked around and saw the girls. "What's up?" he smiled. "You gon' hide up there or can I holla at you."

Cookie came down to the sidewalk looking even better up close. Roni looked her in the eyes while eyeing her sexy body up and down on the sly. "So what's your name, sexy?"

"Cookie. What's yours?" she smiled a bright smile.

"Roni." He said as he glanced down the street. "Let's take a walk."

"You ain't no crazy killer or nothin', are you?" she joked.

Roni loved her vibe off top. "When the last time you seen a crazy killer like me?" Roni's tone was smooth with a touch of conceit. Cookie laughed and took a walk down the streets with him. Walking down Wingohocking Street they got to know one another better. Cookie told him about herself and the kinds of things she was into. Roni gave her some of his background. He'd grown up in one of the toughest part of North Philly--23rd and Diamond. That was before his mother got married and moved him to Logan for a better life.

Roni and Cookie clicked overnight and even as Roni got deeper into the streets Cookie was always down for him. After being put out of Olney High School and being sent to Chesapeake, MD to Job Corp. for two years, Cookie was still his girl. Their love was strong.

Later on, Roni came out of the alley with the hood of his coat over his head and headed down Marvine Street. Avery was just pulling up in his Trooper. Roni cut him off just as he was getting out.

"Avery, let me holla at you for a second." Roni said.

"What's up soldier?" Avery said, stepping onto the sidewalk, giving Roni five.

"Let me get somethin' for five-hundred."

"Cool come in the house wit' me." Avery said.

They headed to the house together.

Inside Avery's basement he gave Roni a $500-pack of caps. "You need to come on and get down wit' the team, Roni. You and Yusuf could get a lot of cash fuckin' wit' me. Cut the bullshit out and get some of this paper."

Roni smiled. "Avery, I got nothin' but love for you, but you know me and Yusuf do our own thing in the streets. We

don't take orders well. That foot solider shit ain't for us. No hard feelings."

"Go 'head wit' that bullshit, Roni. You ain't gotta take no orders fuckin' wit' me. You know better. It's all about family. I'm all about making sure everybody eats. I'm all for the home team. Nothing more, nothing less."

Roni gave Avery five and said, "I like it this way better, big boy."

"I respect that, but anytime you want to step ya' game up I'm here for you."

Roni winked at Avery and headed up the steps.

Two days later, Roni, Yusuf, and a few other young dudes were posted up on Marvine Street hard at work pushing coke. Money was coming fast, but there were so many dudes on the corner trying to get rid of the same thing that money seemed to be coming slow as far as Roni was concerned. His mind was hard at work trying to figure out the next move. Armed robbery was at the top of the list.

Smoking a Newport, Roni looked at Yusuf and said, "It's too many niggaz out here, man. We gon' be all day tryin' to get rid of this shit like this." Roni blew smoke into the air and sighed. "Layin' niggaz down for the paper beats this any day, no bullshit."

Yusuf laughed. "You want everything to come fast. Shit takes time sometime, cannon. Ease up. We gon make out fine. Trust me on that there."

"That's what the drug game is all about, ain't it? Fast money, right? That's why we do this shit, we do this shit for fast money. Fuck all that other shit. I be tryin' to get paid, asap."

"Yeah, you right. I feel you, all the way. I'm just sayin, it's more than one way to look at shit out here."

"This shit ain't movin' fast enough for me, Yusuf. A quick caper ain't never a bad idea."

While Roni and Yusuf were talking, a silver BMW pulled up in front of Avery's house. The windows were tinted so it was almost impossible to see inside. Avery and Vicioso got out and went inside Avery's house carrying shopping bags. Minutes later, Shawn came outside in a huge coat and called a few young boys up the street. They all made their way up the street as if they were marching to the bank on the same team. Avery handed out a few packs and sent the young boys back to work. The shit was a full-scale operation.

"Look at that shit there." Roni said to Yusuf, his facial expression was full of venom.

"That's why the money be comin' so slow. All them little niggaz workin' for Avery and them."

"Yeah, Avery keep that work comin', too."

"You think about what I said about gettin' that Panamanian nigga?" Roni plucked the rest of his Newport in the street.

"Yeah, I thought about it. If that's what you wanna do then you know I'm wit' you. We can do that, but Shawn had a point when he said that we can get some money fuckin' wit' them niggaz. Think about it, if we get the nigga, then we get him one time for whatever bread we come off wit'. If we play the situation for what it's worth then we can get more bread. We can stack paper off the lick just because it's right in our face. It's all about the paper, fuck your feelings." Yusuf said.

Roni sighed. "I see I'ma have to get the nigga by myself. You ain't tryin' to get the nigga for real. That's all you got to say, just say you ain't wit' it." Roni sounded fed up.

"I ain't tryin' to hear that shit you talkin', Roni. You know damn well I'm wit' you all the way. I just think we can get some real money fuckin' wit' Avery and that Panamanian

nigga. That's a real connect. They got that work, let's face it." Yusuf said.

Roni shook his head. "We don't need them niggaz, Yusuf." He didn't want to admit to himself that Yusuf was right.

Avery's young boys were just coming back down the block when Roni saw Vicioso come out of Avery's house. Vicioso was walking toward the corner with a serious look on his face. He and Roni somehow locked eyes. A second later, Avery came out of the house and followed behind Vicioso with a concerned look on his face. Something wasn't right.

Roni and Vicioso seemed to be sizing each other up. Vicioso glanced at everybody on the corner and said, "How many of y'all little niggaz workin' for Avery?" Vicioso was getting back on his Red Hook shit. He wanted the whole block and all the money. A few young boys acknowledged that they were working for Avery while a handful said nothing.

"What about the rest of you niggaz?"

Vicioso waved a finger. No one said a word. With a quick glance, Vicioso said, "Look here, if y'all ain't workin' for Avery y'all gotta get the fuck off the corner!"

Shawn walked up just as the situation was getting heated.

"Who the fuck you think you talking to?" Roni barked. "This my block, I ain't goin' no muthfuckin' where. You gotta be out your fuckin' mind!"

"What?" Vicioso twisted up his face. "You serious, shorty."

"You heard what I said. This is my spot. I ain't goin' nowhere." Roni was fearless. No one would believe that he wasn't strapped. His pistol was in Yusuf's car.

Vicioso smiled and pulled out his Mac-10. Roni saw the long clip hanging from the weapon and began to think twice, but he still didn't back down. His heart was big as Texas.

Yusuf knew that his pistol as well as Roni's was in the car. He didn't know what to expect at this time. They were forced to play the situation out.

"I'ma say this one more time." Vicioso said calmly. "Get the fuck off the corner if you don't work for Avery!" He then studied Roni's eyes for fear. There was none there. A few intense seconds passed. Cutting his eyes at Avery, Vicioso said, "Who the fuck is this young nigga?"

"He cool, P. That's family, he a young cannon." Shawn said.

"Yeah, that's my man. He family, like blood." Avery said. "Him and Shawn grew up together."

"You better let him know what the fuck is goin' on." Vicioso said.

A few young dudes began to step off, fearing the worst. Roni and Yusuf stood their ground.

"Come on, let's go." Avery grabbed Vicioso's arm.

Vicioso and Roni continued to glare at one another for what seemed like minutes. Vicioso then smiled and headed back up the street with Avery and Shawn. In the back of his mind he had to respect Roni. The young nigga had balls.

As Vicioso headed back up the street, he looked at Avery and said, "I like that young nigga. He got heart. I hope I don't have to kill his little ass."

"Don't worry about it. I'ma holla at him. Him and Yusuf are good soldiers. I watched them grow up." Avery said.

Later on, Vicioso and Avery cruised down Marvine Street in Vicioso's BMW. They spotted Roni and Yusuf leaning on Yusuf's car. The young niggaz looked eyes on the BMW.

"Pull over." Avery said. Vicioso pulled over and Avery lowered the window with the push of a button. "Roni! Yusuf! Let me holla at y'all!"

Roni and Yusuf were strapped. This time they were ready to take the situation to the next level. They looked at each other as if they were thinking about opening fire on the BMW.

Not moving an inch, Roni said, "What's up, Avery?" His glare was cold.

"I want y'all to know that that shit earlier wasn't meant for y'all." Avery said. "I told my man, Panama, that y'all like family to me and I watched y'all grow up. I want to clear that shit up, get it out the air."

Roni and Yusuf looked at each other like: Yeah right!

Vicioso was leaning back in the driver's seat checking Roni and Yusuf out. He had a .45 automatic in his left hand that they couldn't see.

"So we supposed to act like that shit ain't happen? Is that what you're tellin' me?" Roni said, not caring how his words were taken.

"Nah, I ain't sayin' that." Avery said. "I'm sayin' that that whole thing was a misunderstanding that we can put behind us." Avery really wanted to smooth things out.

Vicioso leaned over Avery and said, "What Avery is tryin' to say is that I don't have no beef wit' y'all. Can we put that shit behind us? No disrespect."

Roni looked at Yusuf. Yusuf shrugged. Roni looked back at Vicioso and said, "We ain't got no beef, man. Fuck it."

"That's what I'm talkin' about." Avery said. "Look here," he stuck a brown paper bag out the window, "here's a $5,000 pack for you and Yusuf. It's on me. Just to let you know I got nothin' but love for you."

Roni thought about it for a second and then grabbed the paper bag with caution.

"So everything's cool?" Avery asked.

"Yeah." Roni nodded. "We ain't on no sneak shit."

"What about you, Yusuf?" Avery asked.

"Fuck that shit. It's dead." Yusuf said. A week later, Vicioso was on the phone with Yasmin.

"What's wrong?" Vicioso knew something was wrong because Yasmin never called him in Philly. It was understood that Serio only called him in Philly if it was an emergency. No one else was suppose to know where he was.

"The FBI arrested Serio last night." Yasmin shouted, she was nervous and sounded confused. "They raided the Red Hook spot and locked a bunch of people up, like twenty some people. It's all over the news." She gave Vicioso the whole rundown.

"What did they charge Serio wit'?"

"Murders, drugs... a lotta shit. I don't know what to do. I took the kids and checked into a hotel. I don't feel safe right now. Serio has a lot of enemies. I need to get out of here. I can't be here right now."

Without a second thought, Vicioso said, "I'ma come get you. You can stay wit' me until we find out what's goin' on wit' Serio. I'll make sure everything's okay. Don't worry about anything."

"Thank you, Harvey. You are family, I love you."

CHAPTER 17

Standing over the stove in Avery's kitchen cooking a kilo of cocaine, Vicioso had a confused look on his face. Something wasn't right. "What's up, Panama?" Avery asked, standing beside Vicioso.

"This shit ain't right. It's takin' too long to come back. It ain't doing what it's supposed to do. Coke don't do shit like this." Vicioso tilted the Pyrex for Avery to get a better look at what he was talking about.

Vicioso and Avery had copped five kilos from an old Colombian lady that Vicioso had been dealing with for a few weeks. Most of the time the coke was A-1. Two to four, four to eight.

"We takin' this shit back." Vicioso grabbed the shopping bag with the rest of the bricks in it.

"That shit fucked up like that?" Avery asked. He knew the old Colombian lady had no reason to sell them bullshit coke; she'd been around too long for that. Her business was cocaine. She was making a killing

"The shit some bullshit and we ain't spendin' our money on this shit." Vicioso said. "If we just wanted some bullshit we coulda spent our money wit' anybody. We gon' get our money back! We ain't takin' no losses."

Vicioso and Avery jumped in Vicioso's BMW and headed for the old lady's house. They parked down the street from her house a few minutes later. They got out the car and walked up to the house. Vicioso knocked on the door. The old lady opened the door with a confused look on her face. She had to be in her fifties, her hair was gray and her body was frail. She gave Vicioso an evil Colombian glare as she looked from him to Avery and back. She told Vicioso to always come to the house alone. She went off, yelling and cursing in Spanish, telling Vicioso to leave and come back alone. She was pointing her finger at Avery as she went off. Avery didn't understand a word the old lady was saying, but he knew that she was talking about him. "Go sit in the car." Vicioso said to Avery.

As Avery stepped off, the old lady tried to shut the door in Vicioso's face. "Hold the fuck up." Vicioso put his foot in the way and stopped the door from slamming in his face. Pushing his way into the house, he sat the shopping bag on the floor and started speaking in Spanish. He told the old lady that the coke was bullshit and that he wanted his money back. She cut him off and yelled for her nephews to come upstairs. Three young Colombian dudes came up from the basement; one was carrying a shotgun, the other had a chrome 9mm. Vicioso was strapped with a .45 automatic, but the three young Colombians had the jump on him. Playing it smooth, Vicioso tried to finish explaining the situation to the old lady but she wasn't trying to hear any of it. She told him that she wasn't giving him any money back and for him to get the hell out of her house. Her rule was that once the coke left the house there was no refund. However, she told him that the next time she would cook the coke in his face for him. Looking at the three young Colombians standing behind the old lady, Vicioso sighed and agreed to the terms. He had no win. He left the house.

Back in the car with Avery, Vicioso said, "They fuckin' wit' the right one." He pulled off like a man on a mission.

A group of dudes were in front of a house at the end of Marvine Street shooting dice and smoking weed. Roni was making a killing on the dice, hitting point after point as if he couldn't miss. "I can't keep takin' y'all money like this." He joked. "I got other things to do. This shit too sweet, better than Vegas."

"Bet fifty you don't hit that six." Shawn said, trying to up the stakes.

"Bet!" Roni rolled a few times and sure enough the six popped up. "How you like that there?" he laughed. "You wanna bet back?"

"Yeah, bet back." Shawn said.

Yusuf walked up while Roni was on the dice. "Roni let me holla at you when you get a second."

"Hold fast, let me get this money right quick." Roni said, focused on the dice.

"It's s real important." Yusuf said, knowing he was bothering Roni.

Roni crapped out. "Damn, why the fuck you come out here fuckin' wit' me, Yusuf? You know I'm gambling."

"Fuck that shit. Let me holla at you. It's important." Yusuf said.

"Hold up, Roni. You can't just step off. I'm tryin' to win my money back." Shawn said.

"I'll be right back." Roni stepped off with Yusuf and posted up across the street.

"You ain't gon' believe what I just ran across." Yusuf said with a huge smile on his face. He had something up his sleeve.

"What's up?" Roni said. He didn't seem interested, he was still thinking about the point that he'd just missed on the dice. "It better be somethin' good."

"Avery just stepped to me wit' a move that can get us paid, for real!"

"Run it down to me." Roni said, lighting a Newport.

Yusuf told Roni that Avery had stepped to him and told him that his man Panama had a job in the making that involved some Colombians. A little manpower was needed. Avery felt that Roni and Yusuf were just right for the job. At least two bricks were in it for Yusuf and Roni if all went well.

"How we know we can trust the Panamanian nigga?" Roni asked, interested in the move.

"Come on, man. Open your eyes. Avery ain't gon' set us up for no bullshit. You already know that." Yusuf said.

"Why Avery want us to do the job wit' the Panamanian nigga?" Roni asked. "We talkin' 'bout some serious shit fuckin' wit' some Colombians. Why us?"

"Look, Roni, forget all that shit. This is a come up. Our biggest come up, period. We done risked our lives about less. We gotta take this chance." Yusuf said. He already had his mind made up.

Roni thought about the move for a second. He was very leery, but he still reluctantly agreed. "Cool, let's do it. You right, it's a big move. When we supposed to do this shit?"

"Tomorrow."

In the basement of Avery's house, just after 11:00 P.M., weed smoke filled the air as Vicioso, Roni and Yusuf sat around the TV discussing the caper. Vicioso laid everything on the table and told Roni and Yusuf why he decided to rob the Colombian spot. He also made the danger clear. He then told Roni and Yusuf what he needed from them.

"Can y'all handle this shit?" Vicioso asked.

Roni and Yusuf gave affirmative nods; they were down for whatever.

"Okay." Vicioso nodded. "Ain't no time for second-guessing. One wrong move and somebody gon' die. I done dealt wit' these Colombians before, if they get the ups on us they not just gon' kill us, they gon' kill us slow as they can and if they find out who our peoples are they gon' kill them too. So let me know if y'all really ready for this shit." Vicioso paused for a second. He wanted to see how Roni and Yusuf were taking his words. They still looked up to the job. "Avery already told me that both of y'all are soldiers, I trust his judgment, he vouched for y'all so now it's all about us takin' care of business. All we have to do is stick to the script."

"Let me ask you this, Yusuf said, rubbing his chin. "Wit' all the risk you talkin' bout, how much coke you think up in the spot? It gotta be somethin' nice."

Vicioso smiled. Yusuf was on top of his game and Vicioso liked that. A man had to always know what the pro and cons were when dealing with high stakes. "It could be anywhere from twenty to fifty bricks. I'm not sure, but it's somethin' inside that's worth the risk."

"If it's that much inside we gotta get more than two bricks." Roni cut in.

Vicioso nodded. "Whatever we get we gon' split. Don't worry bout it."

"That sounds fair." Roni said. Roni had a bad feeling about the move but tried to ignore it in order to stay focused on getting paid off of the move at hand.

The next day was cold and rainy in Philly, but that stopped nothing. Yusuf headed for Avery's house a little after 2:30 P.M. He was ready to pull the caper off. Pulling his hood over his head and adjusting the .38 revolver as he walked down the street, Yusuf rubbed his hands together and smiled. He was about to step his game up and never look back. At the corner of Comac Street he saw a broad he used to mess with and they spoke for a second, but he really didn't have much time to talk. He was on a mission. He kept stepping and when he got to Marvine Street and saw Vicioso's BMW parked in front of Avery's house, Yusuf began to think about what Vicioso had said about the Colombians. There was no turning back.

A police car bent the corner with two black officers inside. Both cops knew Yusuf as a neighborhood drug dealer. The police car sped up and slammed on the breaks. Out jumped one of the cops. Without a second thought, Yusuf took off running toward 11th Street. The cop on foot gave chase and the one still in the car slammed the car in reverse and gunned it down the street backwards. Yusuf bent the corner at top speed with the cop on his heels. He thought about firing at the cops to get them off his back but his better judgment kicked in and he continued to run for it as his heart pounded.

"Freeze!"

The cop yelled with his gun drawn. He wanted Yusuf so bad he could taste it. He was sure Yusuf was dirty and that meant he would be able to arrest the teenager and send his ass to jail for something. That would make his day being as though he could never catch him dirty any other time.

Yusuf jetted across the street and halfway down the block with the speed of a football player. He then looked over his shoulder and dashed through a yard and hopped over a six-foot high fence. Coming out in the alley he saw that the cop was still on his back. Yusuf dashed out of the alley and across the street nearly getting hit by a car. The car swerved to the side and slammed into a parked car with a loud crashing sound sitting off the car alarm. The close call slowed him down and allowed the cop to tackle him like an All-Pro linebacker. The hit knocked the wind out of Yusuf and slammed him to the

ground with a loud thud. When Yusuf looked up the cop was on top of him smashing his head into the ground. Pain shot through his body as his vision began to blur. He felt like he was about to pass out.

"I got your bad ass this time, motherfucker." The cop smiled as if he had won the lottery.

Yusuf sighed and shook his head, trying to catch his breath.

Vicioso was standing on Avery's porch when Roni arrived, he already knew of Yusuf's arrest. Word moved fast. "I heard your man got locked up." Vicioso said.

"Yeah, man. I'm fucked up about that. If it ain't one thing it's another. That's life though, he gon' be alright." Roni shook his head.

"You got bail money?"

"I'm dead broke right now."

Vicioso pulled a $1,000 out of his pocket and handed it to Roni. "Give that to his peoples. That should be enough, if not just let me know. I'll look out for him, make sure he gets bail."

"Okay. Thanks." Roni said, wondering why Panama was being so cool.

"We still gon' go through wit' the job. You can pull your weight, right?" Vicioso asked.

"Hell yeah. Don't even worry about that. Let's get to it." Roni said.

"Let's take care of business then." Vicioso looked Roni up and down. He liked the little nigga. "You got a gun on you?"

"Yeah." Roni looked at Vicioso like he was crazy. "Why wouldn't I be strapped?"

"Let me see it." Vicioso said.

Roni flashed his .357.

"You ain't takin' that little shit wit' us. I'll be right back." Vicioso snatched the .357 and went inside the house. He returned with an Uzi and gave it to Roni. "Let's get this shit out of the way."

Roni looked down at the Uzi and smiled. Somebody was in trouble.

They jumped in Vicioso's BMW and went around the corner to Yusuf's grandmother's house. Roni went inside and gave the bail money to Yusuf's grandmother. He then returned to the car and he and Vicioso got down to business.

"You nervous?" Vicioso cut his eyes to the side, checking Roni out. Roni was studying the machine gun. He was nice and calm as if he'd been on big capers before.

"Yeah, a little bit." Roni smiled. "But I'm cool. I'm ready. You can bet on that."

"I like that. I wanted to see if you was gon' lie. I'm always nervous before a job." Vicioso smiled. "You never know how shit is going to play out until it's all over."

"Ain't no reason to act like I ain't nervous. I ain't never robbed no Colombians before. I don't know how they gon' act, but I know one thing and that is if they act stupid it's gon' be a murder quick fast and in a hurry."

"That's the idea, just be on your toes. Keep your eyes open. Watch everything moving, be alert. It's life or death at this level. I'm sure you already know that though."

Vicioso made a few changes to the game plan since Yusuf was no longer on board. Turning into an alley behind the old lady's house, Vicioso said, "You ready?"

"No question." Roni checked the Uzi.

Vicioso got out the car, walked up to the back door of the house and knocked on the door holding a shopping bag in his hand as if he was coming to cop. Moments later, the old lady opened the door and rolled her eyes at the sight of Vicioso. It was clear that she didn't care for him. He'd gotten on her bad side. Nevertheless, she still let him in.

Inside, Vicioso laughed to himself, if she didn't like him now she would hate his guts when the day was over, he thought. She let him in and asked him how many kilos he wanted. He said he wanted five and they headed toward the kitchen. Along the way, Vicioso noticed a change in the layout: There was a young Colombian dude sitting on the sofa with an Uzi. This was a big change. Vicioso began changing the game plan in his head. He should have known things would be different after what happened the last time.

In the kitchen, the old lady asked to see the money. Smoothly, Vicioso began to take the money out of the shopping bag. He sat the money on the table. The Colombian dude that was sitting on the sofa came in the kitchen to keep an eye on things. He watched Vicioso like a hawk, as if he wanted Vicioso to make one wrong move so he could kill him. Every second seemed like minutes. As the old lady flipped through the money, Vicioso used one of the oldest tricks in the book and looked out into the living room as if he heard something. The young Colombian dude turned to look toward the living room as well. Wasting no time, Vicioso rushed the young Colombian, grabbing the Uzi and slamming him against the wall. They began to wrestle for the machine gun. The old lady went into a fit of rage, yell and screaming curse words in Spanish. No one had ever tried to rob her spot before. She went for a butcher knife as fast as her old legs would carry her. Suddenly a gunshot went off. Then another.

Outside in the car, Roni heard the gunshots. There wasn't supposed to be any shooting so he knew something was wrong. Roni jumped out of the car, expecting to see Vicioso coming out the back door running at top speed with Colombians right behind him firing automatic weapons. Roni crept up to the back of the house and tried to look through the window. He was startled and almost shot Vicioso when

Vicioso opened the back door with an Uzi to the old lady's head holding her by the collar of her old house-cleaning dress.

"Hurry up!" Vicioso nodded for Roni to come inside.

Roni stepped inside and shut the door behind him. He saw three Colombian dudes on the floor; two were handcuffed with their hands behind their backs while a third was bleeding from the stomach and looked like he was dead. Five kilos sat on the table wrapped in plastic with duct tape around them. The money Vicioso had sat on the table was knocked all over the floor.

"Ain't nobody else in the house." Vicioso said. "Hit the basement and get whatever you see. Hurry up. The cops might be on the way."

Roni grabbed the shopping bag off the table and headed down the steps in a full sprint. With every step he took down the dark basement steps he was ready to shoot. He could hear the TV and smell strong cigar smoke. Once he was in the basement the coast was clear. He saw seven kilos sitting on the floor along with a shotgun and two pistols. Roni grabbed the coke and the money and ran back up the stairs.

"I got everything." He said, still looking around carefully.

Vicioso had already made up his mind about the Colombians. He wasn't leaving any loose ends. He walked over to one of the Colombians on the floor and shot him in the head without a second thought. POP! The loud blast shook the whole room. Pointing at the Colombian dude that was closest to Roni, Vicioso looked Roni in the eyes and said, "Kill 'em." Roni wasted no time; he shot the Colombian in the head twice with no questions asked. The body fell to the floor with a loud thud. Vicioso then shot the old lady and let her body fall to the floor like wet clothes. Vicioso then shot the wounded Colombian dude that he'd taken the Uzi from.

"Let's get the fuck outta here." Vicioso said to Roni. The job was done.

Next to the old lady lived another older Colombian lady, she heard the gunshots and saw Vicioso and Roni run to the silver BMW with guns in hand and go flying down the alley. The lady called the Colombian man that was supplying the cocaine to the spot Vicioso and Roni had just hit. The supplier was a man by the name of Jairo. The older lady gave him the rundown on what had just gone down. Jairo told her that he was sending some men over to clean up and to find out what was going on.

Once Jairo got off the phone he smiled, although he was highly pissed off. He couldn't believe someone had taken his cocaine. It was not something he was used to. Jairo had fought hard for everything he ever had in life; he'd grown up in the streets of Medellin, Colombia, where as a child he was one of the glue sniffing kids that lived off of crime in Barrio Triste. As the drug trade expanded in the 1970's Jairo found a way to make something of himself as the city of Medellin became the murder capital of the world under the watchful eye of the cartels. The cartels gave Jairo his first job at the age of 11 and he became a sicarios—an assassin. In time, the head of the cartel took notice of Jairo's work ethic and sent him to the U.S. to enjoy the fruits of his hard work. Jairo owed all that he had to Pablo Escobar, and he was very connected.

In Avery's basement, Vicioso and Roni sorted things out. They had taken 12 kilos of Colombian cocaine and $45,000 in cold hard cash. Roni couldn't believe his eyes as he looked at the goods. It was the jackpot. In his young mind, he was already rich. The whole thing was just too sweet to be true, he told himself. Vicioso and Roni split everything right down the middle.

"You shouldn't have to look back from here, baby boy." Vicioso said as he smoked a Newport and recounted a handful of cash.

"You really in the game now. This how shit starts."

"Yeah, I know." Roni smiled, wrapping a rubber band around a stack of cash he was placing into a gym bag. "I'm good from here, you can bet that. I'ma sit somethin' to the side for Yusuf and get down to business." Roni stopped what he was doing for a hot second and then said, "Let me ask you this … what we gon' do when all this shit gone? I'm mean like, what's next."

"Don't worry about that. I got that under control. If you want to, you and Yusuf can holla at me once y'all get your money straight. I got some big things in the making. Trust me, Roni."

"Cool." Roni nodded. He was starting to see what Yusuf was trying to tell him. It was a lot of money to be made fucking with the Panamanian.

"Don't forget what I said about that shit we just did." Vicioso said with a very serious look on his face.

"You don't gotta worry about that wit' me. That shit gon' go to the grave wit' me. I don't do no talkin' and braggin'. That ain't my style."

"That's right." Vicioso smiled and gave Roni five. "I like you, Roni. You my kind of guy. You gon' go a long way, I can see it in you."

Within the next few days Roni got down to business. He recruited his cousin, Short Man, and a few young boys from 11th Street that sold coke. He let them know that it was time to get paid and that he was putting the team on. He hit them off with a few packs to see how things would work out. He just wanted to get them started so the money would start rolling in. The coke was so good that it was moving faster

than he could cap it up and hand it out. Aside from that, Roni was able cut it gram for gram and double his money on any amount of the shit.

Panama had told him the yay would double up. Roni couldn't believe how fast the money was coming in. It was an overnight thing, for real. Roni couldn't wait for Yusuf to make bail and see what was in the making. With his eyes open to a new side of the game Roni was ready and willing to take it to another level. He just needed to put his feelings to the side and think about the paper.

Walking down 11th Street to see how things were going, Roni ran into Short Man. "What's up?" Roni gave Short Man five. He then glanced around to see how things were looking on the block.

"Man this shit you got out here movin' like hotcakes. Can't nobody shit fuck wit' it." Short Man nodded and looked up and down the block. Young boys were making hand-to-hand sells left and right in front of the crack house that they had jumping. "You done hit the jackpot wit' this shit here you got. We 'bout to get paid, Roni. For real. This shit is on another level."

Roni smiled and handed Short Man a brown paper bag containing $1,000 worth of caps. "It's our time. You know how that goes. Shit gon' work out as planned."

While Roni and Short Man were talking, a black Jeep Cherokee pulled up and the passenger's side window came down. Vicioso sat there with a smile on his face. "I see what's goin' on, young nigga."

"What's up?" Roni smirked. He and Panama now shared a dark secret and that somehow created a bond between them.

"Avery was right about you, you real sharp." Vicioso smiled, rubbing his chin. "You real crafty." He shook an accusing finger at Roni in admiration. "You got your own spot that fast. All you needed was a little jumpstart. I wish I woulda new that from the start. I would've tried to holla at you."

Roni walked up to the truck and leaned against the door. "I had to put some things in motion on my own." He said, giving Vicioso five. He gave Avery a nod, seeing him behind the wheel.

"You all about getting' money I see." Vicioso said, checking out the young boys that were pumping for Roni.

Roni stood outside of the truck talking to Vicioso and Avery for a while and then looked at his watch. "I gotta go take care of somethin', real quick. I'ma catch y'all later."

"Check this out, Roni." Vicioso said. "I been workin' on a few things, so if you tryin' to put your money wit' what me and Avery spendin' we can get somethin' real nice."

"We can do that." Roni said.

"Cool, we gon' get some money together." Vicioso gave Roni five.

CHAPTER 18

Cookie was standing outside in the cold waiting on a cab after a long day at work. As she watched cars ride by she began to think about Roni and how fast he was moving in the streets. She was hearing more and more stories about him and Yusuf and what they were into. Cookie feared that Roni was on his way to big trouble, maybe even the big house. She wished there was something she could do to slow him down, but that seemed like it was out of the question. As Cookie thought about Roni, a brand-new black Corvette bent the corner and pulled up right in front of her with rap music blasting out of the speakers. Cookie squinted her eyes, trying to make out who was behind the wheel. She couldn't believe her eyes. All she could was shake her head.

"You gon' stand there in the cold or you gon' get in, sexy?" Roni smiled as he let the window down.

"Whose car is this?" Cookie asked in an excited voice as she got in the car. All she could smell was weed and that new car smell.

"It's my car." Roni pulled off smoothly, turning the music down. "Don't ask me how I got it." He joked.

Cookie playfully punched him in the arm and said, "Boy, don't play wit' me. Is this your car for real?"

"Yeah." Roni nodded, his eyes were damn near shut from all the weed smoke.

"You just don't learn, boy." Cookie sucked her teeth.

Cookie had no idea what Roni had done to get the car and the small fortune he now had. She knew that he and Yusuf were on the other side of the law, but what Roni and Panama had hooked up to pull off was a different side of the game.

"What can I say? Say hello to the bad guy." Roni said in his Tony Montana voice.

Cookie laughed. "Shut up, boy!" She shook her head. "I don't know what I'ma do wit' you."

"All you gotta do is enjoy the ride and let me take care of the rest. I got everything under control. Me and you gon' be just fine."

"We ain't gon' be fine if you go to jail. I know how things go in the streets." Cookie shook her head. "I don't care about how much money you got or what you can do for me. All I want is you, I love you."

"Baby, you worryin' for nothin'." Roni rubbed Cookie's leg.

"Whatever, that's what everybody says until they get caught." Cookie rolled her eyes.

Roni softly turned her cute face towards his; she had a pout on her face and turned her eyes away. He leaned over and kissed her lips, saying, "I love you, girl, and I'ma be just fine. Trust me."

When Yusuf made bail Roni had his share of coke and money from the Colombian caper waiting for him. Yusuf was pleased, he was also impressed to see how Roni had the 11th Street spot up and running. Yusuf was impressed with the whole situation and knew that they were into something big. In days, Roni and Yusuf had moved all the bricks they had from the caper and then found themselves in need of more coke. However, Vicioso was having issues getting a connect that could give them the amount of kilos they needed to run

their spots. Vicioso, Roni, and Yusuf made up their minds to go on another caper. It was no other options for them if they wanted to keep the coke spots up and running on a serious level. In Avery's basement, Vicioso laid the plans out for the next caper. "Here's the deal," he said, looking from Roni to Yusuf. "Me and Roni gon' go inside. Since he look so young they not gon' worry too much about him. We gon' go along wit' the two brick deal just to get inside and then we gon' check out the setup. If we can pull off the job right then and there then we gon' do it. If not, we just gon' take notes and hit 'em next go 'round." Vicioso then looked at Yusuf and said, "I want you to stay in the car and watch our backs. I'ma give you a Uzi so you gon' be able to handle your business if push come to shove. Can you handle a Uzi?"

"I got it, I'm cool wit' that." Yusuf said.

"Good." Vicioso stood up. "Y'all be ready at four. We gon' go in and take care of business."

The stick-up game was in effect.

Yasmin was now staying in Philly while Serio fought his cases in New York. Vicioso had put her up in a nice town house close to where he and Niecy where living so that he could make sure she was okay. He made it his business to take care of her like family. It was the least he could do for his brother, and he knew Serio would take care of Niecy the same way if the shoe was on the other foot.

Vicioso let himself into Yasmin's town house and saw her talking on the phone, watching TV. He could smell fried fish and Cajun rice coming from the kitchen. Yasmin got off the phone just as Vicioso shut the door. She got up and gave him a sisterly hug. "I got word from Serio today." She said.

"What's goin' on wit' his situation?" Vicioso asked, handing her a thick envelope full of cash for rent, food and other needs.

"He said to tell you that niggaz ain't livin' up to his expectations. Things are not looking too good at the time. He needs you to lace up your boots, whatever that means."

Vicioso knew exactly what Serio meant, he needed business taken care of in regards to his case.

Yasmin went on. "Serio said that Reego got arrested in connection wit' his case. The feds got everybody scared to even deal wit' Serio. People changin' their phone numbers and everything."

"Oh yeah?" Vicioso said. He didn't like the sound of what was going on with his man. Serio was good to those he truly had love for. It was fucked up that people weren't returning that love.

"Yeah, things are lookin' bad. I can't even sleep I'm so worried about what's going to happen."

"Don't worry 'bout none of that. I'll take care of it. You just let Serio know that I got his back. All he gotta do is let me know what needs to be done and I got it. No questions asked."

An old white Cadillac Deville bent the corner and turned left on 12th Street with three heads inside. A light tint on the windows made it hard to see who was inside the car. Vicioso was in the back seat with a .45 automatic on his lap. Roni was riding shotgun with a 9mm Ruger and shopping bag containing $30,000, which was supposed to be the buy money. Yusuf was behind the wheel with an Uzi on his lap. It was game time. They had their shit together, the game plan was tight and they were all on the same page. They had to be, one wrong move and they would all be in boxes being lowered into the ground.

"We gon' leave the money in the car just in case we need time to stall." Vicioso said, going over the caper in his head. "Roni, no matter what I do inside, I want you to keep your

212

eyes on me. When it's time, I'm goin' to give you the signal and I want you to pull your heat. You gotta be on point at all times."

"I got you, P." Roni said. "You just make sure I understand what's goin' on inside. I don't understand that much Spanish. Just a little."

Yusuf looked back at Vicioso and said, "How I'ma know everything's cool inside?"

"You not." Vicioso said. "You just gotta keep your eyes open, pay attention, go with your gut feelings. If we take too long to come back then you know somethin' is wrong. Simple as that."

"I'm comin' in if that happens." Yusuf said, looking down at the machine gun in his lap.

Moments later, they pulled up down the street from the target house and parked close to the corner. A few young Colombian dudes were outside selling weight in the middle of the block. They were out in the open selling weight like other jokers would be on their corners selling twenty-dollar rocks.

"Don't worry about them. If all goes well they won't even know what's goin' on inside the house." Vicioso said as he checked his pistol one more time. He then looked at Roni and said, "Where's the grip?"

Roni nodded at the shopping bag by his feet and said, "I got that, P."

"You ready then?" Vicioso asked Roni.

"Let's make it happen." Roni nodded. "I'm ready."

"Hello my friend." Alejandro smiled at Vicioso. He was already waiting on Vicioso; they'd met when Vicioso tried to buy more than a kilo from Alejandro's street workers— anything more than a kilo had to go through Alejandro. "I see you brought company." Alejandro nodded at Roni with a suspicious eye.

"This my partner. He watches my back. You know how dangerous this business is." Vicioso was smooth and calm. "I told you I was bringin' one of my men along. It ain't no problem, is it?"

"No, no problem. I understand. That's why I keep my sons close." Alejandro looked Roni up and down, studying him. "Your partner looks kinda young. How old is he? Fifteen? Sixteen?"

"Eighteen." Roni said as he took a seat on the old sofa in the living room.

"Same age as my son." Alejandro smiled and looked at his son that was standing behind him. "Well, let's get down to business." Alejandro's speech was thick with a Colombian accent. He was a tall, fat man in his early fifties with gray hair. "Before we begin, I must have my son pat you down. I don't do business with weapons involved."

Vicioso's mind went into overdrive. There was no way that he was letting anybody take his weapon from him.

"If you have any weapons I ask that you take them back to the car." Alejandro's voice was no longer friendly; it was dead serious as he got down to business. He looked from Vicioso to Roni and then said, "I take it that you have the money in the car as well. Yes?"

It looked like the caper was off. Vicioso was already thinking about how he would try the move the next time. Looking at Alejandro, Vicioso said, "To start our relationship off right I'll put my gun back in the car, but I don't normally do business like this. You know how things go."

"I don't have a gun on me." Roni said, standing up. "You can check me."

Vicioso gave Roni a funny look that no one caught. He was confused. He couldn't believe that Roni left his pistol in

214

the car. Sure enough, when Alejandro's son searched Roni he found no pistol.

"He can stay with me while you go back to the car." Alejandro placed a hand on Roni's shoulder. Roni gave Vicioso a look that told him everything was okay.

"I'll be right back." Vicioso said hesitantly. He headed back to the car wondering what the fuck Roni was up to. Shit wasn't making sense. I truly hoped the young nigga knew what the fuck he was doing.

When Vicioso made it back to the car Yusuf asked, "Where's Roni?"

"He still inside waitin' for me to come back wit' the money." Vicioso said. He told Yusuf how things went inside while he searched the front seat of the car for Roni's pistol.

Yusuf smiled. "Man, Roni got that gun on him, P. I saw him take his pistol wit' him. Don't think for one minute that he ain't strapped." Yusuf looked down the street at the house as if he could see what was going on inside.

"Yusuf, they just patted him down and he ain't have no gun on him." Vicioso said. "My eyes ain't playin' tricks on me. I know what I just saw."

"Trust me, Roni got that gun on him. I done seen him get it in tighter places."

Grabbing the shopping bag with the money in it, Vicioso said, "I gotta go back in here and handle this shit. Hold this." He gave Yusuf his pistol. "I'm just gon' go through wit' the deal."

Vicioso returned to the house. Not knowing what to expect.

"Now we can do business." Alejandro said as he looked at the shopping bag. Roni was still sitting on the sofa, nice and calm. Vicioso handed Alejandro the shopping bag and allowed him to check the money while Alejandro's son checked

Vicioso for a pistol. After that they all headed to the basement.

"You buy a lot of weight?" Alejandro asked Vicioso as he waited for his son to get the kilos from the back room.

"Yeah, but it's been hard to find good product lately." Vicioso said trying to keep his eyes on Roni.

"My product is good. The best around." Alejandro said.

"Everything should work out just right then." Vicioso said.

Moments later, Alejandro's son returned with the bricks. Roni felt as though it was game time. Just as Alejandro's son was about to sit the bricks on the table, Roni pulled his pistol in a flash. "Don't move!" Roni hissed as he stepped around Vicioso and grabbed the young Colombian dude by the shirt, putting the gun to his head. "Be easy! Real easy, I know you understand English. "

Vicioso was caught off guard, but he got right with the program in no time. He put one finger over his lips and looked Alejandro in the eyes, he then whispered, "Don't make a sound." Vicioso then searched Alejandro's son and took his 9mm. "Nobody make a sound or it's gon' be bloodshed."

"What is this?" Alejandro said, he couldn't believe what was going down.

"You know what's up, take me to the stash." Vicioso said, pointing the 9mm at Alejandro. By all means, Vicioso had no problem blowing Alejandro's brains out.

Alejandro was still in a state of shock. He looked at Roni and said, "Where did you get that gun from?"

Grabbing Alejandro by the collar, Vicioso said, "Ain't no time for questions. Let's get the coke!"

Alejandro didn't dare buck, he took Vicioso straight to the stash. In the back room, in an old metal cabinet, Vicioso uncovered seven kilos. He then shoved Alejandro to the floor and snatched down an old clothesline that ran across the room.

After tying Alejandro up, Vicioso went back into the other room where Roni had the son face down on the floor at gunpoint. Vicioso quickly tied the son up as well.

"Grab the shopping bag and let's get the fuck outta here." Vicioso said to Roni.

As Roni got down to business, the son began to scream for help. Vicioso kicked him in the mouth and said, "If you don't shut the fuck up you and your father gon' die!" The son shut his mouth.

After gathering all the goods, Roni looked at Vicioso and said, "How we gon' get out of here?"

"We goin' out the back door."

"What we gon' do about them." Roni pointed at the son with his pistol.

"We gon' leave them tied up."

Roni looked confused.

"If we shoot 'em it's gon' make too much noise. Come on, let's go." Vicioso led Roni through the back room and opened the back door. All was clear. With guns in hand, they jogged down the alley with the goods from the caper. Once they made it back to the car they both jumped in the backseat. Without question, Yusuf started up the car and made a U-turn.

Breathing hard, Roni looked out the back window to see if anyone was on their back. It looked clear. He then looked at Vicioso and said, "We shoulda killed them." Roni didn't feel right leaving any loose ends behind.

"It woulda made too much noise and we would still be shootin' our way back to the car. We don't always gotta kill everybody on a job. Sometimes it has to be in and out."

Roni thought about that for a second and still didn't feel good about it. What was done was done and they had made it out alive. That's all that was important at the end of the day.

"How the fuck did you get that pistol by them?" Vicioso asked as he looked out the back window.

Roni laughed and told Vicioso and Yusuf that when Alejandro mentioned that he didn't do business with weapons involved that he eased his pistol between the cushions of the sofa. After Roni was searched he sat back down while Vicioso went to the car. He wasn't able to get the pistol back until Vicioso returned and all the attention was on him and the money. It was a huge gamble, but it worked.

Vicioso laughed. "You gotta be the slickest little nigga I ever met."

"I told you he had that pistol on him." Yusuf said as he checked the rearview mirror.

"You got balls." Vicioso said to Roni. "I love that right there. Its nothing like having a man that's always on his toes and thinking. That's what a nigga needs out here these days."

"It is what it is." Roni smiled as he lit a Newport to calm his nerves. "I got a few tricks up my sleeve."

Back at the house after getting rid of the car they used for the caper, Vicioso, Roni and Yusuf split the goods.

"Y'all take five bricks and I'ma take five bricks for me and Avery. Sound fair." Vicioso looked from Roni to Yusuf.

They were both cool with the deal. It made all the sense in the world to them.

"Remember, what we do together goes to the grave wit' us." Vicioso said.

"I'm cool wit' that." Yusuf said, tossing a kilo from hand to hand like a heavy book.

Roni looked at his watch and said, "I need to cook some of this shit up and get it on the block." He stood up and gave

Vicioso five. Yusuf did the same. "It's always a pleasure." He said jokingly. "Can't wait for the next time."

Vicioso laughed. "No doubt, I'll talk to you two later. Be safe and keep your eyes open."

After Roni and Yusuf left, Vicioso put some weed in the air and watched a little TV. He looked at the cocaine on the table and thought about what his mother had said about America and its green paper being the reason behind the people changing and killing each other. She couldn't have been more right. The American dream robbed a man of his soul along the way. Vicioso thought about all the dirt he'd done while chasing paper. The memories of some of his deeds still haunted his mind. Thoughts of Pimpo crossed his mind and he began to think about death. Death or prison seemed to be at the end of the road for every hustler, if they stuck around long enough.

Roni pulled up around 11th Street in his Corvette and parked behind Yusuf's brand-new silver Benz 300E. The strip was pumping. They had cornered the market in no time. Yusuf was standing outside of the car talking to Short Man about business. The way Roni and Yusuf had things set up, Roni controlled the street sells by overseeing the young boys on the block through his lieutenant—Short Man. Yusuf had reached out to a few dudes he knew and established a weight operation for him and Roni. They had a nice thing going. Vicioso was impressed with their operation; he never saw that in them, but then again he never gave it any thought either.

Roni got out the car and walked over to Yusuf and Short Man; he gave them both five and said, "What's goin' on out here? How shit goin'?"

"Shit is movin' along just as planned." Yusuf said.

"That's right." Roni said. "I'm gettin' ready to take Cookie shopping; I'll be back a little later on. I just wanted to stop by and see what was up around here."

"Let me get this money for you before you go." Short Man said. He stepped off and returned in a few moments with a brown paper bag. "Here you go." He handed Roni the bag. "That's fifteen right there."

"Good lookin' out." Roni said. "I'll catch y'all later."

Roni rolled out and went to pick Cookie up. They jumped right on the highway to Atlantic City.

"You better slow this car down, boy." Cookie said as Roni took the Corvette to high speeds. "You act like you got a license. If the police pull us over they gon' lock your ass up."

Roni laughed. "We okay, baby."

A short while later, Roni and Cookie were in Atlantic City shopping. Their first stop was the Gucci shop, where Roni dropped a few thousand. After hitting a few more spots they hit the jewelry store.

"Roni," Cookie said, "You don't have to spend all this money on me to show me you love me. You do know that, right?"

Looking at diamond rings, Roni kissed her cheek and said, "It's not to show you I love you, it's 'cause I love you, plus we can afford it now."

Cookie smiled and shook her head. At the counter with the saleswoman, Roni had Cookie try on a huge diamond ring. The white lady seemed like she didn't take the young couple serious. "This ring is $15,000." She said with a fake smile. Her expression made it clear that she thought Roni couldn't afford it.

Roni and Cookie caught her vibe. Roni laughed and pulled a thick knot of cash from his leather coat and said, "Can we

pay cash? Would that make you feel better?" He shook his head with a smirk.

The saleswoman looked like she had just farted in public. "Uh... uh, yes. You can pay in cash, sir."

Cookie almost laughed in the woman's face. Roni paid for the ring and dropped another $10,000 on a Cuban link chain with a diamond covered Jesus piece.

As Roni and Cookie headed back to the car with their hands full of shopping bags, Roni looked at her and said, "Money ain't a thing."

After dropping Cookie off at home, Roni headed home. He was still living with his mother and stepfather, but was in the process of getting his own place now that he was getting paper together.

Roni walked in the house with his hands full of shopping bags and found his mother and stepfather sitting on the sofa in the living room. They had concerned looks on their faces. Roni got a bad feeling in his gut as he sat the shopping bags down and slowly shut the door behind him. He looked at his mother and said, "Ma, what's wrong?"

His mother didn't respond. She just looked down at the floor. Roni's heart began to pound.

"Roni," his stepfather said, "You can't stay here anymore. We're sorry. You have to find somewhere else to stay; your mother and I can't deal with it anymore.'"

"What's wrong?" Roni frowned.

"Someone broke into the house. They only went to your room."

Roni instantly thought about his money. He had $70,000 stashed under his bed in shoes boxes. His knees felt weak as he thought about the money.

"Pack your things and leave by tomorrow." His stepfather said.

Roni looked at his mother who had tears in her eyes. All he could do was nod his head. The last thing he ever wanted to do was bring danger to his mother's doorstep. That's what came with the game. He knew it was time to move out. More money, more problems. "I understand." Roni said. "I'll go pack my stuff up." He looked at his mother one last time and then ran upstairs to his room. The whole room was a mess; it looked like the feds had raided it. He looked under his bed and found that his money was gone. His guns were gone. He was hit for everything. Heating with anger, Roni jumped on the phone and called Yusuf.

"Somebody broke into my people's house." Roni said. "They hit me for my whole stash, guns and all." He was shaking his head in disbelief.

"No bullshit?" Yusuf said. "You don't got no idea who did it?"

"Nah, man. Not right now." He let out a frustrated sigh. "That's everything! I'm back to square one. What the fuck am I supposed to do?"

"Don't worry about it. We still gon' be cool. Shit is still going smooth. I got you. That shit ain't gon hurt us at all."

"I gotta move out. My peoples want me to leave. I'll be over your house in a few." Roni hung up and sighed as he began to pack his stuff.

CHAPTER 19

A **little over a week later there was still no word** on who had broken into Roni's house. However, the show went on. He, Yusuf, and Vicioso tore off some Dominicans for fifteen kilos to keep things flowing and to make up for the loss.

On another note, Serio's trial was about to start in New York. All the drug charges against him had been dropped and he was only facing two murder beefs. One of his workers was the main witness against him; the worker was also running his Red Hook spot while Serio was locked up. Shit was fucked up.

Rob Base and D.J. E-Z Rock's hit, It Takes Two, was pumping through the speakers of the dark-green Park Avenue as it made its way up I-95. Vicioso was behind the wheel, Roni in the back seat and Yusuf was riding shotgun. Three the hard way. It was time to clean house.

"We gon' be in and out like a robbery." Vicioso said as he blew weed smoke in the air. He was taking a huge risk by returning to New York, but for Serio it was worth it. However, Vicioso felt good about having Roni and Yusuf along with him for the job. He trusted that they could handle their end of the deal.

"Be careful wit' that weed." Yusuf said. "Troopers on the highway."

"I got you nigga." Roni said.

"Ay, P, you sure this nigga gon' be right in the projects, even though he telling on your peoples like that?" Yusuf asked. "That don't make no sense to me."

"Yeah, he gon' be right there. You know how these bastards think." Vicioso said. "Serio got him thinkin' everything cool. The raas don't even know that Serio know he's talkin'."

A short while later, they arrived in New York and checked into a Manhattan hotel.

Looking out the window down at the bright city, Vicioso said, "We gon' wait for it to get dark and then we gon' take care of business."

Just after 11:00 P.M., Vicioso and his two Philly comrades headed for Red Hook, strapped with Uzis. If all went well they could be back in Philly before sunrise. However, they knew they had to be on point, one wrong move and the FBI would be right on their asses. The manhunt for Visio so was still very much in effect in New York.

"Y'all gotta keep your eyes open." Vicioso said as they got closer to Red Hook. "Shit might get out of hand around here. Shit goes down at any time around here."

"Just let us know who is who and we got your back. Same shit, different day. This shit like clock work." Roni said, looking around, very alert.

Vicioso smiled as he drove down Columbia Road. He parked and scanned the area. Things were just how he remembered them, except for a few new faces. "All we gotta do now is wait for a little while." Vicioso said.

"What kinda car you say that nigga drive?" Roni asked, looking out the back window. Always on point.

"A red BMW," Vicioso turned and looked out the back window. "Yeah, that's him right there."

MONEY AIN'T EVERYTHING

The BMW drove right past them and parked a few cars ahead. Two dudes were inside.

"We gon' let them get out first, then we gon' move." Vicioso said as he checked his Uzi one more time. His heartbeat began to speed up.

Serio's worker, Martez, stepped out of the BMW with a comrade of his. Martez looked around. His comrade was carrying a shopping bag. Vicioso, Roni, and Yusuf got down to business and jumped out of the Park Avenue. Martez saw the hit coming and tried to pull his pistol as he began to jog backward into the street. "You motherfucker!" he yelled.

Yusuf opened fire first and sent a fully automatic burst of gunfire into his chest, dropping him. More gunfire hit the air from other directions. Yusuf ran up and stood over Martez, sprayed his body one last time without hesitation. Martez's comrade dropped the shopping bag and pulled his pistol, he even got off a few shots before Roni and Vicioso cut him down with flames spitting from their weapons. Workers began to come out of Serio's coke spot firing at Vicioso and his Philly comrades. They exchanged fire for a few intense seconds. Roni ran over and put two more in the head of the dude that was carrying the shopping bag; he then snatched the shopping bag and ran back to the car with Vicioso and Yusuf as they all continued to return fire into the projects. Bullets flew by their heads. As they pulled off, bullets crashed through the back window as they went flying down the street and around the corner, leaving two bullet-riddled bodies behind.

"What's in the shopping bag?" Yusuf asked as they flew through the intersection trying to avoid swiping a car.

Looking in the shopping bag, Roni said, "looks like a brick capped up."

CHAPTER 20

You're one of a kind, Vicioso." Serio said over the phone from jail. His tone was upbeat. His murder charges had been dismissed in New York. However, he was found guilty on weapons charges. His lawyer assured him that he'd get probation for that. Vicioso had saved the day.

"Ain't no thing. You know that." Vicioso said, sitting in Yasmin's living room in Philly.

"I'll be home in no time." Serio said. "Things gon' be right back in motion too. You know how I do."

Vicioso laughed. "Yeah, I know you gon' have some kind of game plan after sitting up in that cell thinking all day. I already know you been playing chess in your head."

"That's exactly what I been doin' too. I got way off track after I started getting' money, but I'm 'bout to take it back to the basics. No shorts is my mind set."

Serio and Vicioso spoke for a while and then Vicioso put Yasmin back on the phone. When she got off the phone with Serio she looked at Vicioso and said, "I guess everything's gonna be alright after all."

"I told you that." Vicioso smiled as he stood up to leave. "Make sure you send that money to my mother before four." Vicioso had been sending money back home to his mother so that she could buy a house and move out the projects. It was a duty that he took pride in. He wanted to do all that he could do to ease the pain of Pimpo's death

226

"I'm goin' to do that as soon as you leave." Yasmin said.

Avery was standing on his mother's porch watching his young boys pump coke at the end of the block. Furniture workers were also moving in the new living room set that he'd just spent $10,000 on. Their big truck was double-parked right in front of the house. Vicioso pulled up and parked a few spaces down from Avery's house in a Jeep Cherokee.

"What's up, big boy?" Vicioso said as he stepped on the porch and gave Avery five. "How things lookin'?"

"Everything runnin' smooth." Avery said.

"Where Shawn at?" Vicioso asked.

He down the street on top of business." Avery watched a few cars ride by. "Some money came up short yesterday."

"That's been happening more and more lately." Vicioso looked down the street and saw Shawn. "I need to check on that." Vicioso stepped off and headed down the block.

Roni and Yusuf pulled up a few minutes later in Roni's Corvette. They parked and got out smoking weed. Avery smiled and shook his head as they walked up on the porch; they were really getting paid now. "What's goin' on around 11th Street?" Avery asked as he took a seat on the front steps.

"Everything movin'." Roni said.

"Movin' faster than expected." Yusuf said. "We gon' need some more coke before the day's out."

Roni and Yusuf went on to tell Avery how they had things running around 11th Street.

Slowly, a dark-blue van came down Marvine Street, cruising right by Vicioso and two young boys. Seeing a Colombian in the driver's seat made Vicioso's antennas go up. Colombians didn't ride through Marvine Street. As Vicioso went for his Ruger the van suddenly stopped right behind the furniture truck and five Colombians jumped out spraying machine guns. Bullets were flying everywhere. Vicioso and the young boys began firing at the Colombian from the blind side and a violent gun battle ensued. Roni and Yusuf fired from the porch as the furniture workers dropped a black leather sofa and ran in the house for cover. All hell broke loose and gunfire was the only sound for blocks. The Colombians sprayed Avery's mother's house with bullets, trying to hit Roni and Yusuf.

Vicioso and the young boys dropped two Colombians as they danced behind parked cars firing their pistols. The other Colombians stood their ground in the middle of the street, they didn't expect to be fired on from both sides. After a few intense moments, the remaining Colombians jumped back in the van and sped away, taking heavy fire from the back as Vicioso, the young boys, Roni and Yusuf flooded the middle of the street firing rounds and leaving shells everywhere.

Once the van bent the corner, Vicioso looked back at the two Colombians that were lying in the street bleeding. One was still alive, but he was hit badly. Vicioso threw Roni the keys to his truck and said, "Get the truck!"

As Roni ran to get the truck, Vicioso told all the young boys to get off the block. Roni pulled the truck into the middle of the street with screeching tires. Vicioso told Yusuf to help him drag the bleeding Colombian inside the truck. Yusuf thought twice about it; he was in a rush to get the fuck out of dodge.

Vicioso sensed that Yusuf was second-guessing. "Just roll with what I'm sayin', I know what I'm doing. We need this bastard alive."

"What the fuck y'all doin'?" Roni shouted in disbelief as he looked back and forth up and down the street. Sirens were already in the air. He thought Vicioso had lost his mind. Was he trying to get them locked up, Roni thought.

Vicioso pulled the Colombian into the back of the truck and Yusuf slammed the door.

"I wanna know exactly who sent these muthafuckas!"

Vicioso, Roni and Yusuf took the Colombian to one of their stash houses in North Philly where they questioned him about who'd sent him and the others. The Colombian was in extreme pain from the bullets in his back, but he still withheld the information. But after being beaten close to death he told his capturer that Alejandro had sent the hit squad. After that the Colombian was shot dead and disposed of along with Vicioso's Jeep Cherokee.

Just after 12:00 A.M., in a gray Caprice Classic, strapped with Uzis and wearing bulletproof vests, Vicioso, Roni and Yusuf headed down Alejandro's block on a mission. However, there was no one outside. As they drove by Alejandro's house they could see lights on inside. Roni was looking around trying to figure out where all the Colombians were; they were normally selling weight on the block. Vicioso made a U-turn at the end of the block and doubled back. He quickly cut off the lights and looked around carefully.

"We gon' spray the house up since they wanna play games." Vicioso said. "Let 'em know we mean business."

"Somethin' don't feel right." Yusuf said from the backseat. He had a bad feeling like it was more to the situation than they could see.

Suddenly, armed Colombians began to come out of the woodwork on both sides of the streets. They were moving in packs like soldiers. They opened fire on the Caprice. The loud popping gunfire exploded like heavy machines. Vicioso started the car with lighting speed and gunned the car for the end of the block while Roni and Yusuf sprayed their Uzis out the windows.

It seemed like the Colombians were everywhere. There had to be at least twenty of them. Vicioso hit the alley at the end of the block and fishtailed as he took the car flying through two intersections. He made a hard right and gunned the car down a small side street. With every bump the car bounced up and down violently throwing them around the car. A red Honda was right behind the Caprice, firing at it. Roni and Yusuf leaned out the window and fired back at the Honda as the car chase covered more blocks. Finally, the Honda turned off and stopped chasing them as they got closer to their section of town. It seemed to back off like a cop car chasing another car into another jurisdiction.

"The streets of North Philly and the Logan area seem to be the battlefield for what police are calling a bloody turf war between Colombian drug gangs and local thugs that has turned the city upside down in the last two weeks. ..." the anchorwoman said as she reported on yet another set of murders in Alejandro's neighborhood. An hour earlier, Vicioso, Roni and Yusuf had went through the block and murdered two of Alejandro's worker. Their plan was to shut Alejandro's operation down since their failed hit had cops crawling all over Marvine Street and 11th Street. Vicioso was using an age-old game plan: Fuck shit up and kill the opponents in order to cut off the competition. In the last week alone, for three days back to back, there had been a number of shootings. Colombians had murdered a few of Avery's young boys, they'd also shot up Avery's mother's house; although she wasn't home at the time. In response, Vicioso, Roni and Yusuf used Alejandro's block for target practice and left three dead. They'd traded in their Uzis for AK-47s. Shit was out of control and no one seemed to be making money. On top of that, even though Vicioso was tripping off of it, the feds were paying very close attention to the situation.

"Somethin' gon' have to give." Avery said to Vicioso as they sat in the living room of Roni's new apartment. "We ain't gettin' no money and we done turned the whole neighborhood into a war zone. This shit ain't good for you either. Don't forget that you on the run. The heat ain't good at all, P."

"Sometimes shit gets heated. It comes with the life." Vicioso said.

"No bullshit." Roni cut in, smoking a Newport with a beer in his hand. "What we supposed to do? Sit back and do nothin'? It is what it is."

"We damn sure can't let them muthafuckas kill us." Yusuf said, playing with an Uzi.

"They got a point, Avery." Vicioso smiled, he loved how firm Roni and Yusuf stood against the odds. He was growing to love them both overnight.

"We need to have a sit down wit' the Colombians and—" Avery began.

"And tell them what?" Vicioso cut him off. "What can we say ... oh, we robbed your spot and killed some of your peoples. Please forgive us. Let's be real here."

Roni and Yusuf laughed.

"Come on, man, I'm serious. Hear me out. What I'm sayin' is this: Them Colombians are all about makin' money, and they fucked up right now too because of this war. If we could talk to them and let them know that this shit ain't gon' stop and ain't nobody gon' get no money I bet you they'll want to talk things out. They'll come to terms. All this heat ain't good for nobody, it's bad for business. This shit gotta stop. Look at y'all. Y'all don't even go outside in the daytime no more." Avery pushed his point for a while longer.

"I don't know, man." Vicioso shook his head. "I think it's too late for all that."

"No bullshit." Roni said.

Avery sighed.

Jairo was in Miami putting together a 400-kilogram deal when he got the news from Philly that four of his weight spots had been raided. One-hundred-fifty kilos and countless weapons had been lost, twelve people had been arrested. Jairo had underestimated the situation with Vicioso, Roni, and Yusuf. It was costing him a lot of money and bringing a lot of heat. Jairo hadn't seen such non-stop violence since he left Colombia. Something had to be done. He refused to let all that he had worked for go to shit because of some small-time drug war. There was a bigger picture as far as he was concerned. The cocaine business was a violent business, but at the end of the day there was also millions and billions of dollars in the business as well.

In his luxury suite, Jairo phoned Alejandro and grilled him about the recent events in Philly. Alejandro stressed the fact that he was doing all he could to put an end to the war, but their foes were operating like street thugs with no central location where they could hit.

"Alejandro!" Jairo snapped with impatience. "Enough with the fucking excuses! I want results! If you can't get me results then I'll find someone who can. I don't care what you have to do, but have that shit in order when I get back! Do you understand me?"

"I understand. Jairo, I was thinking that we should try to talk to these thugs, try to put an end to this mess before we are all in jail or dead. No one is winning right now. We are just killing and losing money. It's not getting us anywhere."

"What is there to talk about, Alejandro? All the fucking money that I'm losing?!" Jairo was in no mood for games.

"They are losing money too. We should try to talk to them so we can get things in order. If not we'll be ruined. This war is bringing too much police attention."

Jairo thought about the situation for a second. Things were out of control. "These thugs have some nerve." Jairo smiled and shook his head. "They're causing me a lot of problems. If we can't get rid of them we might as well sit down with them and try to put an end to this mess. Set up a meeting."

Days later, a meeting was setup by Alejandro. He'd sent a woman to make contact with Avery who explained that the Colombians wanted the killing to stop because it was fucking up the money flow. Vicioso, Roni, and Yusuf were very apprehensive about the whole situation, but they decided to go through with the meeting in hopes of putting the war to rest so they could get back to making money. Their pockets were hurting.

"I still don't feel good about this shit for real. I don't trust nobody that tried to kill us." Roni said to Vicioso as they headed to pick Yusuf up in Vicioso's BMW; they were all going to the meeting with the Colombians. The meeting was to take place in the restaurant of the Four Seasons hotel. Roni lit a Newport and said, "This shit might be a set up. You know what I mean."

"I feel the same way, but we gotta at least try it." Vicioso said. "Shit is out of hand and ain't nobody winnin' for real. Avery's right. Nothin' good gon' come out of this shit."

Roni shook his head. "I just don't see the Colombians overlookin' the fact that we killed their people and took their coke. They going against everything they stand for."

Vicioso said, "The coke we took ain't mean shit to these peoples, they do test runs wit' more shit then we took. Business is always more important to them. As far as the ones we shot, that ain't nothin' but workers. They can always be replaced. What can't be replaced is their operation if the cops destroy it because of all the killin' that's goin' on. Never forget that these people got businesses to run that's far bigger than anything else."

"Yeah, I see where you comin' from, but we'll see how things play out." Roni blew smoke into the air.

Vicioso, Roni and Yusuf stepped on the scene early to check out the layout. They needed to see how things were looking. They put two young boys on post in the garage with Uzis and told them to watch all cars and people that came in and out of the spot. They put three more young boys inside the hotel with .45 automatic and spread them out in the restaurant. If any foul play was to go down things were sure to get bloody.

The restaurant was real laid back with a few white people having lunch. Roni and Yusuf took a table off to the side, right behind the table where Vicioso was sitting.

Moments later, Jairo strolled in with three of his men. He directed them to take a seat two tables away. They were all dressed in suits, yet still had rough looks like they were down with the cartels. Jairo looked more like a businessman than a drug lord. He nodded and took a seat at the table with Vicioso. Taking a look around the restaurant he could tell that Roni and Yusuf were with Vicioso, as well as the young boys. For a few tense moments nothing was said. The other lunchtime diners didn't have a clue what was going on. The danger that was at hand was laying dormant by all means.

"So you are the young man that's been costing me so much money for the last few weeks, eh?" Jairo said in his thick Colombian accent. "I thought you would be older." Jairo took a good look at Vicioso and said, "How old are you?"

"Twenty-three." Vicioso said. He wanted to skip the small talk.

Jairo looked over at Roni and Yusuf and said, "I thought all of your people were Panamanian."

"Nah, just me."

Jairo smiled. "Out of all my years in this business and a Panamanian kid causes me all these problems." He poured himself a glass of water and took a sip. "Let's talk business now."

Vicioso nodded in agreement as he moved in his chair slightly to adjust his pistol as he glanced at Jairo's men out the corner of his eyes. He would be lying to say that he wasn't nervous.

"You and your people have taken what does not belong to you and killed some of my people. Yes?" Jairo folded his hands, noticing that Vicioso was watching his every move.

"We tried to do clean business wit' your people, but they got disrespectful and sold us bad product. We couldn't accept that. Where I'm from you don't let nobody take anything from you and that was taking something from me. I can't stand for that." There was no remorse in Vicioso's voice. "I personally tried to talk things out. That didn't work. What was I supposed to do?"

"So you killed my people and took my cocaine? That was your answer?" Jairo looked from Vicioso to Roni and Yusuf and back.

"What would you do?" Vicioso leaned forward to emphasize his questions. There was no fear in his voice.

Jairo nodded, "You are an old soul, and I see your point. Nevertheless, I want us to stop this war. It is bad for business. What must we do to put an end to it?"

Vicioso shrugged. "You call your people off and I call mine off. It's not complex at all. What do you think about that?"

"And the cocaine that you took?"

"We both know that was small fries to you. Let's be real."

"But it was still mine, nevertheless. Where I'm from, what's mine is mine. I know you can understand that, correct?" Jairo raised an eyebrow.

"You're right, it was yours. But at the time I'm not in a position to just pull that kind of product or money out of my pocket. But since I did take from you and we are comin' to the table, I'm willin' to work somethin' out. It's your call."

"You are strong with the blacks? Yes?"

"Yeah, I'm strong wit' my people. Why?" Vicioso rubbed his chin, wondering where the conversation was going.

"Let's say we end this war by starting a business friendship? How's that sound?"

Vicioso couldn't believe his ears. "Are you serious?"

"Very much so." Jairo said. "How about I front you fifty keys, for starters, and you pay me back what you took and we do business from there. That should make everything right and we can both make money. It will be a clean slate for us both and we all go back to business."

Vicioso smiled. "Shit, I can't beat that." He knew it had to be a catch to the whole situation, but for the time Vicioso planned to play it all out.

Jairo extended his hand and said, "Deal?"

"No question."

"All animosity is behind us." Jairo said as he stood up.

Walking back to the car, on point, with Roni and Yusuf, Vicioso thought about how things had went with Jairo. Life had a way of throwing curve balls that were unforeseen. Nevertheless, Vicioso didn't try to wrestle with fate; he felt that he was always better to play the hand you were dealt.

"So what's the word? Tell me somethin'." Roni asked. He couldn't wait until they got to the car.

"We got a connect."

236

CHAPTER 21

Weeks passed smoothly after the meeting with Jairo. The new business relationship was working out well. At first, Vicioso, Roni, and Yusuf were on edge dealing with the Colombian, but after the first four or five transactions everything was cool. A mutual goal kept things clean and that goal was to get paid. Vicioso was back in position. All it took was a little time. He established a nice core of clientele and was focused on stacking his paper. He knew he had to take advantage of the connect if he wanted to get his stash back like it was when he was dealing with Cortez. In order to do that he had to stay focused.

Roni and Yusuf were on top of the world, seeing more money than they'd ever dreamed of. They had the 11th Street spot doing $15,000 a day, strong. That was aside from the weight they were moving. Some days, they were moving fifteen kilos in total, between the two of them. The money was coming in faster than they could count it; they were living it up at 19-years-old. The more Vicioso tried to get them to save their money the more they spent. Trips to Atlantic City and New York, dropping tens of thousands on shopping sprees, copping $60,000 cars on impulse, it was all at their fingertips. By the end of 1988, Roni and Yusuf both had homes in New Jersey. The sky was the limit. Not once did they think about a rainy day.

Serio came home in the summer of '88 on probation; he and Yasmin moved to Maryland and left Brooklyn behind. Serio needed a new start. It was the only way he could get his operation back on track smoothly. Vicioso hit Serio off with ten bricks when he got out of jail. Overnight, Serio was on top of his game in Maryland and had a whole new La Banda crew that was getting money in Forestville, MD, and parts of Southeast, D.C. Serio and Vicioso rarely got to see each other at this point. Things were moving too fast, and Vicioso was trying to stay far away from D.C. and New York due to the fact that the FBI was still looking for him, their focus was in those areas.

Thinking about how things were going, Vicioso stood in the doorway of his house and watched Niecy pull up the driveway in a red '89 BMW. Melly, Vicioso's mother, was in the passenger seat. Melly seemed amazed as she glanced at the beautiful home. It was a big day for him. To see his mother in person, to see the joy in her eyes, it gave Vicioso a proud feeling to be able to bring his mother to the U.S. to see him.

"You two have such a nice place here." Melly said to Niecy.

"Thank you." Niecy said.

Vicioso welcomed his mother through the front door with open arms and a tight hug. He kissed her and held her tight. He missed her more than word could express. It had been close to three years since he'd seen her last. "How was your flight?" He asked as Niecy took Melly's coat.

"Cold." Melly said. "How can you live in such a cold place? It feels like Alaska or something." She looked around the spacious house and was impressed.

Vicioso laughed. "I still can't stand the cold myself, ma. I had to get used to it though." He stepped around her. "Let me get your bags." He went to the car and returned with her bags.

While Niecy put dinner together, Vicioso showed his mother around the house. It was a dream house, like something out of the movies. Big front yard, big back yard with a pool, two-car garage, the works. It cost him $300,000, but at the time he was "gettin' it."

During dinner, Melly and Niecy talked to each other so much that Vicioso felt left out. Niecy told Melly how things were and how much she missed Panama. Although they had much more in the U.S., there was nothing like home. Niecy longed for the day when they would be able to go back to Panama. She felt the longer Vicioso stayed in the U.S. the greater his chances were of getting killed or going to prison for life. Melly felt the same way. Yet and still they knew and understood that Vicioso was caught up in what he was doing and that being as though it was providing a better life for him and his that there was nothing much they could really say about it.

After dinner, Niecy went to take a shower and left Vicioso and Melly downstairs in the living room. Vicioso and his mother talked about everything. They had one of those real heart to hearts between a mother and her son. He told her how he planned to make the best out of his situation, for what it was worth. He had nothing to hide from his mother. As they talked, tears began to fall from Melly's eyes. She'd spotted a picture of Pimpo on Vicioso's living room wall. The picture brought back tons of memories and emotions. Memories of times when Vicioso and Pimpo were young, sweet and innocent. Before the way of the world had gotten a hold of them. She would gave anything to get those days back.

"What's wrong, ma?" Vicioso slid closer to her on the sofa. "Why you cryin'?"

She wiped tears from her eyes and said, "This is not how it's supposed to be, Harvey." She continued to gaze at the picture of Pimpo. She pointed at the picture. "He looks so young and full of life. His life was cut so short, and for what? I wanted more for him. I wanted more for you. I prayed for the Lord to protect you both."

Vicioso looked at the picture. Rubbing his mother's back, he said, "I ask myself the same thing, Ma. Life deals us bad hands sometimes. I still haven't gotten over what happened to him. I never wanted anything to happen to him either." Vicioso shook his head and sighed. Thinking about Pimpo always made he realize how dangerous the game was that he was in. Life was short and in the blink of an eye it could all be over. That was the price one had to pay when their number was called.

"Is all this worth it, Harvey?" Melly wiped more tears from her face as she waved a hand around the house. "Is the money that you make here in America worth all that comes with it? The death? The trouble? The looking over your shoulder everywhere you turn? Is the stress worth it? Look at all that you have. How long will it last? How long will it be yours? Until the American police or FBI come take it away? Look at what happened to Pimpo, he didn't even get a chance to see this much. Just think, I have the nice house that you bought for me, and I love it, but I don't have you there with me, and I don't know if you will ever make it back home. You may never even see the house with your own eyes. That hurts, Harvey." Melly stopped talking for a second and began to pull herself together. "I don't mean to cry and add to your stress. I'm sorry, I don't want to ruin such a special reunion. I didn't plan to come all the way up here to talk

about this. I know that you have enough problems. Seeing the picture of Pimpo just brought back so many memories."

"I understand, ma." Vicioso nodded, still rubbing her back. "Don't worry about it. I need to hear the things you have to say. They keep me focused on what's really important in this world. It's so easy for me to get caught up in what I do to survive."

"You are really living well though, Harvey. I must admit that. You have done well for yourself." Melly tried to change the subject. "It's much different than Santa Cruz." She forced a little smile. "How much did you pay for this place?"

"Close to three-hundred-thousand."

Melly looked around. "Three-hundred-thousand, plus the cars in the driveway. That's a lot of money." She paused for a second. "How much money do you think you've made up here?"

After a second of thought, Vicioso said, "Not sure, but I know I've seen a lot. I don't even want to try to count all the money that has gone through my hands. Why?"

"With the way you're living you should have enough money to stop what you're doing. This stuff can't last forever, Harvey. From the looks of things, I'm sure you've made over a million by now. What do you have to show for it? Do you something put away for yourself?"

Vicioso tried to calculate the cash that had flowed through his hands since the early Red Hook days. It was no doubt that he had made Serio over a million dollars during those days. He'd seen a lot of cash, but he was not in the million-dollar bracket. However, he should have been.

"Listen to me, Harvey," she placed a hand on his thigh. "You have been up here risking your life for almost three years now. I don't know what it's been like, but I know this: You need to cash in and get out. Put something up for the future. Start thinking about tomorrow. Start making your exit. If you never listened to anything I have ever told, please listen now. I won't beat you in the head with what I'm talking about, I'm going to say that and I'm done. Just take heed to what I'm saying."

Vicioso nodded in agreement.

"What happened to your plan to leave this country and come back home? Your time here is running out anyway." Melly looked him in the eyes.

"I'm caught up right now, but I'm gettin' it together. I just need a little more time." Vicioso said.

A little more time is all he felt he needed to put himself in a position to leave the country with enough money to justify to himself the reason for all he'd been through thus far.Snow covered 11th Street. Drug traffic on the block was in full swing. Since the war with the Colombians, security was at an all-time high. Roni and Yusuf had bought Uzis, Tec-9s and other weapons for the crew. Armed lookouts were inconspicuously positioned up and down the block. Marvine Street was no different.

At the end of the block there was a gas truck, it had been on the scene for days and no one seemed to be paying it attention. Inside the gas truck, the feds were watching the whole operation; Roni and Yusuf were really Big Time now. Pictures were being taking and phones were being tapped.

Melly stayed in the U.S. a little over a week. Vicioso treated her like a queen. He'd taken her shopping and showed her all around. When it was time for her to go back home she had gifts for everybody back home. Vicioso also sent her back home with $100,000 in new bills that she could carry on her person. It was like putting money in the bank.

A few days later, Vicioso walked into the stash house in North Philly and found Roni and Yusuf hard at work, cooking

242

up cocaine. Roni was at the stove whipping and mixing while Yusuf was at the dining room table weighing and wrapping.

"Teamwork." Vicioso joked. "That's a beautiful thing."

Roni and Yusuf laughed.

"We just takin' care of business." Yusuf said. "What's brings you this way?"

"Shawn got some dudes he been dealin' wit' that want three bricks. I ain't have it on hand." Vicioso walked to the back room and returned with a shopping bag.

"Them dudes Shawn been dealin' wit' been spendin' a lot of money, huh?" Roni asked, with his eyebrow raised.

"Yeah," Vicioso said. "They been spendin' on a regular." He sat on the sofa and turned the TV on. What was on the news grabbed everybody's attention. What police were calling one of the largest drug lords in the Philly area and ten of his closest associates had been arrested and charged with running an international narcotics ring that stretched from Philly all the way to Colombia.

"… The investigation into the international drug trafficking ring was sparked when drug enforcement agents intercepted a shipment of more than 500 kilograms of cocaine bound for U.S. streets, coming straight from Colombia," the news reporter said. "DEA sources say this was the second largest shipment of cocaine to be intercepted within the last year. Both are allegedly attributed to the drug ring led by this man"—a picture of Jairo appeared on the screen—"Whom authorities are calling Jairo Diaz. …"

"Y'all see this shit?!" Vicioso looked at Roni and Yusuf with disbelief. They had walked over to look at the news. Just as things were starting to go smooth adversity had to rear its ugly head.

"Damn!" Roni shook his head. He never got close to the Colombians, but he liked their business relationship. All he could think about was the fact that their connect was now cut off. Once again.

"We right back at square one now." Yusuf said with a sigh.

Vicioso just shook his head. His mind was on something different. He was concerned about the investigation that had led to Jairo's arrest. It was no telling if the feds were on everybody that had dealings with Jairo. In Vicioso's mind, he knew his time in Philly was up. It was time to start plotting his next move.

CHAPTER 22

For almost three months, Roni and Yusuf tried to keep things moving without the Colombian connect, and without Vicioso who'd left town with Niecy. Yusuf knew a few dudes from West Philly so he and Roni copped a few bricks from them. They didn't like the coke or the prices so they moved on. They did this a few times and moved on. They found another dude in North Philly but he would only serve them five bricks at a time. They rolled with that for a second and then the heat came down hard and heavy. FBI agents and local police raided Roni's house just before dawn on a Wednesday morning.

Agent Smith, who'd been investigating drug activity on 11th Street and Marvine Street, was standing inside Roni's walk-in closet admiring the fresh collection of designer clothes. Roni's wardrobe was worth more than the agent's yearly salary. As other agents and cops roamed the house, tearing it up, a young white agent walked up to Smith and said, "All we've found is a weapon and a safe full of money."

Agent Smith turned to face the young agent and saw him holding an AR-15 assault rifle. "That's it? No drugs? Nothing?"

"That's it." The young agent shrugged. "The place is clean and there's no sign of Mr. Edwards or his girlfriend." The young agent handed off the AR-15 to a cop that was walking by.

"How much money was in the safe?" Smith asked as he tried on one of Roni's $4,000 leather coats.

"Close to five-hundred-thousand dollars. We're not sure yet."

"Any news from the other raids? Was the Panamanian arrested? That's who we really want. We need his ass." Smith asked.

"No, sir. In fact, it looks like he's left the area. The guy must have a sixth sense about us. The house was clean and looked like no one had been inside in weeks."

Agent smith shook his head. "Were any arrest made?"

"Mr. Avery White was arrested; we caught him with $150,000 and a handgun in his house. A few teenagers were arrested on 11th Street. Mr. Edwards' cousin was also arrested in their stash house. Close to $600,000 was found in Mr. Battle's house along with an Uzi and a few other handguns."

"Yusuf Battle?" Smith asked, hanging up the leather coat.

"Yes."

"Well it looks like we still have some work to do."

Roni was on his way home from the club and was dead tired and drunk. He couldn't wait to get in bed. He could sleep for a few hours before he had to go pick Cookie up from her grandmother's house to take her to get her hair done. As Roni began to turn down his street he saw the feds all over the place. He quickly bypassed the street and grabbed his car phone. His heart was pounding as paranoia began to set in. All he could think about was what Vicioso had said about the feds being onto them. Roni checked his rearview mirror to make sure the feds weren't on his back. All of a sudden he didn't feel drunk anymore. Money was on his mind now. All of his money was inside his house, except for a little bit he had stashed in his North Philly apartment. "Fuck!" He shouted as

he slammed his fist against the wheel. He called Yusuf on his car phone.

"Where you at?" Roni asked with a sense of urgency.

"On my way home. Why what's up?" Yusuf asked with the music blasting in his car.

"Don't go home. The feds done raided my house, you already know what that mean they up in your shit."

"What?!"

"Yeah, you heard me."

"Oh, fuck nah!" Yusuf turned the blasting music down. "I don't believe this shit."

"Vicioso was right." Roni sighed and lit a Newport.

"What the fuck we gon' do now?"

"I don't know. Meet me at the Days Inn." Roni said

A short while later, Roni and Yusuf were in a New Jersey hotel smoking weed, trying to figure out their next move. They'd already learned about what spots were raided and who'd been arrested. Everything was falling apart at once. To make matters even worse, they were wanted men and they were damn near broke. Their options were limited. The walls were closing in.

"I don't know what the fuck we supposed to do now." Roni said. "We broke! On top of the feds gon' be all over us."

"We gotta get the fuck away from Philly, I know that much." Yusuf blew smoke in the air. His mind was made up: He wasn't going to jail, not without a fight.

"I got a hundred-thousand stashed at the apartment. We need to try to get that. That will be enough to make a move with."

"I think we should try to hook up wit' Panama. We can lay low in VA for a while. Somewhere down there."

"That sounds good, but I gotta check on Cookie. I know she worried sick." Roni said.

"Cool, but whatever we gon' do we gotta make it happen quick. The longer we stay here the easier its gon' be to go to jail. I ain't trying to see the inside of a cell no time soon."

Cookie couldn't sit still; she was worried sick and didn't know where Roni was or what the hell was going on. She'd learned of the raids and hadn't heard from Roni yet. She'd beeped him over and over but got no answer.

Sitting in her old bedroom at her grandmother's house, Cookie watched the news and saw the feds raiding all the drug spots that Roni was connected to. They kept flashing his face on the screen as well as Yusuf's and Vicioso's, the reporter was saying that they were armed and dangerous. When the phone beside her bed rang, Cookie jumped. She answered the phone sounding like she'd been crying.

"I'm on my way to get you." Roni said.

"Roni! Where are you? Are you okay? What's goin' on?" Cookie fired question after question.

"I'll tell you everything when I get there. Be ready." Roni hung up.

In a rush, Cookie got herself together and sat in the living room waiting for Roni to show up. Minutes later she heard a horn blow outside. Looking out the window, she saw Roni's Corvette. She ran to the front door and snatched it open. Just as she stepped outside, FBI agents came from everywhere, like swarming bees. They'd been waiting and watching. They even had the phone tapped at Cookie's grandmother's house. Cookie's heart sank as she saw close to twenty agents with their guns drawn run down on Roni's car. She screamed, "Noooo!!!" She started to cry and scream as agents snatched the driver's side door open. "Get off him! "Get off him!" She yelled. "Don't hurt him!" She sobbed. She ran for the car.

"You don't gotta be beatin' on him like that." Two agents grabbed Cookie. "Get off me, muthafucka!"

"Miss, calm down or we'll have to arrest you." An agent said.

"It's not him! It's not him! Another agent called out. The agents began to back off the driver. One of Roni's workers was driving the car. The driver was in his late teens and looked a little bit like Roni.

Grabbing the teenager by the collar of his coat and snatching him off the ground, a tall white agent snarled, "Where the fuck is Edwards, you-son-of-a-bitch?! And you better have something to say."

"I don't know who you talkin' 'bout." The teenager said.

Two blocks away, Roni sat in the passenger seat of a dark-blue Honda Accord with tinted windows. When he saw the FBI run down on his car he knew he had to hit the road without Cookie, at least for the time. Roni looked over at Yusuf, who was behind the wheel, and said, "Roll out. They all over us."

With a sigh, Yusuf carefully pulled off.

Down in Northern Virginia, Vicioso and Niecy had a nice little apartment that was tucked away in the suburbs. Vicioso was laying as low as possible, staying under the radar, but still getting some money. At a much slower rate. He was buying five quiet kilos from Serio at a time, just enough to keep the cash coming in. Vicioso hooked up with two dudes by the name of Slim and Barry; he had dealings with them from when he was first in D.C. dealing with Cortez. Slim and Barry were Vicioso's only clientele at the time.

Slim and Barry were from Southeast, D.C., Vicioso often met them on Atlantic Street when they did business. Pulling up on Atlantic Street in front of the apartment building in his BMW, Vicioso saw the hand-to-hand drug action in full swing. He parked his car behind a black Nissan Pathfinder and placed his hand on the Glock 19 that was lying across his lap. He was a man on the run and he was playing for keeps on all levels.

Slim got out the Pathfinder and jumped in the BMW with Vicioso. "What's up, Panama?" Slim gave Vicioso five and handed him a brown paper bag. Vicioso nodded toward the shopping bag on the floor of the passenger's seat. Slim looked in the bag and said, "Good lookin' out." He then took a second to look down at his beeper before he continued. "I got my man, Jimmy in the truck, the one I said I want you to meet. You tryin' to holla at him now, while you around here? He good peoples, you will like him."

Vicioso looked at his watch and said, "Yeah, we can talk."

Slim went back to the Pathfinder and sent Jimmy to holla at Vicioso. Jimmy got in the car and gave Vicioso five. "What's up, man?" Jimmy said.

Jimmy was a smooth brown-skinned dude; he looked like he could have been a part of an R & B group that sang to the ladies. Slim had been telling Vicioso how Jimmy was trying to hook up with somebody that he could cop bricks from. Jimmy was moving a lot of coke on the South side before his connect got caught up in a federal drug sweep; now he was dry and trying to get back in position.

"I'm good." Vicioso said. "Slim been tellin' me a lot about you."

"Yeah, man, I'm kinda fucked up right now since my connect got popped." Jimmy said. "I got a lotta clientele beatin' down my door, but I ain't got the product to hit 'em wit' right now. I'm tryin' to find somebody to help me out on that end. In return I can bring you a shit load of business."

"Yeah, Slim was tellin' me that, but the problem is that I just got back in the Washington area and I ain't in position to

do a lotta things right now." Vicioso lit a Newport. "I'm working on a few things though."

"How 'bout a few bricks? Can you do that?"

"Yeah, I'm sure I can do that for you. Give me a number that I can reach you at." Vicioso said. Jimmy gave him a beeper number. They sat in the car for a few minutes and threw around some ideas and some numbers. Vicioso could tell that Jimmy was about money by the way he talked business. Jimmy told Vicioso how he used to move close to twenty-five kilos a week before the drought hit. Too much spending and not enough saving had him in a bad situation. However, if he could just get a connect that could keep the coke in rotation then he could make some major shit happen on the south side of town.

"A nigga be thinkin' he gon' have a connect forever, you know?" Jimmy smiled.

"Yeah, I know what you mean." Vicioso smiled, he could feel where Jimmy was coming from. He liked the vibe he got from the dude. "I'ma beep you and let you know somethin' later on tonight." Vicioso gave Jimmy five.

"Bet." Jimmy said as he got out the car. "I'm looking forward to it."

Just after dusk, Yusuf and Roni were exiting I-95 somewhere in Maryland. They pulled into a gas station and parked on the side by the restrooms. Roni got on the pay phone and beeped Vicioso. Vicioso called back almost instantly.

"I been wonderin' when I was gon' hear from you." Vicioso said, he'd heard about the raids in Philly. "Where you at?"

"Me and Yusuf somewhere in Maryland. I'm not sure for real." Roni said. "Close to Washington though."

"Look here," Vicioso gave Roni directions to a nearby hotel. I'll meet y'all there in thirty minutes. Be safe."

"Cool." Roni hung up the phone and looked at Yusuf who was leaning against the car drinking a Pepsi. "Panama gon' meet us at a hotel not too far from here. He already heard about what went down."

"Let's go then." Yusuf said.

A short while later, Vicioso, Roni and Yusuf were inside the hotel talking about the raids in Philly and what was the next move.

"One thing's for sure, its good y'all left Philly." Vicioso said, looking out the window into the dark parking lot. He explained to Roni and Yusuf how things were going for him in the Washington area. "Shit ain't like it was when we was in Philly and had the Colombians backin' us. I'm makin' a little paper, but nothin' like what we had goin' for us in Logan. I'm real low-key right now.

Nevertheless, y'all family to me. Y'all can stay down here, that's no problem. I'll set somethings up and we'll move from there. Where there's a will there's a way."

252

CHAPTER 23

f it wasn't one thing it was another. Serio was Vicioso's coke supply and Serio got locked up in D.C. for a gun charge just as Vicioso was getting his shit in order in the Washington area. Bad news seemed to be the only news Vicioso was getting lately. Nevertheless, he rolled with the punches. Being as though Serio was being held without bond, Vicioso had to reach out to a few people that he'd met through Cortez in order to buy a few kilos until Serio made bond. Coke prices were sky high; the best Vicioso could find was $22,000 a kilo and that came from Cortez's sister, Candice, who picked up where Cortez left off when he got out the game.

Sitting in the living room of an apartment on Chesapeake Street, Southeast, Vicioso, Roni, and Yusuf were getting down to business, trying to put things in motion with Slim and Barry. They planned to get Slim and Barry's old strip pumping again with huge 50 rocks. At the time, the only consistent coke in the area was coming from two Jamaicans around the corner. Slim and Barry had had some issues with the dreads but nothing major. If Vicioso could supply grade-A cocaine the Jamaicans would be out f business.

Smoking a Newport, Vicioso looked at Slim and Barry and said, "If we gon' make this shit work for us all we gon' have to work together, as a team. Y'all gon' have to show my men around the neighborhood so they know what's what. Once we get the spot up and running, money gon' start comin' in like it's supposed to. But like I said, loyalty is everything."

"That ain't no problem, Panama." Slim said, looking at Barry. They both wanted to get the strip pumping again like they had it before Jimmy's connect got locked up. That's when they had weight for sell on the strip.

"We got any fuckin' problems wit' the dreads?" Roni asked. He knew nothing was free and easy. After all he was in a different city, a city where niggaz from out of town went home in plastic bags.

"Fuck them niggaz. They ain't got no say-so around here." Barry said.

Roni smiled. "I hear that, but they might have a problem wit' what we tryin' to do. After all, we talkin' about putting them out of business."

Vicioso knew were Roni was going. "What my man is trying to say is can we get money without killin' them Jamaicans? Can we just make it happen without gunplay?"

"Fuck it." Slim said. "For all I care we can smash them niggaz. I wanted to smash them niggaz a long time ago, but Barry was like let the shit ride."

"Cool then." Vicioso said. "If we have to we'll take care of them. Other than that, we gon' focus on gettin' this shit together."

"That's what I'm talkin' 'bout, one hand wash the other." Slim said. The foundation was laid.

The Deli Den on Martin Luther King Jr. Avenue, Southeast, was a nice little lunch spot for high school kids and D.C. police. There was a lot of lunchtime action in and out the deli when Vicioso stepped inside and saw Jimmy joking with a female cop. Vicioso's stomach turned. There was nothing that could turn him off more than going to meet somebody about business and find them playing with the

police. Without a word, he turned around and walked out. He was on the run for countless crimes; he couldn't be hanging out around a bunch of cops. He couldn't believe that Jimmy had asked to meet in such a spot. In fact, Vicioso was pissed off.

Jimmy saw Vicioso leave and jogged outside behind him. He caught the vibe but wasn't sure what was wrong.

"Panama!" Jimmy called out as he jogged up behind Vicioso. "Hold up, man."

Vicioso turned around with an irritated look on his face. "What's up?"

"Where you goin'? Why you just leave like that?" Jimmy asked.

"Why you ask me to meet you up here and you got all them cops in there? What kind of games you playin'? I don't do business like that."

"Man, them police ain't thinkin' 'bout us. They just eat and roll out, joe. They don't never fuck wit' me. They just support my mother's business. It ain't that kind of party, man."

"Fuck that." Vicioso started to step off. "I don't do business like that, man."

"You not understandin' the situation. Hear me out. Shit is sweet, trust me."

"I don't want to understand it." Vicioso said as he looked up and down the busy street. "I do understand that I saw you all up in that police broads face, laughin' and jokin'. I ain't for all that shit. We breakin' the law wit' what we doin'. I don't need no cops around. Shit is hard enough as it is."

"Listen, that broad is cool peoples. I fucks wit' her like so." Jimmy said. "She wouldn't say shit if she saw me come in the store wit' fifty bricks. On the real, she used to ride wit' me when I used to go pick my shit up, just to keep the feds off me.

She on my team. Me and her been fuckin' wit' each other for a while now. She's part of what I do, Panama." Jimmy looked around the crowded street and lowered his voice. "Let's get in the car and talk so I can explain the situation to you. You got to understand how I do shit"

Vicioso thought about it for a second. If Jimmy had the police broad on his team then shit was on a much bigger level then Vicioso had thought. It grab his attention. "Come on." Vicioso led Jimmy to the car.

Inside the car, Jimmy went into more detail about the role that the police broad, Faith, played in what he had going on. Jimmy and Faith were real close, she was damn near his woman.

She watched his back and kept him on point about police investigations and drug sweeps. When Jimmy was on, he sold coke out of the Deli with no problems and the police inside never knew what was going on.

"So that's your woman?" Vicioso asked. "That's what you're tellin' me?"

"Yeah, in so many words." Jimmy said.

Vicioso nodded with a smile on his face. "I like you. You ain't no nickel and dime hustler. You got a whole operation set up already. We can do some things together."

"I'm tryin' to tell you that. I just ain't got a connect right now."

"I see." Vicioso nodded.

"So can we talk business now?" Jimmy said. "Cause I got a few things lined up."

"Lined up like what?"

"I got a dude tryin' to get a brick right now. Another nigga want a half. I'm bout that paper, it's not a game with me"

"You gon' have to put that on hold for a second until I get some things in order, but I got two bricks in that shopping bag

256

for you. Go 'head and do your thing and holla back at me."
Vicioso said.

Jimmy gave Vicioso five. "We gon' do big things together."

In less than a month, Roni and Yusuf had set up shop on Chesapeake Street and had the smokers going crazy over the huge working-50s they were giving up. The neighborhood was deadly and the police came through more than a few times a day, but Roni and Yusuf had to deal with it. After all, they were playing catch up; trying to get back on their feet from the loss they'd taken in Philly. They were going hard, going hand-to-hand. They'd break down every brick into a thousand 50 rocks and let it all hang out. Slowly but surely, they were stacking their paper in Southeast, grinding hard.

Roni's cousin, Short Man, had made bond in Philly and joined the crew in D.C. They needed the extra eyes and ears in the Southeast. Slim and Barry also put Roni and Yusuf down with a dude by the name of Twan, Twan was a huge help to the team. He knew how to get the strip pumping, plus he knew everybody in the neighborhood. He put Roni and Yusuf on point about who was who and what was what; he also brought in loads of cash. Fast. Twan could move close to a quarter-brick, hand-to-hand, in beeper sales alone.

Shop was set up in the second building from the corner. It was getting all the action, and word continued to spread about the working-50s. The way Roni and Yusuf set things up, they could see everything that came in and out of the apartment. When smokers came in the building to cop, the first thing they saw was Roni in the apartment with an Uzi in hand. It was clear that the crew meant business.

Stepping outside on Chesapeake Street to serve a few smokers, Twan saw a red Benz bend the corner. Two Jamaicans were inside. The one behind the wheel was a dread by the name of Lion. Twan used to do business with Lion and still owed him $15,000.

The Benz pulled up and stopped right in front of Twan. Lion lowered the driver's side window with the push of a button and said, "I see you take me for a joke, Twan, you think rude boy won't send you to the other side." Lion's accent was thick.

Twan looked from Lion to his partner in the passenger seat and said, "I'ma get you what I owe you, slim, you don't gotta be sellin' all that death though."

"Raas claud! Me talk about me money when me feel like it."

A few more harsh words were exchanged and then Lion stepped out of the car with a Tec-9. That was the wrong move. Roni had been watching the whole thing; he wanted a reason to deal with the dreads from day one. Now he had this reason. Roni sent Short Man out the back door to sneak up on the Jamaicans from behind. Short Man hit the scene with his MAC-10 blasting. Twan was caught off guard and got low as the slugs began to fly. Lion tried to spin around and fire but Short Man was all over him. Lion's partner tried to open fire on Short Man, but Roni and Yusuf were already spraying the car with Uzis. Smokers and other people outside took cover as the sound of fully automatics tore through the afternoon air.

When the smoke cleared, Lion and his partner were laying in the middle of the street in their own blood with their guns still in hand.

There were no more Jamaicans in the neighborhood after that. After a few days, the cops didn't even care about the shooting anymore.

Vicioso was a little concerned about the heat after Lion and his man was murdered, but as things cooled down and money

began rolling it was all good. Vicioso was really feeling Jimmy; the dude could move coke faster than anyone Vicioso had ever met. The only thing holding things back was the fact that Vicioso had no real connects. They were still paying top dollar and could only get a limited amount of kilos from Candice. Nevertheless, Vicioso was working on taking care of that problem.

Using one of his fake IDs, Vicioso went to pay Serio a visit at the D.C. Jail, where Serio was still being held without bond.

"What they gon' do wit' you Serio?" Vicioso asked, sitting on the other side of the glass with the phone to his ear in the crowded visiting hall. "You ain't got shit but a punk-ass gun case. They actin' like you got a murder or somethin'. What's that all about?"

Serio sighed; one obstacle after another was always on the horizon. "New York is puttin' shit in the game. They tellin' D.C. I'll disappear if they let me out on bond."

"If it ain't one thing it's another." Vicioso shook his head. "You gon' beat the case anyway so it ain't shit New York can do."

"Yeah, that's how I'm tryin' to look at it." Serio rubbed his chin. "On another note, how's things goin' for you."

Vicioso told Serio that things were slowly coming together for him and his crew around Atlantic Street. He told him about Jimmy and how things were going to take off once they got a real connect.

Serio smiled. "You know how to get back on your feet. I give you that. You been like that since you was young."

"Yeah, I learned from the best."

"So you done brought your Philly crew to Washington, eh?"

"Yeah, they family. We gon' do some things down here."

"I see." Serio nodded.

He really didn't like the fact that Vicioso let some American dudes get so close to his heart. "You still be lookin' out for my man Donald?"

Donald was one of Serio's Forestville workers; he was running things for Serio while he was in jail. Vicioso was making sure Donald had coke for the crew; he even let Donald get a little money around Atlantic Street with Roni and Yusuf.

"Yeah, I can't do much, but that's your man so you know I'ma look out for him while you gone."

"Good lookin' out, Vicioso." Serio cut his eyes at a female C.O. with a pair of tight-ass pants on. "Check this out: I ran into this Panamanian guy that used to deal wit' Cortez. He says that Pete is in the Washington area. He gave me a phone number, I tried to call it but some other dude answered the phone and said Pete wasn't around. He said Pete does come through though. You might want to check into that."

Vicioso smiled. He hadn't seen Pete since Pimpo was murdered. "Give me the number." Vicioso said. "I'll check it out."

Serio gave Vicioso the number.

"The last I heard, Pete was down in Miami doin' some things." Vicioso said.

"Yeah, I heard he was dealin' wit some real good peoples from back home." Serio said.

"You know 'em?"

"Nah, I just heard they had some big things goin' on down there."

"I'll check it out and let you know somethin'." Vicioso said.

Later on, Vicioso pulled up in front of an apartment in Suitland, MD. Pete was standing in front of the building talking to another Panamanian. A huge smiled crossed Pete's

face when he saw Vicioso pull up in the BMW. It was like a reunion of long-lost brothers.

Vicioso got out of the car and hugged Pete. "What's up, man?"

"I'm good, I'm real good." Pete smiled. "What's up wit' you? Last I heard you were in Philly somewhere."

"I was for a minute, but shit got too hot." Vicioso leaned against his car, checking Pete out. Pete looked like he was getting money. "I been down here for a few months now, tryin' to put a few things together. I done took a few losses so I'm not where I should be right now. You know how that go, it's all a matter of time. So what's up wit' you?"

"I was in Miami for a while doin' a few things. It was so much money to be made down there that I didn't want to leave. Me and a few brethren from back home hooked up and put some things in motion. We ran into a little problem wit' the Cubans. We had to do the Red Hook thing." Pete laughed.

"Shit got real heated so I had to hit the road. I'm fucked up I had to leave that behind. That was a good thing. You would love it down there."

"Yeah, I bet I would." Vicioso smiled. "So how long you been up here?"

"For 'bout a month now. I'm dealin' wit' a dude from Miami that's up here. He got a few things goin' on, but not much. He really don't know a lot of people so shit don't move fast. I'm tryin' to holla at a few people I know from Brooklyn to get things movin' 'cause the dude sittin' on bricks out the ass."

Vicioso smiled.

"What's up? Why you smilin'?" Pete asked.

"I knew you had somethin' up your sleeve." Vicioso gave Pete five. "You just what I been waitin' for." Vicioso gave

Pete the full rundown of what was going on in Southeast. He made it a point to stress the fact that Jimmy could move coke like Nike moved tennis shoes. "We been grindin' on the slow tip, but we ain't got no real connect. That's all we need to take off."

"I can introduce you to the dude I'm dealin' wit'. That ain't no problem. You family. I'm sure he'd love to do business wit' you. You might be just what he been waitin' for."

Pete took Vicioso inside the apartment and introduced him to a Panamanian by the name of Paulito. Paulito had a direct connect to a cocaine supplier back in Panama. Whatever Paulito asked for was shipped straight to the U.S. and the price was dirt-cheap. Paulito had been in the U.S. for a while and had spent some time in Brooklyn where he'd heard of Vicioso and Serio as well as the La Banda crew. After Pete introduced Vicioso to Paulito the two of them spoke about doing business.

"So you can move a lot of coke in Washington?" Paulito asked.

"I got a nice team in D.C., we been movin' a whole lotta shit without a connect." Vicioso said.

"How much coke you talkin', Vicioso?"

"Whatever! If the price is right."

Paulito smiled. "For you, since you and Pete are family, let's say… uh… $11,000 a key. How's that sound?"

"Sounds great to me. Let me check wit' my man and I'll get back to you later on today. We can get that movin in no time."

"Good, we'll work things out then." Paulito said.

After Vicioso finished talking to Paulito he went back outside with Pete. They sat in Vicioso's BMW smoking weed and talking business.

"I like how you got shit set up down here." Pete said.

"I'm tryin' to make the best out of the situation. I got the FBI on my ass so I gotta make every step count. I'm fuckin' wit' some serious niggaz in Southeast, they opened up the door for me and my Philly men to get some money.

I told you how we had shit workin' in Philly. Right now we just tryin' to stay as low as we can for a while. I don't have time for one of them federal courts."

"You really fuckin' wit' these American niggaz like that? You trust them?" Pete asked.

"Yeah, I love 'em. They family Pete. I told you how me, Roni, and Yusuf went to war wit' the Colombians in Philly. They stood firm wit' me. They soldiers. The dude Jimmy, this nigga is one in a million. His mind is always on business. You gon' love these niggaz. I'm tellin' you. Now you done put me down wit' a connect shit really 'bout to take off. Watch." Vicioso smiled.

After Vicioso finished talking to Pete he headed back to D.C. and caught up with Jimmy at the Deli Den. In the back room, Vicioso laid all the cards on the table with Jimmy. Jimmy was ready to take things to the next level.

"You don't even gotta ask twice." Jimmy said. "I been waitin' for a connect to come along. I know what to do."

"I'ma introduce you to the connect. I don't normally do shit like this. I want you to know that everything is on the up-and-up. We all in this together to the end. It ain't no big 'I's and little 'YOU's. You see how me, Roni, and Yusuf deal wit' each other. Loyalty is everything. We are a team, first and foremost. Nothing comes between us, not money, not bitches, nothing at all."

"We on the same page. You ain't gotta break it down for me. I'm down for whatever." Jimmy said.

Later on, Jimmy and Vicioso went to see Paulito with $165,000, for starters. They copped fifteen bricks. They then met up with Roni and Yusuf and hit them off with five kilos for their crew; then they hit Barry and Slim off with five kilos for their crew. The ball was rolling. Vicioso and Jimmy went to work with the rest of the kilos, working out of the Deli Den. Just as Jimmy said, the bricks moved with no more than a few phone calls. $25,000 a brick. Vicioso was impressed.

"This ain't shit." Jimmy told Vicioso when the coke was gone. "I can move whatever. Let's get your peoples to hit us off heavy. A lot of niggaz tryin' to cop. It's too much money and not enough product around."

"Sounds like a plan." Vicioso gave Jimmy five.

CHAPTER 24

A few months into 1989, Vicioso and his crew were on top of their game. They had filled the void that was left when other kingpins had gone to prison behind the Rayful Edmond case. All they needed was a strong connect and they could take things to new levels. Almost overnight they were moving bricks of high quality cocaine at the best prices. Out of the Deli Den alone, Vicioso and Jimmy were moving fifty or more kilos a month. Roni and Yusuf were doing the same kind of numbers around Chesapeake Street. Aside from a few minor problems where guns were blazed, the whole operation was running smoothly.

Inside the Deli Den, Vicioso and Roni sat back on the sofa watching Jimmy's back in the back room while he served a few dudes bricks of coke. Two kilos. Five kilos. One and a half kilos. The sells kept coming, like fast foods. The shit was like magic.

"Jimmy knows everybody in the city." Roni said, smoking a Newport. "He got all the contacts a nigga really to get pumped.

"No bullshit." Vicioso said. "He went through twenty bricks yesterday. Niggaz was comin' from all over."

"He the truth, for real." Roni said as Jimmy finished serving a young dude by the name of Chez from Valley Green.

Flipping through a handful of cash, Jimmy looked at Vicioso and Roni and said, "We only got four more joints left, joe." His beeper went off as he was talking. It was another sell.

"I just got a hit for two more joints." He grabbed the phone and called the number back. He told a dude by the name of Cheese to meet him at the deli.

Vicioso looked at his watch and said, "I gotta take Niecy to the hairdresser in a little while so I'ma have to catch y'all later on." He stood up. "Be safe, I will see you niggaz later."

Jimmy put the money he was counting in a brown bag and said, "Hold up, P. You might as well wait till Cheese come through and take all the money to the spot when you leave."

"Nah, I gotta make a run before I go get Niecy. Give the money to Roni." Vicioso gave Roni and Jimmy five and then left the Deli.

Roni and Jimmy talked about where they planned to hang out later on while they waited for Cheese. Jimmy knew Roni loved to party so he would take him to different go-go spots; sometimes it would be the Eastside, then the Metro Club, even the Black Hole every now and then. A short while later, Cheese showed up. He and Jimmy had been dealing with each other for about a year. Cheese normally copped a brick or two every week.

"What's up, young?" Cheese said to Jimmy, giving him five as he walked into the back room carrying a shopping bag with $45,000 in it. He saw Roni and gave him a nod.

"I see you on top of your business." Jimmy said as he handed Cheese a big brown paper bag containing potato chips and sodas. Two bricks were also at the bottom of the bag. Jimmy made sure that everybody that copped from the deli left with a few food items to make things look smooth.

"I'm tryin' to get this paper, joe." Cheese said. "You know how shit go. Money talk. I got this crankin' nonstop." Cheese handed Jimmy the shopping bag with the money in it.

Jimmy glanced inside the bag and handed it to Roni. Looking back at Cheese, Jimmy said, "Check this out: I see you really tryin' to get yourself some paper so I'ma go ahead and front you the last two bricks I got along wit' what you coppin'. Just hit me when you done. Cool? When you come back we gon' do the same thing."

"Good lookin'. I'ma be right back at you in no time." Cheese smiled.

Jimmy got two more kilos and put them in the bag that Cheese was holding. "Next time you see me you should be coppin' five or more of them things."

"No doubt." Cheese said. He gave Jimmy five. "I'm gone. I'll see you in a week or so." He left, giving Roni a nod on his way out.

When Cheese was gone, Jimmy got the money together and put it all in a blue duffel bag. They were sitting on more than $250,000 for the day. Sitting the duffel bag at Roni's feet, Jimmy said, "You got that, right?"

Roni stood up and threw the bag over his shoulder. "Yeah, I'ma go 'head and take this to the spot. Beep me around nine."

"Cool." Jimmy gave Roni five.

Roni left out the back door.

Jimmy made a quick phone call to line some things up for the next day. When he was done he turned around and saw Faith coming into the back room. She was wearing her police uniform, looking good as shit, somewhat like a thick version of Robin Givens. He got up and gave her a hug and a kiss, rubbing her ass. "How you doin', baby?"

"I'm alright. Just missin' you." Faith said.

Jimmy noticed an envelope in Faith's hand. "What's that?" he nodded at the envelope.

Handing him the envelope, Faith said, "That's all the police reports about the murder on Atlantic Street that you asked about. All the witness statements and everything."

A month prior, a dude tried to rob one of Roni's workers that were pumping on Slim and Barry's block. Short Man peeped the move and gunned the dude down with a .45 in broad daylight. The killing was all over the news for a few days.

Jimmy looked inside the envelope and then at Faith and said, "Good lookin' out, baby. I see they really don't have shit."

"Don't nobody know the dude that did the shootin'." Faith said. "No leads for real. It's going to be a cold case in a minute, you can bet that."

"Let's get out of here. You hungry?" Jimmy asked.

"For you." Faith smiled.

Jimmy smiled.

A week later, in Faith's Saab, she and Jimmy followed Vicioso's BMW down Southern Avenue in Southeast, Washington. They were on their way to Suitland, MD. to pick up their shipment from Paulito. Faith was in her police uniform, just to make things look good in case they got pulled over with a trunk full of bricks.

Minutes later, they all pulled into an apartment complex and parked in the back, besides the last building. Aside from a few teenagers that were hanging out, everything was laid back.

Vicioso, Roni, and Yusuf went inside the building. Vicioso knocked on door 303 and Paulito opened it. "Always on time." Paulito said as he let the trio in. Inside the apartment, two Panamanians sat on the sofa watching TV; they were paid to watch Paulito's back. Like clockwork, Roni and Yusuf went in the back with Paulito and returned carrying one duffel

268

bag each. "Vicioso," Paulito said. "Let me have a word with you before you leave."

Vicioso and Paulito went into the bedroom where Paulito told Vicioso that he was having a problem with a dude that owed him $150,000. The money was nothing. Paulito didn't like the fact that the dude was playing games about the money. He wanted to dude dealt with swiftly.

"How can I help you wit' the problem?" Vicioso got straight to the point.

Paulito sighed and rubbed his chin. "I want him dealt with, Vicioso. I want those like him to know that I'm not to be played with. You see my point?"

"Yeah, I see what's goin' on. That's shit like that needs to be dealt with."

"Can you have it taken care of for me?" Paulito asked. "I'll look out for you. You already know that."

"Who are we talking about?" Vicioso asked. Paulito told Vicioso that the dude's name was Sid and that he was doing some things in a Maryland spot called Forest Creek. Sid had a strong team behind him and was supposed to be about gunplay as well. His young niggaz were known to knock head off for him as well.

"Don't worry about it. I'll have it taken care of." Vicioso said. "Consider it a favor."

"Thanks, Vicioso." Paulito shook his hand. "I'm goin' to put five extra bricks with your next re-up, free of charge."

"Cool." Vicioso said.

Moments later, Vicioso, Roni and Yusuf were emerged from the building. Roni and Yusuf took the duffel bags to Faith's car and put them in the trunk. Once Vicioso, Roni, and Yusuf were back in Vicioso's car, Faith pulled out of her parking space. Vicioso followed behind the Saab.

Keeping a close eye on the Saab, Vicioso told Roni and Yusuf about the dude Sid and what Paulito wanted done. "I told him I would take care of it."

"Shit, we gotta treat the connect good." Roni said as they cruised through a traffic light.

Vicioso nodded. "That's what I said to myself."

"That ain't shit." Roni said. "We can take care of that tonight if you want to."

Yusuf wasn't really into what Roni and Vicioso were talking about. He noticed something more pressing at the moment. Tapping Vicioso's leg, Yusuf said, "Look at this shit here." He pointed at a P.G. County police car that was coming up beside them with its lights on. Vicioso, Yusuf, and Roni were all strapped and on the run. There was no pulling over. However, the police car got behind Faith's car.

"Shit." Vicioso hissed as the Saab began to pull over. Vicioso made a right turn and circled back around.

Inside the Saab, Faith's heart was pounding as she wiped her sweaty palms on her thighs and tried to calm herself. She could see the officer approaching the car through the rearview.

"Relax, baby." Jimmy said as he adjusted the Glock in his waistband. "Be cool and tell him you on the way to work."

"Okay. I got it." Faith prepared herself as the tall white cop stepped to her window.

Across the street, Vicioso pulled into a 7-Eleven and parked. He, Roni, and Yusuf watched closely.

"We can't let no one police pop them like that." Roni said, checking his Uzi. He was thinking about killing the cop if things looked like they were going to get out hand. They couldn't afford any more loses.

"He right, Panama." Yusuf said. "We can smoke his ass before backup get here."

270

Rubbing his chin, Vicioso said, "Hold fast. Jimmy got it under control. Let's see what happens first. He said Faith knows how to work her shit."

Across the street, trying her best to be cool, Faith said, "Is there a problem officer?" She was smooth as she handed the cop her ID.

Instantly, the cop noticed Faith's uniform. With his cold blue eyes, he glanced at her ID and said, "I pulled you over because a car like yours was reported in a robbery, but I can see you're not a robber." The cop cracked a smile as he looked over at Jimmy and nodded. Jimmy nodded back, feeling uneasy.

With a fake laugh, Faith said, "Sorry, officer, I'm no robber. Just trying to get to work."

The cop handed her ID back and said, "Have a nice day."

"You too." Faith said.

Across the streets, Vicioso, Roni and Yusuf breathed a sigh of relief.

Serio beat the gun charge after spending a few months in D.C. Jail. In that short amount of time a lot of things had changed on the streets. For one, Paulito was the man to see for kilos. Serio didn't like that. He was used to being the top man. As soon as Serio hit the streets he began to squeeze Paulito, on the quiet tip. Paulito was scared to death of Serio and wouldn't do anything to rub him the wrong way. However, Paulito wouldn't turn Serio onto the cocaine connect back home for fear that Serio would no longer need him.

Sitting in the back of the Deli Den with Vicioso, Serio smoked a cigarette while talking a little business with his young brother/comrade. Roni, Yusuf, and Jimmy had just left to go get some bricks from the stash house.

"Vicioso," Serio said as he blew smoke in the air. "Let me ask you something."

"What's up?" Vicioso said as he counted stacks of money and put them into a shopping bag at his feet.

"I know you gettin' a lot of money fuckin' wit' Paulito, but how do you feel about him as a man?" Serio raised his eyebrows.

Vicioso knew what Serio was getting at. "He cool. He ain't cut from the same cloth as us, but he ain't no bad guy. Besides that, its just business. He's a connect, a great connect."

Serio nodded, as if he was thinking about what Vicioso had said. "Check this out: I just found out who his connect is back in Santa Cruz."

"Serio, I already see where you goin', but it's really no point in that."

"It is a point, Vicioso. He gettin' them keys for $7,000 a pop. I pulled up on him and told him to plug me straight into the connect, since we all from Santa Cruz. He wanna hold the connect to himself and he ain't even paid no dues, Vicioso. Niggaz like us came up here and stood on the front line in the trenches. In spots like Red Hook, when Panamanians had to fight for everything we got ... we supposed to get what our hands call for. Niggaz like Paulito ain't paid no fuckin' dues; if it wasn't for Pete and strong niggaz like us, Paulito wouldn't be able to sell one gram in this country!"

Vicioso thought about what Serio was talking about. Seven thousand a kilo was unbeatable. However, Vicioso didn't want to scare Paulito off or do anything that could cost them the connect. After all, Vicioso and his comrades were making a killing with the current price of $11,000 a kilo.

"Serio," Vicioso sighed. "I see where you comin' from, but we doin' good right now. I don't see no sense in fuckin'

up a good thing. Me and my men on the run. We tryin' to get as much money as we can and stay as low as we can. So what Paulito making a quick $4,000 off the bricks. We killin' the streets. Don't forget bricks goin' for damn near twenty-five and thirty thousand. We ain't losin' nothin'."

"What's wrong wit' you, Vicioso?" Serio looked at his old protégé with disappointment. "You know that only the strong survive in this game, I taught you that a long time ago. If we don't squeeze this coward somebody else will. Remember that. You can't think wit' your heart in this game, Vicioso. It's business, that's how this shit goes." Serio put his hand on Vicioso's shoulder, like he used to do when Vicioso first came to the U.S. and was green to the game. "Niggaz like us—me, you, Pete—paved the way for other Panamanians up here. We gon' always be royalty! If Paulito got a connect for $7,000 then we damn well supposed to have that same fuckin' connect. We entitled to that. Don't forget that niggaz like Paulito need niggaz like us!"

Vicioso thought about how he had hit the dude Sid from Forest Creek for Paulito two weeks ago.

"So what exactly do you wanna do?" Vicioso asked Serio.

"I want to make Paulito understand how important niggaz like you and I are when it comes to doin' business up here in the U.S." Serio smiled. "Like I said, he gon' give us that connect!"

Vicioso sighed. "Serio, you know I'ma go to war wit' you against anybody wit' you at anytime. You know that. But I ain't wit' this one here. It ain't worth it. I don't see no sense in it. We gettin' everything our hands call for."

Serio shook his head in disgust; he couldn't believe the position Vicioso was taking. "You tellin' me you ain't wit' squeezin' this raas for the connect? What? You done caught feelings for this nigga?"

"That ain't the point. I'm tellin' you I don't think it's a good move. What if we scare the nigga away? Then we ain't gon' have no connect at all. We gon' be right back at square one, and for what? I ain't got time for that right now. I keep tellin' you I'm on the run. I gotta stack paper and stay low. You only thinkin' about yourself right now."

"I can't believe you!" Serio said with disdain.

"I can't believe you!" Vicioso shot back. "If you ain't runnin' the show it's always somethin' wrong!"

Serio said nothing for a second, just looked at Vicioso with a mean glare and shook his head. "You losin' your edge, you know that? ... I told you that when you lose your edge in this game you lose your life."

Vicioso gave Serio a confused look. Was Serio threatening him? "When you think you're bigger than you really are you get cut down to size."

The two men glared at one another for a few seconds. Heated.

Serio shook his head and looked at his watch. He then patted Vicioso on the back and said, "I gotta run." He sighed. "I thought I taught you better than that."

"You ain't have to teach me how to think for myself." Vicioso said coldly.

Serio left shaking his head.

After Serio was gone, Vicioso thought about the whole situation and told himself that Serio was going to fuck shit up. Serio's ego was going to be the death of him.

Jimmy dropped Roni off in front of the building on Atlantic Street and then headed for the Deli Den; they'd just came from the stash house dropping off $250,000. Business was booming.

MONEY AIN'T EVERYTHING

When Jimmy got to the Deli Den, Cheese was waiting for him. Jimmy told Cheese to follow him into the back so they could take care of business.

"What's up, baby boy?" Jimmy said once he and Cheese were in the back.

"I'm tryin' t get five of them things." Cheese said.

"Where the money?" Jimmy asked.

"In the car. I ain't walk in here wit' it until I knew you were here."

"Cool." Jimmy went to get the bricks and returned with them in a brown paper bag. "I'll walk to the car wit' you."

Cheese and Jimmy walked to Cheese's car where Jimmy got a shopping bag containing $100,000. Giving Cheese five, Jimmy said, "I'll catch you next time around."

"Bet." Cheese said.

CHAPTER 25

Vicioso was bothered for days after his last conversation with Serio about squeezing Paulito. Serio's mindset was getting back on top by all means. Vicioso didn't knock that, but he had other plans. As far as Vicioso was concerned, it was time to start thinking about what tomorrow would hold. Whatever Serio had planned, Vicioso hoped it didn't get in his way. Their plans were very different at the time.

The phone in the back of the Deli Den rang. Faith answered it and gave it to Vicioso. It was Paulito.

"What's up?" Vicioso said.

"Vicioso, I need to see you. It's important." Paulito said.

"Okay. Is everything okay?"

"I'll tell you when I see you. Meet me at the apartment." Paulito sounded like the situation was urgent.

"I'm on the way." Vicioso hung up the phone.

"What's up, joe?" Jimmy said, he could tell something was wrong by the look on Vicioso's face.

Vicioso sighed and said, "I don't know what's up for real, but I'm 'bout to go check on it. I'll let you know when I get back."

"Want me to go wit' you?" Jimmy asked.

"Nah, stay here and get the re-up money together. Call Roni and tell him and Yusuf to be ready to take that trip when I get back."

276

Vicioso left the deli and headed for Suitland wondering what the hell was going on with Paulito. When Vicioso got to the Suitland apartment, Paulito was waiting for him, looking nervous.

"What's up, Paulito?" Vicioso said, stepping into the apartment, looking around as he sat on the leather sofa. Paulito sighed. "It's Serio."

Vicioso shook his head. He knew Serio was going to be a problem for Paulito.

"Serio's leaning on me real hard, Vicioso. You know how he is. I don't want trouble. I'm a good guy. I'm fair, right? I do my best to make sure everybody eats. I play by the rules. You know what I mean?"

Vicioso nodded. "Yeah, you're real fair to me. I can't complain." "Serio wants my connect. He's planning to take me out if I don't give it to him. You can't reason with that guy. I never met a person like that. What businessman doesn't listen to reason?"

"That's my brother, but he can be hard to deal with at times." Vicioso studied Paulito's fear. "So how do you know he wants to take you out?"

"I know, Vicioso! Take my word. You know how Serio is. It's his way or no way at all. He wants to take over."

"So where do I come in?" Vicioso asked. Vicioso knew that Paulito wouldn't try to get him to take sides against Serio. That would never happen.

"I spoke to Pete and he said that he will have a talk with Serio, I ask you to do the same. For me, can you do that for me? Try to get him to understand that we can all eat together."

"You already know that Serio is his own man. I can't make him do anything he don't want to do, but I give you my word that I'll talk to him."

"That's all I ask. It'll be something in it for you." Paulito gave up a nervous smile. His fear was written all over his face.

"Give me a day or two and I'll let you know something." Vicioso said.

Sitting in the basement of his Forestville, MD home watching the evening news, Serio was thinking about his plans to get back on top of his game. Since he left Brooklyn things were never the same; he seemed to face one bad situation after another. However, once he got the connect that Paulito had, Serio would be able to take control in a way he was used to. Nothing would stand in his way.

"Serio! Yasmin yelled from the top of the basement steps. "Vicioso's here to see you!"

"Send him down." Serio said with a slight smile on his face; he knew Vicioso would be paying him a visit.

Serio looked at Vicioso with raised eyebrows as Vicioso came down the steps and sat on the sofa to the right of where Serio was sitting in a deep loveseat. "What's on your mind, Vicioso?"

Rubbing his chin, Vicioso said, "You're good, real good." He pointed his finger at Serio. "You might be the best to ever do it. I give you that. I love the way your mind works."

Serio smiled. "What are you talkin' about?"

"You know what I'm talkin' about. You put the squeeze on Paulito knowin' he was goin' to run to me and Pete beggin' us to talk to you. In the end you get exactly what you want. Right?"

Serio leaned forward and said, "Always remember this, Vicioso: If you squeeze an orange hard enough you get orange juice. That's how this game goes. You and Pete ain't want to squeeze this raas so I did the squeezin' myself. Now we got juice."

"So what's the next move?" Vicioso asked.

"I'ma take the connect and we gon' pay the price he payin' for bricks from back home. Tell that scared nigga that I want the connect. No questions asked. If he can't live wit' that … tough."

Vicioso smiled and shook his head. Serio was so crafty that he was dangerous. "So are you cuttin' Paulito out?"

"Nah, he can still do what he's doin'. That's his business. What I'm doin' won't affect what you have goin' on wit' Paulito. In fact, you can handle things wit' him however you want to, but if you want bricks for seven I'ma give you that, even though you didn't want to squeeze the coward wit' me."

Serio's game plan worked better than expected. Paulito plugged Serio, Vicioso and Pete directly into the Panamanian connect. They were all getting kilos for dirt-cheap and had access to as much cocaine as they could move. The cocaine still came in through Paulito's man in Baltimore, but Paulito had no control over the prices Serio, Vicioso and Pete paid. The game was on another level at this time.

Jimmy was able to reach out to more people that he knew in the game now that there was no limit to the amount of cocaine they could move. Dudes from Virginia, Baltimore, Philly and New York began to holla at Jimmy at the Deli Den. Deals of twenty-five to thirty kilos were made at one time in the back of the Deli Den. Drug traffic picked up so much for Vicioso, Jimmy, Roni and Yusuf that the actual drug deals of twenty kilos or more had to be made away from the Deli Den. Most of the time those kinds of deals were made at Forestville Mall in Maryland.

As the evening grew dark under a light rain, Vicioso and Jimmy rode in Vicioso's BMW as they followed Faith's Saab. They were on their way to Forestville Mall. Faith was riding alone with thirty kilos in her trunk. Vicioso and Jimmy decided that Faith looked better riding alone if she was pulled over.

"These Virginia dudes you fuck wit' been comin' real strong lately." Vicioso said to Jimmy as they cruised through traffic. His pistol was laying across his lap. "Where they movin' all this shit?"

"Richmond." Jimmy said, keeping a close eye on Faith. "It's a lot of money to be made down there."

"Yeah?"

"Trust me. I used to go down there fuckin' wit' these New York niggaz I used to deal wit'."

"I'd like to go down there and check shit out." Vicioso said. He never liked staying in one spot too long. Things in the D.C. area were going too well and that was too good to be true. He knew that he needed to start thinking about moving on. A change of location always kept him ahead of the feds.

"We can go down there and check it out. I know a few broads down there." Jimmy said.

"Let's do that." Vicioso lit a Newport.

"On another tip, I meant to tell you some wild shit."

"What's that?"

"Remember the broad I told you about that be readin' palms?"

"Yeah, why?" Vicioso was keeping his eyes on Faith's Saab.

"Two weeks ago she told me that somebody I know was gon' die in a fatal accident. Then today I find out that this dude I went to school wit' died in a car crash on Suitland Parkway yesterday." Jimmy rubbed his head and sighed.

"The shit freaked me out."

"Oh yeah?" Vicioso cut his eyes at Jimmy. "You believe that palm readin' shit?"

280

"I don't know. You tell me. This ain't the first time she done called money. One time she told me to be careful and watch out for the law. I caught a gun case the next day."

Vicioso laughed a little. "I see it like this: We can't tell what tomorrow holds so I go through life makin' the best moves I can make at the time. Don't let that shit bother you. Fate is already written."

"I don't know, P., that's some spooky shit." Jimmy said and paused for a second. "That ain't what got me trippin' though."

"What got you trippin' then?"

"The other day she told me to watch those close to me for envy because danger is around the corner."

Vicioso laughed. "Come on now. I could tell you that much. Look how much money we gettin'. We always gotta watch those close to us. We keep our circle tight so don't worry about that shit. Don't freak yourself out!"

Jimmy sighed. "You right."

Minutes later, they pulled into the parking lot of Forestville Mall. The deal went smooth. As planned, they left with $450,000.

Inside the South Capitol Street apartment, Roni and Yusuf were serving Donald, Serio's old worker. Donald was wanted for questioning in connection with a shooting in Maryland. Lying low, he was making a few moves of his own in Southeast. Staying away from Serio's Forestville spot, Donald was buying two or three kilos here and there from Roni and Yusuf. On the strength of Serio, they looked out for Donald.

Sitting in the living room with Donald, Roni and Yusuf waited for Twan to bring two kilos from the apartment next door where they stashed the cocaine.

"You makin' a killin' over there on Southern Avenue I see." Roni said, smoking a blunt with his Nikes on the coffee table. "Tell me somethin' good."

"Yeah, shit pumpin' around there. I'm gettin' money from both sides of the line. A lot of sells be comin' from the Maryland spot across the street." Donald said.

Yusuf looked up from the money he was counting and said, "This only thirty-eight-thousand right here, Donald."

"Oh yeah, I must've missed counted." Donald said. "I'll take care of that the next go 'round."

"Cool." Yusuf said as he put the money back in the shopping bag Donald had it in.

Twan came through the door moments later carrying a shopping bag. He handed the bag to Donald and said, "The joints already cooked up."

"Good lookin' out." Donald said as he headed for the door.

"Holla at you later." Roni said. The phone rang a few moments later. Roni answered it.

It was Jimmy; in code Jimmy told Roni he needed five kilos but didn't feel like going all the way out to Maryland to the stash house.

"I got you." Roni said. "Come down the apartment."

"I'm on my way." Jimmy hung up the phone.

"What Jimmy talkin' about?" Yusuf asked.

"He need five joints. They must've sold out up in the deli." Roni said. He then looked at Twan and said, "How many joints we got left?"

Twan thought about it for a second and said, "Seven."

"I'ma give Jimmy five of them and I'm gone in the house." Roni yawned.

"I been up twenty-four hours. I'm tired as shit." Roni went to get the kilos and returned with them in a shopping bag.

Twan was on his way out the door when Roni came back. "I'ma catch y'all tomorrow." Twan said as he left.

"I'ma call it a night too." Yusuf said as he slid his .45 in his waistband. Giving Roni five, he said, "Be safe. See you tomorrow." Yusuf left.

A short while later the phone rang. Roni answered. It was Jimmy. "I'm out front." Jimmy said.

"I'm on my way out." Roni said.

Roni headed outside and jumped in Jimmy's BMW with the shopping bag.

"What's up, Roni?" Jimmy said.

"You on the clock kinda late ain't you?" Roni asked, sitting the shopping bag on the floor.

"Yeah, I was on my way over Faith's house, but Cheese hit me and said he needed five joints. I might as well grab that money real quick." Jimmy said as his beeper went off. "That's youngin' right there."

"Catch you tomorrow. I gotta go get some sleep before I fall out." Roni gave Jimmy five and he got out the car.

Sitting in his Acura Legend with his man Ray-Ray, Cheese was a little nervous about the move they were about to put in effect. He really didn't feel good about the move, but Ray-Ray kept pressing Cheese to set Jimmy up. Ray-Ray didn't like the fact that Jimmy had niggaz from out of town on his team and were helping them get paid.

As they waited for Jimmy to come serve Cheese the kilos, Ray-Ray looked at Cheese and could see that he was still second-guessing what they were about to do. "Ay, young, stop trippin'!" Ray-Ray frowned his face up. "You act like that nigga really fuck wit' you. It's business nigga. He'd do the same to you if the shoe was on the other foot. Fuck him and them Panamanian niggaz he fuckin' wit'. We gon' snatch him, hit 'em for everything they got up in the deli and ain't nobody gon' know who did it. My man already told me they keep like twenty joints up there. The shit is sweet."

Cheese looked down at the .45 laying across his lap. "You right, joe."

Ray-Ray coached Cheese a little while longer. They were sure they were about to come-up in a big way.

Seeing Jimmy's BMW coming down Martin Luther King Avenue, Cheese stepped out the driver's side of the Legend. Jimmy pulled up right beside him and Cheese jumped in the car with a shopping bag in his hand.

"What's up, joe?" Jimmy said with a smile as he pulled off, giving Cheese five.

"Ain't shit, just trying to get this paper right." Cheese was still nervous, but Jimmy didn't pick up on it.

"The bricks right there." Jimmy nodded at the shopping bag on the floor by Cheese's feet. "Just leave the money on the floor; I'm sure it's all there." Jimmy turned down a side street so he could double back and drop Cheese off at his car. Stopping at a stop sign at the end of the block, Jimmy saw Cheese making a quick move out the corner of his eye.

"What the fuck is up, joe?"

"Pull the car over, nigga." Cheese hissed, putting the barrel of the .45 to Jimmy's head.

CHAPTER 26

Just after 12:00 P.M. the next day, Vicioso was awakened by the phone. It took him a second to gather his senses and reach across Niecy to answer it. "What's up?" he said in a groggy voice, wiping sleep from his eyes.

"Turn on the news!" the voice on the other end shouted.

"Roni, I'm sleep and---"

"Turn on the fuckin' news, P!"

Roni's tone drilled a sense of dread into Vicioso's heart. He dropped the phone on the bed and grabbed the remote.

Niecy was awakened by the commotion. Rubbing her eyes, she said, "What's wrong?"

Once Vicioso cut the TV on he didn't have to say a word.

On the news, yellow tape was around a brand new BMW along with countless detectives and uniform cops. The news reporter on the scene was already into the story: "... In what police are calling a gruesome discovery, 26-year-old Jimmy Porter was found in the passenger seat of his late model BMW. He was shot three times in the head and neck, according to police..."

Niecy covered her mouth in shock. She'd just seen Jimmy hours ago. She couldn't believe he was gone. Her heart dropped.

Vicioso's body felt cold. He was numb for a second and then the pain began to set in. Jimmy was more than a partner to Vicioso, Jimmy was a brother—he was family. Thoughts of Pimpo's murder flooded Vicioso's mind and squeezed the life from his heart. He said, "Meet me at the apartment. Have everybody there!" Vicioso hung up the phone and stared at the thick carpet for what seemed like hours. He felt Niecy rubbing his back as tears rolled down his cheeks.

"I'm sorry, baby." Niecy tried to comfort him. His silent demeanor was scary. Niecy still remembered the night he got the call about Pimpo's murder.

Vicioso stood up and said, "I gotta go. I'll be back later."

"Be careful." Niecy said. She knew the code. It was no sense in trying to talk Vicioso out of what had to be done.

As Vicioso headed for the South Capitol Street apartment all he could think about was what Jimmy was telling him about the palm reader. She was right. Thoughts of who killed Jimmy ran through Vicioso's mind like racing horses. Somebody was going to pay. Every time things seemed to be going smooth something always came up.

When Vicioso got to the apartment, everybody was on the scene. Roni, Yusuf, and Short Man. Jimmy's murder hit the crew hard.

Roni told everybody how he was the last one to see Jimmy alive and that Jimmy was on his way to serve Cheese five bricks.

"Cheese?" Vicioso asked, standing in the middle of the living room with his arms folded. He never trusted Cheese.

"Yeah, he said Cheese hit him for five joints right before he was about to go in the house." Roni said.

"We need to find that nigga." Vicioso said. Looking around the room, Vicioso said, "Where's Slim and Barry?"

"I couldn't catch them." Yusuf said.

"Beep them again for me." Vicioso said. "We gon' put a nigga in the dirt before the day is over about this shit here!"

Word of Jimmy's murder began to spread all over the city in no time. A lot of niggaz were getting paid fucking with him. On the south side, fingers were already pointing at Cheese. He was the last person to be seen with Jimmy. Although Cheese and Ray-Ray only got the five kilos Jimmy had with him, they also got a little over $300,000 from the Deli Den.

Vicioso, Roni, and Yusuf were out looking for Cheese, riding all over Southeast, when Faith called Vicioso's car phone, crying, and told him that she needed to see him. Vicioso told her that he would be right over.

When Vicioso got to Faith's house in P.G. County he left Roni and Yusuf in the car and went inside to see what was up with Faith. He was hoping that she had some information about Cheese's whereabouts.

Faith was still in tears and very emotional when Vicioso came over. She couldn't help it; she loved Jimmy and wanted somebody to pay for what they'd done to him. Sitting on the sofa with Vicioso, Faith told him that homicide detectives were already looking for Cheese and Ray-Ray. A girl from Barry Farms had seen the two of them get out of Jimmy's car thirty minutes before his body was discovered.

"Who is Ray-Ray?" Vicioso asked, he wasn't hip to him.

Fighting back tears, she said, "He's a known stick-up guy out of Barry Farms. Him and Cheese are real close."

"Can you get me the addresses on them?"

"Yeah, I can do that. Both of them have arrest records."

"Do that for me as soon as you can. I want to make sure I catch them muthafuckas before the police." Vicioso said with a serious glare. "They are gonna wish they had never fucked wit' us."

"I want in." Faith stated, looking Vicioso in the eyes.

"What?"

"I want in. I want to help find these bastards."

"I got it. Let me take care of this." Vicioso said. He had no problem with the role Faith played in moving the cocaine, but murder was something that was on another level.

"You know how much I loved Jimmy!" Faith shouted. "Don't act like I'm not hurtin' just as much as you! They took a piece of me when they killed him! I want to make sure they burn in hell!"

"They will." Vicioso tried to end the conversation.

Faith grabbed his arm and shouted, "Muthafucka! You gon' let me help find these bastards or I'ma do it by myself! Please believe me."

Vicioso gazed into her blood-shot eyes for what seemed like hours. He could feel her pain. "You sure you wanna do this? This is where things get messy."

"Do I look like I'm playin'?"

"This ain't drivin' bricks from one spot to another. This 'bout murder. This shit is serious, Faith. Niggaz 'bout to start dyin'."

"I don't give a fuck. I want them all dead." Faith said as she wiped tears from her eyes.

"Cool, but first, get them addresses for me." Vicioso pulled a knot of cash out of his pocket and handed it to Faith, he then said, "I want you to make sure Jimmy's mother has everything she needs for the funeral. I'ma hit the streets and check into a few things. Beep me when you have those addresses and we gon' move from there."

Later on, after riding through Barry Farms a few times, Vicioso, Roni, and Yusuf ended up back at the South Capital Street apartment. Roni was fed up with looking for Cheese and Ray-Ray and was ready to ride through Barry Farms and

light shit up from top to bottom. As far as he was concerned,
they were going to have to go to war with the Farms once they
killed Cheese and Ray-Ray anyway. Might as well get it on.
However, Vicioso wanted to make sure they focused their
energy on finding Cheese and Ray-Ray.

Vicioso's beeper went off and he called the number right
back. "What's up?" he said.

"Meet me in the alley behind the apartment in five
minutes." The voice on the other end said.

"Cool." Vicioso hung up.

"Who was that?" Roni asked.

"Faith."

Barry Farms was alive with drug action under the cover of
darkness. Young dudes stood at the mouth of an alley in the
heart of the Farms, without a care in the world. They didn't
care that it was a war zone. Gunplay and murder was all they
knew. In the middle of the group was Ray-Ray, talking shit
and smoking weed with the young dudes that were coming up
under him. Most of them looked up to Ray-Ray, and now that
he was fronting most of them coke, he was even more
important around the way.

A silver Caprice Classic with tinted window bent the corner
and pulled up a few feet from the alley. All eyes were on the
car, but no one seemed too concerned. A young dude dressed
in all black stepped out and called Ray-Ray over to the side.

"What's up, Mookie?" Ray-Ray said, giving his homie
five.

"Ay, young, I was just up the avenue and niggaz were
talkin' 'bout you and Cheese had somethin' to do wit'
Jimmy."

"Oh yeah, who was that?" Ray-Ray asked, not tripping at
all.

"Slim and Barry."

"Don't trip. Fuck them niggaz. If they wanna see me they know where I'm at." Ray-Ray said

Behind the apartment on South Capitol Street, in the darkness of the alley, Vicioso, Roni, and Yusuf waited with guns in hand. A car pulled into the alley with no lights on. As it approached it became clear it was a police car. The car stopped in front of Vicioso. The window came down and Faith said, "I got his ass." She then nodded toward the back seat.

"Check the back seat."

Vicioso peered through the window with a hand over his eyes and saw a body hog-tied with plastic restraints. "Is he dead?"

"Nah, just knocked out." Faith said. "I hit him with a high-powered stun-gun. He'll wake up in a little while. He's all yours."

Vicioso looked over his shoulder and called Twan and Short Man, who were standing at the back door. When they walked up he told them to take Cheese inside the building. They got on top of it.

"Panama," Faith said. "You need to get his car. I stopped him on Wayne Place. Don't leave the car there like that." She threw Vicioso the keys to Cheese's Acura Legend.

"I got it." Vicioso caught the keys and handed them to Yusuf. He then told Yusuf and Roni to go get the car. They stepped off.

"I told you I was gonna get his ass." Faith said. "I woulda killed that muthafucka myself if you didn't say you wanna find out who else was in on the murder."

"Don't worry. I'ma find out who was with it." Vicioso said as he watched Roni and Yusuf walk down the alley. "I'll let you know what's next." He put his hand on Faith's shoulder

and continued. "I'm gon' find every last one of 'em. That's my word. They not gon' get away wit' this shit here."

Faith's eyes began to water as soon as Vicioso touched her. The pain was killing her. She didn't care about anything else at the time. "Why? Why, Panama? Why Jimmy?" She covered her face and wept softly.

Trying to comfort her, Vicioso said, "I'ma make sure they don't get away. That's on my life." That's all Vicioso could think of to say, but the truth was that no matter who paid, Jimmy wasn't coming back.

Faith took a deep breath and tried to pull herself together. "I'm in 'til the end. Whatever you need me to do."

Vicioso nodded.

"I gave the money to Jimmy's mother. I'ma go check on her first thing in the morning. I'll have those addresses for you too."

"Faith."

"Yeah?"

"Be strong."

Inside the apartment, Cheese slowly came around and was shocked to see Vicioso standing in front of him with his arms folded across his chest. Twan, Slim, and Short Man were also in the room. Cheese was still groggy and delirious from the stun gun. Sitting on the sofa with his hands duct-taped behind him, Cheese said, "What the fuck is up, Panama?" He began to frantically look around the apartment trying to regain his senses.

"You thought we was gonna let you get away wit' what you did to Jimmy?" Vicioso said calmly.

"I don't know what the fuck you talkin' 'bout, man! What the fuck is up?!" Cheese began looking for an exit.

Looking Cheese in the eyes, Vicioso hissed, "Stop lyin', I already know it was you."

"I ain't have shit to do wit' that shit, Panama!" Cheese's voice began to grow shaky.

"Who was wit' you?" Vicioso asked.

"I swear to God—" Cheese's words were cut short when Short Man slapped him in the face with a 9mm. Cheese screamed out in pain.

"Stop lyin', bitch-ass nigga!" Short Man yelled.

Calmly, Vicioso said, "Cheese stop lyin', shit only gon' get worse. Just tell me who was wit' you. I know somebody put you up to it."

Roni and Yusuf walked in as Vicioso was questioning Cheese.

In pain, Cheese said, "I swear to God, I ain't have nothin' to do wit' that shit... aaahhh ..." Roni punched Cheese in the mouth. Yusuf followed with heavy blows to the face and head. Slim and Short Man joined in as well.

While Cheese was getting the shit beat out of him, Vicioso told Twan to step outside and make sure everything was cool. Vicioso then turned to the crew and watched them work Cheese over for a second. After a few moments, Vicioso told the crew to hold fast. Looking at Cheese's bloody face, Vicioso said, "We can do this all night long. All you gotta do is tell me who was wit' you."

Out of breath and spitting blood on the floor, Cheese said, "I don't know what the fuck you talkin' 'bout. I ain't do shit."

"Who the fuck was wit' you?!" Vicioso snapped for the first time.

"This the last fuckin' time I'ma ask you, nigga!"

Cheese broke down and began to cry for his life. He knew death was coming.

"Tape that nigga up, Short Man." Vicioso said.

Short Man grabbed the duct-tape and began to wrap it around Cheese's head, leaving only a small hole for him to

breathe. Cheese began to struggle and Slim and Yusuf had to hold him down.

Looking at Vicioso, Roni said, "We might as well go at their whole crew. We already know the dude Ray-Ray was wit' it."

"You right. That's what we gon' do." Vicioso nodded.

In a flash, Cheese jumped from the sofa and dived out of the second floor window. However, he didn't get all the way through the window; half of his body was hanging out the window. He'd knocked himself out. Vicioso and Roni rushed to grab him before he fell to the ground behind the apartment building. As they tried to pull Cheese back into the apartment, Cheese began to come back around, he began to struggle.

"Fuck it!" Vicioso said. "Shoot this nigga."

Short Man fired his 9mm. Roni fired his .45. Cheese fell two floors to the ground with a sickening, bone-breaking plop.

"Come on," Vicioso headed for the door. "We gotta get the body outta here."

When the crew got downstairs and ran out the back door into the darkness of the alley, two police cars with shining lights were coming up the alley. The bright lights fell upon the crew. They all took flight. Sirens blared as the police hit the red and blue lights. "Freeze!"

A short while later, inside an apartment that the crew controlled on Chesapeake Street, Roni sat on the sofa smoking a Newport. "I know I hit that nigga in the head. He gotta be dead."

Everybody but Twan had met up at the Chesapeake Street apartment after the police chase. Roni had beeped Twan and was waiting for him to hit back.

"Somethin' ain't right though." Yusuf said. "The nigga shoulda been lying right under the window. That's where he fell."

When the crew came out of the building, Cheese was nowhere to be found.

"It's no way the nigga got up and walked away." Short Man said. "That's out of the question!"

Vicioso was sitting back in deep thought. As he rubbed his chin, thoughts of how they were going to hit Ray-Ray and his crew crossed his mind.

The phone rang and Roni picked up. It was Twan. After a few quick words Roni hung up and said, "We gotta go back around South Capitol Street."

Vicioso looked up, snapped out of his thoughts of murder, and said, "What's up, Roni?"

"Twan got the body."

Back around South Capitol Street, in the darkness of the alley behind the building, Twan led Vicioso, Roni and Yusuf down the back stairs that led to the boiler room. Hidden under bags of garbage was Cheese's body.

Twan was out back when the body fell from the window. He saw the police cars and quickly moved the body.

"Let's get the body outta here." Vicioso said. "Yusuf, go get his car. Hurry up." Vicioso and Roni lifted the body as Twan held the door.

Moments later, Yusuf pulled up in the alley, in Cheese's Legend. He popped the trunk for Vicioso and Roni to put the body inside but they found it stuffed with shopping bags that were filled with new clothes. Short Man and Slim started grabbing the shopping bags.

"Nah," Vicioso said. "Leave that shit alone. That nigga died for this punk-ass shit. Let him keep it. We gon' put his ass in the back seat."

Slim and Short Man stuffed Cheese's body in the back seat of the Legend.

294

We gon' leave this nigga in his car just like they left Jimmy." Vicioso said. "I wanna send a message to them bitch-niggaz."

Once the body was in the car, Vicioso, Roni, and Twan got in Vicioso's BMW while Yusuf drove the Legend with the body in it. Slim and Short Man followed behind Yusuf. The three-car motorcade carefully crept through the dark streets of Southeast until they found a spot to leave the car and the body: Under the 11th Street Bridge.

News of Cheese's murder was all over the news the next afternoon. Police were calling it the second murder in a turf war for Southeast drug markets.

Ray-Ray wasn't running though. He was riding around with a 150-shot Calico, ready for war. He had two young guns with him—Mookie and Lil Soldier, both young niggaz were teenagers with bodies under the belt.

Riding up M.L.K. in Ray-Ray's Nissan Pathfinder, Mookie looked to his right and saw Slim on the phone in front of the carryout. "Ay, young, there go that nigga Slim right there." Mookie said.

Ray-Ray took a quick look and made a U-turn. "Air his ass out." he said to his young guns.

In broad daylight, Mookie and Lil Soldier jumped out of the truck and ran down on Slim with their Mac-11s blazing. Slim saw them coming and tried to pull his burner but it was no use. Death was upon him. The teenagers lit ass up and left his bloody body on the sidewalk as they ran back to the Pathfinder.

"That's right." Ray-Ray smiled as he pulled off. "Put that work in."

On high-alert days later, Vicioso, Roni, and Yusuf slid to Jimmy's wake to pay their respects to their fallen comrade. They didn't care how risky it was. Besides, they were strapped like the SWAT team. Everything was out in the open.

After paying their respect, Vicioso, Roni, and Yusuf smoothly stepped off. Outside, as they headed for the car, a young female with tears in her eyes stepped to Vicioso and said, "I told Jimmy to watch those close to him."

Hand in his coat on his Uzi pistol, Vicioso looked confused. The female caught him by surprise. "Huh?"

Roni and Yusuf were on point as well, keeping an eye on everything moving outside.

"My name is Kathie. I told Jimmy that harm was coming his way. I told him to watch those close to him." Kathie still had tears in her eyes.

It became clear for Vicioso. He remembered the conversation he and Jimmy had about the palm-reader.

"Oh, I know who you are." Vicioso nodded. "Jimmy told me about you. You're the palm-reader."

Kathie nodded. "I also told Jimmy that you would sacrifice all for his sake. Did he tell you that?"

Kathie's words sent chills up Vicioso's spine. Even Roni and Yusuf got wide-eyed behind her words. They had never heard such a thing.

"Be careful, Panama." Kathie looked Vicioso in the eyes. "Some of those who now stand with you will not stand by your side when the storm blows through. It will get darker before it gets lighter. I promise you." She wiped tears from her eyes and walked off with a small crowd, she left Vicioso amazed and a little spooked. Her words rang over and over in his head.

Faith came out of nowhere just as Vicioso was about to pull off in his BMW. He lowered his window and said, "What's up? You got any news for me?"

Looking from side to side, Faith said, "The homicide investigation ain't focused on y'all at the time, but I don't know how long that's gonna last. The Deli Den and Jimmy's murder done already came up in Cheese's murder." Faith handed Vicioso a brown envelope. "Those are pictures of the other dudes you asked about. Their addresses are on the back of the pictures. Any thing else you need to know about them just ask me and I can get you their whole file."

Vicioso looked in the envelope and pulled out a picture of Ray-Ray. He studied the picture for a second, locking his face into his mind.

"That's Raymond Jones; they call him Ray-Ray." Faith said. "He's the one that put Cheese up to robbin' Jimmy. He has a lot of pull around here. Be careful dealing with him."

"Who are these young dudes right here?" Vicioso pulled out pictures of Mookie and Lil Soldier.

"Those are two little killers from Barry Farms that Ray-Ray has under his wing. Don't underestimate them either. They will blow your brains out faster than you would think." Faith said. She then pointed to Lil Soldier's picture and said, "He's fifteen and wanted for two murders right now. The other one is seventeen and he just beat a murder last summer. They are dangerous, Panama. Don't pull any punches with them."

"They'll be dead before the week is out. I put that on everything I love." Vicioso said.

CHAPTER 27

Vicioso, Roni, and Yusuf pulled up behind an apartment building on 14th Street Northwest and parked the Buick Regal they were in at the end of the alley. They were on top of business. The information Faith had given them allowed them to track Ray-Ray down Uptown.

Putting his ski mask, Vicioso looked at Roni and Yusuf and said, "We gon' make this quick. Leave nobody alive."

"No doubt." Yusuf said, cocking his Uzi.

"Where the lighter at?" Roni asked, putting on his ski mask.

"Here." Vicioso handed Roni the cigarette lighter. "Let's take care of this business."

Vicioso, Roni, and Yusuf stepped out of the car into the dark alley. They headed for the back of the building and found the door unlocked. They slid up to the third floor and stepped out into a well-lit hallway. Roni saw the smoke detector and pulled the lighter from his pocket. He then lit a brown paper bag on fire and held it up to the smoke detector. In seconds the water sprinklers began to spray water from the ceiling. Yusuf pulled the fire alarm and put the move in motion. Residents began rushing out of their apartments. Roni, Vicioso, and Yusuf stood in the cut at the end of the hall and waited for Ray-Ray to show his face.

298

Moments later, Ray-Ray stepped out of apartment 311 in his boxers and looked up and down the hallway. He looked confused. He must have been asleep.

"I got his ass." Vicioso whispered to Roni and Yusuf. Vicioso stepped out into the open and began walking toward Ray-Ray. No one seemed to pay the man in the ski mask any attention until the .45 automatic went off. Boom! Boom! Vicioso fired shots into Ray-Rays back. Boom! Boom! Boom! More confusion set in as residents began to yell and scatter in all directions. Every shot Vicioso fired was careful and on point, hitting its target.

Standing over Ray-Ray, Vicioso looked down into his eyes and said, "You thought you was gon' get away wit' that shit you did to Jimmy? You got shit fucked up, bitch!"

Ray-Ray looked up into the eyes of his killer but was in too much pain to say or do anything.

"Hope it was worth it motherfucker." Vicioso fired five shots into Ray-Ray's head without a blink of the eyes. He stood there for a second with thoughts of Jimmy on his mind. Slowly, he turned and walked away, smoking gun at his side.

Across town, Barry, Short Man, and Twan were riding in a blue Chevy Impala with a Pizza Movers sign on top of it. From afar, one would think the pizza man was coming through because Short Man and Twan were laying on the floor in the back with AR-15 assault rifles. Barry was out for blood for what happened to Slim.

Bending the corner and driving deep into Barry Farms, Barry saw a crowd of dudes stand at the end of the block. He couldn't make them all out, but he could see Mookie. "Ay, y'all," Barry said over his shoulder to Short Man and Twan. "We got action. I'ma let y'all know when I pull up. Get ready to rock and roll."

"Cool." Short Man said. His heart was pounding, he was ready to let the show begin.

Barry slowly drove down the block. He stopped a few feet away from the crowd and said, "Game time."

Short Man popped the door and opened fire on the crowd, spraying bullets left and right; Twan popped the door on the driver's side and opened fire over the roof. Automatic gunfire cut through the night; it sounded like four or five automatic rifles were going off at the same time. The element of surprise allowed Twan and Short Man to drop three bodies before anyone had a chance to fire back. Mookie was the first on to fall from slugs to the face and chest. As the crowd began to scatter, automatic fire was returned.

"Let's go! Let's get the fuck outta here!" Short Man yelled jumping back in the car. Twan did the same. Barry stomped the gas and took the Impala flying around the corner.

Days after Ray-Ray was murdered, and Mookie and two of his men were smashed in Barry Farms, dudes from Barry Farms came through Atlantic Street, where they knew Barry was from, and opened fire on any and everybody outside, killing two young dudes that worked for Barry. It was a terrible scene. The news covered the murders and called them a continuing turf war.

Vicioso really didn't care about the war now that Cheese and Ray-Ray were dead. His mind was on getting out of town. D.C. was too hot for him at the time. He was thinking about Miami and had talked to Roni and Yusuf about it. They were all for the move. They had a good run in D.C. and made a lot of money. With the connect they had they could set up shop anywhere in the country and have good prices. They made up their minds to collect the money that dudes owed them in the streets and to get rid of the last of the kilos they had and then they would hit the road.

300

MONEY AIN'T EVERYTHING

Sitting at the foot of his bed smoking a Newport while watching the news, Vicioso was in deep thought about Jimmy. They'd only known each other for a short time, but they were close as if they'd known each other for a lifetime. The game had robbed Vicioso of more than he cared to account for.

"Harvey," Niecy said, lying in the bed. "Are you sure about Miami?"

"Yeah, I think it's the best move for us." Vicioso looked over his shoulder. "Serio has some people down there. We can go down there and lay low for a second and then make our way back to Panama. That's the game plan."

"How soon do you plan on doin' that?" Niecy asked, she was ready to leave the D.C. area.

"A week or two at the most. I just want to wrap some things up." Vicioso said.

Short Man stepped out of his silver Pathfinder into the cold winter air on Southern Avenue with a shopping bag in his hand. The shopping bag contained two kilos of powder cocaine. Looking from side to side, Short Man crossed the busy street, walking across the Maryland line toward the gas station.

Out of nowhere, two unmarked police cars pulled up. "Freeze!" The officers yelled as they jumped out with their guns drawn. It was as if it had been planned.

Short Man thought about running but before he made up his mind he found himself slammed to the ground.

"You're under arrest!" an officer said as he put cuffs on Short Man.

A short while later, Roni, Vicioso, and Yusuf were inside the Chesapeake Street apartment wrapping up a few things. They'd just learned of Short Man's arrest and knew that wasn't a good sign. Just like Roni and Yusuf, Short Man was on the run in Philly. The feds had to be closing in.

As Vicioso wrapped up kilos of crack at the kitchen table his beeper went off. He called the number back. It was Faith. She needed to see him. Said it was very important. When he got off the phone he told Roni and Yusuf he'd be right back after going to see what Faith wanted.

"Everything cool?" Yusuf asked.

"I ain't sure. I'll let y'all know when I get back. Stay on your toes."

Vicioso left and headed up to the Deli Den. He found Faith in the back and said, "What's up? You sounded like something was wrong when you called. Are you okay?"

"Something is wrong." Faith said as she shut the door so no one could hear what they were talking about. "Somebody's talkin' to the homicide detectives about Cheese's murder. Homicide knows that Cheese, Jimmy, and Ray-Ray are connected. They also know that a Panamanian had somethin' to do wit' it. The FBI stepped in two days ago so information is goin' to be hard to come by now. What I do know is that the Redrum task force is in town to investigate these murders and some duct-tape murder Uptown. I think you should go ahead and leave town now."

Vicioso felt the walls closing in.

Twan pulled up in a red Nissan 300 ZX and parked on 6th Street. He looked around and spotted Donald sitting in front of the apartment building. Twan waved his hand for Donald to come over to the car. Donald walked over and got in the car, looking like he was up to something.

"What's up, D?" Twan said, giving Donald five. "Where the money at?"

"It's inside I thought you was gon' come inside. That's how me and Roni do it when he come through." Donald said, looking around nervously. "I really ain't wit' all this out in the open shit."

302

"Yeah, I can dig it, but shit real tense out here in the streets right now. You know what we goin' through right now. It is what it is." Twan said, checking the mirrors. "I got the bricks right here." He pointed at the shopping bag at his feet.

"Go get the money. I'ma wait right here for you."

"Come on, man, you don't expect me to come out here wit' sixty-thousand dollars." Donald said. "That shit don't look right. You know how hot it is around here."

Twan sighed and pulled his Glock from his waistband. Looking around to check out the scenery he tucked the Glock in his coat pocket and grabbed the shopping bag. "Come on, man, let's hurry up."

"Bet." Donald said.

Donald and Twan got out and headed for the building. Twan was on point, finger on the trigger, watching everything moving. He refused to get caught slipping. Inside the building they walked up the steps to the second floor. Something didn't feel right. Twan gripped the Glock. Looking over his shoulder, Twan saw a dude with a hood over his head coming up the steps behind him, moving fast. With no questions asked, Twan pulled the Glock and fired into the dude's chest three times, dropping him. Twan turned to fire at Donald but Donald was already running. Twan fired at Donald's back a few times before running down the steps, jumping over the body of the hooded dude, and out the door. Outside, he ran straight for his car.

Minutes later, inside the Chesapeake Street apartment, Twan told Roni and Yusuf how Donald tried to set him up.

"Donald must think we got our hands full!" Roni frowned.

"I tried to take his head off, but he was halfway down the hall." Twan said.

"I can't believe this shit." Yusuf said. "Donald know damn well we ain't gon' let him get away wit' no shit like that."

Vicioso walked in the apartment and overheard what was going on. "Hold up. Donald did what?"

"He tried to set me up." Twan said. "He wanted to get me inside the building."

Vicioso sighed. "Let's go find this nigga. Right now!"

A little after one in the morning a dark blue Nissan Maxima pulled up in Fort Greble Park, not far away from Chesapeake Street. The car's lights went out and two dudes stepped out and walked to the trunk. The taller of the two dudes popped the trunk and they both pulled a duct-taped body out. Duct-tape was wrapped around the head of the body and its hands were cuffed behind the back. Three gunshot wounds were in the top of the head.

"We gon' leave it right here." Vicioso said. He and Roni dropped Donald's body and got back in the car. Just like that.

Late at night the next day, Roni and Yusuf were in the South Capitol Street apartment counting money. They were finished moving the last of the kilos they had. Once they had all their money together they would be ready to hit the road. Things were coming to close.

"I still can't believe Donald tried some shit like that." Yusuf said.

Smoking a blunt, Roni nodded and said, "A nigga will risk his life for money. It never fails. It's the root of all evil. That's what my grandmother used to say."

"Yeah, no bullshit." Yusuf wrapped a thick rubber band around a stack of money and placed it in the book bag on the floor.

"But it's the same everywhere you go. We gon' run into the same shit when we get to Miami."

"You might be right, but we gotta get the fuck outta D.C. before we end up in a box or a prison cell." Roni stood up and looked at his watch. "I gotta go meet Twan real quick and get the last of this money he got for us. I'll be right back."

"Bring some food back wit' you." Yusuf said, rolling a blunt.

"I got you." Roni said as he walked out the door.

Moments later, the phone rang. Yusuf picked it up and said, "Hello."

"What's up, joe?" Barry said.

"Ain't too much. Yusuf said.

"Man I need you, real bad."

"We ain't doin' nothin'. We dead, baby."

Barry sighed. "I can't find nobody to holla at, joe."

"You know how that go. It be like that sometimes."

"How long you gon' be around there?"

"At least another hour. Why, what's up?"

Yusuf lit the blunt.

"I'ma bring you that change I owe you."

"Cool, catch you when you get here." Yusuf hung up the phone. He sat on the sofa smoking weed and watching TV while waiting for Roni to return. A knock on the door grabbed his attention. He got up and walked to the door. Looking through the peephole, Yusuf unlocked the door and opened it. A frown instantly covered his face. "What the fuck is up?" Yusuf said as he was shoved backwards and smacked in the face with a pistol. He lunged for the gunman but was hit with a barrage of bullets that knocked him to the floor. Slowly, the gunman looked around the apartment and then stood over Yusuf. Looking down into his eyes, the gunman said, "Where is Vicioso?"

In fatal pain, struggling to breathe and coughing up blood, Yusuf said, "You...you... think you gon'... get ...away wit' this?"

"I already did." The gunman said before he emptied the clip into Yusuf's face and chest. Looking around one last time, the gunman slowly walked out of the apartment and closed the door behind him.

Stuffing fries in his mouth as he bent the corner on South Capitol Street, Roni looked up and saw police lights everywhere. His stomach began to turn. His heart began to pound. Slowly, he drove by the apartment and saw a body being carried out under a white sheet. A small crowd was gathered on the sidewalk across the street. Roni saw Barry and Twan in the crowd. Roni parked at the end of the block and walked back down the street to find out what the hell was going on.

"What the fuck is up?" Roni asked as he walked up on Barry and Twan.

Twan sighed and said, "Yusuf, joe."

"What?!" Roni's heart dropped. He didn't want to believe his ears. It couldn't be true.

"Yeah, man." Barry said. "When I pulled up the feds was already on the scene."

"Ain't nobody seen nothin'?" Roni snapped. "Somebody had to see something.

"I ain't had a chance to holla at nobody yet." Twan said.

"Meet me around Chesapeake Street." Roni said as he stepped off with tears in his eyes. When he got back to his car he sat behind the wheel looking down South Capitol Street. As tears rolled down his face, thoughts of Yusuf flooded his mind. They'd been partners since back in the day. Before all the money making and killing. "Muthafuckas gon' bleed."

306

Roni said to himself as he started up the car. Shaking his head, he didn't care anymore.

Inside the Chesapeake Street apartment, Roni stood at the window looking down at the drug action that was in full swing outside. Barry and Twan were sitting on the sofa. Twan was telling Roni what a pipehead had seen after the gunfire went off.

"... he say it was only one nigga." Twan said.

Barry spoke up. "I'm tellin' you, Roni, that's them Barry Farm niggaz. We gotta go through there tonight."

Roni said nothing for a second, only rubbed his chin. He was waiting for Vicioso to call back. "Ain't no way Yusuf let one of them niggaz get that close to him like that." Roni said.

Before anyone could say a word, the phone rang. Roni answered. It was Vicioso.

"What's up?" Vicioso said.

"We got trouble." Roni said.

Vicioso sighed, instantly alert. "What's goin' on now?"

"Yusuf, man. Yusuf got hit. He's dead."

"I'm on my way over there right now." Vicioso shouted and hung up.

When Vicioso got to the apartment, he, Roni, Barry and Twan threw some names around, but nobody was sure who could've hit Yusuf alone. When they couldn't come up with a name they took the fight to Barry Farms. They strapped up with Uzis and AR-15s. In a pipehead van, they went through the Farms and jumped out like the A-Team, unloading. The gunfight tore through the night. Niggaz from the Farms seemed to come out of the woodwork, spraying automatic weapons. By the time the van went flying down the street two bodies were left bloody on the sidewalk.

The next morning, the top story on the news was the arrest of Twan and Barry. They were arrested in a number of raids in Southeast in the early morning hours. Their names were mentioned in the killings around Barry Farms. The heat was on.

Inside Vicioso's BMW, he and Roni were headed down 18th Street Northeast. Vicioso looked at Roni and said, "We not leavin' Washington until we find out who killed Yusuf, I don't care how hot it get. I want you to know that."

With an Uzi in his lap, Roni said, "I already know that. Yusuf ain't gon' die in vain. Fuck that. I ain't goin for no shit like that."

"You know Faith said they was lookin' for us too when they raided the South Capitol spot."

"Yeah, that's why I ain't go back around there last night." Roni said. "I knew the law was gon' connect the dots after Yusuf got hit."

"Whatever we do, we gotta make it quick." Vicioso said.

Minutes later, Vicioso pulled up and parked in front of a nice row house. He and Roni looked around and got out the car. The cold wind was blowing hard as they walked up to the door. Vicioso knocked on the door. The door opened and a cute female looked at them and said, "I knew you'd be coming." She let them in and led them to the living room. "Can I offer you two something to drink?"

"No, but thanks." Vicioso said. "We're kinda pressed for time, not to be rude."

"I understand. I sense that a great loss has occurred." Kathie sat in a chair across from Vicioso and Roni who sat on the sofa. They both looked at one another in amazement when she spoke of the great loss. She smiled and said, "You two have come to see if I can identify the source of your loss. Correct?"

"Yeah." Vicioso nodded, still in amazement.

Kathie walked over and kneeled between Vicioso and Roni, softly grabbing their hands, rubbing their palms with her thumbs. "I can't tell you who the person is by name." She closed her eyes as she continued to rub their palms. "I don't see visions in that way. I can only describe the person to you. I can tell you what he is like, what he is about."

"That's all we need." Roni said."Please, don't talk." Kathie said, almost in a whisper. "Just let me feel your energy." She eased into an Indian-style sitting position. A few awkward seconds passed. Then in a calm voice she said, "The person you seek did what they did as an act of vengeance. They lashed out because of a loss as well. The person feels like he has been done wrong"

Vicioso looked at Roni with a skeptical look on his face. For all he knew that someone could be a number of people.

Kathie continued. "The one behind your loss is the one that has always been in a position of authority."

Kathie opened her eyes and gazed into Vicioso's. Her gaze sent chills up his spine. "This time, his position of authority will not benefit him. His time is coming to an end. You will not have to avenge your loss. God has already written it the way he wants it." Kathie stood up and looked at Vicioso and Roni. "I know you two are uncertain about what I've told you, but once you see the light you will understand. Don't seek revenge. Rest your souls. Everything will fall into place."Vicioso cut his eyes at Roni and stood up. It was time to go. He shook Kathie's hand and said, "Thank you for your time."

Roni shook her hand as well. His mind was racing, trying to put two and two together.

As she let them out, Kathie said, "There is nothing good here for you two. Leave this city. Get far away. For Jimmy's sake."

Inside an interrogation room being pressed by aggressive Redrum agents, Short Man was at his breaking point. He was facing life in prison and nothing else seemed to matter to him.

A short, fat white agent leaned over the table into Short Man's face said, "We got you and your crew connected to a number of murders and cocaine deals of up to fifty kilos at a time. It's time for you to start thinking about yourself. The game's over. I can't stress that enough."

With tears in his eyes, Short Man began spilling his guts. The agent pressed harder for more information. Short Man opened up on every detail that he could think of.

"I can give you murders you don't even know about." Short Man said. "This shit goes all the way back to Philly and on up to New York."

"How many? Give me some hard facts or you can forget about any kind of deal."

"At least ten. All drug-related and unsolved, from D.C. all the way to Philly. I can put Panama and Roni on the scene of all of them. If you really want them I can give you them with ease." Short Man said.

"You may have yourself a deal." The agent said as he walked out the room.

A few blocks away from Kathie's house, Vicioso and Roni rode in silence for a while as they headed back to Southeast.Yusuf's murder was weighing heavy on their shoulders. They couldn't let it go unanswered. Yusuf would never let their murder go unanswered.

"Did you get anything from what Kathie had to say?" Roni asked.

"I think so." Vicioso blew cigarette smoke in the air.

"Who you think did it?" Roni glared at Vicioso.

"Serio." Vicioso said. He and Roni looked at one another for a second and said nothing. "Everything Kathie said makes sense. Plus, I knew them Barry Farms niggaz couldn't get that close to Yusuf. Serio is the only one who coulda got up on Yusuf by himself like that."

"Hold the fuck up!" Roni shook his head. "Why would Serio do some shit like that? For what?" Roni was confused. He knew Serio was supposed to be family

"I don't know." Vicioso picked up the car phone and called Serio.

"Yeah." Serio answered the phone as if nothing was wrong.

"I know it was you." Vicioso got straight to the point.

Serio laughed a little bit. "What you talkin' 'bout?"

"We ain't gotta play no fuckin' guessin' games. I know how you work. It had your name all over it."

Serio got deadly serious. "It was meant for you, Vicioso. You gettin' beside yourself. You need a blast of reality."

Vicioso frowned. Serio's words hurt him to his heart. "Fuck is you talkin' 'bout?" Vicioso snapped.

"All of a sudden Donald turns up duct-taped and handcuffed. That had your name all over it."

"You gon' go against me for some nigga you met at a stoplight somewhere? After all we been through?! What the fuck is on your mind."

"Donald was loyal to me. He was one of my people."

"He tried to take from me! You cool with that?"

"Look at it like this: You hit one of my workers and I hit one of yours. All is fare in love and war. Isn't that how they say it."

"That's where you wrong. Yusuf was family. He put in work to get you out of jail. You forgot about that?! How the fuck you gon' look at him like some fuckin' worker and gun him down like that?!"

"There's a price to pay for everything." Serio said coldly. "Donald was family to me."

"Bullshit! Your beef is wit' me! But you right about one thing: There's a price to pay for everything." Vicioso hung up. He looked at Roni and said, "Serio's a dead man."

The car phone rang again. Vicioso answered it.

"I ain't gon' play wit' you like I did when we was in Brooklyn." Serio said in a voice that was cold. "I'm gon' take your ass out this time, Vicioso. You better think this one through. It's late in the game."

"Fuck You." Vicioso snapped. "We have nothing to talk about."

Serio laughed. "I taught you everything you know. Don't forget that. You can't fuck wit' me. Not on your best day."

"We'll see." Vicioso hung up.

Vicioso and Roni set out to hunt Serio down, but couldn't track him down the first night. No matter what things had come to, Vicioso couldn't see himself taking the heat to Serio's house while Yasmin was there. However, Vicioso and Roni did sit down the street from Serio's house waiting for him to show up. He never did. Vicioso and Roni checked Serio's Maryland coke spot and still came up with nothing. Serio was nowhere to be found.

Three days passed after Yusuf's murder with no sign of Serio. The mission to find Serio had to be put on hold for a hot second in order for Vicioso and Roni to head back to Philly for Yusuf's burial.

In Philly, Vicioso and Roni made sure that everything was taken care of and that Yusuf was laid to rest properly. They had to be extra careful while in Philly and even had to sneak to the funeral since they were wanted by the feds.

On the highway back to D.C., Vicioso looked at Roni and said, "We gotta find Serio as quick as we can and hit the road."

"Cool." Roni said. He was tired and ready to put D.C. behind him. The life they were living was getting the best of him. Stress was weighing him down.

Back in the D.C. area, Vicioso and Roni hit Vicioso's apartment and began strapping up. Popping a clip into a .45 caliber Uzi, Vicioso's beeper went off. It was Faith. Vicioso called her right back. "What's up?" he said.

"Have you seen the news?" Faith asked.

"Nah, why?"

"Serio overdosed last night. The police are saying that you had something to do with the overdose. They had your picture on the news. Everybody is talking about it. You need to get out of town as fast as you can."

Somewhere along the line, Serio had picked up a heroin habit, but he kept it on low. Yasmin ended up finding him passed out on a hotel floor where he was laying low.

"Faith, I gotta take care of a few things. I'll call you once I'm done. Thanks for keepin' me up to speed. I haven't been watching TV at all. I will stay in touch."

"No problem." Faith hung up.

Vicioso hung up the phone and walked over to the window. It had started to rain. Looking out the window, Vicioso began shaking his head in disgust. He was tired of all the drama. He and Serio were geared up to kill each other, but as Vicioso gazed out into the rain he had tears in his eyes. He and Serio were brothers from another mother. How had it come to this? Vicioso searched his mind for answers. He began to have feelings of guilt about his plans to kill Serio. Things didn't seem real. What had it all boiled down to in the end? Vicioso asked himself that question over and over.

Roni gave Vicioso a minute and then said, "What's up? Talk to me."

Vicioso told Roni about Serio's death.

"For real?" Roni said, thinking about what Kathy had said. "That's some wild shit."

"Yeah, I know." Vicioso sounded depressed.

"You okay?" Roni asked, seeing Vicioso wipe tears from his eyes.

"Shit wasn't supposed to go down like this. Serio was a brother to me. We had big plans when we came up here. I woulda never thought in a million years that we would be at war." Vicioso took a deep breath and shook his head. "Ain't no sense in dwellin' on what can't be changed. We gotta get ready to hit the road. Shit ain't sweet, the show goes on."

Roni nodded in agreement. "Let's get out of here."

"Me and Roni gon' be on the road in 'bout thirty minutes." Vicioso said to Niecy over the phone. She and Cookie were already in Miami waiting for Vicioso and Roni at a friend's house.

"Be careful." Niecy said.

"Always. I love you."

"See you when you get here." Niecy hung up.

Vicioso hung up and turned to Roni. "We can hit the road now." They'd just counted up a little over $500,000 in money they collected off the streets. It was more than enough to get them in position where they were going.

Stuffing stacks of cash into a gym bag, Roni said, "D.C. made us a lotta money, but it took so much in return. I guess it's a price to pay for everything, you know."

"No bullshit." Vicioso shook his head as he zipped up a gym bag full of money.

"What time is it?" Roni asked.

314

MONEY AIN'T EVERYTHING

As soon as Vicioso looked at his watch countless Redrum agents came bursting through the front door of the Fort Washington condo and stormed the spot with MP5 assault weapons. "Freeze! Don't move! Get on the ground! Now!" The agents yelled. Vicioso and Roni automatically went for their weapons but were slammed to the floor. Guns were put to the back of their heads; knees were jammed in their backs and they were cuffed in seconds.

"Search the place from top to bottom!" An agent yelled as he stood over Vicioso and Roni. He then looked down at them and smiled. "We finally got you two motherfuckers." He pulled a picture from his pocket and nodded. "This is Panama and Roni." He said to another agent. He then squatted to look Vicioso and Roni in the eyes. "The show's over fellas. Nothing lasts forever. I'm sure you know this already. I hope you have something put up for a rainy day." He gave off a funny smile as if he had made a big catch by getting the two fugitives.

Vicioso looked to his left and saw his Uzi on the sofa. It was so close but yet so far. He would've given anything to have a fighting chance. He always told himself that he would never let the feds take him alive. Things just didn't turn out that way.

Roni spit in the agent's face and snapped, "Fuck you cracker! That shit you talking don't mean shit to me. You ain't got shit on us but the word of a bunch of lyin' ass rats that won't make it to court no way."

The agent smiled, wiping spit from his face. "I like you, little guy. You're a real class act. After you've served about fifteen or twenty on your life sentence you won't be talking so tough anymore." The agent turned his head and nodded for other agents to get Roni out of the condo.

The agent looked at Vicioso and said, "We've got murders on you from here to New York. You are done, you do know that, right?"

"Tell me somethin' I don't know. Don't none of this shit mean a damn thing to me. I'll deal with whatever comes my way. I'm built for it." Vicioso said.

"Get the Panamanian out of here, too." The agent said. As agents picked Vicioso up off the floor, the agent that was running the show looked Vicioso in the eyes and said, "You won't ever see the streets again so take it all in on your ride downtown. Somewhere like Colorado or Leavenworth will be life as you know from here on out. Bet your last dollar on that."

"Why don't you go stick your head up your ass and talk that shit to someone that cares." Vicioso said as he was taken out the door.

Vicioso and Roni were the last men standing, but their run was over. In a flash it had all come to an end without warning.

AFTERMATH

n what became one of the longest criminal trials in the history of the District of Colombia Superior Court, Vicioso, Roni, Twan and Faith all stood trial for drug trafficking and murder. Short Man was the star witness in the case against the crew, telling everything he knew. Barry joined the prosecution also and testified at trial in order to cut a deal with the government. He later killed himself by blowing his own brains out over the guilt he carried from testifying against his comrades.

Seven months after trial began for the so-called "Deli Den Gang" the verdicts came back. The jury deadlocked on Faith, although she later took a plea to conspiracy to commit murder and ended up doing close to seven years in federal prison. Vicioso, Roni and Twan were convicted of Cheese's murder and a number of other charges. They were all given multiple life sentences. They were sent off to do their time at Lorton, in Virginia, and then to the federal system years later. They never gave up the fight for freedom in the Court of Appeals. Their trial had been infected with all kinds of prosecutor misconduct that the judge overlooked, despite objections from defense lawyers. Hard work ended up paying off: Fifteen years later, the Court of Appeals overturned all the convictions.

About The Author

Eyone Williams was born and raised in Washington, D.C. He is a publisher, author, rapper, and actor representing urban life in a way that is uniquely his. Known for hardcore, gritty novels, Eyone made the Don Diva best-seller list with his first novel, Fast Lane (Fast Lane Publications). He followed up his debut novel with Hell Razor Honeys 1 and 2 (The Cartel Publications). He then delivered his readers a short story entitled The Cross (DC Bookdiva Publications). He's also a staff writer for Don Diva Magazine, his most notable work is featured in Don Diva's issue 30, *The Good, The Bad, and The Ugly,* where he outlined the rise and fall of D.C. street legends Michael "Fray" Salters and Wayne Perry.

Eyone's first acting role was in the movie *Dark City* (District Hustle). His latest mixtape, *A Killer'z Ambition,* is a sound track to the novel, A Killer'z Ambition (DC Bookdiva Publications) by Nathan Welch. With the release of his fourth novel, Lorton Legends (DC Bookdiva Publications), Eyone reached new heights in his career and won the AAMBC award for Male Author of The Year for 2012.

Always working, Eyone followed up Lorton Legends with another bestseller in Secrets Never Die (DC Bookdiva Publications). Secrets Never Die is soon to be a movie.

For more information about Eyone Williams visit his Facebook page: facebook.com/eyone.williams, also follow him on Twitter @eyonethewriter, and on Istagram at uptowneyone

Order Form

Fast Lane Entertainment Order Form
#245 4401-A Connecticut Avenue, NW
Washington, DC 20008

Name: _____

Inmate ID _____

Address: _____

City/State: _____ Zip: _____

QUANTITY	TITLES	PRICE	TOTAL
	Up The Way, Ben	15.00	
	Dynasty By Dutch	15.00	
	Dynasty 2 By Dutch	15.00	
	Trina, Darrell Debrew	15.00	
	A Killer'z Ambition, Nathan Welch	15.00	
	Lorton Legends, Eyone Williams	15.00	
	Secrets Never Die, Eyone Williams	15.00	
	The Hustle	15.00	
	A Beautiful Satan	15.00	
	A Hustler's Daughter	15.00	

Q, Dutch		15.00	
Hellrazor Honeys, Eyone Williams		15.00	
Hellrazor Honeys 2, Eyone Williams		15.00	
Fast Lane, Eyone Williams		15.00	

Sub-Total $_____

Shipping/Handling (Via US Media Mail) $3.95 1-2 Books, $7.95 1-3 Books, 4 or more titles-Free Shipping

Shipping $_____

Total Enclosed $_____

Certified or government issued checks and money orders, all mail in orders take 5-7 Business days to be delivered. Books can also be purchased on our website at dcbookdiva.com and by credit card at 1866-928-9990. Incarcerated readers receive 25% discount. Please pay $11.25 per book and apply the same shipping terms as stated above.